ACCLAIM FOR RACHEL HAUCK

THE LOVE LETTER

"Enjoyable inspirational romance . . . Jesse and Chloe rewrite Hamilton and Esther's history on screen and their relationship strengthens as reenacting the story helps them reconsider their ideas about a perfect ending. Hauck cleverly uses the play to bring historical flourishes to a strong story about overcoming mistakes through faith and commitment."

—*Publishers Weekly*

"A Civil War love letter is the centerpiece of this delightful read by Hauck as forgiveness, dependence upon God, and second chances are intricately woven together . . . A captivating story line, historical research, and God's truth equal a recommended read for all."

—*CBA Market*

"From its epic opening to its unexpected and wholly satisfying conclusion, *The Love Letter* serves up the perfect blend of modern and historical romance infused with exquisite vulnerability. It sweeps readers into the centuries-old drama of South Carolina and the flash of contemporary Hollywood and delightfully explores layers of social and emotional duality."

—*Booklist*

"Hauck's latest is a gorgeous melding of two timelines into an unforgettable story. She does an incredible job balancing the two, and the pacing works perfectly . . . What makes this story shine is that it isn't what readers will be expecting, but it will be what readers need. Themes of redemption, love, sacrifice, and loyalty resonate throughout."

—*RT Book Reviews*, 4 stars

THE WRITING DESK

"Rachel Hauck enchants us again! Tenley and Birdie are bound together by the understanding that creativity is a guiding force and that their stories must be told. A tale both bittersweet and redemptive, *The Writing Desk* is your must-read."

—Patti Callahan Henry, *New York Times* bestselling author

THE WEDDING SHOP

"Hauck seamlessly switches back and forth in this redeeming tale of a shop with healing powers for the soul. As Cora and Haley search for solace and love, they find peace in the community of the charming shop. Hauck succeeds at blending similar themes across the time periods, grounding the plot twists in the main characters' search for redemption and a reinvigoration of their wavering faith. In the third of her winsome wedding-themed stand-alone novels, Hauck focuses on the power of community to heal a broken heart."

—*Publishers Weekly*

"I adored *The Wedding Shop*! Rachel Hauck has created a tender, nostalgic story, weaving together two pairs of star-crossed lovers from the present and the past with the magical space that connects them. So full of heart and heartache and redemption, this book is one you'll read long into the night, until the characters become your friends, and Heart's Bend, Tennessee, your second hometown."

—Beatriz Williams, *New York Times* bestselling author

"*The Wedding Shop* is the kind of book I love, complete with flawed yet realistic characters, dual timelines that intersect unexpectedly, a touch of magic, and a large dose of faith. Two breathtaking romances are the perfect bookends for this novel about love, forgiveness, and following your dreams. And a stunning, antique wedding dress with a secret of its own. This is more than just a good read—it's a book to savor."

—Karen White, *New York Times* bestselling author

"In *The Wedding Shop*, the storyline alternates between past and present, engrossing the reader in both timelines . . . and the ways that God's provision is shown is heartwarming and can even increase the reader's faith. The weaving in of characters and plot points from *The Wedding Dress* and *The Wedding Chapel* adds depth and meaning to the gorgeously rendered tale."

—*RT Book Reviews*, 4 stars

THE WEDDING CHAPEL

"Hauck's engaging novel about love, forgiveness, and new beginnings adeptly ties together multiple oscillating storylines of several generations of families. Interesting plot interweaves romance, real-life issues, and a dash of mystery . . . Recommend for mature fans of well-done historical fiction."

—*CBA Retailers and Resources*

"Hauck tells another gorgeously rendered story. The raw, hidden emotions of Taylor and Jack are incredibly realistic and will resonate with readers. The way the entire tale comes together with the image of the chapel as holding the heartbeat of God is breathtaking and complements the romance of the story."

—*RT Book Reviews*, 4½ stars and a TOP PICK!

THE WEDDING DRESS

"Hauck weaves an intricately beautiful story centering around a wedding dress passed down through the years. Taken at face value, the tale is superlative, but considering the spiritual message both on the surface and between the lines, this novel is incredible. Readers will laugh, cry, and treasure this book."

—*RT Book Reviews*, TOP PICK!

"*The Wedding Dress* is a thought-provoking read and one of the best books I have read. Look forward to more . . ."

—Michelle Johnman, Gold Coast, Australia

"I thank God for your talent and that you wrote *The Wedding Dress*. I will definitely come back to this book and read it again. And now I cannot wait to read *Once Upon a Prince*."

—Agata from Poland

THE ROYAL WEDDING SERIES

"Perfect for Valentine's Day, Hauck's latest inspirational romance offers an uplifting and emotionally rewarding tale that will delight her growing fan base."

—*Library Journal*, starred review

"Hauck writes a feel-good novel that explores the trauma and love of the human heart . . . an example of patience and sacrifice that readers will adore."

—*Romantic Times*, 4 stars

"A stirring modern-day fairy tale about the power of true love."

—Cindy Kirk, author of *Love at Mistletoe Inn*

"*How to Catch a Prince* is an enchanting story told with bold flavor and tender insight. Engaging characters come alive as romance blooms between a prince and his one true love. Hauck's own brand of royal-style romance shines in this third installment of the Royal Wedding series."

—Denise Hunter, bestselling author of the Chapel
Springs Romance and Blue Ridge Romance series

"*How to Catch a Prince* contains all the elements I've come to love in Rachel Hauck's Royal Wedding series: an 'it don't come easy' happily ever after, a contemporary romance woven through with royal history, and a strong spiritual thread with an unexpected touch of the divine. Hauck's smooth writing—and the way she wove life truths throughout the novel—made for a couldn't-put-it-down read."

—Beth K. Vogt, author of *Somebody Like You*, one
of *Publishers Weekly*'s Best Books of 2014

"Rachel Hauck's inspiring Royal Wedding series is one for which you should reserve space on your keeper shelf!"

—*USA TODAY*

"Hauck spins a surprisingly believable royal-meets-commoner love story. This is a modern and engaging tale with well-developed secondary characters that are entertaining and add a quirky touch. Hauck fans will find a gem of a tale."

—*Publishers Weekly* starred review of *Once Upon a Prince*

THE
MEMORY
HOUSE

ALSO BY RACHEL HAUCK

The Love Letter
The Writing Desk
The Wedding Dress
The Wedding Chapel
The Wedding Shop

NOVELLAS FOUND IN *A YEAR OF WEDDINGS*
A March Bride (e-book only)
A Brush with Love: A January Wedding Story (e-book only)

THE ROYAL WEDDING SERIES
Once Upon a Prince
Princess Ever After
How to Catch a Prince
A Royal Christmas Wedding

LOWCOUNTRY ROMANCE NOVELS
Sweet Caroline
Love Starts with Elle
Dining with Joy

NASHVILLE NOVELS
Nashville Sweetheart (e-book only)
Nashville Dreams (e-book only)

WITH SARA EVANS
Sweet By and By
Softly and Tenderly
Love Lifted Me

THE
MEMORY
HOUSE

RACHEL HAUCK

THOMAS NELSON
Since 1798

The Memory House

Copyright © 2019 by Rachel Hauck

Published in Nashville, Tennessee, by Thomas Nelson. Thomas Nelson is a registered trademark of HarperCollins Christian Publishing, Inc.

Unless otherwise noted, Scripture quotations are taken from the New American Standard Bible®, Copyright © 1960, 1962, 1963, 1968, 1971, 1972, 1973, 1975, 1977, 1995 by The Lockman Foundation. Used by permission. (www.Lockman.org)

Lyrics for "The Old Rugged Cross" by George Bennard. Public domain.

Lyrics for "Good, Good Father," performed by Chris Tomlin, written by Anthony Brown and Pat Barrett.

Thomas Nelson titles may be purchased in bulk for educational, business, fund-raising, or sales promotional use. For information, please email SpecialMarkets@ThomasNelson.com.

Publisher's Note: This novel is a work of fiction. Names, characters, places, and incidents are either products of the author's imagination or used fictitiously. All characters are fictional, and any similarity to people living or dead is purely coincidental.

Library of Congress Cataloging-in-Publication Data

Names: Hauck, Rachel, 1960- author.
Title: The memory house / Rachel Hauck.
Description: Nashville, Tennessee : Thomas Nelson, [2019]
Identifiers: LCCN 2018049926| ISBN 9780785216643 (library edition) | ISBN 9780310350965 (paperback) | ISBN 9780310350972 (epub)
Subjects: | GSAFD: Love stories.
Classification: LCC PS3608.A866 M46 2019 | DDC 813/.6--dc23 LC record available at https://lccn.loc.gov/2018049926

Printed in the United States of America

19 20 21 22 23 24 LSC 6 5 4 3 2 1

Gary and Bonnie Stebbins, giants in the Kingdom of God. It's been an honor to walk with you for almost three decades. Your faithfulness is breathtaking.

CHAPTER ONE

BECK

Manhattan, New York

She was never afraid of the dark. But the light? Now that terrified her. So when the perp ran down shadowed, dark Avenue D, she followed without hesitation.

"NYPD. Stop!"

A sergeant with the Ninth Precinct, Beck Holiday also never shied away from a fight. At least not on the streets of New York. Not in the name of justice.

Her partner's footsteps resounded behind her, each heel crack vibrating against the cold New Year's Eve night. But when the suspect jumped an iron gate bordering a small concrete courtyard between two buildings, Hogan slowed up.

"Beck, forget it." He gasped between each word. "Happy New Year to him. We'll get him next time."

She reached for the bars and sailed over, the edge of her tac pants just clearing the five-foot wrought iron—despite the extra load she carried—with ease.

Adrenaline made her Wonder Woman.

"Stop. Police!"

The perp aimed for a side door of a run-down apartment building. His toe hit a crack in the concrete and he stumbled, dropping a package to the ground.

The item hit with a *thud*, and Beck glanced down as she leaped over, maintaining her pursuit.

"Hogan, get the package!"

1

Just as the lanky, pasty, undernourished perp made the door, she grabbed the back of his jacket and tossed him to the ground face-first, driving her knee between his shoulder blades. "Hands behind your back."

"I wasn't doing nothing." A boy. No more than eighteen. Lately the young ones were getting to her.

"Nothing? So why'd you run?" She slapped him in cuffs, then searched for a weapon, finding a knife, a crack pipe, and a plastic bag.

"I had to pee."

Beck dangled the bag in front of his nose, almost gagging at its putrid smell. "And this?"

"Never seen it before in my life. You planted it on me."

Hogan was hung up on the gate, his pant leg stuck on a spiked iron tip. Swearing, he yanked himself free with a ripping sound and fell to the ground with a grunt.

Beck dropped her head and sighed, then jerked the perp to his feet, shoving him toward Hogan.

"Get him to the car. I'll investigate the package."

Through the yellow glow of apartment lights, she caught a clearer view of her perp's profile.

"Parker Boudreaux."

Go figure. An Upper West Side kid with a serious addiction problem who had nothing better to do on this holiday than run drugs.

"Sergeant Holiday, so we meet again." He stumbled toward Hogan. "I'll be out before the clock chimes twelve."

Beck had no doubt Boudreaux's rich daddy would spring him in time to ring in the New Year with champagne and a blow of coke. But for now he was her collar.

She'd arrested him three times already for running drugs through Alphabet City, working for a sly dealer the Ninth had yet to collar.

"Do your parents know you're down here? Working for your next high?" What a waste of potential, Boudreaux.

Beck stood by the stash he left on the ground expecting to find a couple hundred milligrams of crack—just shy of felony possession.

"High? Why, you have me confused with someone else. I'm visiting a friend who's throwing a New Year's party." Boudreaux leaned against the bars as Hogan tried to work the gate. "Uncuff me and I'll open it for you."

Hogan grunted as he tucked his light under his chin, giving the stuck latch a determined tug.

Beck watched, waiting. "Call the super, Hogan."

"Don't need you to tell me how to do my job, Holiday."

She watched for another second, then bent down to Parker's canvas tote bag. Seemed like a no-brainer to call for the superintendent.

But Hogan was Hogan. An old beat cop who knew more about crime and donuts than any cop she knew.

He'd trained her. Brought her up. Taught her how to do the job. He was the one who listened when her world didn't make sense.

But a bad divorce and a battle with alcohol nearly ruined his career. He'd only recently returned to the Ninth and was eager to redeem himself. Seemed strange to be his boss now. She'd only been a sergeant for a little over a year. But if battling with a stupid gate made him feel like he was a member of the fraternity again—

"Pretty cop lady, hey, how about letting me go?" Boudreaux resorted to whining. "I can make it worth your while. Besides, when did it become a crime to visit a friend?"

Hogan battered the lever with his flashlight and a few choice words. "That kind of talk will get you nowhere. Especially with her."

Especially with her. At one time that may have been true. But lately she'd started to change. Started to *feel*.

It wasn't enough anymore to be a tough cop, to get the collar. Suddenly she teared up over the smallest detail—a kid with a cut or a single mom locked out of her apartment. Forget the hard stuff like a suicide or the death of a family member. A year ago, six months ago, she shook them off with a beer at Rosie's.

But lately she found it harder to look away. Harder to shake off the inhumanity, the ridiculous, the despair wandering her streets. This emerging compassion rattled her and, frankly, ticked her off.

"You need better friends, Boudreaux," Beck said, peeling back the filthy cloth tote, getting a whiff of something . . . dying. She jerked back, covering her nose, then startled when the bag moved.

Snatching her hand away, she leaned right, aiming her light through the opening, finding the dirty, weary face of a small gray dog, his watery eyes pleading.

"Boudreaux!" Dropping to her knees, Beck gently slid the mutt from the worn canvas bag, compassion stinging her eyes.

The dog whimpered and moaned as she examined his protruding rib cage, his matted chest rising and falling, struggling for each shallow breath.

She'd kill him. *Kill him*. "Oh, sweet thing, I'm so sorry. I'm so sorry. What has he done to you?" But she knew. She knew.

Running her hand down the dog's back, she felt every rib, every bone. Again he moaned when she touched his belly. The smell—vomit, feces—emanated from his fur and skin and clung to Beck's nose.

"Hey, Five-O. That's my friend's dog, you hear me? Five-O, you listening?"

Beck raised up, adjusting the stiff waistband of her new cargo tac pants. She'd finally broken down and purchased a larger size to accommodate her expanding middle.

"Your friend's dog?"

"You heard me. I don't stutter."

Beck shivered from the inside, numb to the exterior cold, and balled her hand into a fist. "Did you feed him this plastic bag?"

She held it up, pinched between her thumb and finger, the stench of the bag matching the dog.

"What bag? I haven't seen a bag." His prep-school accent only fueled her disdain.

About then, the gate latch released and Hogan tumbled backward, a broken piece of metal clanging down on the concrete.

"Look here, the po-po damaged private property. I think that's a felony, isn't it?"

"Let's go." Hogan yanked Boudreaux toward the RMP, the boy's protests bouncing between the brick buildings.

"Sergeant, careful with my friend's dog." Parker struggled against Hogan's grip. "Help, police brutality!"

A few apartment windows lit up, and someone shouted an indistinguishable response.

"Easy now, little guy." The dog moaned as Beck tried to pick him up. "What'd that mean ol' Boudreaux do to you?"

Based on the dog's bones-to-skin ratio, he was starving. A fresh wash of tears covered her eyes. This sort of emotion kicked at her steel doors, at her habit of ignoring tenderness, care, or concern. She had her MO when it came to her emotions or sorrowful memories— burying them. Even better, forget them.

From her side pocket, she retrieved a bottle of water, twisted off the cap, and touched the dog's tongue with a few drops. He lapped it up, and she poured out a little more.

"Beck, let's go." Hogan peered between the bars. "Call animal control for the dog."

Beck ignored him. How could she leave the pooch? He'd die. The dog's sad condition reached deep and unwound her tight heart. Where she'd been hard and controlled, she was now soft and impulsive.

The night's cold dipped between the buildings and the dog shivered. Beck shimmied from her coat to cover him up before scooping him, and the scent of death, into her arms.

He cried as she stood, making her way toward the gate. And darn if she didn't feel the dog's tears dripping against her hand.

"I'm sorry, so sorry, sweet boy. I'm going for help. Just stay with me. There's a vet over on 15th—"

From inside the patrol car, Boudreaux shouted against the glass. "That's my dog. You hear me? Just because you're the police doesn't mean you can steal a man's dog."

"Is he alive?" Hogan peeked beneath Beck's jacket.

"Barely." Beck swore, kicking the car door with such force Parker jumped back. "Did you feed this dog drugs? That bag?"

Hogan took the moaning pooch in his arms and under Beck's flashlight glow, examined him. She stroked the dog's ears, telling him everything would be all right, fighting another grip of tears. Last thing Hogan, or Boudreaux, needed to see was feminine emotion.

"He's in bad shape, but I've seen worse. He's weak and hungry," Hogan said. "Probably just gave back that bag. Wouldn't surprise me if Boudreaux was about to feed him his next haul. Or worse, just stuff it up his—"

"That's it!" Beck wrangled Boudreaux from the back seat by his hair and slammed him against the car, her knee boring into his thigh as she pressed his face against the trunk. "You think your daddy can get you out of this? Huh?" She slammed his face against the cold metal.

"You can't treat me this way." Boudreaux struggled against her hold, and it took every ounce of strength to maintain her grip.

"Yeah? Who says? I can treat you the way you treated that dog." Every molecule in her body was on fire and racing through her. If she didn't defend the weak and helpless, then who would?

"Sergeant." Hogan yanked her back, sounding like his former-sergeant self. "Put him back in the car."

But Beck shrugged him off. "You think you're a big shot running drugs—for who, Vinny Campanile? He's the devil himself. Feeding crack to sweet, innocent animals will not keep you alive. Or out of jail. People will cry for your head when they hear what you did."

"He's a mutt," Boudreaux said, raising up enough to spit at her.

"That's a step above the gutter you live in."

"Okay, we've had our fun." Hogan shoved her out of the way

and turned the kid toward the open back seat door. "Get in the car, Boudreaux, and shut up."

Parker cackled and snarled at Beck. "He's a mutt. A *stinking*, nobody-wants-him mutt. I was planning on barbecuing him for dinner."

Beck flew at Parker, swinging with the full force of her ire, driving a wild punch to his face. Boudreaux yowled as he toppled forward and cracked his head against the top of the door.

"Sergeant!" Hogan shoved her back, gripping her collar in his fist. But the dog in his left arm handicapped him. And Beck was too quick.

"This is for the dog," Beck snarled over Parker before ramming her boot into his ribs. When he buckled she drove her knee against his nose. "That's for squandering your life." Beck extracted the pup from Hogan, whispering in the dog's floppy ears. "I got you."

"Sergeant—" Hogan lifted Boudreaux from the sidewalk and shoved him into the RMP. "I told you to shut up." He slammed the door and chased Beck to the melody of Parker's muted complaints. "Beck, talk to me. What's going on?"

"I'm taking this poor animal to the clinic on 15th." With each step, her stride lengthened. She never felt more right about anything in her life.

But Hogan's firm grip pulled her back. "We've got Boudreaux. His fourth arrest. He'll give us Vinny for sure this time. Happy New Year to us. We need this. I need this. Come back with me and I'll help cover for you."

"Cover what? That I gave him what he deserved?" But she knew. Hitting a man while he was cuffed was the *worst* offense. She could feel the steam rising from the hot water waiting for her. "Do what you have to do. I'm getting help for this dog."

"Beck, wait." Hogan sounded more like a father than a partner. "What's gotten into you? This sort of stuff never put you over the edge before. You've always been so controlled."

A tear leaked from the corner of her eye. "I'm . . . I'm still controlled. Maybe my priorities are shifting." She raised her chin in subtle defiance. "Can't a girl change a little?"

"Sure, but not when it comes to procedure. You've been by the book since the day I met you."

"Well, maybe the book needs some new pages."

She'd been fine with life, ensconced in her routine and cop identity until this past summer, when a nine-month sting operation to take thugs like Boudreaux and Vinny Campanile off the street went bust.

The team met at Rosie's to drown their sorrows, and she ran into—

"What?" she said, her gaze meeting Hogan's through the ghostly drift of street lamps and the low yellow of apartment lights, the honks and motor sounds of the city boxing them in.

"Nothing." Hogan squinted. "You just seemed different there for a second."

"I'm the same old me, but I'm not abandoning this dog. Take Boudreaux in. Get the collar. My New Year's gift to you. I'm going to the vet." She whirled away as the dog emitted sounds of pain. A cold tear slipped down the side of her nose.

At first her steps were weak, undecided, as she marched down the avenue, her knuckles still stinging. But as Beck passed through swaths of dark and light, her confidence grew. The weak and weary pup nestled against her breast, and she felt as if she carried a piece of her own soul in her hands.

CHAPTER TWO

BRUNO

January
Scooba, Mississippi

For a kid who grew up on the wrong side of happiness, he had done well for himself. Graduated with honors from Florida State. Made the *Law Review*. Mentored by the best sports agent in the business, Kevin Vrable, which landed him in the 90210 zip code.

Yeah, for a while he had the world on a string.

"I'll make you the best sports agent in the business."

"When I retire, all of this is yours, Bruno."

"You have a gift, son. A gut intuition."

Then last year things started going sideways. For no real reason other than his precious ego, Kevin started cutting Bruno out of the loop, closing *his* deals and walking away with the money and the glory. All for himself.

He lived with it until Kevin also cut his bonuses. Last year Kevin only paid him once. When Bruno called him out, Kevin fired him, ending his eight-year career at Watershed Sports.

Kevin Vrable was a petty, jealous, greedy man who saw no value in honoring his word. But Bruno was a survivor of broken promises. Crushed and stunned, he determined to rise above and carve a new path for himself.

After all, he was the top sports agent for the last three years. He had clout, reputation, and skill.

Which was how he found himself in a cheap rental car on his way to Scooba, Mississippi. Population 697.

He'd flown up to the Golden Triangle in a tricked-out, custom Gulfstream owned and piloted by his buddy Stuart Strickland. Then it was a clanging rental car and country roads the rest of the way.

"You're here. Good, good." Coach Brown clapped Bruno on the back as he stepped out of his car, stretching, the cold wind relieving his warm, road-weary legs. "Thanks for coming out. I half expected you to change your mind."

"I almost did." Bruno slung the strap of his leather case over his head and clapped the car door closed. "Did you know you're in the middle of nowhere?" He fell in step with the coach, entering the field house offices, his loafer heels scuffing over the tile floors and echoing against the painted cinderblock walls.

"Yep. The boonies." Coach Brown motioned for Bruno to set his bag in his office, then trek with him down the hall. "But we run a great football program."

"You know I'm only doing this as a favor for Calvin Blue." Calvin was an All-American footballer from Florida State. A must-get for Bruno and his fledgling agency, Sports Equity.

The tailback would go first round of the NFL draft this April, and that meant big money for Calvin. Bruno, too, if he could convince the kid to sign. Not to mention the restoration of Bruno's reputation.

It was one thing to part ways with Kevin and Watershed and launch out on his own, but another to combat Kevin's venomous whispers, poisoning top university pro liaisons against Bruno.

"Lost his touch."

"Can't close the deal."

"A one-man agency? Who's he kidding? He can't do anything for your boys. He's scraping the bottom."

Nevertheless, he limped along with his clout, reputation, and skill.

"Calvin's a good kid," Coach Brown said. "Talented. I'm grateful he's trying to help his old teammate." Brown ran a junior college program that redeemed Division 1 dropouts, players who failed at the big schools for one reason or another. "Did you review the tapes I sent you? This Tyvis kid . . . He's got it all."

"I watched the tapes. He's got an arm, but my main concern is why he's here with you." Bruno walked with Coach through the weight room to the outdoor practice field, zipping his jacket against the wind.

"Anger issues. Got in a few fights with his coaches, then went on a little robbery spree, hitting up convenience stores. God was on his side in court, because the judge gave him community service if he returned all the money. Which he did. He worked all last year to clear his record and name, then showed up here."

Brown's job at this esteemed community college, or JUCO, was to straighten out the boys and send them back up the line to major college programs for a chance at the NFL.

According to Brown, Tyvis Pryor was his most esteemed protégé.

"Have you reformed him in one season?"

Coach grinned. "I don't like to brag, but he earned a B-plus GPA while becoming the conference's leading passer. Broke every record on the books."

About the fifty-yard line, Bruno watched a big kid with long arms, thick legs, and a graceful throw.

"Six five, 230," Coach said. "I'm telling you, he's the next Tom Brady and no one's looking at him."

"He's a JUCO kid, Coach. Of course no one is looking at him. If he's this good, send him up to FSU or down to Florida. They need a quarterback."

"He's twenty-two and wants a shot at the pros."

Of course he did. Along with every other college kid.

"He does know Cinderella is a fairy tale, right?" Bruno followed the ball as it spiraled toward a narrow target.

Yet after a year and a half of hustling, he'd signed exactly zero clients. If he came out of this recruiting season with nothing but a JUCO kid, he might as well bring in the Sports Equity shingle and hang his head. Kevin Vrable, and Bruno's father for that matter, would be right.

Bruno Endicott was a nothing.

"Did you see him thread that target?" Bruno shook off the word *nothing* and give his attention to Coach. "Hit the hole from the fifty-yard line. Come on, just give him a chance."

"Yeah, sure, why not?" Bruno agreed, arms folded, his stance stiff as he observed Tyvis going through drills.

This whole venture screamed desperation. No agent in his right mind would sign a kid out of junior college. It was career suicide.

But if signing Tyvis Pryor won the favor of Calvin Blue, the player Bruno really wanted, he just might do it.

"Come on, Calvin, join your friend Tyvis at Sports Equity. Let's shake up the NFL."

Coach blew his whistle and waved Tyvis to the sidelines. "I've got someone I want you to meet." The quarterback loped off the field. "This is Bruno Endicott, the sports agent I was telling you about."

Bruno clapped his hand into the player's. "Your buddy Calvin Blue speaks highly of you."

Tyvis's smile was quick and sincere. "We been friends since freshman year at Florida State." His voice matched his physique—booming, elegant, and controlled. "He said you used to be one of the top agents in the country. Worked with Watershed."

"I still am one of the top agents." Bravado worked every time. "You know Jack Stryker? Luke Mays? Dustin Clever?" With each name, the NFL hopeful's eyes widened. "Signed them all."

"They're some serious ballers."

Bruno flipped Tyvis his card. "I have my own agency now. Sports Equity."

"Fernandina Beach, Florida?" Tyvis made a face. "Where's that?"

"Just outside of Jacksonville." Seriously? The kid was interviewing him? "What happened with you at FSU?" Even though Coach Brown had filled him in, Bruno wanted to hear Tyvis's version.

"Gentlemen, can we face off over dinner?" Coach slapped Bruno on the back. "My wife makes the best lasagna you ever tasted, and my mouth is already watering. Let's head on over to the house, and you can talk over meat, noodles, and ricotta cheese. Bruno, when was the last time you had a home-cooked meal?"

"What year is it?"

As a sports agent, he lived on the road, eating out of boxes and cartons. When he was home, Mom sometimes cooked for him, but her day job with Mrs. Acker was rather exhausting, and cooking was low on her priorities.

"Hit the showers, Tyvis, while I give Bruno your stat sheet."

The man-boy nodded and jogged toward the field house.

"Kid runs everywhere," Coach said, motioning for Bruno to follow him to his office.

Despite his reservations, Bruno was impressed with what he'd seen on the field. The kid was quick with good feet and could throw a shot.

Coming from the right school with the right trainer, Tyvis *might* be a contender. Hard to tell with what little he'd seen this afternoon. But coming from a JUCO with a troubled past? Yeah, Bruno couldn't see any future for him.

"So what happened at Watershed, Bruno?" Coach Brown walked into his small, boxy office littered with equipment and papers.

"We didn't see eye to eye."

"Does anyone see eye to eye with Vrable?" Coach sat with an *umph.* "I heard your mother was ill too."

"She was in a car accident. Broke her leg in two places. She needed me. Kevin didn't."

"You came home to take care of her?"

"Something like that." And to figure out how eight years at

Watershed ended with Kevin shouting him down in front of the entire Watershed staff.

"You're a nothing, Endicott."

"Here's his stat sheet from FSU and here. Also his forty time as well as his vertical, bench press . . . Well, read, you'll see."

Bruno took the folder and sat in the nearest chair. "He doesn't want a year at a D1 school first?"

"Like I said, he's twenty-two and wants to try at the league. It's now or never for him. At least that's how he sees it. I think you might know what it feels like to want a chance." Coach arched his brow. *Hear me?* "You two have a lot in common, you know."

"Tyvis and me? Like what?"

"His dad walked out on the family, like yours. Died a few years later. You came home to take care of your mom after her accident. Tyvis works after practice to send money to his mom, sister, and brother. Last summer he worked three jobs and showed up for the first day of practice in the best shape I've ever seen." Coach Brown dug through some papers, shuffling things around, finally producing an image of Tyvis. "Can you imagine how he'd look with proper training? He was built for football, Bruno."

Bruno scanned the grainy image printed on regular printer paper. No denying Tyvis's physical stature, but that didn't make him a pro QB.

"And like you," Coach went on, taking the picture back, "he's hungry for more. For success. He won't give up until the last door has slammed in his face."

Coach Brown looked too closely. Saw things Bruno didn't know he revealed.

"What other agencies are you talking to, Coach?"

"Just you."

Bruno sat back with a short, sarcastic laugh. "Then you really don't believe in Tyvis like you say."

"No, I just think you're the guy to take him all the way." Coach shuffled through more papers and manila folders, moving one large stack on top of another. Bruno braced for them to topple over. "My wife is a retired paralegal and she loves to research. Ah, here we go." Coach held up a thin, new folder. "This is your file."

So the man cheated. Didn't have the eye of a magi like Bruno thought.

"Almost every player you signed went in the first round. Most of them in the top ten. You're the only agent in the last five years to accomplish such a feat. You have a gift. An eye. And every one of those players has similar stats to Tyvis Pryor."

Coach dropped the folder on the desk with smug satisfaction.

Bruno leaned forward, arms propped on his legs, and reviewed Tyvis's stats again. They were very similar to a first-round pick he signed three years ago. But that kid led his team to the national championship.

"I don't know . . ." The burn of humiliation ran under his skin. How in the world did he get here?

Why had he stayed in Fernandina Beach? It was an out-of-the-way oceanside community forty minutes from the outskirts of Jacksonville.

Why did he stay, propping up his fledging reputation and business when he had other offers?

Why did he give in to the invisible tug telling him to stay put? The whisper that told him he was home?

He suspected Mom's prayers had a hand in some of this, but she never spoke to him about God. Or church. Instead, she did something more effective. She talked to *God* about her son.

"On top of everything else," Coach said, whether to Bruno or the office walls was unclear. "I've got Tyvis talking to Jesus. Hope you don't mind me saying. Seems the scourge of society today to mention the Holy Man."

Bruno filed Tyvis's folder in his shoulder bag. "Why would I mind?"

"Didn't know where you stood on things. Anyway, Tyvis joined the choir." Coach rocked back in his squeaky chair. "You should see him standing in the back with the rest of the men, towering over them. But he's got a sweet bass."

"How long have you been practicing this pitch?"

"Since you agreed to visit." In his midsixties, Coach Brown had the vitality of a younger man with a passion for football in his eyes. "Call me crazy, but I think he can make it."

"You're crazy." Bruno moved to the window and stared out over the field. A sleeting rain had just started to fall. "You think I'm a miracle worker, Coach? No NFL team will consider him. He won't get invited to the combine, and he won't have a Pro Day at his college because JUCOs don't have Pro Days. What's your plan to get scouts and coaches to look at him?"

"I thought I'd leave that up to you."

Bruno laughed. "You're a bigger dreamer than Tyvis."

"How many clients do you have now?" Coach stood, looking at his watch, then patted his belly.

"I'm in a building phase."

"So zero?"

"Calvin is close, and if I sign him, I *might* take on Tyvis. Might."

"My guess is you won't get Calvin if you don't sign Tyvis. Those boys are thick. Problem with your age group is you think too small. You want only what you see, what others are doing. You think the Wright brothers worried that no man had flown before? What if Edison said, 'Yo, y'all, candles are good. Been working for a thousand years.'"

"Edison would say *yo?*'"

Coach propped against the edge of his desk and tapped his temple. "You've got to think outside the box, get Vrable's voice out of your head. Listen to me, you know as well as I do the NFL will take any player who is good enough. Got guys in the league who didn't even go to college."

"That's a rare case, Coach."

"Tyvis Pryor is rare enough. Stop believing the only guys you can rep are the thoroughbreds. Take a kid who is not in the limelight and break all the rules."

Bruno listened with one ear. Break the rules? No, he was a by-the-book man. So much so he called out Kevin for inconsistencies and impropriety. Which, *again*, was how he ended up in a JUCO coach's office in Scooba, Mississippi.

". . . get him a Pro Day. Florida State. Jacksonville State. University of Central Florida. Didn't you recruit the state of Florida for Watershed? Isn't that your backyard? Tyvis is from Destin. That's your turf."

"You talk as if you know me, Coach." Bruno flipped his hand toward the folder on Coach's desk. "But you don't. Because if you did, you'd know a junior college player will not satisfy me."

Coach sighed and walked around his desk. He powered off his old computer and collected his keys.

"You're right. I don't know you. A few facts and quotes off the internet don't connect one man to another. Any other player, I'd not bother you. But Tyvis is special, Bruno. I've never seen a kid work so hard for so little. Hitting the weight room at five a.m., working in the cafeteria before and after class. Always ready for practice. Makes every study table. Day after day after day. For crying out loud, he still carries a flip phone. You can't text him because he doesn't have a text plan. He messed up, and he wants to make it right. He wants to provide for his mom, sister, and brother. He wants to try for the dream he's had since he was nine years old. Tell me this. Why are you a sports agent? Why not a corporate lawyer or a litigator? The money's way better, and you get to be home on weekends and holidays."

Bruno shifted his stance. Did they have enough time to list his reasons? But in truth, his answer was simple. "I love it," he said.

"Then give Tyvis the same consideration. He loves it. I've seen players, and I've seen *players*." Coach's voice resonated with conviction. "He was born to play the game. Why sit in an office or drive a truck when you know you belong on the field?"

The door opened and Tyvis peeked inside. "Ready?"

"Let's go," Coach said, jingling his keys and flicking off the office lights, ordering Tyvis to follow him to dinner.

Walking to his car, Bruno checked his email. Besides Calvin Blue, he was chasing a player at Ohio State and another at Florida. There were no updates.

Pulling out behind Coach's big F350, Bruno called his mom. "How was your day?" Ever since her accident, when she lay in a ditch for two hours before anyone found her, he kept one part of his heart toward hers.

"Mrs. Acker wanted to plant roses."

"In winter?" Even in Florida, there were seasons for sowing.

"Next week she'll have me pull them up and plant orchids. When are you coming home?"

"Tonight."

"In that small plane?" Mom moaned. "I know you say Stuart is an excellent pilot, but oh, the very idea makes me quiver. Can you wear a parachute?"

"In case we get shot out of the sky?"

"An engine could blow up. Or fall off."

Bruno chuckled to himself. "Stu is an excellent pilot, and the Gulfstream *jet* is an excellent aircraft. You do realize he's flying me around the South for free simply because he wants to log hours? He's saving me time and money. Since I'll be home tonight instead of driving or waiting for a commercial flight, I can take you to breakfast tomorrow at Bright Mornings Café. How about it?"

"Fine, but I still don't like you flying around in a private jet." A bit of the tension eased from her voice. "It'll be good to see you."

He'd been gone all of December. Bowl game after bowl game had him on the road. Even Christmas Day.

They chitchatted while Bruno followed Coach down winding two-lane roads lined with bare-limbed maples and tall pines.

He'd was about to say good-bye as they pulled into Coach's driveway when Mom said, "Bruno, I've been keeping some news from you."

"Like what?" He parked behind Coach's truck and cut the engine, his adrenaline spiking a bit. Was she sick? Cancer? *No, no, don't go there.* Did she meet someone?

Her voice had the same timbre as when she called about the accident. As when she told him Dad had died.

"It's Miss Everleigh, son. She died."

"Miss Everleigh? When?" Bruno glanced out the window as Coach waved him inside, but he lowered his head to the steering wheel instead of getting out.

He'd just lost a sacred piece of his childhood. The cherub-faced woman had lived across the street his whole life. The woman in the memory house—as he called it as a kid—had taught him how to make chocolate-chip cookies, roast marshmallows, and construct Noah's ark out of Popsicle sticks.

The sprawling Victorian with turrets and spirals was where he spent his afternoons after Dad walked out and Mom worked two jobs. It was in her yard where he fell in love at first sight at eight years old.

Beck Holiday. He hadn't thought of her in years.

"Right after Thanksgiving."

"Thanksgiving? You're just now telling me? Did I miss the memorial?"

"The memorial is Sunday afternoon. Miss Everleigh didn't want a fuss, but Pastor decided otherwise. But with the holidays and folks traveling, the memorial was delayed. Will you be home Sunday?"

"Absolutely." He wouldn't miss saying good-bye to the only "grandmother" he'd known.

He finished the call and stepped out of the car, gazing toward the rainy gray horizon.

"Rest in peace, Miss Everleigh." He'd meant to visit her more when he returned to Fernandina Beach. The recruiting trail gave little pause to consider his own life, let alone another's.

"Bruno! Dinner's on," Coach beckoned from the opened garage door. "And it's starting to rain. Didn't your mama teach you better?"

"Coming."

Inside, Tyvis laughed with a slender woman with reddish hair and inquisitive eyes. His sculpted, dark form dwarfed her, but he exuded gentleness. The scene was a cheerful balm to Mom's news, and Bruno stepped into it wishing he had more moments like this in his life. Maybe even a family of his own.

But that would require slowing down. It would require a relationship with a woman that lasted beyond one date. It would require him opening his heart.

"I hope you're hungry," Coach said, pushing Bruno into the room.

"I'm starved." He shifted his gaze to Tyvis, then to Mrs. Brown. "Ready to eat."

CHAPTER THREE

BECK

Light flooded her East Flatbush bedroom as she awoke, grumbling, squinting against the brightness. Burying herself under the covers, Beck bumped against a warm body curled next to hers.

She sat up, tossing the blankets aside as last night's events swept through her groggy haze. Boudreaux. The dog. Four hours at the animal clinic.

"Hey, little man. Happy New Year." She rubbed the pup's ears with tenderness. "Did you sleep well?"

With a small whimper, he tried to open his eyes, but exhaustion and the meds still claimed him.

He was a mini schnauzer, according to the vet. Five to six years old. Malnourished and dehydrated. Flea infested and full of worms.

They x-rayed and ultrasounded his battered insides, then treated him with antibiotics and fluids, finally sending Beck home with special food and recovery instructions.

Bring him back in two weeks. We'll do a more thorough exam.

While the little guy seemed to respond to hydration and food, the vet was concerned about unforeseen complications.

Stepping from her bed, Beck drew the curtains closed, then returned to curl up next to her new friend.

He sighed as she stroked his paw. She'd called him Beetle Boo on the mile walk to the clinic, and when the doctor wrote it on his chart, it was settled.

A light knock sounded on her door. "Happy New Year, Beck. You awake?" Mom peeked around. "You got home later than—" Her lips pursed, and she looked like an angry Popsicle in her pink nurse's uniform and pale winter skin. "A dog? Beck, please, you know Flynn is allergic."

"Happy New Year to you too, Mom." Eyes closed, Beck pressed her forehead against his tiny face, inhaling his sweet, clean fur. She'd had to leave the room when the vet tech started to clean him up by shaving off the clumps of matted fur. Beetle Boo had moaned and cried.

"Is there a story with this dog?"

"Don't worry, I'm looking for my own place. You won't have to endure a pet for long."

"You don't have to get defensive. It's just that Flynn is allergic to dogs."

Living with her mom, stepdad, and baby brother at thirty-one had never been the plan. But when Sara, her best friend from college and her Stuytown roommate, got married last year, Beck returned to her old East Flatbush bedroom *temporarily*.

But days and weeks turned into months, and then a year passed. She'd saved enough to get her own place and was about to sign a lease when she realized the night at Rosie's and the collision with Hunter Ingram had come with consequences.

Maybe that's why she wanted to care for Beetle Boo. As a distraction from the truth she'd so far ignored with her head monumentally in the sand.

"Beck?" The side of the bed sagged under Mom's light weight. Beck peeked at her with one eye. "Did you hear me? I'm heading to work, but dinner is in the Crock-Pot. Flynn should be home by six. The fridge calendar says you're working tonight. Please eat before you go. You're a rail. Flynn said he thought you'd been sick off and on last month—"

"Yeah, I ate too much street vendor food. Didn't sit well with me. Have fun at work, Mom."

"As fun as a twelve-hour shift at Kings County can be. But it is New Year's Day. There's always lots of good eats. Speaking of eats—"

"I heard you five seconds ago." Beck sat up, shoving the loose ends of her dark hair from her face. "Eat before I go to work."

"So, what's going on here?" Mom glanced at Beck, who tugged the sheet over her belly, then inspected the dog. "He's in bad shape."

"Took him from a perp who was feeding him drugs to poop out later."

Oh, right on time. Nausea. Within ten minutes of waking up. She thought she should be past it by now but—

"Why didn't you call animal control?"

"Because—" Breathe in, breathe out. Breathe in . . . And the moment passed. For now. "I felt he needed my help."

Beck glanced at Mom, a nurse, a caregiver, a lover of life. She should understand someone needing help.

Though the two of them had never been close. Beck was a daddy's girl—or so she was told. Then came 9/11, a layered disaster that touched them to this day.

The collapse of the North Tower forced mother and daughter together *and* apart in ways neither of them completely understood.

So they gave each other space, the benefit of the doubt, and overlooked how the other walked with a permanent limp. Mom by moving on with her life and never looking back. Beck by forgetting.

"Interesting," Mom said, standing, straightening her scrubs top. "You've never been sentimental about animals or babies. You hardly looked at your baby brother until he was two."

"Maybe I've changed. A little."

"Miracle of miracles." Mom checked her watch. "So is the dog a permanent addition?"

"I don't know. Maybe. Like I said, I have enough saved for my own place."

"Did I say you had to move? I just need to know what to tell Flynn. He's—"

"—allergic. I know."

And so it went between them. Ever since Beck was fourteen and Dad died. Any attempt to talk or connect came with an unseen tension, yet somehow laced with a soft patience and love.

"What kind of dog is this again?" Mom stretched her hand to Beetle's nose. But he was too weary to lift his head. "Maybe he's the kind that doesn't shed."

"A mini schnauzer." Beck smiled, warming her own soul a degree or two. "I appreciate all you and Flynn have done for me, letting me stay rent-free. But I want—need—to be on my own."

Mom nodded once. "I remember chomping at the bit to fly my parents' coop. I was twenty when I met your dad and fell head over heels." She leaned over to kiss Beck's forehead, bid Beetle Boo good day, and walked to the door. "Oh, you have some mail downstairs. A registered letter."

"From who?"

"A Florida lawyer." Mom checked her watch again, making a face. "I've *got* to go. Don't forget dinner is in the Crock-Pot."

When the door closed, Beck bolted out of bed and banged into the bathroom, dropping down beside the toilet. Relief. How was it possible the worst thing in the world—throwing up—gave her such sweet comfort?

Stretching her T-shirt over her expanding middle, she examined herself in the mirror.

She was in trouble. Big, layered, no-way-to-get-out-of-it trouble. The baby was making itself known, and she could not ignore her any longer.

The first two months she thought she was just working too hard, battling fatigue. Then the nausea started.

If she had her way, she'd hole up in her room with Beetle Boo until winter and all of her woes had passed. But by all accounts, labor was more than a mere woe.

Labor . . .

She'd have to go through it alone.

After brushing her teeth and washing her face, she returned to bed and curled up with Beetle. She stared at the ceiling, trying to think of nothing.

When she was little, her parents tucked her in with good-night prayers. The memories were vague and distant, and none of them had images of her father. Just Mom.

Beside her, the dog shifted with a light whimper and tried to jump down. Beck set him on the floor and watched as he teetered a second before trotting over to his water bowl.

She'd have to take him outside soon. He needed help to do his business. His back leg still didn't work right from being dropped on concrete. X-rays showed it'd been broken twice before. *Burn, Boudreaux, burn.*

Without a thought, she whispered a prayer for the pup. Then for herself. She heard enough desperate pleas on the job from dying vics, scared perps, and grieving loved ones to believe the notion of appealing to heaven was somewhat legit.

"Happy New Year, God, it's me, Beck Holiday. I need help."

Closing her eyes, she waited for some sort of voice or feeling, a response from the Almighty. But the only sound was the *ping* of a text.

With a groan, she rolled over to the nightstand. The series of one-line texts were from her lieutenant, Hunter Ingram.

Beck?
Call me.
Where are you?
What happened?
I need to know.

I can't cover for you otherwise.

Not sure I can anyway.

Sergeant?

WAKE UP!

Lifting Beetle Boo back onto the bed, she weighed her options.

Run away from home? No, she was too old for that. She'd *love* to run away from home and emerge into a new, surreal, almost perfect life where being pregnant made sense and gave her hope instead of dread.

Where she had her own home, a husband to be the baby's father—*if* she even decided to raise this baby—the return of her childhood memories, and a moment with Mom where the pain of Dad's death didn't silently send them to their opposite corners.

Was she just dreaming? Demanding too much of life? After eighteen years, she didn't hold out hope.

This was why she loved being a cop. She knew the job. Knew what was expected. Found a piece of herself in the day to day.

She'd created trouble for herself because of one stupid night. She had no one else to blame. Well, except *him*. They were both drunk, but if her vague memory served, she'd been the one to initiate things at Rosie's.

In the middle of Ingram's texts was one from Hogan.

How's the dog? Call me. Boudreaux's lawyer showed up

before I finished paperwork.

She was about to text him back when her phone rang. Ah, Ingram. She could tell by the ring he was losing patience.

Nevertheless, Beck hit end, tossed her phone beneath the tissues, papers, books, and essential oils in the nightstand drawer, and buried her burdens in her pillow.

Thanks for the help, God.

She must've dozed off, because a knock startled her from a dreamless sleep.

"Yeah?" She cleared her throat with a gaze at the clock. Seven p.m.

Her stepfather, Flynn, entered, dressed in his Brooklyn captain's uniform. "Did you walk off the job?"

"So they're calling captains in Brooklyn now?"

"Ingram, yes."

Beck moved the blankets, exposing Beetle Boo. "I didn't walk off. I just took this little guy to the vet. Hogan took the collar into the precinct. Which was a waste of time and money. Is there any justice in the world, Flynn?"

"There's justice. And everyone gets their day in court." He nodded to the dog. "You should've called animal control. That's their job. Yours is to—"

"Ignore an innocent, hurting, pleading animal to collar a multiple offender? Who, by the way, walked before Hogan finished the paperwork. No, Flynn, no. I was saving this guy right here." She scratched Beetle's nose and he raised his head, touching her hand with his pink tongue.

Flynn stared at her for a moment, caught between police captain and stepfather.

He'd been Dad's best friend since high school. They joined the force together at twenty-two and became members of the Cemetery Club, chasing coffee and trouble from midnight to eight a.m.

After 9/11, Flynn came around a lot to check on "Dale's widow." He and Mom married a year later.

"What happened?" he said with a deep sigh.

"Caught a repeat offender dealing again. He dropped a tote while I was in pursuit. This little man was inside, half dead. A drug mule."

Flynn leaned in for a look but stayed on his side of the room. "He's a sorry-looking pooch. What'd the vet say?"

"'That'll be fifteen hundred bucks.'" Beck jammed her feet into her slippers, flaring her T-shirt away from her middle, and reached for her robe. "Sent me home with some meds and food, along with instructions. He already looks ten times better."

"You know I'm allergic."

"Yep." She walked out of her room. Coffee, please, coffee.

She'd switched to decaf a month and half ago. Mom raised an eyebrow when she poured herself a cup one morning. Beck doctored it with creamer and told herself she had enough caffeine running through her veins to last two pregnancies.

Beef stroganoff aromas permeated the kitchen and for a moment, an overwhelming peace. Beck did love home. The cozy, safe place one went to hide from the world's troubles.

She wanted what Mom and Flynn had, a place to recover from the unexpected and build a life, maybe raise a kid.

There was the place on Rockaway Avenue, but it was a far cry from the swanky apartment she had shared with Sara in Stuytown.

Flynn moved about the kitchen, setting up for dinner, his broad, strong presence causing the peace to linger.

"Wyatt won't be home," he said, taking two plates from the cupboard and setting the table. "He and some of the boys went to Judah Maas's to watch the national championship semifinal."

"Who's playing?" Beck lifted the empty coffee carafe from the machine. So sad. So very sad. She returned it to the burner and opted for an orange juice.

OJ was better for her, right? At least that was the word on the street.

"Ohio State and Texas." Flynn took salad and a beer from the fridge. "Want one?" He held up his dark bottled brew.

"No, I'm working tonight."

He made a face. "Sorry, I thought you were off. Happy New Year, right?"

"I've worked every New Year's since I joined the force. Wouldn't know what to do with myself if I wasn't on shift."

She gulped the last swallow of OJ and tossed the bottle in the trash. "I need to feed the dog before dinner."

"Beck, you can't keep him. Forget my allergies. We work all hours in this house. He'll be by himself most of the time. We fight to spend time with each other as it is, never mind a dog." Flynn walked to the thermostat in the dining room. "Your mom is determined to turn this house into a summer resort."

"I'm getting my own place." A small flutter tickled her belly, and Beck reached for the high-back chair at the kitchen island. The baby. She moved.

"How are you going to take care of a dog with your schedule? Especially one that's sick?" Flynn eyed her over a sip of his beer. "Are you feeling okay these days?"

"I will. Lots of cops have dogs."

"Yes, and they have families to help."

"I can take care of him." She ran her hand through her hair, then adjusted her robe, loosening the belt. "I-I can move to days."

"For a dog?" Flynn's laugh was more sweet than mocking. "Call me the day you ask your lieutenant for that. Why don't you let me ask around the department? Remember Michael and Esther Greaves? They came to our Fourth of July bash last summer. You played basketball with their special-needs son. Mike told me the other day their therapist recommended a pet for him."

"I don't know." She glanced down. "I-I'm not sure I could trust anyone with him. He's been through so much."

"They're good people. You should see them with their boy. Your pup would thrive there."

Beck nodded and started for the stairs. "I'll think about it."

In her room she knelt beside the bed, gently waking up Beetle

Boo. He regarded her with sad brown eyes, though they were brighter and more alive than twelve hours ago.

"You hungry?" She opened a can of puppy food, then lifted him with care from the bed. Cradling him in her lap, she fed from her hand, then let him stand, wobbling, for another drink.

Afterward, she carried him out front, stepping into the cold, crisp night. Christmas lights still garnished the houses along the street.

He hopped toward the grass, and she held his backside as he squatted.

Then she gathered him up, kissing his head. "You and me. I won't let you go."

Back in her room, she cozied the blankets around him, then showered, the warm water flowing over her body, over the baby.

But reality was taking hold. Beck sank to the shower floor and pressed her head into her hands. Darn it. How'd she let this happen?

She was caught, trapped by a circumstance she did not want. And, in true Beck Holiday form, she'd ignored the problem, willing it to go away. She'd put it out of her mind. After all, she was good at forgetting.

She was supposed to have been a Wall Streeter, majoring in international finance at Columbia. She was law school bound until she interned with Goldman Sachs.

What a world. Like the ninth circle of hell. She hated every minute of it. On a whim she took the NYPD exams and earned the second highest score ever. Seven months later she graduated at the top of her class.

She loved her job. It gave her a sense of purpose. She loved the camaraderie of the officers and the unique fraternity of a few in the city of millions.

Mom reasoned Beck joined the force to be like her dad.

"Now why would I do that when I can't even remember him, Mom?"

But as the hot water turned her winter-pale skin pink, she

wondered. By being a cop, was she trying to find something she'd lost? Was it wrong to be like her father? Was it wrong to want to remember him, still, after eighteen years?

But she had more pressing concerns at the moment. Could she be a single mom and a cop? Flynn didn't even think she could look after a dog.

Beck stood and cut off the water. The heat and steam only made her more tired, only made her complications more pronounced.

She'd just finished dressing and drying her hair when Flynn called up the stairs. "You ready to eat? I've got the game on."

"Coming." She grabbed her backpack and set it by the door. Beetle Boo gazed up at her with a lost expression. "I'm right here, buddy. Don't worry."

She carried him downstairs and settled him on the sofa while she fixed her plate. Just as she stuffed the first delicious bite in her mouth, two texts rolled in.

The first was from the doctor's office, reminding her of the appointment on the third. She should consider going to this one since she blew off the last two.

The second was from Lieutenant Ingram.

When you get here, my office.

Beck sighed, tossing her phone to the other end of the couch, the creamy, rich goodness of beef stroganoff turning sour in her mouth. It was going to be a long night.

Meanwhile, Flynn was perched in his chair, wearing his favorite Ohio State sweats, cheering for the men in scarlet and gray.

"Can you watch the dog while I'm at work?" Beck said. "Please?"

"Touchdown!" Flynn tossed his hands in the air, flinging a small noodle across the room. "I'll get Wyatt to look in on him."

"Then remind him. He's sixteen and rather self-absorbed." Her much-younger baby brother was charming, lost in his own world of being a popular athlete who was the "desire of the *lay-dies*." His words, not hers.

"As I recall, you were self-absorbed at that age." Flynn retrieved the noodle, dabbing his napkin against the spot on the hardwood.

"At sixteen I'd lost my dad and any childhood memories associated with him. My mom was absent, working, grieving. Then she brought home a stepfather and gifted me with a bratty little brother. So yeah, maybe I was a bit lost in myself."

Flynn shifted his attention from the game. "Was it really so horrible?"

She grinned, taking a bite of food. "Wyatt's not so bad."

Her stepfather chuckled. "Well, that's good to know." Then he shouted at the TV. "Throw the flag, ref."

Beck had just finished her plate and was contemplating seconds when the game gave way to a commercial.

Flynn carried his dishes and empty beer bottle to the kitchen. "Did your mom tell you about the registered letter?"

"Oh, yeah, she did." Beck set her things in the dishwasher, deciding to forego seconds so she could have a donut on her way to work. She'd been craving a Brooklyn Blackout from the Doughnut Planet for a couple of days.

Finding the letter on the hall table, Beck glanced up at Flynn as he passed with another heaping mound of stroganoff. "Do we know people in Fernandina Beach, Florida?"

"You used to vacation there when you were a kid. When your dad was alive." Eyes fixed on the TV, Flynn sat with his food in his lap, then threw his napkin at the screen. "Come on, ref, let the boys play ball."

Beck stared at the envelope. So legal looking. Mom had once talked of how the two of them spent Beck's summer vacation in Florida. About six weeks, was it? Then Dad joined them for the last three.

But Mom rarely, if ever talked about the past or strolled glassy-eyed down the memory lane of her life, or Beck's, before 9/11.

Beck drew a breath and tore open the envelope, unfolding the long document. "This is the will of Mrs. Everleigh Callahan."

"What?" Flynn shot her a fast glance, then turned back to the game. "Everett who?"

"Everleigh, you goofball. Watch your game. It says . . ." The words caught in her throat. "I-I'm her sole beneficiary." She reviewed the envelope and the letterhead one more time. Yes, it was addressed to her. "This has to be a joke."

A commercial came on, and Flynn reached for the document. "I'm not a lawyer, but it looks legit. You inherited her house at 7 Memory Lane, Fernandina Beach, Florida." He made a face. "And her possessions, including her financial accounts." He handed the notice back to her as he went to the kitchen. "Guess you'd better talk to your mom about this. Who in the world is Everleigh Callahan, and why did she leave you everything?"

"Good question, Flynn. I was wondering the same thing."

CHAPTER FOUR

EVERLEIGH

May 1953
Waco, Texas

Marriage suited her. A notion she had never doubted. It filled her with joy and light. Yes, so much light.

Eight months ago Everleigh Novak walked the aisle of the First Baptist Church to her rancher cowboy and became his wife.

Tonight she would expand their fairy tale. *"Rhett, darling, I'm pregnant."*

Her pregnancy was confirmed by the doctor this morning when she'd already planned a romantic dinner with her man. They'd actually have the Applegate ranch house all to themselves. Her in-laws, the formidable Mama Applegate and congenial Daddy Applegate, queen and king of the Circle A, were dining with friends in town.

Everleigh pressed her hand to her still-flat belly as she gazed through the brilliant afternoon sunlight flooding Waco's downtown streets.

God smiled on her the day Rhett invited her to the dance. Miss Everleigh Novak, of all people, caught the eye of one of Baylor's most sought-after men. And Rhett chose her above all the beautiful girls vying for his attention.

And now her womb carried his offspring. Perhaps a son, the next heir to the Applegate ranching family. Or a daughter, who, in these modern times, may very well take over the ranch one day.

Their son, a future star fullback at Baylor University. Like his father.

Their daughter, *unlike* her mother, a future homecoming queen. Though make no mistake, as a rancher's daughter she'd be one part princess and one part tomboy. Sugar and spice.

Everleigh half decided she'd spoil their son and leave the daughter's indulgences to Rhett. Yet when all was said and done, this child and any future children would be loved. So very loved.

She frowned as rebel clouds gathered beyond her window, obscuring the sunlight and casting a thick shadow over the town, over her drawing table.

Everleigh glanced down at her work, the latest ad for Kestner's Family Department Store. If she didn't get these proofs to her boss by the end of the day . . .

Ink pen in hand, she returned to shading. She couldn't afford to lose her job as an ad artist just yet. She and Rhett were saving for their own home.

They'd tucked her earnings into a savings account while living with Rhett's parents. In his boyhood bedroom.

"I never thought I'd have a girl in here," he said to her on their first night back from the honeymoon.

"Well, I'm glad to be the one and only." Then she kissed him as if for the first time.

Everleigh laughed softly at the memory. He'd been so funny when they returned from their honeymoon, locking the door before crawling into bed, then climbing out again to wedge the small desk chair under the knob.

"This is Mama's house. If she wants to come in, believe you me, she's coming in."

Everleigh inked in the boot heel with vigor as another memory drifted across her mind.

Rhett had come home for lunch one afternoon, and seeing that Mama Applegate had gone into town, he thought the coast was clear to carry his new bride up to their room for a bit of afternoon *ravishing*.

Caught up in the moment, he didn't bother to bolt the door, and well . . .

Four months later, Everleigh bristled if Rhett showed her the slightest affection in front of his parents. Especially his mother.

"Everleigh, Mr. McCann wants to know if you've finished those boots." Betty Jo handed Everleigh a mock-up for next week's newspaper display ad. She was grateful for the distraction from the embarrassing memory. "He said to make sure you have the right dimensions. Your drawing last week bled into the gutter." The woman grabbed Everleigh's ring hand. "You know, I thought that boy of yours was all hat and no brains, but he sure brought it home when he gave you this ring. It's stunning."

"He saved for a long time." Everleigh drew her hand away and examined the mock-up for the *Tribune-Herald*.

"Know what my husband gave me for our engagement? A kid." Betty Jo propped herself against the drawing table, smacking her gum. In her early forties, she was a Southern spitfire with Marilyn Monroe hair and red lips. Her skirts were so tight she had to fall into her chair, and her blouse, well, let's just say the cut of the neck exposed what shouldn't be given away for free.

"A kid?" Everleigh set the mock-up aside and reached for her pica ruler. She had set the ad's border six points too long. "Like a goat?"

"A goat? Please!" Betty Jo cackled and patted her belly. "He gave me a kid-kid. That's why we got married. It was a rough start, but we've survived. That kid, or goat as you called him, is almost twenty and a sophomore in college." She took a cigarette from the snap case she carried. "A goat? Heavens to Betsy. Do I need to review the birds and the bees with you?"

"I'm well versed in the birds *and* the bees. But we were far from having a *kid* at our wedding."

"Then you're a better woman than I." Betty Jo sighed, examining her lacquered fingernails. "I know you're happy now, still in the newlywed stage. What's it been? Six months?"

"Eight."

"Well, just you wait."

"Wait for what?" Everleigh laid the ruler against the bottom of the ad and with her X-Acto knife, sliced off a half pica. "Rhett and I are in love. We're going to stay in love and have a *perfect* life."

"Perfect? Oh my goodness. Please, Pollyanna, take off your rose-colored glasses." Betty Jo blew smoke in Everleigh's face. "The young ones are such dreamers. Darling, all brides think their marriage is going to be candy and flowers, tender kisses and weekend honeymoons. That he'll help with the dishes and the kids, and tend to every household chore whistling a tune. Then little by little, like a frog boiling a pot, ten years have passed and your man comes home tired and grumpy, kicks off his stinky boots, and asks, 'What's for dinner?' He barely kisses you hello. On the cheek if you're lucky. And while you finish cooking, setting the table, yelling at the kids to come in and wash up, he's sitting on the john reading the paper until his legs go numb—"

"Betty Jo!" A glob of ink dropped from the end of Everleigh's pen smack in the middle of the drawing. "Don't rain on my parade just because there's no sunshine on yours." She reached for a cloth to wipe away the ink. But it stained. She'd just have to make it part of the boot.

"Suit yourself. But when you come to me begging for ol' Betty Jo's advice, I promise not to say, 'I told you so.'" She winked at Everleigh, dropping her cigarette to the old wood floor and smashing it out under her shoe. "At least not too many times."

With that, she left, the dark, heavy oak door closing behind her while her cackle lingered in the art room.

"What does she know? 'Know what my husband gave me? A kid.'" Everleigh pictured Betty Jo's man, Jeb. She winced at the image of him on the toilet. Have mercy but that woman could paint a verbal picture.

Everleigh liked Jeb, a hardworking oil-field man who spoke more in deed than word. Betty Jo may have her issues with him, but Everleigh was charting a different course with Rhett.

Since their first date, they all but finished each other's sentences. They spent hours and hours talking. When they weren't together, they talked on the phone. Right before their wedding, Rhett started mailing her short, sweet notes.

Thinking of you. Two more months! Always, Rhett.

No, the day would never be when Rhett came home tired and grumpy, barely kissing her hello before kicking off his boots on his way to the bathroom, where he'd sit until his legs were numb.

"Never going to happen, Betty Jo."

Everleigh propped her elbows on the drawing table, studying the boots. How long would she have to wait before bragging to Betty Jo that Rhett kissed her smack on the lips every night?

In the meantime, what was she going to do with this ink stain? She didn't have time to start the drawing over. She'd just decided to paste white paper over the stain when a broad pair of rancher hands slipped about her waist.

"Hello, beautiful." Rhett pressed his warm lips against her neck.

Everleigh turned, gazing into his august face. How did he still take her breath away? "What are you doing here?"

"Can't a man visit his wife at work?"

"Not when it's the middle of the afternoon. Not when he's supposed to be mending fences in the south pasture."

"I took the afternoon off to tend to something else."

"What kind of something else?" She searched his eyes for a hint of his secret. Good? Bad? "What? Tell me?" He wore his second-best Sunday shirt under a casual sport coat. "But listen here, mister." Everleigh linked her arm through his. "No matter how long we are married, I want a proper hello kiss when you come home at night. And no sitting on the commode reading the paper until your legs fall asleep. And a house . . . Oh, Rhett, I wasn't going to say anything because I know we've been saving, but I really want our own home. Can't we—"

"Hey, hey, sweetheart, what's all this?" He raised her chin and kissed her.

"Betty Jo was saying how—"

Rhett laughed against her hair. "Ol' Betty Jo. What's she been saying now?"

Everleigh inhaled Rhett's scent of sweet hay and sunshine. "The usual. All boo-hoo about marriage." She looked up at her husband and combed the front of his hair with her fingers. "She claims the honeymoon will end and one day, like a frog in a boiling pot, you'll come home tired and grumpy, forget to kiss me, kick off your stinky boots, and ask what's for dinner, then read the paper on the toilet."

Rhett pinned her against him with his arms. "Honey, I promise you a proper kiss in the evening no matter what, and sitting on the toilet reading the newspaper is my father, not me." He crossed his heart while his blue-blue eyes searched hers. "Believe me?"

"With all that I am."

He kissed her cheek, then whispered in her ear, his warm breath giving her chills. "You know I can't stop thinking about you." He nuzzled her neck again, then found her lips. "You're a distraction. Dad keeps assigning me chores, and I forget to do them because I daydream of you."

Everleigh searched his eyes, feeling in her belly the love she saw there. Forever she'd remember this moment. "How did I get so lucky to marry you?"

"I'm the lucky one. But will you do me a favor? Stop listening to Betty Jo, please."

"Done. But you can't blame me when you forget to do your chores."

Rhett laughed. "Deal. But it's true. You're all I can think about." The glint in his eye sparkled and teased, and raised her desire for him. "Doesn't *seem* like the honeymoon is over yet, does it?"

"Not by a long shot, Mr. Applegate." She raised up to kiss him, grateful for the solitude of the square, empty room.

She loved her power over him, but there was no denying Rhett's sway and charm over her. She'd walk to the ends of Texas for him. Barefoot. Or, as it were, endure life in his mother's house.

She'd chored-up, doing whatever asked without complaint. When Mama Applegate spoke as if Everleigh were a guest rather than a family member, she embraced it with grace.

Because at the end of the day, she was Rhett's wife. She alone shared his dreams, his heart, his life.

And at night, when she couldn't sleep, his soft breathing was her lullaby.

"Darling, I have to get back to work or I won't make it home in time for our dinner." She tugged at his shirt collar. "Are you going to tell me why you're here?"

"I was going to wait until tonight, but I got so excited . . ." Rhett stepped over to the desk in front of Everleigh's and held up a long white canister. "Here. Open it. I feel like a kid at Christmas."

"Rhett, what have you done?" She pried away the cap and slipped out a set of drawings.

"Here, let me." Rhett unrolled a rendering of a cozy house with a wraparound porch nestled between two cottonwoods. "Our house, Ev. I took those sketches you made after we were married and gave them to the architect. What do you think?"

"Th-this is our house?" She wrapped her arms around his waist, leaning against his thick arm as she studied the drawing.

"It's our house, darling."

It was just like she imagined. "Are you sure?" She gazed up at her husband. "I didn't think we'd saved enough money."

"We've saved every penny of your salary, and I finally sold the stud bull to Jacob Marshall. He's been after me for a year . . ." Rhett held her with one hand while flipping through the drawing with the other. "I bought the ten acres by the stream. You know, the one with the trees we loved. Dad wanted to give it to us, but I said no strings. I wanted to buy it so he can't hold it over me. Not that he would, but family business can get tricky."

Everleigh leaned to see the name of the road. Memory Lane. "Darling, the section right off Memory Lane? The spot I wanted?"

Rhett's grandmother named the dirt road years ago, when she imagined a large family with lots of grandkids running around. She envisioned an Applegate community.

But her sons, Melvin and Earl, went to war. Only Earl—nicknamed Spike—returned home the fall of 1918. He inherited the ranch, married Mama Applegate, and fathered Rhett, an only child.

Grandma's two daughters married and moved away.

"Your granny would be proud, darling," Everleigh said. "We're beginning her dream."

"Sh-she would." Rhett cleared his throat, pressing his fist over his cough. "So, w-what do you think?" He flipped to the page showing the first-floor layout. "Here's the back porch with a screen. We can watch the pink sunset over the water without the mosquitos." He took a pencil from the holder on her table and pointed out the lines of the porch. "Here's the living room, dining room, and kitchen. I told the architect to give you a big kitchen with all the latest appliances so you can bake and cook to your heart's content. I know Mama is a bit stingy with her kitchen."

"Oh, Rhett, I've never seen anything so grand."

"Here's my den and a powder room. Upstairs we have three bedrooms with a hall bath. But here is our domain, sweetheart." He waved the pencil over a large square at the end of the second floor. "This is a bay window overlooking the pond and the north meadow."

"Rhett, darling, it's *huge*. Can we afford such a place?"

"With a small mortgage, yes. We've earned this, Ev. Besides," he said, kissing her temple with tenderness and adoration, "nothing is too good for you. Look at this attached bath with a tub and a shower. No sharing with any of our dastardly brats when they come along." His laughed. His easy glee tickled Everleigh.

Tell him! The timing was perfect.

"Rhett, sweetheart—"

He jerked his wrist up, checking his watch. "Oh, Ev, sorry, sweetheart, but I promised Dad I'd pick him up from the hardware store thirty minutes ago." He gave her a quick, passing kiss. "I'd planned to show you these tonight, but I just couldn't wait." He rolled up the drawings and tucked them into the canister. "What is it you wanted to say?" On reflex, he checked his watch again.

"Nothing," she said, smiling. "I'll see you later. We can talk then. I have work to do anyway."

"You sure?"

Everleigh fell into him and pressed her cheek against his chest. "You make my dreams come true, Rhett Applegate."

He kissed her one more time, then held her at arm's length. "Distraction, girl, you are one beautiful distraction."

"Go, your dad's waiting." She watched him go, then in a flash of love and excitement, ran after him, her low heels echoing down the hall and down the stairs until she caught him in the street, standing under the slanting light of the Texas afternoon.

"Rhett!"

He turned and caught her in his big embrace. "What is it, darling?"

"I can't wait. I just can't." Her heart thumped in her ears as she drew a deep breath. "I'm going to have a baby, Rhett. Come November, you're going to be a daddy."

He whooped as he scooped her up in his arms and twirled her

around. "I'm going to be a daddy." When he set her down, he hollered at the shoppers hurrying past the storefronts. "I'm going to be a daddy. This here's my wife, Everleigh. She's going to have a baby."

The passersby laughed, offering congratulations.

Everleigh kissed Rhett good-bye one last time and hurried back to work. See, her life was perfect. Just as she dreamed it would be.

CHAPTER FIVE

BECK

"Holiday!" Lieutenant Ingram stood in his office door, arms akimbo, his expression drawn and tight.

Leaving her desk, Beck braced for the chewing-out of the decade. Then she'd drop her bomb and duck away from the shrapnel.

She'd debated telling him. After all, he didn't need to be involved, but her condition would affect her future with the department. And maybe, if she was lucky, gain her some sympathy after punching a cuffed offender and leaving.

"Close the door," he said, using his desk as a barrier between them. "Want to tell me what's going on? You hit a perp, then walked off the job. The captain was all over me about this. Misconduct, dereliction of duty—"

"It was a rough night." She kept her eyes low and averted, her dropping adrenaline giving her small tremors.

"Rough night? Beck, I've seen you hold a dying man in your arms as he bled all over you. The next hour you chased a known drug dealer down a dark alley. Two years ago you broke your wrist wrestling that woman who was beating her man with a bat. You went to the hospital and came right back to work." He bent to see her face. "You have to give me more than 'rough night.'" Besides being her boss, Hunter Ingram was her friend. More than a friend by some estimations. They'd . . . *tangoed* . . . one night. In a closet. At Rosie's Bar.

"I wasn't feeling good and Boudreaux had this dog—"

"So you punched him?"

She raised her chin and propped her hands on her belt. "Yeah,

I punched him. He deserved it, and I'm not sorry. He fed the dog crack. How many times do we have to arrest him only to see him out on the streets within twenty-four hours? It makes our job worthless, Hunter."

"You can't whale on a cuffed offender, Beck." Hunter came around to the front of the desk. "You of all people should know that. You're by the book, Beck."

"Did you hear what he did to the *dog*? His drug mule? The poor thing was in so much pain I could barely pick him up. He was half dead, smelling of feces and vomit." She turned away from him, arms folded, facing the door. "It was too much. Just too much. Then Boudreaux said he was going to eat him for barbecue and well, I snapped."

"I hope it was worth it." Beck glanced back at him. "You're suspended. Four weeks without pay."

"Four weeks?" She whirled around to meet him face-to-face. "What the—" Choice blue words flowed over her lips. "Without pay? Tuttle was arrested for public intoxication and only got two weeks *with* pay."

"Different time, Beck. This is coming down from 1 PP. Zero tolerance for anything smacking of police brutality."

"Hunter, look, I knew *something* was coming. After all, I do know the book." She air quoted *the book*. "But Parker Boudreaux is a *known* drug runner in this precinct. He's hurt a lot of people. Way more than the punch—"

"Or two." Clearly the lieutenant had all the details.

"Or two I gave him."

"And you walked off the job."

"To save a living being. A sweet, innocent dog. I don't see how any of this merits me four weeks without pay. I want my union rep in here."

"He's already signed off on your suspension. Hogan confirmed the events after the kid's parents lawyered up and filed charges for police brutality. We have his body cam footage, and yours as well."

"Hunter, this is crazy. You know it is. Boudreaux is a scumbag.

Who knows what homeless, innocent animal he'll lure into his lair next? If this is some PR stunt, then why don't we tell New York about the dealings of this Upper West Side rich brat who's squandering his life and harming dogs, huh? How many families are destroyed by the product he sells? How many lives lost? Everyone in the city would be on my side."

Hunter reached back for a copy of the *New York Post*. "If you'd answer your phone, you'd know the Boudreauxes already went to the papers."

Front page above the fold was a picture of Beck and the headline POLICE BRUTALITY: ATTACK ON SON OF PROMINENT MANHATTAN BUSINESSMAN.

"You've got to be kidding me." She tossed the paper back at Hunter. "I thought his parents were good people."

"I thought you were a good cop. Smashing Boudreaux, no matter what he did—"

"A defenseless animal, Hunter." Against her will, hot tears surfaced. "I thought we were supposed to protect and defend. You should've seen him. All matted and in pain." Beck held up her hand. "His . . . his tears dripped right here."

"Dogs don't cry like people, Beck."

She lunged at him. "I'm telling you he was crying."

Hunter stepped back, hands raised. "Okay, okay. Sheesh, I never knew you to be so emotional over a dog. Or anything else for that matter."

Beck turned away. It was the baby hormones. Had to be. "So, four weeks without pay?"

"Yes. We dropped the charges against Boudreaux with the condition he goes to rehab. That should keep him away from Vinny for a while. But to make the lawsuit go away, we had to suspend you."

"Rehab? Oh joy. A holiday in a luxury resort where he'll blame his parents for everything. In six weeks they'll give him a gold star and put him right back out on the streets." Beck swore and kicked Hunter's ficus, knocking the tree into the wall. "Who's running this city? Rich businessmen? We've been trying to collar Vinny for years. Boudreaux was our best bet. We had him. Why didn't the DA dangle *that* in front of him? Talk or prosecution?"

"Because he had police brutality as his trump card." Hunter filled a small paper cup with water from the cooler in the corner and offered it to Beck. "This incident goes into your record too, Beck. When you get back, you'll be on probation for a year."

"This is such bull." She drained water from the cup.

"Any repeat offenses could result in termination."

She crunched the paper cup into a wad and slammed it into the trash can. "So I'm the whipping girl?"

"They're holding you up as an example. I probably, *unofficially*, agree with everything you did, but you picked the wrong time to swing. The commissioner's office is eager to advance our good reputation in the city and really, the world."

Beck reached for her service weapon and shield and tossed them onto Hunter's desk. If she waited to be asked, she'd crumble with humiliation. He may as well strip her naked and parade her round the squad.

"Go home, get some rest, Beck. You don't look well." His sympathy was evident in his tone and expression. "I'm sorry about this."

Beck dropped into the chair across from his desk, head in her hands. "Not your fault."

Hunter was fifteen years her senior, handsome and confident, a poster boy for the NYPD. He ran marathons and volunteered at a local boys club. On his credenza was a row of pictures with his smiling, beautiful wife, Gaynor. By her expression she respected and adored her husband.

Guilt and shame welled up. She'd take a year's suspension without pay to undo what she'd done. To undo the growing consequence.

"What are you going to do on your month off?"

Beck crossed her arms, feeling insecure without her NYPD credentials. Badge and gun. Who was she if not a cop?

"I just learned I inherited a house in Florida of all things."

"A house?" Hunter said. "From who?"

"Some lady we knew back in the day."

"The days you've forgotten?"

"Something like that." She stood, fighting a wave of despair and nausea.

Hunter was one of the few in the Ninth who knew about her memory loss. She had to tell him when he tried to reminisce with her about her old man.

"He had this giant, drunk man down on the ground before I could say, 'Stop. Police.'"

"Where in Florida? You know Vinny has connections in north Florida. You could go down, keep an eye out for any suspicious activity." He chuckled and Beck snarled.

"I'm suspended, remember?"

"I think you should check it out. Forget this dingy place for a few weeks. Get out of winter."

"Maybe. But in my mind the house is a broken-down hovel with nineteen cats roaming the rooms. I'm not even sure the will is legit."

"Talk to legal. Have them snoop around."

"Again, suspended." Sarcasm eased some of the pain.

What was she going to do with herself for four weeks? With nothing consuming her days, she'd have to face the truth. She was almost five months—*five months*—pregnant.

Beck peered at Hunter. "Um, there is something I need to tell you. At least I think I *should* tell you."

The door rattled with a heavy knock, and Sergeant Anstruther barged on in. "Holiday," he said, tipping his head to one side, feigning some sort of sympathy. "I heard you popped Boudreaux."

"Get out." She jumped up and slammed the door in his face, almost catching his fingertips against the frame.

"Beck, what is the matter with you?" Hunter yanked open the door, advising Anstruther to come back in a few minutes.

"I'm pregnant." She dropped back down in her chair.

"You're—" His complexion washed white as he reached to steady himself. "Excuse me?"

"I'm pregnant." This time her confession came soft and low.

"H-how . . . can you be . . . Wh-who's the fath—?"

She shot him a wry expression, and he stumbled backward into his filing cabinet. *He* was the father.

They'd been teasing each other for a year, engaging in a bit of *harmless* flirting. Then last summer they met up at Rosie's bar after the failed bust. They drank and complained, then danced and flirted, drank some more, and well—

She scrubbed the image of them entangled in the utility closet from her mind.

"That was five months ago." He frowned as his eyes drifted to her middle. "Are you sure?"

Beck twisted her fingers together and nodded. "I'm sure."

"Beck, my wife—" He yanked her to her feet. "How could you let this happen?"

"Me?" She jerked free. "I don't recall being in that closet alone."

"You said it was safe."

"Did I? I don't remember anyone pausing to ask birth-control questions. We were trashed, Hunter."

Hunter ran his hands over his face. "W-what are we going to do? My wife, she's . . . I can't . . ." He sat hard in his chair. "She knows about the night at Rosie's. I couldn't keep it in any longer. We built our marriage on trust and—"

"You told her? Oh my gosh! It was one night. One stupid night."

"Because one evening she looked at me with those big brown

trusting eyes and asked what I wanted to do for our anniversary and all I heard was, 'Cheater, cheater, cheater.'"

"So you broke her heart to clear your conscience?"

"After she punched me out of the bed—"

"I like this woman."

"—we talked all night. We'd been ignoring some issues in our marriage and knew we had to get some help. Believe it or not, she's forgiven me."

Beck regarded him for a long moment. "But she won't if you tell her about the baby?"

"I don't know. I assured her you were not—" Another deep sigh echoed in the room. "This will crush her. You don't know . . . You don't know."

"Then don't tell her. I've got this."

"Do you? Really? You've just been suspended for four weeks. You're on the edge, Beck. You still live with your parents. Are you sure—"

She shot to her feet, knocking over her chair. "I don't need a lecture on my life from you." She gave him a mock salute and turned for the door.

"Wait." Hunter stepped to the door, blocking her exit. "How? How are you going to go this alone?"

"I don't know. Guess I have something to think about on my suspension."

"This baby is not *just* your problem. It's mine too. You know it or you wouldn't have told me."

"I don't know why I told you."

"Because I'm going to be a father." He swore, shrugging out of his suit coat, loosening his tie. "So what's the plan?"

"Well, since rolling back time isn't an option—"

"I've never done this before. Cheated." He pressed his hand to his chest, drawing in short, quick breaths. "The captain will have me—"

"Hunter, there's no need for anyone to know. I plan to say it was an old boyfriend."

"You don't need to cover for me."

"It's not for you. It's for me. You think I want a rep of sleeping with my superiors? I've never done this either."

"What about the baby? Doesn't he deserve to know his father?"

"In a perfect world, yes. But this is far from perfect. Hunter, I'll take care of this." She tried for the door again, but he refused to move.

"Let me know what you need, Beck. I'll try to be there for you. Have you seen a doctor?"

"I have an appointment on the third."

"Will you keep me posted?"

Their eyes met and she saw his guilt, his apology, and the layers of pain they'd inflicted on his wife. On the baby.

"I think you should just let me take care of this myself. I'm not even sure I want to raise it. I've been considering adoption."

"Adoption? Are you sure?"

"No, but nothing about this feels sure or right."

Hunter stepped aside and Beck left without another word, making her way through the squad room, past the desks loaded with papers and dirty coffee cups, past the detectives and sergeants to the civilian employees answering phones.

In the locker room she changed her clothes and exited the precinct into the dark, busy streets of the city. Descending into the subway, she felt one with the black shadows, with the nearly empty cars as they raced underground through the city that never sleeps.

CHAPTER SIX

EVERLEIGH

May 1953

She awoke late and stretched in the midmorning sunlight streaming through the bedroom windows.

Rhett's side of the bed was empty, the sheets cool under her palm. He rose before dawn to start work. The life of a rancher was not one of ease.

Pushing back the mass of curls falling over her eyes, she glanced across the small room to the bouquet of flowers he'd handed her yesterday before they left for church.

"For your first Mother's Day."

Mama Applegate scoffed at Rhett's extravagance. "She's not even showing yet."

Rhett defended his actions with vigor. "If being pregnant doesn't make you a mother, I don't know what does."

The woman softened afterward. After all, Everleigh was carrying her first grandchild. Kind of gave her a bit more leverage in this strong Texas family.

She slipped from the blanket to peer out over the endless Applegate ranch. He was out there somewhere. *Her* man.

Since she'd told him she was pregnant, Rhett worked the ranch during the day and their house plans at night.

Next week the contractor would break ground. Everleigh pressed her fingers to her smiling lips.

It was happening. Her *own* home. Any more happiness and she might burst. Was it right for one woman to feel so much love and joy?

The soft knock at her door had her reaching for her robe. Mama Applegate stepped through without waiting for a response, tugging on her white lace gloves.

"How are you feeling, my dear?"

"Well, thank you. Still no morning sickness." Everleigh cinched the belt of her robe and looked around for her slippers. Monday was her day off from Kestner's. Rhett insisted she rest, but as the wife of a rancher and the daughter-in-law of Heidi Applegate, lying about was no such luxury. There were chores to be done.

"Then you're blessed. I had a devil of a time with morning sickness. Anyway, I set saltines on the counter just in case."

Mama regarded her with a level of compassion Everleigh had not seen before. A sort of tenderness that said she understood what it took to bring new life into the world.

"I've errands to run in town. When you collect yourself, please feed the chickens and weed the garden."

"Yes, ma'am."

"I won't be back in time for lunch so help yourself. Spike and Rhett went into town about an hour ago to meet with a new breeder. Apparently he came into town a day early. Rhett said to tell you to go through the catalogs he gave you. He wants to finish picking out building materials tonight." Mrs. Applegate reached to close the door, then paused. "Take care of yourself. Take a nap if you need."

"I will. I do get a bit tired in the afternoon."

The older woman's eyes glistened as she nodded, a slow flush spreading across her cheeks. "I remember . . . Oh, can you peel the potatoes and carrots for dinner? And the apples for the pie. I made the dough this morning and put it in the icebox." Mama Applegate lingered a moment longer. "Let's make tonight's dinner a celebration. The first Applegate grandchild." She surveyed Rhett's cramped boyhood room. "You'll be happy to be out of here, I know. Well, I'd best be off—Oh, Spike gave one of the puppies away this morning. There are only four left. I told him this litter is the cutest Lola's ever had. I've a mind to keep one." She set her forefinger to her lips. "But, shhh, let that be our secret for now."

Everleigh locked her lips with an imaginary key.

Her mother-in-law smiled, and the two of them shared another tender moment as the woman bid her final good-bye and closed the bedroom door.

After her bath Everleigh dressed and made the bed, then used one of Rhett's dirty T-shirts to dust the bedside tables and the old desk by the window where he examined the house plans each night.

"I love this house more and more," he'd say, crawling into bed next to her and patting her belly before turning off the light. "What do you think, son? Do you want to grow up in the house on Memory Lane?"

"Stop, what if it's a girl? She'll think you don't like her."

Rhett would kiss her, laughing. "She'll be the apple of my eye."

Everleigh flinched at the stirring in her abdomen. Did she feel her child for the first time? The doctor said it was too soon to feel movement, but maybe her child was letting her know he, *or she*, was eager to live in this glorious new house where they'd create memories of family dinners, board games before bed, birthday and holiday celebrations, warm fires in the winter, and homemade ice cream in the summer.

Well, enough daydreaming. She had chores to do. Wrapping her hair in a kerchief, Everleigh headed downstairs.

First she'd tackled the kitchen, cleaning the iron skillet Mama A. used to fry bacon and eggs for the boys. Besides Rhett and his daddy, Uncle Floyd, cousin Mike, and three hired hands worked the ranch. Mama and Aunt Millie took turns feeding them breakfast and lunch.

Next she peeled the potatoes, carrots, and apples, snatching cut pieces for her own late breakfast, and removed the dough from the fridge, before she headed for the outside chores.

By the time she cleaned the chicken coop, weeded the garden, and played with the puppies, and napped briefly on the picnic table under the cottonwoods, it was late afternoon and she was starving.

Inside, she took a loaf from the bread box, staring out the window, clouds mounting against the sunshine. How she loved an afternoon rain shower.

After lunch, she'd play with the puppies, and when the rain came, she'd make the pie, then pick out the materials Rhett requested.

Everleigh's belly rumbled as she layered two slices with ham and cheese, then poured herself a cold glass of milk. Carrying her lunch outside, she lifted her face to the cooling, rain-scented breeze.

The first bite of sandwich made her heart sing. She shouldn't go so long without eating a proper meal. She had a child to grow. Meanwhile, Lola's border collie puppies gathered at her feet, yipping, trying to climb her leg for leftovers.

She'd already decided to take the runt of the litter with her to Memory Lane. Rocco, she called him.

The wind tousled the tree limbs, flipping the leaves over to their paler underside. Sure sign of rain. Plus, the threatening clouds mounted higher and higher.

Everleigh's napkin blew from her lap and skipped across the grass. Rocco chased his brothers and sister as they ran after the linen cloth.

Finishing her last bite of ham and cheese with a swallow of milk, she snatched the napkin from the biggest puppy, who wanted to play tug-of-war.

"Give me that now, little darling." Everleigh laughed as he sat his wee bottom in the grass, growling with all his might.

But the tone in the wind had changed, and she was anxious to get inside. Scooping up the puppies—tucking Rocco and the other small pup into her apron pocket—she hit the kitchen door as the clouds broke, dropping a thick wall of rain over the ranch.

Everleigh set her dishes in the sink and the puppies on the waxed linoleum floor before moving quickly through the house to close the opened windows.

Mama A. didn't permit the dogs inside—*"They have a fine house in the barn."*—but Everleigh didn't have time to run them back to their hay beds.

Arranging the kitchen chairs as a barrier, she corralled the terrified puppies under the table and gave each one two cuts from last night's chicken.

"Now behave while I make the pie."

Rain splattered the window as Everleigh worked. More than once she glanced out the window as she rolled out the dough.

The moan in the wind had morphed into a howl with an echoing screech.

She'd just set the pie in the oven when a gust slammed the house so hard the windows rattled.

Wiping her hands on her apron, Everleigh snapped on the kitchen radio for a bit of news. But the only sound was crackling static.

Again the wind howled and screeched, haunting and ghostly. Almost angry.

The house shook so hard the chandelier swayed. Then a glass fell from the open shelf by the sink. Everleigh carried the larger pieces to the trash as another knock of the wind against the southern corner produced a loud shatter upstairs.

With her pulse in her ears, she pulled the kitchen chairs aside and crooned to the huddled, trembling puppies. "Come."

Holding their wiggling bodies against her breast, she backed out the screen door, intending to go to the cellar.

The gale drove the hard rain into her skin and knocked her into the porch post. She nearly lost her grip on little Rocco.

The cellar. She must get to the cellar. Leaning into the wind, she stepped from the porch, but her foot slipped on the wet boards. She toppled backward, losing her hold on the big puppy. He cried out as he scampered in a frantic circle.

She called for him, but the wind jerked her words away.

Anchoring her arm around the porch post, Everleigh stashed Rocco in her apron pocket, and clinging to the other two squirming dogs, she stretched for the terrified big boy, lifting him up by the scruff.

Then with a wild shriek, fear claiming her senses, she ducked her head and ran toward the cellar, soaked by water and wind.

When she reached the in-ground doors, she gripped the rusty metal handle. But her fingers slipped and she stumbled, catching herself on the edge of a heavy gust, and lunged forward.

Again she tried the cellar door, her soaked skirt clinging to her legs and the puppies wiggling and yipping.

Adrenaline surged, then faded, leaving her arms trembling and legs weak, trapped by her heavy, rain-soaked skirt.

The howl in the wind deepened, its dark, swirling finger snatching at the ground.

For a moment Everleigh couldn't move. A twister! Then she became Hercules, raising the cellar door against the tyrannical force. She tripped down the narrow stairs and landed on the cold dirt floor. The puppies scrambled free as the storm slammed the door with a resounding *clang*.

Shaking, she fumbled in the dark for the flashlight, finding it on the shelf where Rhett had set it six months ago. They'd come down here for canned goods and ended up, well, behaving like newlyweds.

But there was nothing cozy and romantic about the space now. Clicking on the light, Everleigh waved it over the walls and floor, spotting the puppies huddled by an old horse blanket.

Overhead the wind raged, stomping over the metal cellar door, causing it to rise just a bit before slamming shut.

Joining the puppies, she huddled in the dark underground and with one long, anxious breath, released her fears with a scream that rivaled the fury raging above.

———

BECK

She slept the first day of her suspension, trying to adjust to daytime hours. On day two, she was restless and searched online for a cheap ticket to Florida.

On day three, she went to her doctor's appointment, rebuffing the scorn of the nurse who scolded her for neglecting her care.

The ultrasound proved what she already knew. She was pregnant with a girl. The doctor prescribed prenatal vitamins and set up an appointment for next month. But Beck pushed it out two weeks.

"I'll be in Florida."

Guess she was going then. Why not? Even if this house business turned out to be a joke—which it most certainly *had* to be—a trip to Florida could be fun. Escape the New York winter. Escape Hunter.

On the fourth day, she called Miss Everleigh's lawyer, a Mr. Joshua Christian, and confirmed her inheritance was real. He said he'd be more than happy to pick her up from the airport, but she opted for an Uber ride instead.

The afternoon of the fifth day Beck took the train to Brooklyn Heights and knocked on Phil Hogan's door.

Even though he had ratted her out to Internal Affairs, she needed his advice. She needed his fatherly shoulder. She needed him to tell her what to do.

Though she'd already talked with Mom and Flynn—about the house, not the baby—who urged her to go.

"Shoot, I might punch someone to get suspended," Flynn joked, his eyes dashing toward Mom, doing what he always did. Easing the situation.

Mom agreed in her pragmatic way. "Maybe being at the house will help you remember things, Beck. Miss Everleigh loved you. All of us really, but especially you."

———

"Why?"

"Your dad always said you seemed like twin souls born sixty years apart. Of course, he was Miss Everleigh's summer handyman. I ask you, who goes on vacation to do chores around an old house? But that was your dad. Spent most of his vacation with a hammer in his hand, or a paint brush. He loved it. I read books, helped with the cooking, took you and the neighbor kid, Bruno, to the beach . . ." Mom sighed. "It really was a lovely time in our lives."

The door opened and Hogan stepped aside, inviting her into his warm apartment. "Didn't expect to see you."

"I should've called." She inspected his bachelor pad, wanting him to have a cozy, welcoming place instead of one furnished like a man who lost everything and didn't believe he deserved a real second chance. The furniture was sparse and secondhand but nice. There were pictures and paintings on the wall.

"Were you sleeping?" Beck said, choosing the chair by the door.

"I've been up for a while." He moved to the small kitchen just off the living room. "I don't sleep well without Claudia. Not sure that will ever change. Can I get you something to drink?"

"Water." Beck set her backpack on the floor and slipped from her coat.

Her old friend, her mentor, returned with a cold bottle of water for her and a pop for himself and reclined in his chair. Silent seconds ticked by as they pretended to slake a raging thirst with their drinks.

"I need to leave for the precinct in an hour," he said.

"Yeah, of course." Beck sat straight backed on the edge of the chair, hand tucked between her knees. "I just wanted to ask you—"

"Look," he said, sitting forward. "I had no choice. My body cam captured you punching Boudreaux."

"I know. I know—"

"They knew the story before they asked. Then witnesses called to complain, all on Vinny Campanile's payroll, make no mistake, but the boys at 1 PP weren't letting this one go. Besides, you walked off the job, and I couldn't cover that, Beck."

She nodded, the loose ends of her chestnut hair falling over her shoulder. "I'm sorry I put you in that position."

"You know my past. I can't step out of line even once. I have to look like one of New York's finest."

"I'm pregnant, Hogan."

He stared at her with his pop bottle pressed to his lips. "What?"

"I'm pregnant." She winced at having to repeat herself.

"H-how? When?"

"How? The old-fashioned way. When? Last August at Rosie's after the failed bust."

"With who? Don't tell me Detective Myron. He's such a—"

"Mryon? Ugh! Please." Beck made a face. "You think I'd go for that—"

"Okay, okay." Hogan held up his hands, defending against her barrage. "So who? When I left the party you were playing pool with Lieutenant Ingram. Pretty lit up too."

"Who doesn't matter." He had stepped way too close to the truth. "It happened." She'd said too much. Why'd she bring up Rosie's? It narrowed down the field tremendously.

"Who's the father, Beck?"

"A man."

"A requirement. Does he know?"

She nodded. "I told him, but I wonder if I should've kept it to myself."

"What'd he say?"

"It's complicated. I'm handling this on my own."

"Tell me who." Hogan set his pop bottle down with force. "He can't have all the fun and none of the responsibility."

"It's handled, Hogan." Beck gripped her water between her hands, rocking forward with nervous energy.

———

"Guess it makes sense now why you punched Boudreaux. Hormones."

"No, that was all Boudreaux. Hormones or no hormones, he deserved it." She bounced up, paced toward the kitchen, then leaned against the wall. "I don't know what to do, Hogan. Every time I sit down to think about it, I go crazy. I feel like I'm going to cry, then I get angry because I hate crying. I'm a cop. A member of the NYPD. I bring justice to the world. I don't crumble and fall apart. It's my way of serving, of honoring Dad even if I don't remember him."

"Everyone crumbles and falls apart now and then. Everyone needs justice, Beck. Don't think you're above wanting wrongs to be made right for yourself. Just because you're a cop doesn't mean you have to be callous and cold. You're a woman first. It's okay to act like one. You don't have to be the Ice Queen. Or measure up to some idea you have of your father's heroic legacy."

"Ice Queen? Who said I was an ice queen? Are people saying that about me?" From her first days on the force she'd been all fight and no finesse, but she wasn't cold or uncaring. "And how can I not live up to Dad's legacy? It's all around me. The old guys *still* tell stories about him."

"But it's okay to be *you*. We expect nothing more or less. As for the Ice Queen . . ." Hogan smiled. "I thought you knew that one. So, you're going to be a mother?"

"*That* one? How many are there?"

He raised his hands in surrender. "Just the one, and it's not true, you know. You're not as icy as you want people to believe."

"Maybe." She finished her water in one gulp. "Hogan, I never saw myself as a mom. Not to mention, she'll be without a dad, and I don't want that for her. Every girl needs her dad."

"Then don't let the father off because it's complicated, Beck. Let him man up."

"He's married." There. Happy?

"Ah." Such a simple but weighted word. "Then how can I help you?"

A small tear collected in the corner of her eye. "Tell me what to do."

"Seems you've already decided. How far along are you? Got to be close to five months if it was around the time of the sting. Have you told your mom?"

"Not yet. Not in the mood for a lecture."

"Come on, Beck, give her some credit."

"We've never been close, Hogan. Especially after Dad died. We lived to exist, then Flynn came around, and next thing I know she's getting married and I can't remember anything of my childhood." Beck returned to her chair and unzipped the backpack. "What do you think about this?" She passed Everleigh Callahan's will over to him. If she kept the conversation moving, her tears had to submit. "I inherited a house in Florida."

"You inherited a house?" Hogan reached for the document. "I didn't know you had any relatives in Florida."

"The house isn't from relatives." Mom had finally spilled more details this morning over eggs and bacon. "Dad had an uncle, an aunt, and a cousin in Florida back in the late fifties, early sixties, but they moved to New York somewhere along the line. Anyway, there was an older woman across the street who was like an old aunt or granny to the family. Dad vacationed there with his family for a few years, I guess until his uncle moved, Mom couldn't remember. Anyway, when I came along he wanted to go back down to this . . . this Fernandina Beach and give me the memories he had growing up. Apparently we stayed with this old lady, Everleigh Callahan. She died over Thanksgiving, left me her house."

Hogan looked up from reading the will. "Your dad tried to get a couple of us to go down for fishing one spring. Never worked out." He passed the will back to Beck. "Do you have any memories of this place?"

She shook her head. "Any memory Dad touched is gone."

The words were true, familiar, so much so she often forgot the depth of their meaning. Any memories associated with her father were wiped away eighteen years ago.

After 9/11, when Dad was found crushed at the bottom of the North Tower rubble, Mom went dark. Grieving, scared, alone, trying to figure out her new reality, she didn't see her daughter wandering aimlessly behind her.

Beck tried to find comfort from her mother, but Mom's light was not shining. So at fourteen, Beck found comfort in the shadows and shades of night. She found peace in forgetting.

They lived in a functioning but emotionally void world, their conversations shallow, centered on practical and logistical concerns.

"How are you getting home from practice?"

"Ellie's mom."

"Can you clean the house? I'm working overtime."

"Can I get a raise in my allowance?"

"No, I need every penny to keep this house."

Beck spent many evenings alone dining on popcorn and Diet Coke, *not* feeling and *not* remembering.

"You should go," Hogan said. "Check it out."

"That's what Mom and Flynn said." And Hunter.

Flynn's love brought Mom back to life, but not Beck. They tried to include her into their fairy tale, but she was fifteen and her shades were already drawn.

"I think this will-thing deal might open up some things for you. Hey, Vinny Campanile has connections in north Florida. You could keep your eye out for—"

"You sound like Ingram. Besides, I'm *sus-pen-ded*, remember? If I go down, I'm going as a civilian."

"Good, you're going."

"What will I do when I'm down there?"

"What anyone would do on vacation. Beck, you don't have to have all the answers before trying something."

"Yes, I do. It's too scary otherwise." Dad ran into the North Tower without knowing . . .

"This from the girl who runs down dark alleys without hesitation? Come on, you live on taking a chance." But did she? The dark alleys were a different kind of unknown. Merely barriers to catching a perp or rescuing a victim. "Take a chance. Be surprised. See what life, even God, might have in store for you. Try a little faith. You just might—"

"I've had my fill of God's surprises, thank you."

"—start remembering."

She winced, moving to the window, looking down to the car-lined street. She rarely talked about her memory loss. It was second nature to her now. But since he brought it up . . .

"That scares me the most, Hogan. What heinous thing lurks beneath the amnesia?"

Her entire childhood wasn't wiped. She remembered riding her bike through the neighborhood, sleepovers with Ellie Yarborough, singing in the fifth-grade Christmas pageant.

But Christmas mornings, birthdays, vacations that included Dad's face had become black holes. He was a character in a story Mom referenced once every blue moon.

"Don't overthink this, Beck. Go to Florida, soak up some sunshine, breathe, eat, think, pray. You can't grow a baby on a diet of coffee and donuts."

"I eat a hot dog now and then." Beck returned to her chair. "Aren't you a bit worried the sun might melt the Ice Queen."

Hogan laughed. "Let's hope so."

"I'm taking the dog."

"Good. He could use some R and R too."

Beck pictured herself approaching this unknown Florida home—

an old Victorian according to Joshua Christian—with her suitcase and a jittery Beetle Boo. "The place is probably haunted."

She imaged the wind howling around the eaves, the floor creaking beneath her feet.

"With what? Your lost memories?" Hogan arched his brow, then glanced at his watch.

"W-what if remember him? Dad?" Beck took the cue and reached for her coat.

"Wouldn't that be a good thing?" Hogan helped her on with her coat.

"Unless I forgot for a reason."

"Like what? He adored you, and you idolized him." Hogan drew her into a hug, and Beck relaxed against his stable frame. "Go, have fun, let light fill your life for once."

"I'm telling you, I'll melt."

She resisted a rising sob. But when Hogan pressed a kiss to her head, she broke, gripping at his shirt. He held her, one arm hooked around her shoulders, whispering words she could barely hear.

Then she collected herself, wiped her eyes, and headed for the subway. Sitting in the dark, rattling car, she breathed a question against the window.

"What should I do?" She spoke to no one yet everyone. The fates, the universe, God.

Go to Florida.

The thought was soft, almost pleading. The more she meditated on the urging, the more her adrenaline flowed. Almost with a kick-butt-and-take-names force.

All right, she'd go. She'd pack her bikini—okay, maybe not, but a couple of pairs of shorts and flip-flops—book her ticket, buy a pet carrier, and spread her wings, flying south for the winter.

CHAPTER SEVEN

BRUNO

He never liked good-byes. Especially permanent ones. But Miss Everleigh deserved his respect, his attendance.

He hung around the back of his boyhood church, watching the mourners file in and greet one another with hugs and tears.

He'd resented this place growing up—Mom dragging him to Sunday school and youth church until he went off to college—but today the familiar sanctuary walls were his comfort.

As he got older, he understood Mom's need for the church, for the Almighty, as she raised a man-child alone. God and His people seemed like a good option.

The sanctuary, once an old warehouse, was filled beyond capacity. The side loading doors were pushed back so the January breeze blew through with the scent of heaven.

The western door framed the fiery-orange sunset. A perfect tribute to Miss Everleigh.

Mom and her crew had transformed the rustic sanctuary into a wonderland, crisscrossing the thick old beams with twinkle lights and lining the walls with candles.

Up front, the stage was set with singers and musicians and a large framed picture of Miss Everleigh in her younger years. She was a beauty.

Bruno's phone vibrated as he nodded to Mr. Smock, who tucked in beside him.

It was a text from his Ohio State recruit, Todd Gamble.

You used to work in LA?
Yes.
Can you introduce me to Sabrina Fox?

Typical of high-level recruits. Asking for the stars and moon. Wasn't anything for a kid to want money for family bills or to dance in a music video. One year Watershed had a top draft pick ask to meet Beyoncé. And Bruno made it happen.

Yeah, sure, I'll see what I can do.

It was one thing if a player wanted things or connections. If an agency had enough money, they could make anything happen. But a one-on-one romantic fixup was another ballgame. It made Bruno nervous. As did most matters of the heart.

Yet he was desperate to sign top talent, and if Todd wanted to meet a beautiful starlet, then a beautiful starlet he'd meet.

Besides, Sabrina owed Bruno. Getting her to at least talk to the player seemed simple enough.

As the mourners still gathered, Bruno tapped another message to Todd, an All-American defensive end.

Flying up Tuesday. Private jet. Sending a limo to pick you up from campus. Bring whoever you want with you as long as we have time to talk some business.

Cool! See you then.

As he tucked his phone away, Mrs. Gunter patted his hand. "I know you adored Miss Everleigh. Wasn't she like a grandmother to you?"

"Yes, she was."

The woman watched him with a pinched expression, as if waiting for him to break down. If she wanted tears, her cheap perfume might do the trick.

He turned slightly away, clearing his throat. "Sh-she'll be missed."

"Our prayer group won't be the same without her. Oh, there's Letty Macintosh. Let me go say hi."

Alone again, Bruno shot his pilot friend, Stuart Strickland, a quick message.

Tuesday? We good? I really appreciate this, man.

Who'd have thought losing his lucrative job, moving across the country to his old beach condo, and starting over would come with the bonus of a personal pilot.

God bless Stuart's rich grandfather.

Stu hit him back.

We're on. 10:00a.

He might as well reach out to Sabrina while he had his phone in his hand.

S, got a player who's dying to meet you. Good guy. Out of Ohio State. Thoughts? Hope you're well and remember, you owe me.

She didn't really *owe* him, but he'd rescued her from a drunk LA Laker a few years ago during a Sportswood-meets-Hollywood party. Young, innocent, new to the Hollywood scene, she put herself in a precarious position with a giant, hungry, used-to-getting-his-way athlete.

They'd been good friends ever since.

Bruno scanned the room, his gaze falling on the cross at the back of the nave. Was it right to ask for something personal during the memorial of such a holy, sweet lady?

Mom appeared, gently touching his arm, looking pretty even in black.

"I saved us two seats up front. Look at all of these people."

"I think we're violating a fire code." Bruno moved off the wall when Mom linked her arm through his.

"We're good. Fire Chief Hayes is on the front row." Mom pointed to the somber man in full dress uniform. He greeted Mom when they got to the row.

"Natalie, you're a saint for pulling this off. Miss Everleigh tended my mama when she was sick. Don't know what we'd have done without her."

"Half this room has the same story. When Stone left me, then passed away, she was my rock. My new stone. Of course, she pointed the way to Jesus every day."

Mom walked around to the chairs she'd saved. Bruno took the vacant seat at the end.

Pastor Oliver called the room to order. As the room hushed, Bruno's phone pierced the silence.

"Turn that off," Mom said with her best scowl. "Work can spare you for a few hours."

He acknowledged with the just-a-minute sign. In sports agenting there was no such thing as "not now" or "not today." One missed call could cost him a key client. Young men with millions of dollars on the line waited for no one.

Bruno moved toward the wide bay door as he answered.

"Mr. Endicott, it's Tyvis Pryor. How you doing? Hope I'm not disturbing your Sunday."

"I'm at a memorial, Tyvis. Can I call you back?" Bruno scanned the cars jamming the street, his gaze stopping on a lanky brunette with flowing hair and smooth curves striding his way.

There was something familiar about her. The way she carried herself with bravado, yet not quite sure where she was going.

"Y-yeah, sure, that'd be great. Listen, I hate to bother you but . . ." Tyvis's hesitation and lack of confidence felt odd, so unfamiliar in this biz. "I just wondered if you decided to take me on. I promise to work hard for you."

A voice rose in the background. "Tyvis, need you on the grill."

"I have to go, Mr. Endicott."

"Bruno. Call me Bruno."

"Sure thing, Bruno."

He slipped his phone into his pocket, watching the woman approach. He knew her. But how? Where?

As for Tyvis, well, he felt for the guy, but Bruno couldn't build a business on a JUCO kid. He'd be crazy to sign him, pay for his training and living expenses, when there wasn't a snowball's chance he'd ever make a pro roster.

The woman walked past with a clean, meadowy fragrance and stopped at the bay door.

Bruno bent to see her face, his heart blipping with familiarity. "Can I help you?"

"No, thanks." Her reply was blunt, almost cold, and she didn't even look at him.

Bruno's attention lingered on her profile a moment longer, then returned to his seat. How did he know her?

At the metal pulpit, Pastor Oliver spoke eloquently of Mrs. Everleigh Callahan—*Miss Everleigh* to all who knew her—as a slideshow of her life played on the screen behind him.

"She was born Everleigh Louise Novak on June 15, 1929, in Waco, Texas . . ."

A young, beautiful Miss Everleigh smiled at them in black and white. The slide shifted to another image—a faded color shot of her sitting on a porch with her arms wrapped around a handsome, John Wayne–looking dude.

Bruno nudged Mom. "Do you know the woman at the door?"

"Shhh." She pressed her finger to her lips, and her eyes fixed on the repertoire of Miss Everleigh's life.

Bruno angled forward with a clipped glance toward the woman. *She* remained, leaning against the doorframe with a stoic expression.

"I loved her soft strong hands," Pastor Oliver said. "I could always tell when Miss Everleigh touched my shoulder after service. Even before she said, 'Good word, Pastor.'"

The falter in his voice rammed through Bruno, and everything he loved about Miss Everleigh flooded to the surface.

Her kind eyes and gentle voice. Her patience. Her bone-crushing hugs. How she left her back door open every afternoon for him to run in after school, a plate of homemade cookies and a glass of milk waiting.

How she laughed when he came in muddy after football practice with the entire offensive line.

"Sit down, boys, sit down. Let me bake more cookies. Does anyone want a sandwich?"

Every hand would shoot up.

He clenched his jaw against the emotion rising in his eyes, against the tight grip of regret in his chest.

He should've come home from LA more often to see Mom and Miss Everleigh. But he thought he had time. Thought his career was more important.

When Mom sobbed and crushed her white handkerchief against her wet cheek, Bruno took her hand and braced against his own sorrow.

"She was known as a woman of character and integrity, a woman of prayer," Pastor Oliver went on. "If you were impacted by Miss Everleigh's life, her powerful prayers, please stand."

The entire room lifted.

A young man with a guitar stepped up to the mike and started a hymn. "Sing with me. 'The Old Rugged Cross.' One of Miss Everleigh's favorites."

"On a hill far away, stood an old rugged cross."

The rising voices, the melody, the lyrics battered Bruno's resolve. He ached for his old friend, for the days gone by, for her backyard Bible school and unconditional love.

He caught the tear trickling from the corner of his eye. Tears changed nothing. They didn't grant wishes, bring fathers or old women back from the dead.

Miss Everleigh is worthy of your tears.

As the singing went on, Bruno let his emotions go and fall from his chin. Just then his phone vibrated, bringing him back to reality.

Releasing Mom's hand, he stepped toward the bay doors. "Endicott."

"Coach Brown here."

Bruno sighed, staring down at the cracked, stained concrete that had once been a loading dock.

"I'm at a memorial."

"My condolences." And the line went silent.

Bruno guessed Coach probably wanted to pitch Tyvis more, brag about how he volunteered at a children's home between two and four a.m.

Tucking his phone away, he stood a few feet from the familiar stranger and yielded to another glance her way. This time he thumped with recognition.

"Beck?" he whispered. "Beck Holiday?"

She shifted her attention to him. "Yes?"

"Wow, I can't believe it." He stepped toward her, lowering his voice. "How long has it been? Eighteen, nineteen years?" Her blank stare almost deterred him. "You came. So sad about Miss Everleigh, isn't it? Did Mom get ahold of you?"

Seeing her up close, he fell a little bit in love. Just like the first time he saw her. He was eight, riding his bike up and down Memory Lane, while she stood in Miss Everleigh's yard flying a kite with her dad.

Then again at nine, ten, eleven, twelve, thirteen, and fourteen. Every summer he fell deeper. Then came 9/11, and he never saw her again.

Dressed in dark-blue slacks with a matching jacket and a fitted white blouse, she exuded something hard beneath her mature beauty.

"Your mom? No, coming was a last-minute decision." She faced the church as the congregation sang the chorus one last time.

"So I'll cherish the old rugged cross."

"Can you believe she's gone?" He stood next to her, imitating her protective stance, arms folded, amused *and* annoyed at his driving pulse. Was he still part teenager? "When Pastor Oliver started talking, I was flooded with memories." He glanced at her. "Remember the time—"

Her hard glare knocked the words from his lips. "I'm sorry, who are you?"

Bruno lowered his arms, cracking a small smile. "Okay, I get it. We lost touch. But you didn't write me either. Wait a minute—" He turned to her. "I did email you. Right after 9/11, but you didn't email back. I emailed you again when my dad died."

She scowled, her expression hardening even more. "Look, whoever you are, I don't know or remember you."

It was his turn to scowl. "You *are* Beck Holiday, right? Daughter of Dale and Miranda Holiday? You spent summers at Miss Everleigh's place? Sat next to me at Backyard Bible School? Road bikes up and down Memory Lane? Called her place the memory house?"

She hesitated, then nodded toward the church. "I think that woman wants your attention."

Mom waved him inside. What did she want? Whatever it was, it couldn't be as intriguing as this exchange with Beck. Bruno studied her another moment before returning to his seat.

"People are sharing," Mom whispered in his ear. "You should say something."

"No thanks. I'm a behind-the-scenes guy."

"Who were you talking to out there?"

"Beck Holiday."

Mom's eyes popped as she leaned around him. "Land sakes, I've not seen hide nor hair of the Holidays since '01. So awful about Dale. Is that her there?"

"Don't stare."

Mom arched her brow and nudged Bruno. "She turned out well."

Pastor Oliver walked the warehouse-sanctuary with a microphone in hand as a dozen hands shot up, volunteering to share.

"Trilby, I know you have a testimony." He passed off the mike to Trilby Thomas.

"I'll try to make it short." She wiped under her eyes. "My husband and I had been married about ten years and found ourselves fighting over everything. I thought divorce would be our end. After one particularly bad night, I got in my car to drive. Just drive. But I didn't go two miles before I found myself at the old memory house. Miss Everleigh's. It was raining cats and dogs, but she must have seen my headlights because here she came running with an umbrella and invited me in for tea. It was as if she knew I was coming. She listened to my sob story, then she prayed for me and sent me home. She told me, 'Find wherever you stashed your big-girl pants and put them on. You're not a school girl. You're a woman. Act like it. Work this out, and stop being so selfish.'" Laughter rippled among the many bobbing heads. "I see I'm not alone in that advice. Well, I went home and we worked it out. I'll always be grateful to her for her advice, her strength, and her prayers."

Trilby sat to a light applause, and the mike moved to Scott Harrell. Bruno checked on Beck. She remained just outside the door.

Next thing he knew, Pastor Oliver stood next to him. "Bruno

Endicott, why don't you share? Miss Everleigh was your neighbor and adopted grandmother."

Mom pushed him to his feet as the good preacher shoved the microphone into his hands.

"Well . . . ," he said, facing the at-capacity room. "Like Pastor Oliver said, she was our neighbor and my adopted grandma." He peeked toward Beck. Nothing about her composure had softened or reflected any sentiment for the women they honored. "I spent a lot of time at her house while Mom worked. Um . . ." He inhaled, gathering his emotions, trying to find a memory that would make them laugh instead of cry. But all he saw was Miss Everleigh's sweet, lined face. "She was safe, warm, and compassionate. Made the best chocolate-chip cookies in town." Nods and agreement bounced around. "One year Beck Holiday and I—" He pointed to the door. Heads turned. "We ate about five boxes of Popsicles to get enough sticks for backyard Bible school." He teared up, laughing softly at the memory. "Miss Everleigh talked about Jesus like He was real. Alive." He couldn't control the warble in his voice. "I was fifteen when my dad died, and I *exploded* out of our house, angry and lost. I don't know how it happened, but suddenly she was there"—he glanced at Trilby—"like she knew. I put my head on her shoulder and sobbed. Snot sobbed. She told me Jesus loved me and that I had a Father in heaven. I'll never forget the way her arms felt around me and the peace she exuded." The memory surprised him. He'd not talked about that day in seventeen years. "Mom and I never knew much about Miss Everleigh's life before she moved to Fernandina Beach, but she must've gone through something intense to carry such peace and empathy. I hope to live in a way that would make her proud."

He passed the mike back to Pastor Oliver, convicted by his own confession. *Live in a way* . . . Really? When? Because if he was honest, he had no plan to start living for others above himself.

Pastor cleared his throat and patted Bruno's shoulder. *Well done.*

———

"Miss Ilene, I know you have a story . . ."

As he sat, a slow trickle traced down his cheek and Mom squeezed his hand.

After a few more testimonies, the song leader returned to the stage and invited everyone to stand and sing.

"You're a good, good Father."

Closing his eyes, Bruno raised his voice. This was a confession he needed. A truth he must embrace. God was a *good* Father.

As the last note rang out, he checked for Beck, but she was gone. He resisted the urge to run for the door and scan the street for her.

Whatever happened after Dale died must've been horrendous. The hard glint in her eye told the story.

But surely beneath the toughness was the remains of a bright-eyed, freckle-faced girl who ran through the sun and waves with abandon. The girl he taught to surf. The girl who shared his first kiss under twinkle lights at the music festival. The girl who made him laugh just because.

Would he see her again? Perhaps too much time had passed. It happened. People changed, drifted. Bruno wasn't sure Beck Holiday was anything like the girl he'd once loved. He glanced again at the door, then toward the fading blaze of the orange-and-red sunset.

She'd been gone a long time. Maybe it was good she didn't remember him. Whatever childhood dreams he had of Beck Holiday were a thing of the past. Better to leave them be, alone and undisturbed.

CHAPTER EIGHT

EVERLEIGH

As quickly as it began, it ended. The cellar door ceased rattling, and a sliver of white light slipped between concrete and metal.

The puppies squirmed from her lap, yipping, tussling with one another. It was over. *Yip, yip!*

But Everleigh could not move. Huddled into herself, she pressed her back against the hard, unrelenting cellar wall and waited, shivering, not bothering to dry her tears.

Rocco hopped over and sniffed her hand before trying to climb into her lap. She cradled him close and held on tight, too tight. He squirmed and nipped at her hand, so she let him go.

Get up, Everleigh.

But her arms, her legs, her very being remained pinned to the wall. Rhett would come soon. Then she'd move, fall into his arms, and know everything was all right.

A twister! She'd lived through a twister.

The moments collected into hours. The whitish-blue light falling through the cellar faded to a pale gray. The puppies sniffed about, playing, until they settled into a pile and fell asleep.

Time ticked on as she waited, frozen, her stomach rumbling, her legs aching.

Rhett will come.

He was probably in town, helping with the aftermath. The Applegates were good that way, always extending a helping hand to anyone in need.

At last sleep came to claim her and she surrendered.

"Everleigh!"

She jolted upright, fumbling with the flashlight, tossing off the blanket. "I'm down here! Rhett? Darling, I knew you'd come."

The hinges moaned and a bold white beam flooded the cellar.

"Everleigh?" Duke Cartwright, owner of the DC Ranch southwest of the Circle A, descended the steps. "We've been looking all over for you. Are you okay?"

"Yes, I'm fine." Her voice wavered as she stood, her leg tingling from being curled under her for so long. "I decided to stay here until Rhett came. Is he up top?" She peered up, through the cellar opening, to the stars scattered across the night sky.

"Why don't we get you and these here pups up out of this hole. Y'all must be starving."

"As a matter of fact . . ." Everleigh climbed out with Rocco and the big pup while Duke carried the other two.

They emerged into darkness under a full complement of stars and a white, glowing moon. How was it possible only a few hours ago terror twisted over her?

On the ground, however, Everleigh's landscape was black and eerie, save the headlamps shining from Mr. Cartwright's trucks and those coming up the driveway.

"Lea, darling, can you get these poor things some food and water?" Mr. Cartwright passed the dogs to his wife. "Everleigh, we brought sandwiches and a cold jug of fresh milk." He escorted her toward his truck.

"How'd your place do, Mr. Cartwright? The rain was so thick I didn't see it was a twister until it was nearly too late. There was nothing on the radio but static."

"It was a twister, all right. An F5. Three quarters of a mile wide. Cut right through town before heading up this way. A granddaddy of a storm. Never seen one like it in these parts. The whole town's—"

"Duke, let the girl eat." Mrs. Cartwright wrapped a blanket over

Everleigh's shoulders while her daughter handed over a sandwich wrapped in waxed paper.

"W-what happened to the town, Mr. Cartwright?" Everleigh said, but her eyes were on the truck pulling alongside her.

"Rhett!" She tossed her sandwich aside and ran straight into Mr. Cartwright's arms.

"Do you know what time it is, Everleigh?"

She squinted up at the moon. "Eight? Nine o'clock?"

"It's two a.m."

"What? No. I couldn't have been in that cellar ten hours." She whirled around at the sound of a clapping door, straining against the rancher's hold. "Rhett?"

"I need you to take a deep breath and look around, Everleigh." He swept his flashlight across the terrain—the vacant, barren terrain.

She turned a slow circle. "Where's the house, Mr. Cartwright? And the barn?"

"Gone."

Everleigh jerked away from him. "No, the house is-is-is . . ." She shielded her eyes against the blaze of truck lights. "Is right here." She ran to the cellar to get her bearings. All that remained of the Applegate home was the foundation. "Mr. Cartwright, where's Rhett? Where are my in-laws?"

"They're coming in that truck there." He pointed to the last truck as it left the gravel driveway and cut across Daddy Applegate's lawn. "I hate to ask you, but we need to know what you want to do."

"What I want to do? About what?" In her heart, she knew. But her head refused to accept what was coming. Her eyes filled as the driver parked Rhett's truck, a huge dent in the hood, next to her. "No—" She broke, covering her lips with her hand, and collapsed into Mrs. Cartwright's strong embrace.

It couldn't be. No. Simply no! They were building a house. She carried his baby!

"The bodies, Everleigh. We thought you'd want to see them before calling the funeral home. I hope we were right. We got Spike, Heidi, and Rhett in the back. I'm so sorry. So very sorry."

"No!" She collapsed through Mrs. Cartwright's arms onto the wet, tough Texas grass, a soft, gentle breeze whispering over her.

BECK

"Sign here and here." Miss Everleigh's lawyer, Joshua Christian, passed Beck a gold pen.

Cradling Beetle Boo in her lap, she accepted the house and the massive property that went to the end of the lane, Miss Everleigh's accounts, the ancient car in the garage-barn-looking building out back, and the rest of her worldly possessions.

"Mr. Christian, do you know? Why me?" Beck handed him the pen.

"Because she said so. She had a lot of affection for you, for your family, and she understood the loss of your father was devastating."

"See there, how did she know? My mother said they exchanged Christmas cards for a few years, then nothing. Mom hadn't heard from her in ten years."

The man with the bright aura smiled, collecting the papers. "Miss Everleigh had a good memory and a big heart."

"I don't remember her." Beck set Beetle on the floor, but he whined to be picked up again. She had carried him on the flight from New York, a journey he did not appreciate, and since then he'd barely let her out of his sight.

"Yes, I know."

"Again, how do *you* know?"

"You'll remember in time." He took another set of papers from his attaché. "You don't have to question everything, Beck. Just enjoy this gift. Now, there's about a hundred thousand dollars in her money market. The stocks and bonds listed here. Her husband, Don, bought in to the tech world early on and did quite well. Everleigh designated some of the bigger stocks and some cash to her nieces and nephews, but the rest she left for you. Here's the monthly draw from her annuity. About seven thousand."

"Excuse me?" She snatched up the account printout. "Seven thousand a month?"

Mr. Christian, the most peaceful, unassuming man Beck had ever met, confirmed the amount even though Beck could read it with her own eyes.

"How do I have a right to any of her money? This is nuts."

Mr. Christian pointed to a note on the bottom of the legal papers. "Go to this bank. Ask for Rebekah. She'll give you the cards to sign. And here." He flipped the page. "Sign here, and I'll get these sent off to the investment firm."

She peered at him, his posture a blend of old Southern lawyer and a savvy New Yorker. He wore a simple blue suit with a crisp white shirt and a red tie. Silver threads laced his otherwise reddish-brown hair, and his eyes were the most brilliant blend of green and gold.

But it was his presence that both drew her in and confounded her. He was a force under his gentle demeanor, an otherworldly power that filled the room and almost consumed her.

"Who leaves a stranger her fortune? The remains of her life?"

"But you're not a stranger to her. See the world through her lens."

"I haven't been in Florida or talked to Everleigh in eighteen years."

"Yes, well, that was unfortunate. You might enjoy this more if you remembered her."

She glared at him. "How did you know I don't remember her?"

His smile pierced her, weakening her barriers. "I'm a lawyer. It's my job to know. Now, be a wise woman and accept this gift. Can you do that? With some modicum of grace?" He collected his copies of the papers along with his fancy gold pen.

She felt properly rebuked yet, strangely, loved. "It's just a little overwhelming." The woman's gesture humbled her. Broke down her lie that the world was a hard, selfish place of loss and pain.

"You know, there's a story," he said, pausing by the ornate, polished front door. "About a man who died living under a bridge. When the investigators came along, they learned he had a million dollars in his bank account. Why, they wondered, would he live like a homeless pauper under a bridge when he had such wealth in the bank?"

"Maybe he didn't know. Maybe he wanted to give the money away. Or live without the constraints of wealth."

"Those seem like the obvious answers. But in the end, they learned he was prideful and refused to accept a gift. Don't make the same mistake, Beck."

Their gazes crossed, locked, and the lawyer's words sank into her. "I-I won't." She stopped him just as he stepped onto the veranda. "Wait, Mr. Christian, can I sell it? The house?"

"Why would you want to?"

"Because," she scoffed. "I have a job and a life in New York."

"Do you?"

After he'd gone, the man's presence, his *je ne sais quoi*, lingered, and his simple, two-word question nagged her. Did she have a life in New York? Was the job still her passion?

Yes, of course. Once a cop always a cop. What else was she going to do with her life? Until this strange inheritance, it was her only connection to her father.

But things were changing. She was having a baby. And no matter what she decided—to raise the baby herself or put her up for adoption—she would never be the same.

Her life needed assessing, and it'd been a long time coming.

Closing the door, Beck reached down for Beetle, who heeled after her. "Well, what do you want to do now?"

With the dog in her arms, she explored the house. It was beautiful. Nothing like the haunted, broken-down shack she imagined.

The sun fell through the windows and bounced off the hardwoods with a warm reddish hue.

A broad staircase split the foyer in two. On one side was a bedroom with a private bath. On the other side was the large formal living room with an antique breakfront and upholstered furniture.

Through the living room, Beck came to the kitchen with a high-tray ceiling and a ginormous butler's pantry. She wasn't a decorator, but the kitchen looked recently updated with marble counters and white cabinets.

The back door led to the veranda and a massive backyard with the garage-barn building.

Beck opened the fridge. Empty. She'd have to find a way to shop. Maybe take an Uber, or see which grocery stores delivered.

Back through the living room, she climbed the stairs, finding an angled wall and a window seat overlooking the backyard on the second-floor landing.

There were three bedrooms on this level, plainly furnished, looking as if they hadn't been used in years, and an entryway into another living-room-slash-library.

The eastern wall—four window panes above a bench seat—faced Memory Lane. The opposite wall was a bookshelf. Overhead, the coffered ceiling was framed with gold crown molding. It was both elegant and ostentatious.

The room had two doors. One from the main hall and another to a small alcove leading to a very private, large master bedroom.

Beck walked through, taking it all in again in the light of day, a slight sensation flipping through her.

This is mine?

The master was part of the exterior turret and had lots of windows framed with lacy white curtains. No matter how she tried to position herself in the house, she couldn't hide from the light.

There was a large empty closet constructed of cedar shiplap. Mr. Christian must have done something with Everleigh's clothes.

Beck ran her fingers over the dark cedar, inhaling the fragrance. A hazy memory tried to surface. Had she been in this room? Hiding?

She left the door open as she exited and inspected the bathroom. Very nice. Also recently updated. Everleigh had exquisite taste, especially with the throwback claw-foot tub.

The house was really spectacular. She could sell it, rent it out, turn it into a B&B. Beck shivered. A B&B sounded so *eighties*.

Out of the room, she paused to examine the wainscoting of dark panel under a white wall. To her right was a set of narrow stairs going up to a third floor.

She was about to go up when the doorbell chimed through the upstairs. Leaning over the railing, she called down, her cop instincts kicking in.

"Hello?" She glanced around for a weapon. Man, she felt naked without her Glock.

She picked up a pillow from the window seat, then tossed it back. Maybe there was a cane in the master closet. No, it was void of any long, sturdy sticks.

Back to the stairs, she waited, listening.

The bell rang again followed by, "Beck?" The masculine voice was muffled by the thick front door.

"You should know I'm armed." With a shivering dog, but still, it was something.

"Armed? Beck, it's me, Bruno Endicott. From yesterday. The memorial service?"

She jogged downstairs and opened the front door to find Bruno on the steps with hands raised.

"Is that your weapon? A quivering dog?"

"He bites." She petted his ears. "Sometimes."

He motioned toward the door. "Can I come in?"

Beck regarded him for a second before stepping aside. He wore his dark hair short and loose, and he smiled easily. She liked that about him already.

"How'd you know I was here?"

She set Beetle down, and the dog hobbled toward the kitchen, disappearing under the table. She'd found him this morning hiding in the butler's pantry, shivering for no apparent reason. After a life with Boudreaux, the poor thing was terrified of dust bunnies.

In the week and a half she'd owned him, Beck had learned he distrusted strangers and downright hated men. He wouldn't let Wyatt near him, and when he had to go potty, he'd rather fall face-first down the stairs than let Wyatt help him.

"Miss Everleigh's lawyer stopped by my office. A Joshua Christian?"

"Please don't tell me you inherited the house too." Wouldn't Mr. Christian have told her?

"Too? You inherited this place?" Bruno inspected his seating options and chose the couch. "Mr. Christian told me you were here. Said he thought I'd like to know."

"Why would you like to know? And do you know him?" Beck sat in the wingback chair opposite Bruno.

"I don't, but maybe Miss Everleigh said something to him. You and I used to be friends back in the day."

"Friends, yes, of course." Her words contained zero sincerity.

"You don't remember, do you?"

She shook her head. "What did you think of Mr. Christian? Did he seem legit to you?"

"I've only recently returned to Fernandina Beach after living in LA for eight years, and I'm on the road ninety percent of the time, so I don't have a clue what goes on in this town, but he seemed solid enough. Had this quality, a—"

"A *je ne sais quoi*." So Bruno saw it too.

His smile lit his expression and stirred Beck with something familiar. "I'd was going to say 'vibe' but yeah, a *je ne sais quoi* will do." He leaned forward, arms on his legs, fingers loosely laced. "Tell me about inheriting this place. I didn't know you were in touch with Miss Everleigh."

"I wasn't."

"But she left you the house?"

"And her money."

"Wow, good for you. Miss Everleigh had some nieces and nephews in Texas, but I never saw them. I wondered who she'd leave the memory house to when the time came. I'm surprised she picked you but—"

"Did you think she'd name you in her will?"

"No." He paused and laughed softly. "Well, maybe. Or my mom. She *was* like a grandmother to me."

"Are you going to protest the will?"

He made a face. "If Miss Everleigh left the house to you, then who am I to challenge her? So, Beck, where have you been? What do you do?"

"I'm a sergeant with the NYPD."

He arched a brow. "Like your dad?"

"Something like that. And what do you do, Bruno? Endicott, right?"

"Sports agent. Had a falling out with my boss in LA about the time Mom was in a serious car accident, so I came home to help her and start my own agency."

"How's it going?"

He sat back with a sigh and gazed toward the windows. "Not as well as I'd like."

"I can't imagine this small town is the place to launch a sports agency."

"My location is not the problem. It's my old boss. He keeps knocking my legs out from under me, spreading rumors. Beck, tell me, honest, why haven't we heard from you since your dad died?"

"Life wasn't easy after 9/11. Mom and I were barely hanging on. But I grew up anyway, made a life for myself—"

"You're married?" He nodded to her slightly round middle.

Beck stretched her top over her belly. "No."

She was just starting to surrender to his charm and sincerity until he noticed her condition.

Suddenly he was on his feet. "Well, have you seen the car?" He marched through the living room toward the kitchen. "It's a classic. Wish I had the funds to buy it from you. That is, if you wanted to sell."

"Car? No, I haven't seen the car." She followed him, their steps resounding over the hardwood in unison. "Doesn't matter really, I don't drive."

He stopped short in the arched kitchen walkway, a stray beam of light rising up from the porch boards and catching the hint of red in the short beard dusting his cheeks. "You're a cop. How do you not drive?"

"Okay, I can drive if I have to, but my partner loves being behind the wheel. Personally, I want to know who's big idea it was to build a combustible engine and steer it with a teeny-tiny wheel while going seventy miles an hour?"

"Beck, next to the light bulb and American football, the combustible engine is the greatest invention known to man."

"You want the car? Take it."

Bruno balked. "Are you serious?"

"Yeah, take it." From the butler's pantry came a tiny growl. Beetle hovered against the cupboards, a suspicious eye on Bruno, who glanced at the dog, then at Beck, waving off her offer.

"No, I'll buy it. When I have the funds. Come on, you have to see this." He headed out the door. Beck peered at Beetle and hurried after Bruno. There was something about him . . . What was it? Besides the fact he acted as if he knew her. As if she knew him.

Down the steps and across the green grass, he talked. "Do you remember the time Miss Everleigh let me drive the car up and down Memory Lane? I was a month away from getting my permit, but did she care? Nope. She handed me the keys and said, 'Young people should have fun.' We drove up and down the lane, the top down, music blaring." His laugh billowed.

Beck smiled. She couldn't help herself. It sounded fun. Real. A small ache twisted around her heart, a longing for her forgotten childhood.

"Now that I think about it," he said, "you didn't want to drive back then either."

"I'm a New Yorker. We like being chauffeured."

Bruno walked past the garage-barn door to a birdbath, tipped it back, and retrieved a key from underneath.

"This is the emergency key." He worked the padlock, slid the door open, powered on a bare bulb with a pull string. "Isn't she a beaut? A 1960 convertible Studebaker Lark. Three on the tree, V-8, 180 horsepower, leather seats, slightly worn as you can see, but this here is automobile royalty." He propped his hands on the passenger door with a look of admiration that Beck envied. What did he see?

She ran her hand down the length of the sleek vehicle. It *was* pretty for a car. And with the top down she almost yearned for a sunny afternoon drive.

She glanced out the door. A day like today. The sun was high in a blue cloudless sky, and the temperature sat at a crisp sixty-something. And the breeze was fragrant and light.

"Miss Everleigh kept the car in pristine condition," Bruno said.

"How much is it worth?" But could she sell it? What would Everleigh think? Or Mr. Christian?

"Twenty grand or more. Can you hold on to it for me?"

"Maybe. Until a better offer comes along." She laughed. It was easy to tease him. As if they understood one another.

"Beck?" Bruno walked around the car with intent. "You don't remember any of this, do you? Me? Miss Everleigh?"

She turned away from his inspection toward the door. He was too much of a keen observer.

"Do you live near here?"

"I have a condo on the beach. My mom lives across the street. You must remember her, Natalie Endicott?"

"Yeah, sure."

"Liar." He was next to her now. "What happened, Beck?"

She tucked her hands into her jeans' hip pockets, feeling the north Florida cold in the garage shadows. "I have selective amnesia. Happened after Dad died. Any memories he touched are gone."

"Amnesia?" Bruno looked incredulous. "Serious? Who gets amnesia?"

"Me. I can't remember him or this place." Her gaze met his. "Or you."

"Wow. Well, I remember you." Bruno walked past her into the yard. "I have a ton of summer memories of fishing on the river. I taught you to surf, you know." He pointed to the house. "We used to crawl out the bay window and lay flat on the roof to keep from sliding off and counted stars." He turned to her. "You were my first kiss at a music festival."

"I remember going to school, playing with my friends," Beck said. "I remember my mom and the dog we had from the time I was one to twelve. But my dad? Nothing."

"How can you . . . I mean . . ." He squinted at her. "Do you want to remember?"

"It's been eighteen years, Bruno. I don't know any different. This is my life."

The moment she spoke, a *kerplunk* resonated through her, and just over Bruno's right shoulder, she saw an image unfurl, the light and shadow parting to reveal a girl laughing with her dad.

"Come on, Beckster, you can do it!"

"I'm not old enough to drive."

"We're only going up and down Memory Lane. Now press in the clutch."

Her soft scream was followed by grinding gears. "Dad, this is cray-cray."

"Up and over for second gear. Straight down for third. There you go."

She stalled again, but Dad nodded his approval.

"Look, you moved a foot. A hundred more times and we'll be at the end of the lane." Their laughter blended, deep man-cop with giggly teen-girl. "Here we go."

"Beck, you okay?" Bruno snapped his fingers. "I lost you there."

The vision rolled up, and the only sound in Beck's ears was the song of a distant bird.

"Sorry." She shook her head and tried to focus on Bruno. "W-what were you saying?"

"I asked if you wanted to take the car for a spin." He bent over the driver's side door. "Yep, the keys are in the ignition. Don't know why she kept them in here but—"

"Me? No, no . . ." What just happened? Where had that scene come from? "You go ahead." She needed a moment to think. To process. "I'll . . . go inside. Beetle doesn't like to be alone."

Her mind had played a trick on her. The doctor told her it could happen. But this was a first. It was this place. Coming back here. It was Bruno and his stories. Her subconscious must be trying to conjure up some sort of matching sentiments.

"Are you sure you don't want to come?" Bruno had popped the hood to inspect the engine.

"Maybe another time." Or never. "Lock up when you bring it back, okay?"

Inside the house, she slid down the closed door to the floor, the roar of the engine pressing against the glass. Beetle emerged from the pantry and crawled on her lap.

Beck rubbed his ears, then buried her face in his soft fur. "I thought the house might be haunted, Beetle, but maybe I'm the one who's haunted. I heard his voice, and he called me Beckster."

CHAPTER NINE

EVERLEIGH

February 1960

"Coming down like cats and dogs out there." Connie tied on her rain cap, then opened the cooler door. "I'm off with Mr. Childers's order. See you tomorrow."

Mr. Childers, a widower and long-time customer of Reed's, maintained his beloved wife's weekly flower order. Everleigh and Connie took turns delivering to him personally even though Reed's owned a fleet of delivery trucks.

"Drive safe. See you in the morning." Everleigh finished counting the cash drawer and bundled the money for the safe. "Mr. Reed will be pleased. We're having a banner Valentine's week."

She was the store's afternoon and weekend manager, working alongside the family for the past six years.

"Do you have any fun plans this weekend? A date?" Connie paused at the office door, flowers in hand.

Everleigh ignored her not-so-subtle probing. "The usual. Dinner and TV with Mama."

She set the cash drawer in the safe and twisted the lock.

"All work and no play ain't healthy, Ev."

"What do you and Rand have planned?"

"The girls are fixing us dinner. They're so cute. Gina is taking home economics, and I think she's planning an ambitious seven-course meal. I'll probably have to put out a fire or two, then eat burned meat, but it'll taste like love." Lightning cracked the window, causing Connie to jump. "I hate storms."

Everleigh peered outside. So did she. Time could pass into infinity and she'd never come to peace with a south Texas storm.

"Well, I'm off. Ev, do something fun, will you?" Connie made her way to the back door. "Even if it's the movies with your girlfriends. What about your friend Myrtle?"

"We went to the movies last weekend. She's gone to El Paso for her brother's wedding." Myrtle was the only other unmarried woman in Everleigh's circle. While they liked each other well enough, it was kind of sad and depressing to step out together too often.

"See you in the morning."

"Hey to Rand."

"Hey to your mama."

With the shop silent, Everleigh finished an order for three corsages, wrapped the stems in pink ribbon, and set them in the cooler.

She cleaned the work area and swept the floors, then decided they needed a light mop before she locked up.

As she finished up in the workroom, Mr. Reed appeared in the doorway, jiggling his keys.

"Can I see you in my office, Everleigh?"

"Yes, sir." Her eyes followed him. He was straight and good as the day was long, but something in his voice . . .

Wiping her hands, she checked her appearance in the mirror before joining him. Last year he'd talked of promoting her to buyer, but she was too timid to ask if he'd given the matter further consideration.

"You're embarrassing me, Everleigh," he said.

"Excuse me?"

"You show up to work early, stay late. You double count the cash and recalculate the deposits. You clean even though we have a crew to do the job. I could invite the queen for tea this very moment and be pleased as punch to serve her off your clean floor."

"I like to keep busy." The year after, well, *everything* she nearly

---

went crazy, sitting at home with Mama like a mummy in pearls and low-heeled pumps.

She needed to work to pay the bills but also to keep her mind occupied, to balance the emptiness of being a widow at the age of twenty-three. Working gave her simple little life a bit of meaning.

After a year of mourning and starting to go stir-crazy, she'd tried to go back to Kestner's Department Store but couldn't make herself cross the threshold. It reminded her too much of Rhett, of their hopes and dreams.

Then a friend put her onto Reed's and six years later—

"But I don't pay you for all of this. I feel like I'm cheating you."

With such a confession, how could she not have the confidence to inquire about the promotion? "Have you given any thought to making me a buyer?"

"I'm glad you asked." He leaned forward, his expression unreadable. "Everleigh, I, well, hmm, I guess I'll just say it. I'm promoting my son to buyer."

"I see."

"He needs to learn the business. One day all of this will be his. Besides, he's useless in the store. Impatient with customers, sloppy with the cash count. And I know you rework all of his arrangements. He needs to find something he's good at or Reed's will not survive."

"He's a good kid, Mr. Reed. He'll get the hang of it."

"I'm not sure he's cut out for flowers." He smiled. "He's more of a dirt-and-shovel kind of man."

Everleigh nodded, holding her hands neatly in her lap. "Nothing wrong with that, sir."

Mr. Reed opened the middle desk drawer and passed her an envelope. "I am giving you a raise. Fifty cents more an hour. The envelope has a bonus check from Christmas. You deserve it."

"Fifty cents. Mr. Reed, sir, that's very generous. I'm much obliged." She pinched the envelope between her fingers.

"My wife and I were talking about you the other night. Said how much we appreciate you, but can't help but wonder if there's something more for you."

"More? Like what? Mr. Reed, I'm very content here. This job has been a blessing to Mama and me."

"Everleigh, we value you very much." He cupped his hand over hers. "But I hope you know there's more for you than this place." His tone was fatherly and sincere. "Now, get on home. Sleep in. I don't want to see you until nine a.m. No, ten."

"Yes, sir. And thank you." She held up the bonus. Whatever the amount, she would put it straight in the bank.

As the sole breadwinner, Everleigh policed the budget with vigilance. After Rhett and the Applegates died in the '53 storm, along with Daddy and about 130 others, she and Mama survived only by her prudence.

Daddy left them a small savings, but not enough to get them through the years ahead. The ink wasn't dry on his new life insurance policy that May day when the twister tore up Waco, so there was no payout.

As for Rhett and the Applegates, they'd just mortgaged the ranch for expansion. They made plans for living, not dying.

The bank owned the Circle A now. Everleigh drove by a couple years back, heartbroken to find the land wild and overgrown. She never went back.

As for her job at Ketchner's . . . she just couldn't.

As she buttoned her coat, Everleigh checked the weather through the back door. The wind drove the rain down Austin Avenue at a good clip, but it appeared to be letting up.

The lightning and thunder had moved on when Everleigh called good night to Mr. Reed. But his words remained with her.

I hope you know there's more for you than this place.

What did he mean? More for her? No, there was *nothing* more for her. She'd walked her rainbow path only to find destruction at the end. Not a pot of gold or happily ever after.

Hurrying across the two lanes of traffic to her car, Everleigh moaned as her foot landed in a cold puddle. The water sloshed over her shoe and soaked her stockings.

Isn't this just the way?

But she kept moving, shaking off the rain, shaking off Mr. Reed's comment, and climbed inside Daddy's old DeSoto.

After cranking the engine, she moved the heat lever all the way over and drove, shivering, down the avenue toward Lauderback's.

Mama had called that afternoon with a shopping list. She typically had them delivered, but she wanted a pie, and the last time she ordered dessert the delivery boy turned the cake upside down.

Everleigh parked by Lauderback's entrance and dashed inside. Snagging a shopping buggy, she dug Mama's list from her bag and moved slowly down the first aisle.

Potatoes, carrots, green beans, apple pie, and ice cream.

It was Thursday, and in the Novak-Applegate house that meant pot roast. Everleigh would be too late with the potatoes and carrots. Mama could live with mashed potatoes this week instead of roasted. And who needed carrots? Everleigh didn't like them as a kid, and she didn't like them now.

In the past six years, she and Mama had developed a sensible routine. Everleigh worked; Mama ran the household.

Mondays she did the laundry and made some sort of chicken dish—fried, baked, roasted, fricasseed.

Tuesdays they ate fish.

Wednesday morning Mama had bridge club, so dinner consisted of sandwiches or scrambled eggs before they headed off to evening church, where Everleigh sang in the choir.

Thursdays Mama volunteered at the library, and dinner was pot roast. Also the only night Mama allowed them to indulge in dessert. *"We'll be two fat old widows if we're not careful."*

Everleigh resented the notion. It was one thing to be a widow at thirty-one. It was another to be lumped in with her fifty-eight-year-old mother. And to be called fat.

Glancing around to see she was alone, she peered down at her belly. It was rounder than seven years ago. And she had a collection of pretty dresses she could no longer wear.

Maybe she should skip the ice cream on her pie tonight.

Fridays Mama conquered weekly household chores and ran errands. She dropped Everleigh off at Reed's in the morning and picked her up that night. Dinner consisted of leftovers or dinner at Elite Café downtown, where so much had changed since '53.

A phantom thought from *that* day floated through her. The morning started out so beautiful and peaceful. She would never be free of the tornado. It'd permanently marked her life. Changed her course forever.

Everleigh paused by a new cereal on display at the end of the aisle. Heart of Oats. She dropped a box in her buggy.

Where was she? Oh yes, on Saturdays they dined on pizza. A new dish Everleigh discovered in *Good Housekeeping*. It became a fast favorite.

Sundays after church she and Mama splurged, eating at Lavender or White's cafeteria.

"Pardon us." Everleigh glanced around as a young couple tried to pass. She'd stopped dead center in the canned goods aisle.

"I'm so sorry." She shoved her buggy aside as they went by, laughing, touching, being in love.

Connie was right. She needed to get out and have some laughs. Except for Myrtle, all of her girlfriends from high school and college were married with young children. The single men in town her age were single for a reason. Heaven help her. Not that any of them came calling.

In a blink, Everleigh Applegate was old before her time, lost in a tunnel of grief with the ruins of what should have been.

Two more women passed, their hair bright and shiny, styled in the new bouffant way.

Everleigh touched the tight hair knot on the nape of her neck. It'd been months since she'd gone to LuEllen. *Months.* Honestly, a year. Yes, it'd been that long. Well, of course, the Christmas before last, when she sang the lead in the cantata.

She turned the buggy down the toiletries aisle and slowed before the shelves of Miss Clairol.

"Everleigh?"

She whirled around and peered into a million-dollar face with high curved cheeks, a lean jaw, crystal-blue eyes, and a crisp, sincere smile.

"It's me, Don Callahan." He offered his hand. "I was friends with your brother in high school."

"Yes, of course." She hesitated, then shook his hand. "I didn't expect to see you here. How are you?"

She fixed on his face, remembering. Names and faces came to her easier these days, while events and past dates remained a struggle. If she concentrated hard enough, she'd find a thread to pull.

"I'm well. Still in Dallas working for Dewey Motors. Your brother keeps in touch. Well, his wife sends Christmas cards."

"Alice is good at correspondence. I call her the perfect woman."

"They do seem happy. Tom Jr. is doing well with his job."

"He's a born salesman." Everleigh's attention lingered on Don's face, then drifted down his immaculate coat to the crease of pressed slacks and the shine of his polished shoes.

She remembered him sitting with Tom Jr. at the dining room table working on various school projects. He was always so nice and polite. And very cute. Linda Taylor found a reason to come over whenever Don was at the house, pretending her mother needed a cup of sugar or cooking oil. Which she invariably left behind.

Mama used to play bridge with Don's mama. But it'd been a while since the name Sher Callahan was spoken in the Novak-Applegate house.

"What are you up to these days?" he said.

"I'm a florist at Reed's." The flower shop was a Waco staple. Nothing more needed to be said.

"I bought my prom date's corsage there."

"I just finished up three for a Valentine's dance."

"Are you married?" he said. "Rather, remarried, I guess."

Her hands twisted around the buggy handle as she shook her head, lips pinched. But when she looked up, their eyes met and said more than mere words.

Sorry about Rhett.

Me too.

"I'm not married either," he said with a soft laugh. "Much to my mother's consternation."

Everleigh was suddenly conscious of her old, faded work dress, the matronly bun on the back of her head, and the squeak in her soggy shoes as she adjusted her stance. "Mama's waiting dinner. I'd better go."

"I hear you. Mom sent me on an errand for coffee. I'm thirty-two and live in my own home in Dallas, but that doesn't stop her from ordering me around." He laughed and joined step with Everleigh as she walked down the aisle. "Know what? I still can't get used to all the parking lots around here where businesses used to be."

"You're not in Waco enough, I suppose."

The F5 twister rearranged Waco forever. Beyond the lives lost, buildings collapsed and the owners moved on. The town cleared away the rubble and paved the barren places into parking lots.

"I'm in town for my niece's dedication," Don said, still walking with her. Didn't he have a mama chore to attend? Surely Everleigh held no interest for him. "Pearl's daughter, Mia."

"Pearl has a daughter?" The news soaked in. Don's sister, two years younger than Everleigh, had a daughter.

"She has three actually. The latest is six months old. Has her uncle Don wrapped around her pinky already." He chuckled. "They all do."

"Three daughters?" How did she not know? She must've heard but forgotten.

Nevertheless, her friends, her classmates, her cousins, the *world* had moved on while she remained rooted in a soil she could not escape.

"You've never met them? Don't our mothers still play bridge? Come by the house Sunday afternoon. The family would love to see you."

"I'm not sure."

"Then you should definitely come. Dad has a new grill, and I know he'll make more hamburgers and hot dogs than we can eat."

"Don, thank you, but we couldn't intrude." Everleigh pushed the buggy with intent. She *must* be going.

Don's exuberance and charm, the way he looked at her, rattled her. What was he seeing? Did he feel sorry for her? Consider her existence sad and pitiful? Lonely?

"If you change your mind, we're still at 21 Whitehall Road. It was nice to see you, Everleigh."

"You too." She rounded the end of the aisle before glancing back. Don had not moved and watched her with a measure of intensity.

When he smiled, she ducked her head and raced toward the bakery. *What in the world?* Another day, another time, another woman, and she'd say he was flirting.

She asked Marla at the bakery counter for Mama's pie—forget the ice cream—then made her way to the checkout, her heels in a rhythmic *click-squish* against the floor.

———

Unloading the groceries, she settled down, the routine of the checkout counter grounding her in her small but familiar world.

Quite a charmer, Don Callahan. He must sell a lot of cars up there at Dewey's.

Getting out her checkbook, she caught her reflection in the store's darkened pane glass.

She looked old with the baggy shirtwaist and her brown hair pulled tight. Two weeks ago she noted a deep V between her eyebrows along with dark circles under her eyes. She looked like a creature from the Black Lagoon.

But to be fair, though—and who didn't want to be fair when the assessment was so bleak?—the dress was a work dress. As were her shoes. She wiggled her toes against the damp leather. And if she didn't wear her hair back, it fell around her face and neck all day.

Frankly, it was a miracle Don even recognized her. She looked nothing like her former days as a vibrant high schooler then college co-ed.

"How're you doing, shug?" Madeline greeted as she rang up the groceries. "How's your mama?"

"She's well. I'll tell her you asked after her."

Mama . . . Not *How's Rhett?* or *How're the kids? You know my Jimmy's in class with your oldest.*

No, it was "How's your mama?" That was Everleigh's world. Not a husband. Not children. Not even a career. But her *mama.*

"Did you get everything you need?" Madeline said.

"No, Madeline, I didn't." Everleigh started filling out the check. "Sadly, I probably never will."

"What? You just tell Mr. Lauderback and he'll get it in."

"I don't think Lauderback's sells what I'm looking for." Mr. Reed's same sentiment echoed as she handed the check to Madeline.

Was she looking for something more? Since when?

Madeline prattled on as she bagged the groceries, handing the single brown paper sack to Everleigh.

"Be careful with the pie now. Keep that bag upright."

When she arrived at her car, Don stepped out of the dark folds between the exterior lights.

"Mercy, you scared the what's-it out of me." Anxiety throbbed in her throat.

"Sorry." He reached for the grocery bag, opened the passenger-side door, and set the groceries inside. "I didn't mean to frighten you. I'll set the pie on the seat so it doesn't get smashed."

Everyone was so darn concerned about that pie. Forget the pie. What did he want?

"You best get on home with your coffee. Your mama will have your hide." She fumbled with her keys, dropping them to the wet asphalt.

Don bent for them and walked her around to the driver's side. "What are you doing tomorrow night?" He opened the door as he handed over her keys.

"T-tomorrow night? I-I don't know. Leftovers and television with Mama."

"Have dinner with me."

"Dinner? With you?" Her nervous laugh betrayed her.

"The Ridgewood has a nice menu on Friday nights. Some of the old big bands come play. Do you dance?"

"Dance? Yes. But don't tell my pastor." She chortled with a nervous energy. "He doesn't know Jesus approves."

Don's laugh was a song. "I'll pick you up at seven."

"Seven? Well, okay."

Neither one of them moved. Did she just say yes?

She ducked into the car, exhaling only when he closed the door.

"See you tomorrow night at seven."

Fingers shaking, she slipped the keys into the ignition. *What are you doing? What would be the point? Tell him you can't go.*

She was a mess. Dull hair. Chipped nails. She'd have no time to visit LuEllen's, and the last time she tried on one of her party dresses from the Korean War era, the side seams ripped.

Ridgecrest had a high standard. She couldn't possibly go to the country club in one of her old frocks with a metropolitan man like Don.

Besides, it was the place where Rhett proposed and she'd not been back since—"Don, wait." She crashed open the door and stepped out.

He turned, walking backward, arms outstretched. "It's just dinner, Ev. A steak and nice baked potato. You like steak, don't you?"

"Well, yes, but—"

"Great. I'll pick you up at seven."

"Don." Her voice echoed across the parking lot. "I didn't say yes."

"You just said, 'Well, yes.'"

"Followed by a *but*." She *would* win this mini debate.

"No, no," he said with a shake of his head, flashing his gleaming smile. "I accept no buts."

"Can we please stop yelling 'but' in the public parking lot?"

He laughed his merry laugh. "Then just say yes."

CHAPTER TEN

DON

As a kid, Don Callahan wanted one thing. To make his dad proud. So he worked hard, got good grades, starred on the football team, did his stint in the army, then graduated Baylor with honors.

At his father's request, he moved to Dallas to work for Standish Dewey of Dewey Motors, to learn firsthand from the larger-than-life businessman how a big, successful dealership worked. One day, when Dad beckoned, Don would usher Callahan Cars into the modern age.

So far, so good. He'd made Dad proud. Especially when Standish Dewey called to say he thought Don might be his heir apparent and the perfect match for his one-time beauty-queen daughter, Carol Ann.

That's when Dad started talking merger.

"I think we can make it work. Standish has been after me for a couple of years now."

So Don had done well. Performed his duty. But lately—

The status quo was cutting off his air. He had ideas of his own. His life was becoming a replica of his father's. But at the dawn of a new year and a new decade, Don had a new opportunity. Yet if he told Dad what he was thinking . . .

He turned up the radio as he passed by the old Waco silos. Someday someone should buy those things and do something great with them.

He passed the paved lots where buildings once stood. Drafted in '48, he had been in Korea when the tornado tore through downtown.

The Callahans were spared death and destruction, but many of their friends suffered loss. Like the Novaks. Like Everleigh. He couldn't imagine what she'd endured.

Turning into the Callahan driveway, he parked his new Corvette behind Dad's Impala. Coffee in hand, he stared at the lights of his childhood home.

The large plate glass, framed the family gathered in the living room, the fireplace crackling. In his mind, he could hear them all talking at once—Dad and Mom, his sister, Pearl, and her husband, Mamaw and Papaw, Aunt Florine and Uncle Doley.

He loved them all, and except for his time in the army, he'd never missed a holiday, birthday, or family barbecue. Not a baptism or dedication.

But lately he chomped at the bit for something more. To go out on his own without disappointing them. Especially Dad. How could he be his father's son while bursting to be his own man. He'd been to war, for crying out loud.

At first he dismissed his itching for adventure as a wild thought. Crazy dreams. Why leave Dewey when he had everything a guy could want?

Success. A beautiful girlfriend. A solid future. All he had to do was stay on the straight and narrow.

When George Granger, a college buddy, approached him about starting an insurance business, he brushed it off at first. Then he could think of nothing else. Now he believed he'd explode if he didn't try.

Don walked around back to the kitchen, where the aroma of roasted meat and baking bread made his senses tingle. In the far corner by the toaster, the radio was tuned in low to KBGO, the Big Go.

"Mom, coffee's here."

She bustled in. "Where have you been?"

"Took the long way home. Drove by the old silos."

"When you knew I was waiting for coffee?" She dug the can opener from the big drawer and hooked it over the lid.

"I ran into Everleigh Applegate at Lauderback's."

Rhett hit the jackpot when he married her. She was beautiful ten years ago and still was beneath her plain appearance and faded dress, beneath the death that tried to steal her shine.

"Did you tell her about Carol Ann?" Mom scooped coffee into the percolator.

"Why would I tell her about Carol Ann? 'Hi, Everleigh, I know we're in the middle of Lauderback's shopping, but can I tell you about my girl?'"

Mom grimaced, swatting at him. "Don't sass your mama. I just meant in the course of how-are-yous, did you mention you'd be engaged soon?"

"No." His folks believed a proposal was imminent, but Don wasn't sure he'd ever drop to one knee for Carol Ann Dewey.

"Well, there's time." Mom raised the lid on the boiling potatoes. "Go change if you want. I'll whip these up while the rolls and coffee finish. And we have cake from Mrs. Keaton's."

Don started down the hall to his old room, slipping out of his sport coat, then stepped back to ask a question before he lost his nerve. "What happened between you and Mrs. Novak, Mom? You two were thick as thieves once. Everleigh didn't know Pearl had three girls."

She glanced back at him as she retrieved the butter and milk from the fridge. "We still play bridge in the same club."

"Yeah, but seems after losing her husband and all you'd be—"

"Don, I know full well what happened to the Novaks." She opened the oven for the rolls. "The rolls are ready. Grab that bread basket, son."

"I'm taking her to dinner tomorrow night."

"Who? Irene Novak?" Mom dumped the steaming rolls into the basket and covered them with a cloth. "Take that to the table."

"Everleigh, Mom. Everleigh." He ducked into the dining room, greeting his sister and her husband, Troy. Mom was waiting for him when he came back through to change his clothes.

"What do you mean you're taking her to dinner? You have a lovely girlfriend in Dallas. Don't mess that up, Don. Women like Carol Ann don't wait for any man. And is it fair to Everleigh? Don't toy with her affections. Mark my words, Don, Carol Ann is the kind of woman you need by your side."

"Doesn't hurt she's my boss's daughter, does it?"

Mom patted his face. "Not at all. You treat her right and your future is set, my handsome boy. Now, go change."

Don tugged at his tie, the comment, the warm kitchen suffocating him. How did he tell Dad he wanted to do something else? To work with George Granger?

In his old room he hung up his starched work shirt and tugged a light sweater over his T-shirt. Back in the kitchen Mom had Dad carving the meat.

"Did Standish tell you we're moving ahead with the merger?" Dad dropped a thick slice of beef onto the platter.

"Dad, I've never understood why you want to merge with him." Dad was successful in his own right yet somehow viewed Standish as the popular kid he wanted to pal around with. But this wasn't sandlot baseball. This was Callahan Cars. "He's a hard business man, Dad. It's his way or no way."

"Exactly. What we need at Callahan. Together we'd own the south central Texas car business. He has the business mind while I possess the gift of a salesman. You're the heir to both businesses, so why not merge? It's a good decision, Don. I'm surprised you can't see it."

"Oh, I can see it. But for Standish. Look, Pop, I know you're old friends, but he can be, well, *cunning.*"

"And won't it be great to be on his team?" Dad waved the knife, slicing the air. "Once you marry Carol Ann, the sky is the limit. I've waited my whole life for this kind of opportunity."

"Dad, Callahan's is doing well. Why give up control to Dewey?"

"Son, if a kid comes along while you're playing marbles and says, 'Can I play?' then shows you his bigger, better marbles, what're you going to say? No? You partner with him and play against all the other kids. Next thing you know, you're at the drugstore buying Sugar Daddy's and jawbreakers with money left over for the piggy bank."

"So we're stealing the other kids' lunch money now?"

"You're inviting them into a game of chance. Such is life. You have to be better than the other guy. Dewey is better than the other guy. This is a good strategy, Donny-boy."

"Harold," Mom said, hands on her hips. "That meat isn't going to carve itself."

"On it, Sher." Dad motioned for Don to move close while he sliced more meat. "Don't tell your mother, but I'm talking to a builder. Going to move her into Castle Heights like she's always wanted."

"How do you propose to keep that a secret?"

"Shhh, she'll hear you."

"What are you two going on about?" Mom inspected the meat platter. "That's enough for now, Harold. Oh, the gravy, I forgot to make the gravy." She shoved Dad aside and dropped a skillet on the burner. "Five minutes. Pearl," she called, bending toward the dining room. "Come get the meat. Cover it with the lid from the breakfront."

Dad glanced at Mom as she frantically concocted the gravy and pulled his pack of rumpled cigarettes from his pocket.

"Smoke on the porch, Harold. Not in my kitchen."

Don followed Dad into the cold, crisp air.

"I was thinking of a summer wedding," Dad said, propping against the porch post, striking his match and setting the flame to the end of the cigarette. "You're saving for the ring, aren't you? Can't go cheap with a girl like Carol Ann."

"Granny gave me her ring."

"That ring is older than Methuselah, and looks it too." Dad tapped ashes over the railing. "Use that for a Christmas present or an anniversary. Carol Ann needs a new ring. From Tiffany's. I've a meeting in New York next month. Want to tag along?"

"I'm working." Through the kitchen door came the sounds of

laughter, the sounds of love. All the things that anchored Don during boot camp, during the cold, dark nights when he was a million miles from home, during his first days on Baylor's campus as an old man in his early twenties.

"You sure? I'll bring you a catalog then." Dad squinted at him through cigarette smoke. "Everything okay, Donny?"

"Sure, why do you ask?" *Coward. Come on, fess up. Just say it. You want to go into the insurance business with George Granger.*

"I sold three trucks to Cameron Air and Heating today," Dad said, tapping the loose ashes over the flower bed. "That'll look good on the books for the merger."

"Dad, listen, be sure to read the small print with Dewey. Remember three years ago when he bought Trainor Trucking? Flick Trainor was supposed to get a cut of the profits for twenty years."

Dad regarded him, listening, smoke twisting through the cold night air.

"But not if sales dropped below a certain number—and don't you know Standish made sure no one bought a Trainor truck for over a year. Totally cut Flick out."

Dad chuckled. "I'm sure there are two sides to that story. Standish is savvy, I'll grant you, but he won't cheat me. And if I have any doubts, son, you're my ace in the hole. Sher, how's that gravy coming? I'm weak from hunger."

Ace in the hole? *Speak up, you idiot, before the merger.*

"Put out your cigarette and come on in."

Dad took a long drag and stamped out the burning tobacco.

"You know you should give those up," Don said, aiming for a soft segue. "They cause cancer."

"Doctors are always going on about something." Dad dropped the dead Marlboro into the standing ashtray and clapped Don on the back. "My grandpa smoked, my father—you better get going, son, you're breaking tradition."

"You can keep that one." *Say it now.* "Dad, I'd like your advice about something. George Granger called and—"

"Can we do it later?" The screen door clapped as Dad went inside, leaving Don to face his back. "You know my advice is no good on an empty stomach."

"Yeah, sure." Don hesitated with his hand on the latch.

He'd been to war. Slept in the open. Waded through rivers and streams with water up to his chest. He'd killed the enemy.

Yet he couldn't find the words to tell his father he hated working for Standish Dewey. Or that Carol Ann, while as comely as any dame in Hollywood, bored him silly. Fifty years married to her would make him a madman.

He couldn't tell his dad he'd met a woman tonight who made his heart feel soft and warm, and maybe, if he was lucky, she'd look back at him and see something worth having.

CHAPTER ELEVEN

BECK

By day three, she still felt like an interloper in someone else's life, but she was getting used to the house, the quiet, the gobs of light spilling through the many windows, and the song of the night birds.

She went by the bank as Mr. Christian instructed and asked for Rebekah. She signed the bank card and took two hundred dollars from the account just because.

But it didn't feel right. Peering out the upstairs bedroom window, she held Beetle in her arms.

He sniffed her neck, then stretched to see out, barking when a black Mercedes eased into view, under the sprawling bare limbs of an oak.

"What? You don't like that black car? Did Vinny drive one like that?" She scratched his ears and kissed the top of his head. "Don't worry, he won't bother you again."

Beck watched the car for another minute as it crept slowly down the lane, and her cop senses tingled. One of Vinny's connections?

Beck, stop. That's crazy.

The lowlife dealer had bigger worries than a suspended NYPD sergeant.

Pulling the curtain closed, she set Beetle down and headed for the shower.

Let's see . . . what else?

Oh, yesterday afternoon Everleigh's broker called to see how Beck wanted to handle the annuity.

She talked shop with him, calling upon her decade-old Columbia finance courses before deciding to keep going with the minimum monthly payments. He verified her New York address and social security number, and just like that she was, as they say, "in the money."

How could she do good with this windfall? Share the blessings?

She ordered groceries from Publix and had them delivered.

Last night Beck popped a big bowl of popcorn—carb lovers unite—and sat down to season one of *Gilmore Girls*. The ninety-year-old Everleigh was no slouch in the techno department. She had internet and cable and a smart TV with Netflix and Amazon Prime.

"Show me what you got, Gilmores."

In high school her friends were gaga over some guy named Luke, the diner owner, gruff but sweet. There was also a Dean, Jess, and Logan, who divided her friends into teams. Suzie Gunter had a huge falling out with Gracie Fausnaugh over Team Jess versus Team Logan.

Beck had been too busy for television and fights over TV boyfriends. She had sports and schoolwork, and the business of adjusting to a stepfather, a baby brother, and Wednesday afternoons with a therapist. Which did no good. She still had no memories of her father.

In between *Gilmore Girls* episodes, Beck slept—growing a baby was exhausting.

She explored the house more, curious about photos in the upstairs bedrooms.

Photos of smiling faces, women with linked arms, men holding fishing poles. One in particular captured Beck's attention—a large black-and-white picture of a young couple in a gilded frame. Everleigh and Don?

Beck had no idea what the woman looked like, and while the walls downstairs were decorated with paintings, these were the first personal photos she'd seen.

Most were black-and-white. Beck examined the backs looking for clues. One said, *Tom Jr., Alice, and kids.* Another had the word *Pearl* written on the back, but nothing more.

There were no notations on the other four photos. Beck recognized the Studebaker in one. A woman wearing a nice suit and heels leaned against the hood, her handbag dangling from her hand. It had to be Everleigh.

She was pretty, with an expression that was more than smile-for-the-camera.

The last photo was small. Not even in a frame. Just tucked between the others. A little blond boy rode his tricycle toward the camera's eye. The color was faded, and the make of the car in the background was old-school. The date stamp on the yellowing edge was 1960. Stepping into the shower, she soaked herself in warm water.

"Everleigh, if you meant to leave me your life, why didn't you at least call me?"

Maybe Joshua Christian could answer a few more questions. It was one thing to deal with her own whitewashed past, but making assumptions about someone else's seemed unjust.

She glanced down at her growing belly. While her past had blank spots and her present, question marks, her immediate future seemed clear.

In four months she was having a baby, and she had absolutely no concrete plans.

"This wasn't supposed to happen," she whispered to the shower wall, to herself.

She wondered how, or if, Everleigh faced a crisis. Did she have an unexpected blow? Did her parents die young? Did she lose a sibling or a friend?

A baby? If she was childless, chances were she knew some sort of grief.

Mom might know, but Beck doubted her memories. While she didn't have amnesia, Mom had done a good job of stuffing things away, never to be recalled.

Bruno's mom was her best bet for Everleigh's history. They'd finally met yesterday when Beck took Beetle Boo for an evening potty break. They talked briefly on the curb just after Natalie arrived home.

Stepping from the shower, she wrapped in a towel. She dressed in yoga pants today—her jeans were too tight—and a loose top.

From the edge of the bed, Beetle Boo stared up at her, his pink tongue peeking out. He grew stronger every day but still maintained a vigil on Beck, whining if he lost sight or scent of her.

Last night he slept with his paw on her face.

She dried her hair and clipped it back, then scooped him from the bed. "Let's see what Lorelai and Rory are up to this morning."

She paused by the second-floor master bedroom window and pulled back the lacy curtain, squinting against the light. This room was entirely too bright. She still preferred her night.

They settled in the BarcaLounger, Beck pausing to check email, then Facebook on her phone. She didn't post much, but last night she couldn't resist a snapshot of the endless sunset over the river.

She had a bunch of comments like "wow" and "Where are you?" Her friend Ellie posted, "Call me."

But she didn't want to call anyone. She wanted to just *be*. Hide. Unpack this unexpected gift, like Mr. Christian said, and really contemplate her future. She wouldn't have this kind of time ever again.

Of course, the biggest question was about Baby Girl. Should Beck give her to a family ready, eager, and desperate for a baby? A family with a father and mother? Where no secret would destroy their love?

She'd looked at a house to buy in her old Stuytown neighborhood. With the money she'd saved along with Everleigh's windfall, Beck could buy a decent place. Hire a nanny.

But—

Amazon came up on the TV screen, and Beck aimed the remote at Lauren Graham's face and hit play. At the end of her mental debate, nothing felt right.

The *Gilmore Girls* theme song had just started when the doorbell chimed *and* her phone rang.

She whacked Beetle in the head trying to pause on a view of Stars Hollow.

Hunter's name appeared on her phone screen. She answered as she went for the door, Beetle yipping and hobbling alongside her. She scooped him up before descending to the main floor.

"How're you doing?" Hunter Ingram sounded contrite and humble.

"Fine. Can you hold on? Someone's at the door."

She opened to find Bruno on the porch, wearing an LA Lakers jacket, leaning against the porch post.

He straightened. "What are you—oh, you're on the phone."

She waved him in, unsure what else to do. Slamming the door in his face seemed a bit rude, even though Hunter was on the phone.

"Take a seat," she said, walking through the kitchen and out the back door, fixed on a brick fire pit on the side of the garage-barn. "Hunter?" She stopped somewhere between the house and the garage-barn. The air was cold but the sunlight warm.

"Beck, yeah, I just wanted to see . . ." He sighed. "Are you okay?"

"I am. Don't worry."

"But I do worry. How's Florida?"

"Nice. Colder than I imagined but warmer than home."

"What's up with this house?"

"Hunter, please." She pressed her hand to her forehead. "You don't have to be my partner here. You're my boss. You're married. Let's not pretend we are intimate friends even though . . ." She flashed on the moment they stumbled, drunk, into Rosie's utility closet—Beck squeezed her eyes shut and crushed the images.

Baby Girl might see and demand an explanation.

"I know, but it's my child too, Beck."

"So what are you saying? You're going to tell your wife and make us a threesome?"

"No, no, I don't know, but I don't want to be left out completely. Do you need anything?"

"Hunter, you were left out the moment you hooked up with a woman not your wife in a broom closet."

He sighed and the conversation wilted.

"Let's not complicate this," she said. "I'm fine. In fact, this Florida woman left me some money, and until I decide what to do with this house, my job, Baby Girl—"

"It's a girl?"

Beck smiled, facing the salty breeze. "I had an ultra before I came down. She's healthy, Hunter, and very grainy with shades of gray."

His short laugh was sweet. "I'm sure she'll come out in living color."

"Beck?" Bruno came through the back door. "Your dog is crying and I can't—"

She turned with a nod, holding up the just-a-minute finger. "Hunter, I need to go. Someone stopped by."

Bruno stepped back inside.

"I see." He cleared his throat. "You'll tell me if you need anything?"

Hunter was a man's man, a cop's cop. It wasn't in his DNA to shirk his duty, no matter how uncomfortable. It was one of the things that had drawn her to him.

"I-if you want, I-I'll try."

"One more thing. I'm transferring. Midtown. Captain Leeds has approved the move. I'll be on days. The change will be good for my—"

Marriage? He didn't say the word, but Beck felt the guilt in his confession. She hated that she was part of their story.

"Good for you. Leeds is a great cop. You'll learn a lot from him. Good luck."

"I'm not ducking out on you."

"I know."

"Without me at the Ninth, you can come back with no awkwardness."

Why did he have to be so nice? So supportive? She'd rather there be a wall between them, an unspoken resentment driving them to opposite corners.

"See you, Ingram."

"See you, Holiday."

"Everything okay?" Bruno said, stepping back out onto the porch as she approached.

"Of course." She forced a smile and tucked her phone away. "A work issue. So, what's up with my dog?"

"He's in the pantry, hiding, growling at me and whimpering for you."

"He's got issues." The wind blew her T-shirt against her middle, and Beck tugged at the hem, pulling it away from her body.

"Don't we all?"

"So, what's up? Aren't you off chasing some future NFL superstar?"

"As a matter of fact, yes. There's a kid in Tallahassee who's this close to signing. Calvin Blue. He has some free time this afternoon. Care to drive over with me? We could take the Studebaker, blow out the carburetor."

"Why would I want to drive over to Tallahassee with you? I've got the *Gilmore Girls* waiting on the big screen."

"*Gilmore Girls*? You can watch them anytime. I'm inviting you on a road trip." He raised his hands and gyrated his hips in what might have been an attempt to dance. "Tallahassee is beautiful. And it impresses the players if I come around with a gorgeous girl."

"Ha, now you're a *lying* sports agent."

"How's that?" He jumped off the porch steps, heading for the birdbath and the hidden key. "You are, you know. Beautiful."

She tugged at her T-shirt again, he gaze following him.

"What do you say?" He worked the padlock and opened the garage door. "I'll buy dinner."

"How far away is it?"

"Three hours."

"Can Beetle Boo come?"

"We can't leave him hiding in the pantry, can we?"

"Do you think a sixty-year-old car can make the trip?"

"When I took her out the other day, she drove like a top. This old beauty will be around another sixty years."

"Bruno, did she ever have children?" Beck asked, joining him at the garage-barn opening.

"Not to my knowledge. Mom might know more." He got behind the wheel and revved the engine. "Was that your boyfriend on the phone?"

"No."

His stepped out of the car, leaving the engine to idle. "The baby's father?"

Her face burned with his direct question. "If we're going to be friends, you need to ask less questions."

"How far along are you?"

"Whatever happened to less questions?"

"If we're going to be friends, you need to trust me."

"I barely know you."

"You know me, Beck." He gaze captured hers and she felt it. She *knew* him. She just didn't remember him.

"It's complicated."

"All the more reason to have a friend on your side."

"Why do you care? Why do you want to know? I'm only here for a month. Then I'll be gone and—"

"Because you're in all my favorite childhood memories. Because you own the memory house. Because, Beck Holiday, you and I shared our very first kiss."

Her first kiss. And she couldn't remember. How should she respond? Lie. Obfuscate. Tell the truth. What would Lorelai Gilmore do? Better, what would Beck Holiday do?

"The father is my lieutenant and he's married. It was one stupid, *stupid* night, and we both regret it. He was on the phone, checking up on me."

"I see."

"You see? What, Bruno? What do you see?" She walked back into the house. "I shouldn't have told you."

"Beck, wait. I'm not judging you. Just taking it all in." He followed her inside, jumping sideways when Beetle Boo snapped at his heels. "But for the grace of God there go I. I'm no saint. I've made plenty of mistakes." When she stopped in the kitchen to pick up Beetle, he set his hand on her shoulder. "How can I help? What are you going to do?"

She peered up at him and her heart released. Everything about the past five months flowed out.

How she ignored the pregnancy until the baby made herself known. How she punched a perp and got suspended the same day she read Mr. Christian's letter about her inheritance. How she never wanted to be a mother, but lately she'd begun to change, to wonder if there was more for her. A different path even.

"Yet I bust perps for a living and I like it. I never saw myself raising a kid, much less alone. I miss my dad every day, especially because I can't remember him. I don't want a fatherless life for her."

"I hear you. My dad walked out when I was eight. He wasn't around much. Then he died when I was fifteen."

"I'm sorry. I didn't know."

"I emailed you but." He shrugged. "You never wrote back."

She gave him a wry smile. "I was a mess at fifteen."

Bruno raised his hand. "Double mess. But you know what? Miss Everleigh, this house, got me through some of the darkest days."

"Did you live here? Were any of the upstairs rooms yours?"

"I slept in the downstairs bedroom if I stayed over. But at fifteen I was old enough to be home alone." He leaned against the kitchen counter. "I came here after school for cookies and milk, maybe a sandwich. She made me do my homework before letting me go home to play video games." He nodded toward the door. "Still want to go on a road trip. I promise, no more invading questions. All fun, all the time."

"Sure, why not. Let me get Beetle's water bowl and some food. He's on a special diet, so no sneaking him people food."

Ten minutes later they were in the car ready to go, the top down, Beetle curled on the floor by Beck's feet, baring his teeth every time Bruno looked his way.

"Just don't try to pet him."

"Wouldn't dream of it." He'd just shifted into gear when he peered over at her. "I was going to marry you."

"Really?" She turned sideways in her seat, squinting at him through the sunlight, pulling her hair back into a ponytail, and the tension she'd been carrying released a bit. "Did you tell me?"

"I wanted to but chickened out. We were fourteen, and it was your last night here before going back to New York. It took every ounce of my courage just to kiss you, never mind a marriage proposal. Plus, I didn't have a job and had to finish junior high."

She laughed. "Tell me about this kiss? How was it?"

His slow grin made her heart quicken. "Awkward at first, in that junior high way where you're all lips and teeth."

Beck laughed. "Now that I'd like to remember."

"You think you'll ever get your memories back?"

"I stopped trying. Hey, thank you for telling me you wanted to marry me. It's sweet."

"Thanks for keeping me company on this road trip." He reached over and squeezed her hand. "Thanks for telling me your story. It means a lot."

"Why? Why does my story mean a lot, Bruno?"

"Because it's you. Beck Holiday."

She settled back and raised her hands into the wind. She didn't entirely understand his answer, but for now, it was enough. They'd shared something special, and maybe in time, she'd understand.

An hour later they were on I-10 West with Big Gulps and Pringles, the old AM radio tuned to an oldies station.

The cold air passing through the open top at seventy miles an hour made her shiver, but oh, it was crazy, wildly freeing. She reached down to make sure Beetle wasn't shivering. Bruno blasted the heater, and most of the air went to the floor. Yeah, the sweet dog was nice and toasty.

They talked some, mostly chitchat. It was hard to hear with the wind ripping through, breaking up their words. Then a Bon Jovi song came on, and Bruno upped the volume and drummed on the wheel.

At the chorus they leaned toward one another and belted, *"Woah, we're halfway there, woah, livin' on a prayer . . ."*

She knew it was a reflex, but when Bruno snatched her hand as they finished the chorus, electricity fired through her, and for one blissful moment, she felt one with someone beautiful and grand.

CHAPTER TWELVE

EVERLEIGH

Why hadn't she canceled? Well, it was too late now. It was almost seven and surely Don was on his way.

Since stuffing and buttoning herself into an eight-year-old evening dress twenty minutes ago, she had yet to take a long, deep breath. If she made it through the night without passing out or busting a seam, she'd claim a bona fide miracle.

She paused for one last glimpse in her dressing table mirror and tried not to groan. She wasn't twenty-two anymore, when this dress was flattering and elegant. Now her bosoms were smashed behind the tight bodice and the sleeves gripped her elbows so tight she couldn't raise her arms.

Since she didn't have time for an appointment at LuEllen's, she washed and set her hair with pin curls that night before. The style had been popular when she dated Rhett.

But when she removed the pins this morning, she looked like Shirley Temple. However, the curls eased throughout the day, and by midmorning they looped about her face with a softness. She felt quite pretty.

Then a flash shower caught her on her way home from a lunch and turned the curls into long, droopy puppy-dog ears.

"Ev?" Mama came into her room, adding her face to Everleigh's reflection in the mirror. "What are you doing? Why are you wearing that old dress? You look like a prom queen at her twentieth reunion trying to reclaim her glory days." Mama picked at the strained seams. "I might be able to let it out a little. Not much. When do you need it?"

"Tonight." She'd not mentioned the date with Don to Mama.

"Tonight? It's leftover night. I saved the potatoes and gravy for you." Mama held Everleigh by the shoulders and turned her around. "Everleigh, what are you doing?"

"Going out."

"In that? Where?"

Everleigh shifted her brassiere, hoping the movement would free her bosoms a bit, but they only looked flatter. "I'm dining at Ridgewood."

"With who?" Mama ripped a tissue from the box on the dressing table. "What's with all the makeup? Your lips look like Rudolph's nose."

"Mama, stop." Everleigh swatted at her mother's hands. "I look perfectly fine. Besides, he's on his way."

"Who?"

"Don Callahan."

"What? Last night you never said anything about dinner. Just that you ran into him at the store."

"He asked me to dinner. It's not a big deal. Steak and a baked potato." Everleigh brushed past her and down the hall. Mama's contradiction battered her already weak confidence. But it was *just* dinner.

Everleigh had repeated that phrase to herself throughout the day when she caught herself picturing Don's handsome face and jocular ease.

"You can't wear that dress. It's not decent." Mama followed right on her heel.

"It's all I have."

"Then put on a Sunday dress. If people see you in that—"

"A Sunday dress isn't dressy enough. Shoot, half of mine aren't dressy enough for church." In the living room she grabbed a beaded clutch from the coat closet and took her driver's license, a five-dollar bill, lipstick, and a handkerchief from her everyday handbag. She could feel the heat of Mama's watching. Of her silence.

"You know that's where Rhett proposed."

Everleigh rose up, the clutch dangling from her hand. "You don't say, Mama. I'd forgotten. Thank you for reminding me."

"I don't need your insubordination." She stamped her foot. "I demand more than 'It's just dinner.' How long has this been going on? Have you been corresponding with him without telling me?"

"No, Mama, for pity's sake. I told you, I ran into him at Lauderback's. He's in town for his niece's dedication. By the way, thanks for telling me Pearl has three little girls."

"I thought you knew." Mama folded her arms, pressing one hand to her cheek.

"You're the one in the bridge club with Sher."

"I don't see her all that much these days." Mama sat with a sigh, then reached for her knitting. "So you're going on a date?" Emotion weighted her voice.

"Mama." Everleigh knelt next to her, pressing her hand on Mama's. "Really, it's just dinner. I think he wants to talk about old times."

Mama's eyes glistened as she managed a wide smile. "I suppose. He did spend plenty of evenings here when you all were in school." Mama stroked Everleigh's cheek. "Seems like yesterday. And you, you've not been on a date since—"

"I know." Everleigh stood, batting away her own tears. Losing Rhett would always draw sorrow from her well. "But it's not like I'm going to marry the man. He'll be back in Dallas on Monday and it'll all be a pleasant memory."

Mama chuckled as she worked her knitting needles. "I hope if he wants to reminisce you'll play along. Even if it's a nod and a forced laugh. You're horrible at reminiscing."

"I'm getting better." Everleigh went to the kitchen for a glass of water. What if Don did want to reminisce? Or talk about Rhett and everything . . .

After the funerals—Daddy's, the Applegates', and Rhett's—Mama's way of dealing with grief was to talk about *everything*. She pulled out the old home movies, the slide projector, and for a year took stroll after stroll down memory lane.

Everleigh chose the opposite path. Silence. For almost a year she remembered nothing about Daddy, Rhett, or her life at Circle A. It was too painful to recall.

Mama said the shock knocked the memories out of her.

But on the anniversary of the tornado, the images came rushing back. And she was grateful. So much so she guarded the images, the sensations and emotions, the distant sounds of music and laughter, the timbre of a voice like treasure, speaking of them only when necessary. She hid them in her heart with all the associated affections and locked them away with the key of silence. To keep them from growing old, worn, and faded, she rarely visited.

Over the years when she remembered, quietly and to herself, she *knew* the love she had for Rhett still existed. After seven years, she still wasn't ready to let him go.

Not all the memories were treasures. Some were hard and dark, yet worth keeping.

The day her baby boy came into the world? She never worried about this one fading away. It would remain with her forever. She never discussed him with Mama, the only one in their social circle who knew.

When it was all said and done, Mama held her as they cried and said, *"It's done. Over. For the best. Let's leave it be and go on with our lives."*

"What if he knows?" Mama's voice jettisoned into Everleigh's thoughts.

"Knows what?" How could she possibly ask about *that* day when Everleigh was just thinking on it?

"You know."

Everleigh sat on the couch, her back straight to keep the seams from tearing, and spread the wide skirt over the cushions. "You and I are the only ones who know."

"People talk."

"I can't imagine who. I went to Austin for the last half of the pregnancy. I don't think Alice put in her Christmas card, 'It's been seven years since Everleigh delivered her baby.'"

"There's no need to be snide."

"There's no need to be paranoid either. It was a closed adoption. There's nothing more to say. Can we just leave it?" But they'd wondered. Only Mama and Daddy knew she was pregnant, along with Rhett and his parents.

And of course the doctor, who she'd not been back to since.

"Well, if he brings it up—"

"He won't bring it up." Everleigh glanced at the door, tense with anticipation. It was seven o'clock. The bell would ring any second.

Mama's needles clicked in rhythm to the clock. "You know Don is dating Carol Ann Dewey, Miss Texas runner-up."

The doorbell chimed, and Everleigh jumped to her feet. Mama motioned for her to sit down. "I'll get it."

Don was seeing Carol Ann Dewey? What was he doing taking her to dinner? She sucked in her gut and adjusted her biting girdle.

"Don, welcome to our humble home." Mama stepped back as he entered, rolling her eyes at Everleigh, smiling.

"Evening, Mrs. Novak." He gripped his hat between his hands. "Everleigh, you look lovely. Ready?"

"Yes, my coat is right over there. Mama, don't wait up."

Don aided her with her coat, then walked her to the car with a light touch at her elbow. His cologne reminded her of summer nights by the river.

Situated in the car, he tuned the radio to the Big Go and shifted into reverse.

"I'm looking forward to this evening," he said.

"Don't expect too much, Don. I've not danced in years."

"Then we'll stumble around together."

A Ricky Nelson song came on the radio, and Don belted out the lyrics.

"Well I've been thinking, whatcha gonna do little girl on our first date."

Everleigh pressed her fingers to her lips, hiding her smile, as Don's off-key melody filled the car.

But his unabashed joy put her at ease, and by the time he pulled up to Ridgewood, she was singing with him.

At the door, the maître d' bowed and called him Mr. Callahan, then led them to a table with a view of the water.

"You're smiling," Don said, passing her a menu.

"Am I?"

"What are you thinking?"

"It's impolite to ask a woman what she's thinking." Everleigh scanned the entrée options. She'd forgotten the women's menu came without prices.

"I thought it was impolite to ask her weight or age." Don set his menu aside and took a sip from his water goblet.

"Or if she colors her hair."

"Do I need to make a list?"

Everleigh flipped her gaze at him as his smile widened, charming her. "I would if I were you."

She decided on a petite filet and a baked potato. Not that she could eat anything in this dress. "But beware the list does change. Perhaps you should resign yourself to the fact we are the mysterious sex."

"Mysterious, charming, enchanting."

Goodness, he was flirting with her. "Frankly, I'm surprised you men put up with us."

"The gratitude is all ours." He leaned forward to squeeze her hand again. He was definitely flirting. Well, for one night she could go along with it. Pretend her gown fit. Pretend he wasn't linked to an extraordinary Dallas beauty.

He seemed delighted in her, and she rather relished the feeling and gave in to the Cary Grant romanticism created by the flickering candles.

The waiter served them a house wine with a plate of cheese, then took their order. Don ordered a rib eye with a baked potato and the house salad. Everleigh, the filet.

Then Don regaled her with tales of his day with his nieces. Everleigh talked about the twenty bouquets she'd made for Valentine's Day tomorrow. All the while, soft house music floated above, around, and through them.

"Did you come here with Rhett?" Don said without pause as he buttered a piece of bread.

Everleigh stared out the window toward the campus lights. "Yes."

"I'm sorry, I shouldn't have asked—"

"To be honest, Don, I don't talk about Rhett or the Applegates. I don't talk about Daddy either, much to Mama's dismay. I lost my memories for a while after burying the loves of my life, and when those memories returned, praise God, I locked them away for safekeeping." She sat back, adjusting her position so as not to strain against her dress. "I don't want to lose them again."

"I can't imagine what you've been through."

"Thank you, Don, but I don't want to sound defensive or high and mighty, as if Everleigh Applegate has suffered more than anyone else. I merely mean—"

"To guard your heart."

"Yes, exactly." She smiled softly. "I almost canceled on you."

"On Valentine's weekend?" He slapped his hand over his heart. "I'm so glad you didn't."

"Look at me, Don." She drew attention to her dress. "I'm

ridiculous. My hair is a mess, and my dress is out of style and entirely too tight."

His gaze roamed over her, intense and slow. Everleigh glanced away, the heat of passion rising on her skin.

"You look beautiful to me."

"You're too kind."

"I'm telling you the truth." Don sat back as the waiter set down their iced teas and salads. Then taking up his fork, he caught Everleigh's attention with a glance. "There's a woman in Dallas. My boss's daughter. Carol Ann—"

"Dewey. Runner-up to Miss Texas 1955. I watched the pageant."

"We're something of an item."

"Mama may have mentioned it." Everleigh stabbed at her salad, gritting her teeth as the tomato wedge tried to escape. "You don't owe me anything, Don. This is just dinner."

"I know, but I want to be upfront, Ev. You deserve that."

"Don, it's *just* dinner." She stabbed another fork full of lettuce and cucumber, then tugged at her sleeves, hoping for a bit more wiggle room.

"Doesn't feel like *just* dinner, though, does it?"

She froze, then slowly set down her fork. "But it is." It must be. She was in love with her husband and would always be in love with him. She wiped the edge of her lips with her napkin. "So, tell me about you and Carol Ann."

"What do you want to know? She's Dewey's daughter. We met at the dealership. Standish asked me to escort her to the governor's balls, so I did. One thing led to another." His tone dragged on as if recounting something humdrum, or unpleasant. "Everyone expects us to marry. Especially my folks."

"I'm sure your parents are very proud." Everleigh regretted all the fussing over her dress and hair when in fact tonight truly was nothing more than dinner. "You have a bright future."

"Except it's not the future I want." He sat back with a glance at the bandstand. The musicians had returned and were warming up. "I have this opportunity . . . with George Granger. In Florida. Do you know the Grangers?"

She shook her head. "I don't, no."

"George is a great guy, smart, savvy. An entrepreneur. He called me a few months ago to invite me into an insurance business with him in Florida. The Jacksonville area. He's got connections there, and the town is booming. It's a real opportunity."

Now his voice contained energy and excitement. A spark lit his blue eyes.

"How exciting." Everleigh speared another tomato. "What about the car business?"

"Yeah, that's the problem. I'd be letting Dad down if I leave Dewey. Callahan Cars is about to merge with him, and, Ev, you should hear him talk." She liked the way he used her nickname. "I'm the heir apparent and the hope of all his dreams." The color drained from his cheeks. "It's too much . . . too much."

"And they've already selected your queen?"

"Yes, yes, you get it, don't you? Feeling trapped with no way out." He slapped his napkin on the table and leaned toward her. "Tell me what to do."

"Don," she said with a swallow of tea. "I can't be responsible for your life. Besides, if I tell you what to do, wouldn't that make me just like your father and Dewey? You have to decide on your own and then talk to your father man to man. Me? No, I have enough just managing Mama. Don, I'm sure your father will understand. He'll see what I see when you talk of this endeavor. Excitement with a spark of life."

He winked at her, then grimaced. "Will you come with me when I talk to him? Ev, my entire life he's preached one message to me. That I'm his hope and future. He built the car business for me to take over. He's worked twelve hours a day for twenty years, six days a week, for *me*. His father owned a dealership and made Dad work for pennies, which he gladly did, thinking he'd inherit the business. But when Grandpa retired, he sold everything, took the money, and moved to Arizona. Dad had to start all over. So now, with me, he's built something his son can just step into. But it's not the step I want to take." He spoke like a man who'd been holding in his thoughts for a long time. "Listen to me go on about myself." He picked up his fork and inspected his salad. "What do you dream about, Everleigh Applegate?"

Dreams? She'd buried them on May 17, 1953. Even when she slept, she dreamed of nothing.

But *nothing* sounded so maudlin. "Shoes," she said. "Sensible shoes." She glanced up as the waiter refilled her tea glass.

"Sensible shoes." Don's eyes caught his laugh. "You dream big, Everleigh. Come on, you must have something you want, secretly hope for."

She tapped her fork through her salad. "I'd wish for Rhett to be alive, living in the house we designed on his parents' property. Well, our property, because he bought it. Our own piece of heaven right on Memory Lane with a pond and room for kids to run. Instead, he's buried in Oakwood Cemetery next to his parents."

Don's fork clattered against his plate as he sat back, motioning for the waiter to clear the table. "I keep stepping in it, don't I?"

"It's all right. It's just dinner." Everleigh glanced toward the dance floor. "I can't tell you what to do, Don, but don't wait for someone else to give you what you want. Chase your dream, whatever it may be, because you never know when it all might end. When an F5 tornado might take it all away."

"Come on." He slipped his hand into hers as the band eased into a slow, soft rendition of "Starlight" and walked her to the center of the floor, taking her in his arms.

She resisted at first, holding herself stiff and awkward, the dress barely giving her room to rest her hand on his shoulder.

But as the music played, Don stepped closer and closer, and Everleigh leaned against him. Funny how her cheek fit nicely against his chest.

She closed her eyes as the melody hypnotized her and as Don's heartbeat sounded in her ear.

In that moment she was not Rhett's widow, nor Mama's daughter and provider. She wasn't Mr. Reed's weekend manager nor the owner of a dozen dresses from another era that no longer fit.

In this moment, she was the Everleigh she used to be. Young and hopeful. Beautiful. Her gown fit and her hair flowed over her shoulders like Lana Turner's.

She knew true love would never come her way again, but for now, it was nice to have this one magical evening dancing and dining with a dear old friend.

CHAPTER THIRTEEN

BRUNO

Just off the shoreline, a pilothouse boat motored north with a string of red, blue, green, and white lights left over from Christmas.

Bruno stepped through the glass deck doors of his condo into the damp, salty January air that sank a wicked chill into his bones. Inside, a fire flickered in the fireplace, and his vintage hi-fi played a Glen Campbell album.

Lowering into the Adirondack chair, he loosened the cords of his work day and let his thoughts run. Straight to Beck.

After the road trip to Tally, he knew the hard glint in her eye wasn't rooted in anything real. Caution maybe, fear, but she was kind and sweet underneath. All he had to do was watch her with Beetle Boo to see her inner self.

The weird thing was how her pregnancy hit him. Like Beck, he hadn't considered parenthood. Didn't see himself in the daddy role. But over the last few days, he wondered if he'd be a good father. Bruno swigged his beer. He might like a try at fatherhood. If he found the right woman. If he fell in love.

He gazed through the open sliding glass door toward the fire. He'd much rather sit by the fire with his wife than alone. But *alone* he knew. Truth be told, it was his dearest and oldest friend.

Another swig of beer, and he pictured Beck, with her flapping ponytail, singing Bon Jovi at the top of her lungs. His laugh echoed in his chest.

Of all the people he imagined running into at Miss Everleigh's memorial, Beck Holiday wasn't even on the list.

The fact she was a cop kind of explained her demeanor that day, but hearing how she lost her dad twice—first in a burning tower, then from amnesia—gave him a deeper level of understanding.

Seeing her again also forced him to admit something about himself. He'd changed. He wasn't the ambitious, driven, hair-on-fire sports agent he used to be. He actually wanted more out of life than fame and fortune.

Granted, he wanted Sweat Equity up and running. He still aimed for success. But he didn't want to be a Watershed kind of agency but an intimate, unique boutique firm where his clients were friends and family, not just numbers on a roster.

He laughed against the quiet. "You're a dead man, Bruno."

Calvin Blue had been impressed by Beck. Especially when she told him she was an NYPD officer. He should thank her for raising his esteem in Calvin's eyes.

The music stopped and Bruno headed back inside, setting his beer in the sink. He stoked the fire, snapped off the record player, then sat on the couch with his laptop.

But instead of working, he stirred up memories of Beck. The good, sweet ones of riding their bikes to the beach, running through downtown puddles after a summer rain.

A few bad memories surfaced as well. Like the time Dad bawled him out after a junior high football game.

"If you're going to play the sport, then play. Learn the game. You're embarrassing yourself. You're a nothing otherwise. A nothing. And I don't have time for nothings."

"Knock, knock." Mom rapped on the sliding door. "Can I come in?"

Mom's timing was amazing. She rescued him from that stupid memory. He envied Beck for a moment. He'd love to have amnesia about his father. God rest his soul.

Mom entered with a grocery bag in hand and set it on the kitchen island. Then she plopped down on the sofa with a sigh. "Mrs. Acker decided we should start spring cleaning."

"It's January."

"She wants to get a jump on everyone. Like it's some sort of contest." Mom rolled her eyes and pulled a Diet Coke from her tote. "I brought you a surprise."

"What sort of surprise?"

"I found an original iPod and two dinosaur cell phones in Mrs. Acker's attic. Spring cleaning paid off for you." Mom hoisted the plastic bottle before taking a long swig.

"You're kidding." Bruno moved to the brown bag Mom set on the kitchen island.

"There's a Motorola and something that looks like an old car phone."

"Any chance it's a Dynatac 8000x? They're nearly impossible to find." Bruno set the contents on the marble and smiled. Sure enough, she'd found a Dynatac 8000x and a Motorola Microtac. "Merry Christmas to me." He held them up, dancing side to side, making his mother laugh.

"My handsome, sports agent son, the cell phone collector geek." Mom pulled a package of almonds from her bag and dumped a few in her hand. "What do you do with them besides collect dust?"

"Take them apart. Fix them up. Sell them." He returned to the couch. "I've found some interesting messages before. Job offers, breakups, proposals." He kept his collection lined up on the credenza of his downtown office. When he needed a distraction from his lack of success, he tinkered with the phones. "I've given some to charity. It's a fun hobby."

"You've seen Beck Holiday is at Miss Everleigh's?" Mom said.

"Yep."

"Have you talked to her?"

"Yes." And so his thoughts went full circle. From Beck to Dad to Mom to phones and back to Beck. "You?"

"A few times. When she's out with that cute, gimpy dog. She said she inherited the house."

"Did you know about Miss Everleigh's will?"

Mom twisted the cap back on her soda and stored the half-full bottle in her bag along with her almonds.

"She never shared details, only that she left the house to someone who really needed it. I figured it was a charity or one of the families at church, maybe one of her nieces or nephews. But they rarely came around. I never imaged it would be Beck Holiday. No one's seen hide nor hair from her in almost twenty years."

"She has amnesia, Mom. Can't remember anything related to us, the memory house, Miss Everleigh, or her dad."

"Amnesia." The low glow from the fire highlighted Mom's surprise. "You could've offered me a million dollars and I'd never have guessed amnesia."

"I know, sounds like *As Your Life Turns* or whatever soap you watch at Mrs. Acker's, but I believe her."

"We watch fixer-upper shows now. So she really doesn't remember anything?"

"She said any memory related to her dad is gone. She found out about the house right when she was suspended from her job. So she came down to check it out."

"Suspended? For what?"

"She's a cop and apparently took issue with a perp who was using the dog as a drug mule. She decked him."

Mom laughed. "Now that's the spunky Beck Holiday I remember."

"She's also pregnant." Might as well tell the whole story.

"I noticed." Mom faced Bruno, propping her arm on the back of the couch. "Is she married? In a relationship?"

"No, she hooked up with her lieutenant one drunken night. But good news . . . He's *married*."

"Lawd a mercy."

"I told her I wanted to marry her back when I was fourteen." Bruno got up to stir the fire, dropping on one more log before bed.

"Are you sure that was wise? To tell a single pregnant woman you wanted to marry her?"

"Eighteen years ago? I think she can process it okay, Mom." Bruno sat on the hearth, the heat from the flames hot on his back.

"I wonder if Miss Everleigh knew," Mom said. "About the amnesia. Or that Beck would need a connection to her past as she faced being a mother."

Bruno made a face. "You make it sound like she died on purpose so Beck could inherit the house."

"That's not what I mean, but life, *miracles*, have a way of coinciding. Beck needs a miracle. She needs her memories. Miss Everleigh's mission on earth ended the way she lived. Giving."

"Wouldn't Beck have a better chance of remembering if Miss Everleigh were alive?"

"God works in mysterious ways." Mom glanced at her watch and scooted off the couch. "I didn't realize it was this late." She kissed Bruno on the head on her way out. "I want to finish my book before going to bed."

"So God set this up? Miss Everleigh died in order to bring back Beck's past? That's a stretch even for you, Mom." He walked her to the door, arm draped around her shoulder.

"Not her past, her memories. There's a difference. No one can ever bring back the past. But you know what else is odd?" Mom patted his cheek. "You coming home when you had no intention of ever living here again."

"I can leave if you want."

"Don't be smart. I'm just saying God has a way of taking the worst situation and turning it for good." With that, she slid open the patio door and headed for her car. With a short toot of her horn, she drove off.

Back inside, Bruno faced his silent, sparsely furnished condo, the crackling fire the only sound.

Mom was right. He'd never wanted to come back to Fernandina Beach. It was a lousy spot to run a sports agency. He kept a post office box in Jacksonville for his business cards.

So what was he still doing here? Mom's leg had healed. She didn't need him to hang around. His little office on Centre Street was costing him more than he could afford.

Having a personal pilot was nice, but he didn't know how long the luxury would last. Maybe he was here because Dad and Kevin Vrable were right.

He was *nothing.*

That one word lodged in his psyche, and no matter how much he achieved, it reared up when Bruno was at his weakest.

A text ping pulled him from his mental spiral. It was from Calvin Blue. *Let this be a sign.*

Your girl was hot. Whatever you do, hang on to her.

Bruno grinned. She's not my girl. Just a friend.

Then get busy.

He returned that comment with an emoji and tossed his phone aside. It rang a second later, Beck's name on the screen.

"Hey, what's up?" Was he smiling? Yeah, he was smiling.

"I have a thought."

"Just one?"

"Ha. About your client, Calvin."

"He said you're hot, by the way."

"Whatever. Listen, maybe you already know this, but you need to play to his mom."

Bruno flashed through the meeting highlights. The other day was his first sit-down with Calvin's people. His high school coach (a guy named Max Benson), his parents, and two siblings.

"His mom? No, trust me, he was taking his cues from his coach and his dad."

"Yes, but when she spoke, his posture changed. I arrested a hard-core perp once. I mean, you name it, he'd done it. No one could ever get him to talk. But we had him for a murder he didn't commit. All he had to do was give up evidence, take a plea, and be on his way. He refused to deal. I knew his mother from the neighborhood, so I told the detective to bring her in. He broke before she even sat down."

"Calvin's not a criminal, Beck."

"But didn't you see his posture change every time she spoke? When his coach or his dad suggested something like being drafted by that team in New England—"

"The Patriots."

"And how he wanted to be like the Brady Bunch."

"Tom Brady."

"He'd be puffed up, all jock-like. Then his mother would say, 'What about his education?' and Calvin humbled up, shrank down a little, and echoed her sentiments. 'What about my degree, man?' He wants to please her. Bruno, his mama is running the show."

"You're crazy. He's prime for a major NFL contract. I appreciate your cop senses here, but his dad and coach—" He stopped, seeing the scenes from the meeting from a different angle. "I guess he did look at his mom a lot." How did he miss this? Reading people was Bruno's super power. But desperation could wreck a guy's strength. "Any advice, Officer Holiday?"

"It's Sergeant Holiday and yes. Send her the biggest bouquet of flowers you can afford and tell her you are committed to her son's education. That you'll make sure he goes to classes in the off-season. She seemed concerned about his money too. Tell her you'll help him with his finances. She kept saying how Kobe Bryant put his first paycheck in the bank."

"Beck, I owe you one."

"You owe me two. I went with you on your little drive, didn't I? And now I'm telling you who's going to influence your player the most. I thought you said you were a top agent, Endicott."

He grinned. "One round of good advice and you're talking smack? I *was* a top agent. I'll be back on top again. Calvin's my ticket."

"Just make sure you keep the main thing the main thing."

"What's the main thing?"

"If I have to tell you, you've already lost sight."

"What's your main thing, Beck Holiday?"

"Being a good cop, I guess. Being a good friend. Loving my family. Though it's not always easy with Mom. More recently, doing what's right for this baby."

"Worthy attainments. I guess mine would be to be a good son. A good agent. A friend. Try not to be a nothing."

"A nothing?"

"Yeah, a nothing." He sank down into the sofa cushion and propped his feet on the narrow coffee table. "I wanted to play football since I was ten. Wanted to be a big-time star." Talking to her on the phone made it easy to be real. "But there was a disconnect between my ambition and my ability. I learned my lesson after one particular game when I fumbled the ball for the third time and my dad chewed me out afterward. He called me a nothing."

"In front of everyone?" By her tone, she was appalled.

"Not everyone, but enough. When we got home I crawled under

my bed and cried. Know the weird thing? You called me about five minutes later. Mom answered and passed the phone to me without a word." He stopped, choked by the intimacy of retelling one of his darkest memories. "You told me how you wanted to play ice hockey but couldn't skate."

"Really? I don't remember. I do know I don't have any ankle strength. What did I say?"

"Within two minutes you had me laughing, something about doing the, what, Chinese splits, right on the ice? Twisting and sliding toward the opponents' goal with the puck under your foot."

"Maybe it's a good thing I forgot this one."

"You scored their only goal, the game's only goal. They won."

His laugh mingled with hers and released the tension of being a nothing.

"Sounds like we had fun together," she said.

"We were best friends. At least for six weeks every summer."

"Was it fun?"

"Yeah, it was." He waited, listening.

"Hey, I should go. Lorelai Gilmore just ran out on her wedding to Max."

"Poor Max."

"Poor Lorelai. And, Bruno, you're not a nothing. That's the main thing you can't forget."

After hanging up, Bruno closed the fireplace doors and reached for his laptop, feeling the good residuals of talking to Beck.

He'd just settled on the couch when his phone beckoned again. Bruno winced to see Coach Brown had texted.

Are you going to call Tyvis back?
In a few days.
Don't forget.

Come on, Coach. Be realistic. The man had to know Bruno took the meeting with Tyvis to win *Calvin's* allegiance. Signing the JUCO player was never on his agenda.

He searched the internet for a florist near Calvin's Texas home town and ordered a big bouquet for his mama. Then he texted Beck.

Order flowers. Check.

She returned with a thumbs-up.

I feel so bad for Max!
Max who?
Gilmore Girls!
Oh right. I'm sure he'll survive. It's in the script.
Haha.

He did a little bit more work, but his thoughts kept drifting to Beck. A little after eleven, with the fire dying, he shut off the lights and headed to bed.

He'd plugged in his phone to recharge when it rang, this time with an unknown number.

"Endicott," he said, slipping from his jeans and tossing them into the laundry.

The caller cleared his throat but said nothing. Voices murmured in the background along with the clink of glasses.

"Hello?" The caller didn't answer. "Can I help you?" Bruno glanced at the screen to see if the call was still alive.

"Tyvis? Is this you? Hello?"

The line died, and Bruno's attempts to call back went to a mechanized voice mail.

"The person at this number . . ."

He deleted the call and switched off the lights, then fell into bed, picturing Beck as she slid across the ice toward the goal, the hockey puck stuck under her skate.

———

DON

On the green of the Dallas country club, Don leaned on his putter, waiting for Standish Dewey to line up for his shot. The angles of the course ran parallel to a clear blue sky and the late-February temperature soared into the low sixties.

Three feet away, Carol Ann, dressed in a plaid shirt and tight sweater, chatted with a group of women playing behind them.

Standish knocked the ball with his putter and Don watched it curve toward the hole. Only Standish. His ball broke toward the cup at just the right time.

"That's par." Standish slapped him on the back. He was a Texas-size man with a Texas-size pride and Texas-size clout.

Until now Don had only worried about Dad's response to his alternate career plans. But for the first time, he considered his boss. Standish would be a force.

"Darling? Don?" Carol Ann waved her hand in front of his face. "Your shot."

Don walked toward his marker and set down his ball.

"You're distracted, my boy." Standish hovered over him, puffing on his cigar, tinting the air with tobacco.

"Thinking of work."

"Well don't. Take a load off. I own the place and I'm not thinking of work. Carol Ann, can't you get this boy to have some fun?"

"I try, Daddy, I do. But he's so serious. Ever since he came back from Waco I can't get five words out of him." Carol Ann traced her finger down Don's arm as he tested his swing. She was a charmer, well

———

trained by her Southern-belle mama, a former Miss Texas herself and Miss America runner-up.

Don gently tapped the ball, but it found a divot in the pitch and rolled left of the cup.

"Too bad, Don." Standish prattled on, giving him a wordy lesson on how to sink a putt.

"Carol Ann, let's see what you can do." Standish waved her forward, the smoke from his cigar swirling like a locomotive.

The man was always in charge. At the dealership, on the golf course, with his family. And it would be no different when Callahan Cars merged with Dewey. But Dad couldn't see it.

While she busied herself with her putt, Standish turned to him, the jovial cheer gone from his voice, his eyes glinting.

"Carol Ann said you left her alone Valentine's weekend."

"I sent flowers, took her to dinner before I went to Waco. It was my niece's christening." He resented this accounting. Resented Standish trying to command his personal life.

"Why not invite her to Waco? Our families will be bound together in more ways than one soon enough."

"She didn't want to go."

Carol Ann twirled her putter like a baton as she pranced over to the men. "I sank the putt while you two gabbed." She draped her arm over Don's shoulders.

He smiled down at her. She was picture perfect with her dark hair and green eyes, skilled and polished in social etiquette.

"What was Daddy going on about?"

"Nothing," Don said, glancing around to see Standish had moved ahead to the next hole.

"Did he bring up Valentine's Day? I told him you took me to dinner and sent a beautiful arrangement of pink alstroemeria and white daisies. Know what he said?"

"I can only imagine."

Carol Ann pretended to puff on a cigar and lowered her voice. "'What, no roses?' Don, it's okay. I-I told Daddy you were saving up for my birthday. It's only a month away, and well, *shiny* things do cost money."

There it was—the Rubicon. And Carol Ann invited him to cross it. Engagement. Marriage. The beginning of his end. The loss of his soul. To be honest, he was pretty sure Carol Ann didn't love him.

"Shiny things do cost money." He withdrew his arm from hers. "Come on, your dad is teeing off."

"When the two dealerships merge, everyone will expect a wedding."

"Then I'll give them a wedding."

At the next hole, as Carol Ann prepared to tee off, Don approached Standish. "So, this merger with Callahan. Did you and Dad agree to terms?"

"We're working it out. Carol Ann, adjust your grip."

"Standish, Dad's building Mom a big new house. I don't want him to get lost in the shuffle. Nor the Callahan employees."

"Don, what are you implying? I've known your dad for twenty-five years and he's built a great business. I intend nothing but the best for him and Callahan Cars. Plus, look, I'm angling to have his prize possession marry mine."

Carol Ann swung, sending her golf ball arching into the water.

"Ah, baby, call a mulligan. Do it again." Standish patted Don on the shoulder. "Your parents have worked hard all their lives, and I aim to give them a share of my gold. That's just how I am, Don. Plus, your dad could sell a car to an Amish man." He chewed on his stogie and leaned toward Don's ear. "It goes without saying a lot of this rides on you. You and my little princess over there. Carol Ann, tighten up your grip."

Rides on him? Precisely as he feared.

"I'm not sure Carol Ann wants to marry me, Standish."

"Posh, she's crazy about you." Standish walked over to his daughter and tried to give her a lesson, but she wasn't paying attention. Instead, she made faces behind his back, and Don laughed.

Friends. That's what they were more than lovers. And she deserved more. A man who loved her outside the pressure of a car kingdom. One who could stand up to her father.

In the six months they'd been together, neither had mentioned love. Just marriage. Carol Ann was sucked into her father's vortex, same as Don.

He felt guilty, really. What man his age wouldn't want the kingdom he was offered? But he didn't. He wanted the opportunity George Granger dangled in front of him.

And he just might want Everleigh Applegate, the girl with the sensible shoes trying to find her way back to happiness, to take the leap with him.

"Darling," Carol Ann called, "are you playing or staring?"

"Playing," he said, striding forward. "Playing."

CHAPTER FOURTEEN

BECK

She jolted awake to the sound of a motor. Stumbling from the bed over to the window, Beck shoved back the lacy curtain and gazed down to the yard.

A crew of three worked the yard. One on a riding mower, one with the buzzing weed whacker, and another with the blower.

The guy on the mower finished in, like, two seconds and parked the machine in the back of the truck before inspecting Everleigh's flower beds and the shrubbery, bending to eliminate an errant weed.

When they packed up and drove off, she sat in the rocker to study the day. She could bend and see Bruno's mother's carport beneath the tree branches. Her car was gone so she must be at work.

The women had talked again yesterday when she was out with Beetle Boo. Natalie didn't ask a lot of questions. Bruno must have filled her in on everything.

Tomorrow marked her first week in Fernandina Beach, and the mystery of Everleigh Callahan remained.

Bruno turned out to be a nice surprise. She hadn't planned on making any friends while she was here, but he made her feel . . . known. There was something comforting about being remembered. He possessed pieces of her childhood she did not.

And he'd wanted to marry her. The idea made her feel light and fuzzy.

"Come on, Beetle Boo. Let's go." Where? She didn't know except away from *that* feeling.

Cradling the dog, she walked him outside, let him do his business, the air fragrant with newly mown grass.

He'd filled out this past week and a shine had returned to his coat. His eyes no longer pleaded for someone to love him.

Funny thing about love, real love—it filled every soul with courage.

She fixed eggs and bacon for herself, then sat on the back porch steps, eating breakfast while layers of sunshine fell through the morning chill and over her bare feet. The air was crisp and promised a perfect day.

Last night Mom texted a photo of their snowy backyard.

> Flynn went out to shovel and never came back. I think a snowbank ate him.
> Ha!
> How's it going?
> Good. The house is huge. In great shape. There's money too, Mom. Still wondering why Everleigh left me this stuff.
> Just embrace it. Got to go.

Beck may have lost her memories, but Mom lost her sentimentality. She did what was required by the counselors and therapists, but she found her own unique way to deal with Dad's death and move on. She rarely strolled with Beck down memory lane.

Munching on the last piece of bacon, Beck set her plate down for Beetle Boo to wash and laid back in a patch of yellow sun.

Maybe it was the freezing-cold road trip to Tallahassee with Bruno, singing oldies at the top of their lungs, or possessing this old house all to herself, or perhaps it was merely the consequence of blue skies and sunshine, but Beck felt different. Changed from when she'd arrived.

Beetle finished his chore and leaned against her side. She stroked his ears, her eyes filling up. Two weeks ago he was a weak, abused, and starving pup, moving drugs instead of real sustenance through his bowels, his dirty, matted fur wrapped around his protruding ribs.

Today he licked plates and attempted to chase squirrels across the lawn. And she was on the edge of big changes in her life.

Beetle barked at a bird, then tumbled from the porch steps, hop-running toward a mossy tree.

The sun had moved and the shadows on the porch caused Beck to shiver. "Beetle Boo, let's go inside, see what the Gilmore girls are doing."

She'd finished season three and so far tolerated the fast-talking mother-daughter duo. Maybe she would be a Lorelai and Baby Girl a Rory. Only Beck would be the stalwart but tender cop, and Baby Girl the athletic and musically gifted genius.

After collecting the dog from where he'd collapsed by the garage-barn door, Beck headed inside.

She'd had no more flashes of memory like that day beside the Studebaker, and she was relieved.

The boards on the second-floor landing creaked under her foot-steps as she crossed to the living room.

Beyond the window, a low thunder rumbled and Beetle hid under the ottoman. Beck moved to the window. Sunlight still drenched the backyard despite the dark clouds in the distance.

She had just sat down when she heard laughter. She leaned forward, listening.

When she heard it again, she peered out the window into the front yard. Seeing no one, she walked to window seat at the end of the hall.

The sunlight dimmed as the storm moved closer with thunder and lightning.

There was no one in the backyard either. Even so, Beck listened a moment longer. She was about to return to her TV perch when she heard the laughter again, bouncing against the window. Beck dropped to the window seat and peered out to see children sitting at a table in the yard.

Despite the clouds they sat in a bowl of sunshine, and a woman in a house dress passed around Popsicle sticks. Two of them, a boy with sun-kissed brown curls and a girl with dark pigtails, clashed their sticks like swords, laughing and falling backward off the bench.

"Beck, Bruno, are you all right?" The woman helped them up. "Thick as thieves and twice as ornery. Come on now, we're going to make Fruit of the Spirit sticks. Now, grab the marker and, Beck, sweet girl, give poor Bruno a chance. Bruno, give up, she's knocked your stick to the ground twice. Now, tell me what the Fruit of the Spirit are."

"Love, joy, peace, patience, kindness, goodness, gentleness, faithfulness, self-control." Beck's breath steamed the pane, and as soon as she uttered the last words, the sun bowl vanished in the storm.

Backyard Bible School with Miss Everleigh. The clipped scene was real. She remembered. Barely. Shaking with adrenaline, Beck went to the bedroom with the pictures and studied the gilded-frame photo. The woman looked like Everleigh, but it wasn't her. Maybe the woman leaning against the Studebaker. Beck stared at the image, wished she could make it larger. This could be the woman she just saw in the house dress. But younger.

None of the other women resembled her. Beck exited the room with a whisper.

"All right, God, or whoever. Tell me, why am I here? What's going on?"

Thunder clapped, shaking the house, and sure as she stood, Beck heard a voice.

"It's what you said to your father."

The strange pronouncement electrified her. Wha—*What* she said to her father?

"I don't know what that even means."

Behind her, the wind drove the rain against the bay window and sent an eerie feather over Beck's soul.

She had to go. Get out of here. Down the stairs, she burst through the front door into the wet cold air of the veranda.

"I don't understand. None of this. It doesn't make sense!"

Then she heard her name drop from the clouds as a thick sheet of rain began to fall.

Beck!

"What?" Her reply came from the deepest, darkest part of her soul. "What do You want from me? I don't understand."

She dashed off the porch and into the winter rain. "Hello? What? First Y-You take Dad, th-then my memories, and leave Mom and me to fend for ourselves. Aren't You on the side of helping people? On the side of good? Huh?"

Water soaked her hair and her clothes, her skin. She didn't care if she trembled, if she shook with cold, if she looked a fool.

For eighteen years she'd pretended losing Dad was okay. That amnesia was okay. That she'd found a way to live with it. What good were the memories of her dead father anyway? Yet right here, right now, was all a lie.

Life, God, Everleigh, fate had landed her in a place where she had nothing to do but confront her past and contemplate her future. Despite her confusion and complete lack of understanding, it seemed the force of the unseen might be her only hope.

"You have my attention. You called me, didn't You? Beck? That was You, right? What do You want?" Another slap of thunder was followed by lightning streaks.

"God? What? I don't understand." She waited, listening, more soaked, more cold than the moment before.

It's what you said to your father.

This time the words came from inside, quiet but just as loud and more real than before. Beck dropped to her knees.

"I don't know what I said to my father."

Somewhere in the distance, a screen door slammed.

"Beck, are you all right?"

She looked up to see Natalie running across the lane with an umbrella, water from the street staining her yoga pants. "My stars, are you hurt?"

"No. I'm not hurt."

Bruno's mom hooked her arm through Beck's and urged her to stand. "You'll catch your death out here." Without asking, she led her to the little house with the big awnings. A welcoming light radiated from the windows. "These Florida storms can come out of nowhere."

Beck pulled up on the carport, shivering and numb. "I-I'll just go home. I don't want to drip on your floor."

"Don't you worry about my old floors. They've seen way worse than rainwater." She closed the umbrella and leaned it against the side of the house. "You're soaked through. Come in and I'll fix you some tea, grab you a towel. What were you doing kneeling in the rain?"

"I think the house is haunted."

"Miss Everleigh's place?" Natalie laughed. "Mercy no. I wouldn't be surprised if an angel or two hung around, but a ghost wouldn't dare."

Weary and shaken, Beck dropped her forehead to the kitchen table's veneer surface. Water dripped from the ends of her hair and pooled on her already soaked pants.

"Bruno said you have a slight case of amnesia." The kettle clattered against the burner, followed by the *tick-tick-tick* of the pilot light.

"Selective."

"Well, some memories are best forgotten. Now you hold on and I'll be right back."

Okay then. That went well. From a peaceful breakfast with sunshine to a sudden storm, disembodied laughter, an apparition, quoting a Bible verse from memory, and last but not least, thunder proclaiming it's what she said to her father.

What did she say? When? Where?

The kitchen door opened and closed. "Mom?"

Bruno. What was he doing here in the middle of a Saturday

morning? Didn't he have football players to chase? Beck almost sat up, then considered her options.

If she sat up, cold and drenched, her T-shirt clinging to her, he'd want to know what was going on, and she didn't have an answer. At least not a sane one. She'd rather not talk about the morning's events until she figured them out.

"Upstairs." His mother's call echoed deep within the house. "Can you get out mugs for some tea? Did you get wet? Do you need a towel? Did you say hi to Beck?"

"I don't need a towel. I wedged my car in next to yours. What's going on with Beck?"

"I'm not really sure but leave her alone, son. She had a rough morning. She might have seen an angel."

"You don't say?"

Head still down, Beck watched Bruno's feet go by, each step resounding in the small space. The cupboards opened. The mugs clattered against the counter. A canister lid banged.

Then he sat in the chair across from her and stretched out his legs. "Hello, Beck."

She raised her hand, waving drops.

"So, Mom," he called. "Anything else happen today?" He peered under the table, catching Beck's eye, grinning as she made a face.

"What's up?"

"Not much, you?"

"Did you see an angel?"

"Her words, not mine."

"Bruno?" Natalie called from somewhere in the house. "Have you eaten? I can make y'all something."

Bruno sat up. "Grabbed a bite in town. Stuart and I are on our way to Athens to meet with a Georgia player."

"Not in that small plane again, Bruno."

"Mom, it's a top-of-the-line Gulfstream jet. Perfectly safe."

"So you've said. But still—"

"Look at it this way, I'm here in your kitchen instead of stuck in I-75 traffic or in some crummy hotel."

"Just be careful." Her voice still reverberated from the bowels of the house. "Oh, there was one weird thing that happened this morning."

"Only one?" Bruno drummed his fingers on the table and Beck peeked at him from under her hair. The glint in his eye warmed away her chills. "I can't imagine."

"I picked up Mrs. Acker's dry cleaning on my way home last night so I decided to run it over to her this morning after the gym. As I was leaving, she tried to give me her old fur coat. Said she wanted to give me a *bonus* for stopping by on a Saturday. I was like, 'Got any cash in those pockets?' Really, what am I going to do with a fur coat? In Florida? But that thing was pure mink. Has to be worth thousands."

"You know how people feel about furs today."

"I'm one of them. Anyway, her daughters would hunt me down if they found that coat missing. But she did give me the change from the dry cleaning. Eight dollars and fifty-two cents. I was thinking of booking a trip to Hawaii."

"Want me to see if Stuart will fly you out? He needs those long hours."

"He'd have to pay *me* to fly over the Pacific. So, are you hopeful about the Georgia player?"

Beck exhaled softly, gaining peace and balance from this causal mother-and-son exchange. Her thoughts settled. Her pulse relaxed. Still, what was taking Natalie so long? She just went for a towel.

"Not really. I'm pretty sure he'll sign with Jack Bechta, but it can't hurt to build a rapport with him. If Jack doesn't work out, maybe he'll call me."

"You'll get him, son. Your experience and good character will win him over."

"Hopefully. I don't mind losing a client to Jack. Word on the street is Kevin Vrable has a new protégée and the two of them are doing everything possible to ruin my good name. Hey, remember when I told you about Calvin Blue at FSU?"

"Sure? Any news?" Her voice was muffled, as if buried in a pile of clothes.

"Someone wise told me to order flowers for his mother. Got a text today saying she was bowled over. I'm first on his list now."

Was this where Beck should lift her head for an I-told-you-so?

Beck gave him a thumbs-up as her mind's eye drifted above the kitchen, observing Bruno conversing with his mother's disembodied voice while she sat there with her head planted on the table, cold and shivering. What a sight.

From the stove, the kettle shimmied and whistled.

"That'll be the tea," Natalie called.

"I'll get it." Bruno's legs and feet disappeared. "I forgot to tell you when you came by the other night, Mom. Beck and I drove the old Studebaker to Tallahassee."

"Nice. How'd she drive?"

"Like a dream."

Well, that was the last straw. Beck sat up with a laugh, shoving her hair away from her face, hooting all the more when her gaze met the smirk in Bruno's blue eyes.

"How do you take your tea?"

Then Natalie appeared, her arms laden with clothes. "Sorry it took so long, but the towel I grabbed was ratty on the end, so I hunted down a good one. Go figure, they're all in the laundry. Then I remembered I had some clothes—"

With a cackle, Beck toppled from the chair, face to the floor, and laughed and laughed and laughed.

There was nothing normal about this weird scene, but everything about it screamed life and family.

Natalie draped a towel over her shoulders. "You think the cold got to her? Maybe the angel vision?"

"Here, hand her this. I hope you like cream and sugar, Beck."

Natalie set a steaming mug by Beck's head. "Careful now, it's hot."

She laughed, no longer caring about voices from heaven, or visions of Backyard Bible School, or the way "love, joy, peace, patience . . ." rolled off her tongue as if she'd recited it yesterday, or Natalie's delusion of an angel sighting.

She laughed until it didn't matter she still had no idea what she said to her father. Until the rain stopped and the thunder was long gone over the waters.

CHAPTER FIFTEEN

EVERLEIGH

Since Monday was her day off, Everleigh typically slept in, took a long bath, watched a soap or two, ran some errands, maybe visited a friend. She often met Myrtle for lunch.

But this particular Monday morning Everleigh woke with a mission—to address her tired-mule appearance.

After breakfast, she washed the dishes, made her bed, and dressed in her Sunday best for a trip downtown. Though her Sunday look definitely needed a refreshing too.

Mama looked up from her crossword when Everleigh came in search of her handbag. "Where are you going?"

"Seeing to some errands." There were times when she and Mama were just too close. In each other's business.

"What kind of errands? If you're going to be downtown, pick up—"

"I'm running errands for me, not you, Mama. I'll see you later."

"If you want dessert on Thursday, you best pick up some flour."

What if she didn't want dessert on Thursday? What if she wanted to lose a few pounds? It was one thing to bulge out of her dress that night at the club, but it was another to have Don's hand resting on a soft roll of back flab.

She drove down Franklin Avenue toward LuEllen's Beauty Salon. Parked and walked in with determination. She knew the hairdresser and salon owner would make a fuss over her long absence, so she braced herself.

"I saw your name on my book but refused to believe it until you darkened my door. Everleigh Applegate, where have you been?"

LuEllen wore tight capri pants and a fitted sweater. Her blonde hair was teased into a hairy mountain and her red lipstick left a stain on her coffee cup.

"Busy. Working." Everleigh hung her coat on the rack by the door. "It's good to see you."

"Darling, by the looks of it, you've needed to see me for a long, long time." She patted her chair. "Go on, take a seat. I'll get the hammer and chisel."

Everleigh winced, leaning toward the mirror. Was she *that* bad?

LuEllen set Everleigh's handbag on the shelf and wrapped her in a cape, prattling on about her son, Ryan, and his new wife.

"They are the cutest lovebirds. Now, what do you want? Cut and color? Of course. We should set up a standing appointment. Let's not have this mess again."

Everleigh slid down in the chair. Did LuEllen have to talk so loud? The two ladies under the hair dryers raised the lids to hear what was going on.

"LuEllen, I was thinking of a wash and set. Nothing drastic."

"Wash and set?" LuEllen curled her lip and pointed at the two under the dryers. "That's what I do for those old cronies."

"I heard that."

"I said it loud enough so's you could, Jean." LuEllen spun Everleigh's chair around. "You're still young, honey, and under all this brown dullness is a beautiful woman. Have you forgotten how to be *her*?"

Yes. She'd forgotten. Yes! Everleigh squeezed her eyes shut, resisting the urge to run. What was she doing here? One date with Don Callahan and she was assessing her appearance, her wardrobe, her life.

LuEllen handed her a magazine. "Look through here. See what you like?"

Everleigh fanned the pages. "I-I think just a nice wash and set." She ran her fingers through her hair. "Maybe a trim?"

"Absolutely not. I've been waiting a year to get my hands on you.

We're dolling you up but good this time." She took the magazine. "Let's see."

"Beauty is more than the latest hairstyle, LuEllen."

"You took the words out of my mouth." She gazed at Everleigh through the mirror, tapping her heart. "If you don't have it going on in here, don't matter what you got going out here." She circled her face with her hand. "You could be Lana Turner or Marilyn Monroe on the outside, but if you ain't got Jesus on the inside? Well, just leave your lipstick and mascara at home. Do you have Jesus on the inside, Everleigh?"

"Y-yes." Since Mrs. Soja stuck a flannel Jesus, complete with red felt stripes on his back, up on the board during Vacation Bible School, Everleigh believed.

But in truth, she could do better. Live with a greater faith.

"Well then, that's eighty percent of the battle. The rest is getting this mess into shape." LuEllen ran her fingers through Everleigh's hair. "How about a lovely auburn? Or blonde?" She snapped the pages of the magazine, then showed it to Everleigh. "Kim Novak. This is a perfect look for you. You share a name and the same shape eyes. What do you say? Holly, get Ev a Dr Pepper, will you?"

"It's rather drastic, don't you think?" Everleigh stared at the blonde, green-eyed bombshell. She looked *nothing* like her. "Tell you what, LuEllen, you decide. I put myself into your hands." Everleigh handed back the magazine.

"Second wisest thing you've done today. Now, let me mix up some color and eradicate that church mouse from your hair."

Being a church mouse was easy. Simple. Cheap. Was she really going to keep up with beauty appointments? Spend precious dollars to look good for who, the customers at Reed's? They didn't seem to mind her dull appearance.

Was it for Don Callahan? Hardly. When would she ever see him again? Besides, he was spoken for by a true beauty.

Everleigh stared at her reflection, LuEllen's voice resounding from the back room, and battled the familiar sensations of guilt and condemnation.

She didn't deserve a makeover or any kind of second chance. Being a blonde or brunette wouldn't bring back Rhett or change what she'd done with his son. She was now, and always would be, a mousy brown childless widow.

———

DON

The first week in March, Standish sent Don to Waco with legal papers for Dad to sign. Since Valentine's Day, the merging of the two dealerships hit the fast track.

Don rehearsed his speech to Dad on the way down.

"Are you sure you want to merge with Standish? Look, I was only supposed to work for him a few years, then come back here, take over Callahan Cars. I could come now. But to be honest, Dad, there's this business venture in Florida with George Granger—"

But when he faced Dad at the Callahan offices, he said nothing. Not one blame word. He just watched him sign. Posed with him when he called Judith to bring her camera.

One word of dissent and he could see Dad's face. Hear his argument.

"My dad left me with nothing, son. This merger gives you a dealership twice as big as Callahan Cars. Don't look a gift horse in the mouth."

Don set his briefcase beside his boyhood bed and slipped off his tie. If all Dad wanted was a path to retirement, then maybe it didn't matter if Don went his own way.

He fell back on his pillow and stretched out. Five thirty. *Wonder what Everleigh is doing?*

———

He'd not called her since their Valentine's dinner. He wanted to, but every time he picked up the phone he set it back down.

What could he offer her? His life was in motion, planned out, and moving fast. The Carol Ann engagement hints intensified, and he needed to settle things with her before pursing another woman.

She said something the other night that made him wonder if she'd also like the relationship to end. His heart skipped with hope.

He'd just dozed off when voices echoed down the hall. Plates rattled against the kitchen table.

"Don? Dinner," Mom called, rapping on his door.

He sat up, shoving the sleep from his eyes. "Be right there."

He followed the delicious aroma to the table.

She patted his shoulder. "I'm not used to seeing you twice in a month. This is a treat."

Don raised the lid of the Pyrex dish, releasing a beef-and-pasta-scented aroma.

"Harold? Put the paper down. Dinner's on the table." Mom handed Don the bread basket. "How's Carol Ann? You know, we still need to meet her. Well, meet her *again*. She was a girl when I last saw her."

"Who was a girl?" Dad came in smiling, folding the newspaper, his reading glasses riding low on his nose.

"Carol Ann. I was telling Don we need to meet her again."

"You'll see her at Dewey when we celebrate the merger, Sher." Dad scooped the casserole onto his plate. "I signed the papers today."

"How exciting. When do we start building in Castle Heights?"

Dad chuckled. "Let the ink dry a little, but we can start talking to the architect."

"He tried to keep it a secret." Mom beamed, and Don hoped her expression was worth the price he feared Dad was paying.

She had worked in a factory when he was young, helping support the family while Dad built up Callahan Cars. Took care of the house, all the washing and shopping, cleaning and cooking. Helped Don and Pearl with their homework. Meanwhile, Dad worked from seven to seven, six days a week.

Build her a castle, Dad. She deserves it.

"Which one of you is going to say grace?"

Dad volunteered, uttering his standard prayer, then dove into his dinner, reaching for a hot roll.

"When do you head back, Don?" he said.

Don swallowed his first bite. The taste, the warmth, the aroma made him a little homesick for the days of his youth, before the army, college, and a career in Dallas. When disappointing Dad was never an option. When he was an energetic, good kid who came home every day to loving parents and a halfway decent sister.

"Thought I'd stay for the weekend. Baylor has a basketball game tomorrow night." He reached for the iced tea pitcher and filled everyone's glass. "Maybe see the nieces."

"Standish doesn't mind you taking off a few days?"

"I've got time coming to me."

"And you want to spend it here?" Mom hopped up for the salt. "I'd think you'd want to spend more time with Carol Ann. Listen, when you propose, give me time to get into LuEllen's. I'll need a makeover for the society page pictures."

Don turned her words over in his head. At least he could be honest about Carol Ann.

"Mom, there aren't going to be any society page photos. At least not with me and Carol Ann."

"Sure there will be. WACO BOY DOES WELL, SET TO MARRY DALLAS SOCIALITE AND BEAUTY QUEEN. You better believe the photographers will come out."

"Well, focus on Dad's big news. Callahan Cars merging with Dewey Motors. Get gussied up for that story. You've called Bill Davis over at the *Tribune,* haven't you, Dad?"

"Talked to him this afternoon." Dad buttered his roll. "Son, your mama's right. Get moving with Carol Ann. You'll need her by your side as you step into more and more of the business. What's Standish going to have you doing?"

"He's not said."

Dad frowned. "You don't say. He told me he was making you senior sales manager. Maybe I'm spoiling the surprise."

Senior sales manager? "I don't know, Dad. Mo Bryant is doing a great job, and he has twenty-five years' experience. Not to mention a wife and kids in college."

"You're family now, Don. We need you in a key position." Dad swigged his tea. "Sher, you're married to a genius. I've set our son up for a prosperous future."

"I never doubted you." Mom went on to talk about the Waco library charity dilemma. What event to have as a fund-raiser. "The committee wanted to bring in Elvis again, but he's too big for us now."

Then they talked about the unusual weather and an update on the grandbabies.

Don helped Mom clear the dishes until she shooed him out of the kitchen. "Keep your father company."

He folded the dish towel and set it on the counter. "Mom, don't be disappointed if things don't work out with Carol Ann and me."

She regarded him with a stern expression. "What are you saying?"

"I'm just not sure she's the one."

"The one? Of course she's the one." Mom fussed, plugging the sink for soapy water. "I hope this doesn't have anything to do with Everleigh Applegate."

"What if it does? And how do you know Carol Ann's the one?"

"Because I know her family, know she comes from good stock."

From the living room Dad blared the TV. Douglas Edwards from CBS announced things were going well with talks between South Vietnam and the Vietcong.

"Don, son, she's not for you. There are better, more upstanding girls."

"Upstanding? I can't think of anyone more upstanding than Everleigh Applegate. Look at what she's been through. I tell you, I couldn't lose one of you, plus my wife and in-laws, and go on living."

"If you had to face it you would. You're a Callahan. Don, listen to me, I *know* things, things I cannot share. I don't wish ill on Everleigh, not at all. But let another man take her on. Frankly, I think she likes being an old widow with her mother, arranging flowers at Reed's. Probably will be there her whole life."

"I don't think any woman wants to be an old widow, Mom. Maybe she's the way she is because no man's tried to court her." He half believed her austere hairdo and sensible shoes were more of a reflection on his gender than on Everleigh.

"Now you listen to me, Donald Callahan." Mom shut off the water but left her hands in the white suds as she faced him. "Your father has worked his whole life to leave you with a legacy his father never left him. He's worked hard for this merger. He wants you, me, all of us, to be set for life. Don't you dare jeopardize it." Her glistening eyes pleaded with him.

"I hope my wife loves me as much as you love Dad." He kissed her forehead. "Make Dad take you to dinner once a week. He won't be working as much with this merger in place, and you deserve a night out."

Mom scoffed and waved him off with a splatter of suds. "Well now, there's no reason to go all crazy."

Don walked out back and leaned against the porch post, jiggling the keys in his pocket.

He glanced through the kitchen window. Dad was at the sink making Mom laugh. She dried her hands and removed the cover on the cake plate.

Don sighed and knew he'd do what they wanted. He couldn't let them down.

The edge of the moonlight caught his eye, and he hankered for a drive around town. And perhaps stop by his old friend's, Everleigh Applegate's?

He made tracks for his car before Mom called him in for cake, before she started up about Carol Ann again.

Perhaps he could sacrifice for his career, but not his heart. He'd end things with Carol Ann, and it sure would be nice to know if the twisting in his heart for Everleigh was anything close to real.

CHAPTER SIXTEEN

BRUNO

When the rain let up, he walked Beck home, carrying her wet clothes. She was dressed head to toe in one of Mom's rhinestone-encrusted sweat suits from the eighties.

"Stop laughing! That's what we wore back then."

"What were you doing in the rain, Beck?" He leaned against the open door, handing in her damp clothes as her little dog yipped from the top of the stairs.

"Come in. I'll change so you can take back your mom's stuff." At the top of the stairs, she scooped up the little dog and held him close, crooned something to him Bruno couldn't hear.

"That's not an answer," he called after her.

She peered over the railing. "It's an answer. Just not the one you wanted." She disappeared with Beetle growling a warning.

Bruno picked a spot on the couch and spotted the remote. He turned on the TV and spent a few minutes watching ESPN before switching over to the Big Ten Network.

So-called experts were surmising about the top draft picks. An image of Todd Gamble, Bruno's Ohio State prospect, popped on the screen.

"His stock is really high. He's going in the first round."

"Word is he just signed with AJ & Co., a top sports agency—"

"What?" Bruno reached for his phone. *Seriously.* After connecting the guy with Sabrina Fox, he didn't even have the courtesy to let him know he signed with an agent? Bruno fired off a text.

Hey, just heard you signed with AJ & Co. Congrats, man.

Yeah, thanks. I was going to text you.

How's it going with Sabrina?

Good. Thanks for the intro man.

Invite me to the wedding.

Ha!

So he was back to one major candidate. Calvin Blue. If he could just get him to sign . . .

Agitated, he changed the channel, landing on a nineties sitcom rerun, and tried to focus, but his gut burned.

Was Vrable right? That he was a *nothing* who owed all his success to Watershed?

He glanced up when Beck came back down with her hair turbaned in a green towel and a growling Beetle tucked under her arm.

She wore gray sweats and a white T-shirt, not bothering to hide her baby belly. Bruno resisted the urge to touch her. What did it feel like to carry a growing baby? Women were amazing.

Beck sat next to him, passing over his mom's folded burgundy sequined sweats.

"Doesn't your mom ever get rid of her old clothes?"

"She's sentimental. She probably wore this on a date with my dad or something. Even though I can't imagine why she'd want to remember him." He set the outfit on the coffee table.

"That bad?"

"He walked out on her. Then had the nerve to die." He peered at Beck. "What were you doing in the rain?"

She tightened her jaw. "I'm not sure I want to talk about it."

"Was it an angel?"

She laughed softly. "No. But I did see something, Then I heard something."

"I'm going to need more details."

She regarded him for a long, intense second. "I saw a backyard Bible school with Everleigh. Or someone I think was Everleigh. You and I were sword fighting with our sticks."

"You saw it? Where?" He glanced around at the pictures on the walls. Mr. Don was a photography buff, had cool camera equipment he'd allow Bruno to see but not touch.

"Not on the walls. With my eyes. Or in my mind's eye. I don't know, it's hard to describe."

"What'd you see?"

"It was cloudy, but all of a sudden there was a picnic table with about eight or so kids. Two of them, me and you, were sword fighting with Popsicles sticks. And I knocked you—"

"—off the picnic bench." Bruno muted the television. "You saw that?"

"Maybe." She cradled a throw pillow in her lap.

"That's why you were in the rain?" Concern marked his tone.

"Wouldn't it drive you out of the house?"

"Yeah, maybe."

"Then I heard something."

"What did you hear?"

She started to speak, then closed her mouth. "No, you'll think I'm crazy."

"I hate to tell you but—"

"You already think I'm crazy?" She smacked his arm. "Only because you're well down that road yourself."

"No doubt. What'd you hear?"

"I heard, 'It's what you said to your father.' I have no idea what that means. It freaked me out, so I ran downstairs and onto the veranda, kinda yelling at God, then I heard my name. Loud, Bruno, like thunder."

"But it wasn't thunder."

She shook her head, her greenish eyes searching his. "It was *like* thunder. Booming. Thick. 'Beck!' Then I heard the father comment again, but gentle, like a feather."

"What did you say to your father, Beck?"

"I have no idea. Thus my adventure in the rain."

Her towel turban slipped from her hair, and the longer Bruno regarded her, the louder his desire hammered in his ears. Her round, girlish features had matured, and the painting of freckles on her cheeks had faded. And she still mesmerized him.

"I think you do."

Her expression hardened. "No, I don't. Don't tell me what I do or do not remember, Bruno."

"You've buried it."

"I've forgotten it."

"Then try to remember."

She fired from the sofa. "What do you think I've been doing for the past eighteen years? You think it's easy to live with gaping holes in your mind? I can't just remember because I want to, Bruno. Haven't you been listening to me?"

"Then why the voice? Why those words? This vision? They must have come to you from somewhere."

"It's this house. It's haunted."

Bruno laughed. "Come on, Beck, you know the house isn't haunted."

She pursed her lips. "Then why doesn't He tell me if He knows?"

"He?"

"God. That's who I was talking to when I heard the words."

"I don't know, but as my mother loves to say, 'God works in mysterious ways.' Keep talking to Him."

Beck returned to the sofa, reaching down to pet Beetle. "So Calvin's mom liked the flowers?"

He sat back, stretching his legs to the coffee table. "Loved them."

———

"I told you."

"What are you doing tomorrow?"

"*Gilmore Girls*. Rory has met this hottie named Jess and—"

"I'm driving down to Gainesville. Let's take the Studebaker. I'll pick you up at nine. No, make it eight. Central Florida is beautiful."

"What's in Gainesville?"

"University of Florida. The pro liaison called me yesterday, saying a player actually *asked* to meet with me." Making eye contact with Beetle, Bruno slowly reached to pet him, but the dog snarled and snapped. "The last road trip was a success so I thought you'd like to come along." Besides, he loved her company. Almost craved it.

"As your good luck charm?"

"Yes. You *and* Beetle, of course."

"Of course." He stood, collecting his mom's clothes. "I'll see you in the morning, Beck, and your little dog too."

"Can't wait."

He paused, gazing down at her. He could kiss her if he had the courage. But he used all he had to keep his head above sports agenting waters.

———

BECK

She walked with Bruno toward the University of Florida's field house, his long stride anxious.

"Come on, we're a little late." Frustrated Bruno was an anxious Bruno.

Beck didn't blame him, though. He was kind toward Beetle Boo who caused their tardiness. The little guy got sick on the drive down. They spent a half hour at a BP station cleaning out Everleigh's car.

Next road trip she felt sure he'd go alone. Because Beck didn't travel without her Beetle Boo.

———

Inside the field house, Bruno caught up with the pro liaison, who led them to a meeting room at the end of a long echoy hall.

Beck stepped back when Eugene Rotherham V rose from his seat to greet Bruno. Wow. He was a brute of a man—six six, three hundred pounds—and nothing at all like his aristocratic-sounding name.

She expected him to wear a sweater knotted at his neck and boat shoes without socks while ordering around His Man Friday. But G-Ro, as he was called, was regal and intense, aloof with the air of an elite athlete.

"G-Ro, man, thanks for meeting with me."

"Calvin Blue recommended you."

"I'll have to tell him thanks." Bruno sat across from G-Ro with a backward glance at Beck. See what one big bouquet of flowers will get you? "This is my good friend Beck and her dog, Beetle. He's had a rough year, so she can't leave him alone yet."

"Nice to meet you." Beck offered her hand.

"You too." G-Ro was polished and smooth, his easy grip like steel.

"Well, I'll let you two talk. Beetle and I will scout out the place."

One of the men at the table wearing a Gator shirt hopped up. "I can show you the snack and soda machines in the cafeteria."

Beck selected a bag of chips and a bottle of water, then walked Beetle outside, setting him down on the grass. She twisted the cap off the bottle and took a long swig, then tore open the chip bag.

In the last week her appetite had doubled. She'd eat all day if she gave in to every craving and pang. This morning she braved the old scales she found in Everleigh's bathroom closet. She'd gained five pounds.

"Come on, Beetle," she said. "Let's see the field."

She'd just taken another bite of chips when Bruno came flying past her, grabbing her arm and yanking her around toward the parking lot.

"Hey, what's wrong? Bruno, you're making me spill my drink."

He spun around, snatched her chips and water. "Pick up the dog. Let's go." Fire blazed in his eyes.

Without a word she scooped up Beetle and followed, walking behind at a safe distance. She had a partner once who blazed with fire when he was mad. Beck learned quick to let him cool off before asking questions.

She'd give Bruno the space he needed. But when they got to the car, he was on his phone.

"—nice blindside, Sam. Thanks for wasting my time." He ended the call and climbed behind the wheel, slamming the door. "To think I did him a ton of favors when I worked at Watershed." He gunned the gas, revving the engine to match his mood.

Beck eased into the passenger's seat, gently settling Beetle on the floor. "Who's Sam?"

"The pro liaison."

"What happened?"

"G-Ro already signed with an agent."

"What? Then why did he ask to see you?"

"Curious. Keep his options open. Maybe his new agent spooked him in some way. Or he thought he'd get something from me he couldn't get from him." Bruno barreled out of the parking lot, taking the exit heading for US 301.

Beck reached for the radio, but Bruno stopped her. "Please. Silence." He peered at her with a visual apology. "Just for a while."

About an hour in, he turned on the radio and seemed to let go of his tension. His shoulders relaxed, and he no longer gripped the wheel as if for dear life.

When they arrived home, Bruno parked in the garage-barn, then padlocked it closed.

Beck gathered Beetle's things and started for the house, then paused, turning back to Bruno, who stood by the garage, arms akimbo.

"I know it's part of the job, but this one . . ." He shook his head, finally, slowly smiling. "Maybe my dad was right. I'm nothing."

"Is that what you truly believe?"

"No, I don't know. I knew starting out on my own would be difficult, but I wasn't prepared for zero clients in almost two years." The soft Florida breeze tugged at the hem of his pullover. "Remember that kid's story where he thinks he's brave and ferocious, and when he faces his bullies, they go running? But it's really because his dad is standing behind him?"

"Yeah, I think it's about a lion or something. Was it the *Lion King*?"

"I can't remember, but maybe I'm that kid. I thought I was the one drawing in all the clients, but really it was Kevin and the might of Watershed."

"I wish I could contradict you with some lofty you-can-do-it plat-itude, but I can tell you if you don't believe in yourself, no one will believe in you."

"Mom used to tell me, 'If you go around saying you can't, don't be surprised when you fail.'"

"Bruno." Beck closed the distance between them, standing close enough to smell the clean scent of his shirt. "For what it's worth, you don't want a guy like him."

"You mean a guy whose potential worth will be in the, oh, twenty-five million range?" He swung around, arms wide. "Forget the money, he'll be a legend, a player younger guys want to emulate. He's a poster boy for any agent. Why wouldn't I want a guy like him?"

"He's a player."

"No kidding. One of the best in the country."

"No, a player-player. He may have a fancy name and lots of amaz-ing stats, but he's trouble. I've seen it with the rich ones, the talented ones, the guys who have it all."

"Where? On the streets of New York? You chase the rich guys down dark alleys, Beck? Are they your main offenders?"

"As a matter of fact—Ah, forget it." She turned for the house.

"Wait, Beck." His touched her with a gentle hand. "I shouldn't have let this get to me."

"Tell you what . . . Ten bucks he fails his first drug test."

Bruno smiled, shaking his head. "He's already passed his drug tests. And if he's using, he knows how to clean out his system."

"Sure, but once he starts having some success—"

"He is successful."

"In the NFL. Trust me, he won't last."

"Are you that good?"

"Ten bucks." She set Beetle on the ground and stuck out her hand. "He'll be in trouble his first year."

"Deal. And since he's not my client, I won't mind if I lose. But I won't." He winked at her as he clapped his hand into hers.

She wouldn't mind losing either. Not to him. Why didn't she remember *him*?

"Sorry for my attitude on the way home. It just gets me every time I lose—"

"You're somebody, Bruno. To your mom, to your friends, to Calvin. To me."

"To you?" He stirred the air with his intimate tone.

"Y-yes." Beck stepped back. "I know what a nothing looks like, and you're far from it." His nearness made her yearn. "When I found Beetle he was in the care of a Park Avenue junkie whose parents are as rich as the dickens. He could've done anything he wanted, gone anywhere. But he chose to waste his life running drugs for a lowlife dealer in Alphabet City. That's how I know about rich guys, about the G-Ros of the world. They're the nothings, Bruno. Not men like you who give up your career for integrity. Or to take care of their mothers."

"Beck—" In one motion, his arm was about her waist and he pulled her to him.

"Bruno, wait." She flattened her palm against his chest.

He pressed his forehead to hers. "I've been waiting. For eighteen years."

His confession made her laugh. "Please don't tell me you've been pining for me since a teen kiss at a music festival."

"I didn't know until now." He ran his hand down her arm and intertwined their fingers. She gasped when he kissed her forehead.

"Bruno." She set Beetle on the ground and averted her gaze. "I'm pregnant with another man's baby, a situation that is sticky and complicated, with decisions looming. Besides all that, I'm leaving in three weeks, going back to my life and job in New York."

"Today is just filled with bad news for old Bruno." He touched her chin, gently drawing her attention. "I don't care. I'll take what I can get in the next three weeks. You're the best thing that's come into my life in a long time."

"Bruno, please." She lowered his hand. "Stop, take a breath. Think about what you're saying." If he realized the impracticality of his implications, then she wouldn't have to tell him. She couldn't be another disappointment in a long line. "We're not kids making innocent summer memories."

"No, I guess we're not." He released her and stepped away. "What was I thinking? It's January."

"Exactly." There, let him down gently.

He faced the house. "We made a lot of memories at the memory house. Remember?" He glanced over at her. "No, I guess you don't. But memories or not, it's true, you can't go back again."

"Say, I have a friend at home who does metal work. I can get him to make me a plaque for the front. The Memory House. Who started the nickname? Me or you?"

"Miss Everleigh. She called it her memory house. It fits, doesn't it? The memory house on Memory Lane. The place where we had some darn good times."

"I want this baby to have those kind of moments in her life. Running around outside, chasing her cousins, chasing fireflies and the ice-cream truck. Going to ballgames and family picnics."

"You're just not sure you're the one to give them to her?"

Beck shook her head. "No, I'm not, and part of it breaks my heart. But I've always been honest with myself."

"Except for what you said to your father."

"I don't know what I said to him, so no, I guess not."

"It'll come to you," Bruno said. "Beck, do you ever wonder why you forgot?"

"What do you mean?" At the base of the oak by the back porch, Beetle barked at a squirrel.

"I don't know, but not remembering is a whole lot different than forgetting. Did you forget, or do you just not remember?"

"You're raising more questions than I have answers."

His hands slipped into hers. If she exhaled, she could tip sideways and rest her head against his chest. Wouldn't that feel good? To drop her burdens someplace strong and steady. On someone with a tender heart. Just for now. Tomorrow, next week, in three weeks she'd have to walk her journey alone, but for now—

"Beck?" Their eyes met when she looked up, and there was no resisting. He'd kissed her with his heart long before his velvet lips covered hers.

His arm encircled her as he bent toward her. He kissed her without hesitation, taking her with a husky passion.

She surrendered to the moment, resting in his embrace, locked in the sensation of being known and wanted.

Then at her feet, Beetle barked and snarled.

Bruno broke away with a laugh. "I think he's jealous."

"He knows he's my number one." She stooped to pick him up but kept her right hand on Bruno's waist. She wasn't quite ready to let go.

"The second was better than the first."

"The second?"

"Kiss. Way better than the awkward first," he said. "And just as memorable."

"Bruno, should we start something we can't finish?"

"Who says we can't finish?"

"Me. You. Us. This whole crazy situation."

"You're right. Let's just slow down and see where things go."

"O-kay." She swirled with a blip of disappointment despite his perfect answer. Of course they had to go slow. See where things headed. But oh, what if he'd refused? What if he fought for her? "I'd better go." Beck motioned to the house. "I need to eat and take a nap."

"I'll call you later. Maybe we can have dinner."

"Yeah, maybe." She turned to go, but a strong hand came around her waist and turned her around.

Bruno kissed her again and again, his physical affection fighting for her in a way words could not.

"Beck, I think I—"

"Bruno." She kissed him, drinking in the word she'd never let him say aloud. Love. It was too soon, too impossible.

In mid-embrace, as their affection tumbled to greater depths, Beetle Boo had enough. With a guttural growl, he lunged at Bruno, snapping at his shirt pocket, and with a quick shake of his head, ripped it clean away. The dark-red square dangled from his teeth.

"Beetle!" Beck covered her laugh. "B-bad dog." But she didn't mean a word of it. "Bruno, I'm so sorry. I'll buy you a new shirt."

"I'll take that," Bruno said, yanking the square from the dog's grip. "This was my only Sports Equity shirt."

"Please, let me buy you a new one. Two new ones."

He sighed and smoothed his fingers over the logo. "Don't worry about it. Maybe Beetle's right. I have no business starting my own agency." He peered at Beck. "Or kissing you. I can't support myself, let alone a wife and kid." He scanned the blue afternoon sky. "You think God sees me? That He'll call my name from the clouds?"

Beck grabbed him by the collar. "You listen to me, you're going to have a great sports agency, and when you do, you're going to go on national television and tell everyone I told you so."

He cut her off with another kiss. Slowly Beetle slipped from her grasp as she raised her arms around Bruno, the sensation of the moment more than the best wine.

"Can I tell you I'm falling in—"

"Good night, Bruno." Beck brushed her hand over his chest, patting where the pocket had been.

He ran his hand over hers. "Night, Beck."

Inside, she set Beetle down and stared out the kitchen window as Bruno got into his car and drove away.

When she'd devoured a quick snack and climbed the stairs for a nap, she saw his face and marveled how his kiss felt like her very first time.

CHAPTER SEVENTEEN

EVERLEIGH

She parked Dad's old DeSoto under a string of bare white bulbs on the Callahan Car lot and stepped out, straightening her new skirt and fluffing her hair.

Everleigh had no plans to trade Daddy's reliable DeSoto until she walked out of LuEllen's weeks ago as a bobbed platinum blonde with red lips and tweezed eyebrows.

She felt like a new woman until she climbed into the old DeSoto— God bless its Firedome, hemi, eight-cylinder engine. It was a tome to her widowhood as well as Mama's, and perhaps now was the season for change.

She broke down when LuEllen turned her to see herself in the mirror.

"There you are, Everleigh Louise Novak Applegate. Your youth has not expired."

And she suddenly craved . . . life.

She started slow. First with updating her wardrobe and beauty products. After the dresses and shoes, slacks and blouses were hung in her closet, the products organized in the bathroom, Everleigh took a good look at the old car.

But letting go was harder than she imagined. So tonight when she left Reed's, she gave herself permission to just look. If she found something she liked for the right price, she'd try to make a deal.

Confession? She was a bit nervous. She'd never negotiated for a car before. Daddy had always bought the family cars from Harold Callahan, so of course that was her first stop.

"Harold will give you a good deal," he always said.

Walking across the lot, Everleigh was immediately drawn to the shiny line of Studebakers, especially the red one with a white convertible top. Goodness if she didn't fall a little bit in love.

Moving for a closer inspection, she ran her gloved hand over the butter-soft white leather seats. Wouldn't she feel rich in this machine, in this symbol of change?

Then she braved a look at the price tag and gasped. She patted the gleaming red door.

"It was nice knowing you."

"Can I help you, ma'am?" A salesman hurried toward her, swinging on his jacket, buttoning the top button of his white shirt.

"Can you loan me $2,600?"

His grin lit his pale-blue eyes. "That can be arranged. Is your husband with you? I'd be more than happy to talk details with him."

Everleigh leveled her gaze at him. "You'll be dealing with me."

"I see." The man offered his hand with a slight bow. "Glenn Harmon, at your service."

"Everleigh Applegate." She couldn't say for sure, but it seemed blondes did have more fun. No man had bowed toward her when she was a dull-headed brunette.

"So you like the new Lark?" He walked around the car. "She's a beaut. Drives like silk. Can you handle a manual shift?"

"See that DeSoto over there? I drive it every day. Three on the tree. I have truckers' arms."

Beyond the dealership's main showroom, a row of salesmen gathered, watching with pie-eating grins and their arms folded.

Ignore them. If they thought a woman didn't know how to negotiate a car deal, they had another thing coming. Yes, she was new to the game, but she'd done her research, talked to Mr. Murdoch next door as well as her banker, who kindly gave her a letter of credit.

She'd resisted the urge to call Don. But she'd not heard from him since Valentine's Day, and calling him seemed like a ruse to get his attention.

Never mind the fact that a woman in 1960 should be able to negotiate her own car deal. And if Don wanted to communicate with her, he knew where she lived.

"I take it you want to trade in the DeSoto." Glenn walked toward the steady old machine sitting under the lot lights, looking like a relic from another time.

In fact, Daddy used to say, *"Wrap a scarf around the hood ornament and stick a pipe in the grill, and Grandpa Novak would be back from the grave."*

"If the trade is fair, yes." She followed Glenn, holding her cards close.

When she arrived, she'd been more than willing to walk away from a deal. But with each passing heartbeat, she wanted the Lark more and more.

She'd drain the savings account if need be. Never mind Mama had announced at dinner that Dutch Borland inspected the leak in the roof and said the whole thing needed to be replaced.

Bless it all, ever since the night out with Don, she'd changed. She was tired of being practical. Tired of hiding. Even from herself.

You see me, Rhett? I'm making a move.

He never would have wanted Everleigh to hole up and quit living. He'd tell her to get out there, make the most of things.

Glenn opened and closed the DeSoto's doors. Inspected the interior. Kicked the tires.

"What does that do?" she said, chasing him around the vehicle, her new red pumps clacking against the concrete.

"Tests the quality."

"They are top of the line, I assure you. Who drives around on cheap tires?"

"You could've swapped them before bringing the car in."

"Why would I spend money on tires just to trade it in?" Everleigh retrieved the DeSoto's documents from the glove box, as well as the banker's credit letter. "You'll see the purchase date and price, the mileage, the maintenance. I took the car to Wayne's Classic Auto for regular oil changes and tune-ups. The belts and plugs aren't a year old." Glenn reviewed the papers with hmms and uh-huhs. "The carburetor is only two years old. The seats are clean, with no tears or scuffs. Of course, there's the regular wear and tear, but she's in pristine condition, I assure you."

Listing the old car's qualities stirred a bit of sentiment. The sweet old thing deserved her loyalty. It started every morning, rain or shine, hot or cold. The old girl hauled Mama and Everleigh all over Waco and to Austin twice a year.

"Mrs. Applegate," Glenn said, making notes on the DeSoto's documentation. "Let me see what I can do." He winked at her. "You'll look mighty fine wrapped up in that Studebaker."

She caught her smile. *Steady now.* "We'll see. Depends on the deal you offer. I suppose you're looking to make a sale this week too."

"Every day." Glenn walked off and huddled with the men under the lights, showing them the papers, pointing at Everleigh, then toward the Studebaker.

The tall man in the middle scanned the DeSoto's documents while another went inside and came out with a book, flipping pages. After an eternity, Glenn returned.

"I can give you a trade-in of fifty dollars."

"Fifty dollars? For an entire, well-maintained DeSoto?"

"She *is* ten years old, Mrs. Applegate. We'll have to put some work into it. Resale markup isn't that much."

"I saw an ad in the paper for one older than mine going for one twenty-five."

"You're welcome to sell it on your own."

"Then I won't have a trade-in deal." Why did she get her hopes up? She had no idea what she was doing.

"The good news is we can give you a bit of a discount on the Studebaker." Glenn started for the convertible.

"How much?" Everleigh walked beside him, desperately rejecting any and all excitement.

He took the sign from the window—$2650—and wrote over it with a big black marker, turning the six into a five. "Twenty-five fifty with the trade-in. I assume you'll want to pay on time."

Twenty-five fifty? Everleigh hugged her handbag to her chest. She had five hundred in her savings account. If she put it all on the car, she just might be able to afford it.

But . . . the new roof. And sooner rather than later, the kitchen appliances all had to be replaced. The stove was going on twenty-five years, and Mama complained the oven cooked unevenly.

"H-how much would the monthly payments be?"

Of course everyone needed a bit put by for emergencies.

"Around eighty."

Steady, Ev. Eighty dollars a month? She only brought home fifty a week. But the house was paid off, so there was no mortgage. Mama cleared that debt after Daddy's funeral with the entirety of their savings.

"No bank is ever going to kick us out." She had a steel resolve about debt and dealing with banks that came from marrying and birthing babies during the Great Depression.

"You're getting one of the best cars of the year, Mrs. Applegate. Well worth it. Quality has no price tag."

"What can you do to get the payment down to forty dollars a month?" She preferred thirty, but forty was her absolute top end.

Glenn chuckled. "Forty a month? I could put you in this nice Ford over here, or a Studebaker from the used lot. Just put one out today in excellent condition. Only three years old."

"I'd rather keep the DeSoto." If she mentioned the five hundred, Glenn would have the upper hand. No cause to dicker. She wanted his best price before she delivered her down payment. She turned to go. "Thank you for your time."

"Hold on now, Mrs. Applegate. Let me talk to the boys, see what I can do."

So it began, the back and forth. Glenn showed her the used blue Studebaker, just in case, but it wasn't a convertible and the black seats had small tears.

Next he gave her a seat at a desk in the showroom and brought her a coffee and a stale donut. She sat alone while he tried to negotiate the monthly payment.

"Can you put any money down?"

"Get me to thirty-five a month and we'll see. I'd like a hundred for my trade-in. And if you could, knock another hundred off the Lark sticker price."

Why not bob for all the apples? She'd resigned herself to drive home in the DeSoto.

"Mrs. Applegate, you're killing me here."

Two hours later, Glenn could go no further than seventy-five dollars on the DeSoto trade-in, twenty dollars off the Lark sticker price, and a seventy-dollar payment.

By now Everleigh was hungry, tired, and ready to go home, change into her pajamas, and watch TV with Mama. What made her think a bottle of bleach and a new tube of Avon's red lipstick could turn her into a modern woman?

Even if she offered the five hundred down payment, which she was beginning to reconsider, the monthly payment still wouldn't be low enough.

"Glenn," she said, standing and straightening her skirt. "I think we've wasted enough of each other's time." Her voice sank with disappointment. "Thank you for trying."

"Mrs. Applegate, we'd love to show you something slightly used if you'd be willing."

"What's going on here, fellas?"

Everleigh steadied herself as Don walked across the showroom floor, his back straight, his shoulders square, looking stylish in slacks and a sweater, his blue gaze scanning her from the top of her bleached head to the tip of her red heels.

"Everleigh." His whistle was slow and steady. "You look . . . Wow." He kissed her cheek. "I went by your house. Your mom said you were running errands."

"How'd you find me here?"

"I didn't. I was driving by and decided to stop in. Must be a divine appointment."

She smiled. "Must be. So, do you like it? My hair?"

"Very becoming."

"Don." Glenn marched toward his boss's son. "Didn't expect you tonight."

The rest of the salesmen popped out of their offices and out of the break room where they played poker and drank beer.

"Are you giving my girl a good deal?" Don roped his arms around Everleigh. "Darling, you should've told me you were coming in tonight."

"I didn't know you were in town . . . *sweetheart*." They shared a glance, a joke, a camaraderie.

"Came down on an errand." Don walked her over to the showroom window. "So, what's your pleasure?"

"Champagne on a beer salary, I'm afraid."

"We tried to get her in the convertible Studebaker, Don," Glenn said. "But her budget doesn't quite stretch."

"Well, let's see what we can do. How much do you want to spend, Ev? Let's get my girl in the car of her dreams."

He was joking, surely, trying to mess with the boys.

"Don." Everleigh leaned in to him. "Really, Glenn has worked hard to meet my demand but—"

"How much?"

———

"Forty dollars a month." She winced, giving him a five-dollar wiggle room. Her previous notion of thirty-five dollars a month was just unreasonable. Forty would be a steal.

Don pressed his hand on Glenn's back. "Let's talk to Bruce. See what's holding up this sale."

Bruce, Everleigh gathered, was the sales manager. Don met him in the middle of the showroom, then walked with the man to his office and shut the door. The rest of the crew scurried about, trying to look busy.

She pressed her hand over her lips. What was going on behind the closed door? Should she let him do this? He was a friend, and a favor of this magnitude might make her beholden in some way.

On the other hand, it had been so long since a man, since *anyone*, had come to her rescue, Don's gesture made her feel treasured.

After Daddy and Rhett died, she had to be her own knight in shining armor, as well as Mama's. If Don wanted to ride in on his white steed, his Corvette, and do her a favor, why not accept?

Ten minutes later he exited Bruce's office. "How's thirty-nine dollars a month strike you?"

"You can't be serious! For the brand-new convertible Studebaker?"

"That's the car you want, isn't it?"

"Y-yes, it is." She studied his expression. He seemed sincere, even excited. "What's the catch?" she said.

"No catch." He directed her over to one side while Bruce and Glenn bustled around with the paperwork. "Why didn't you call me, let me know you wanted a new car?"

"And say what? 'Hello, Don, can you help little ol' me buy a car from your daddy's lot?'"

He laughed, reaching to touch the ends of her hair, searching her face. "That's what friends are for, Ev." He kept calling her Ev as if they were well acquainted and intimate. "I really like your hair."

"LuEllen went a little crazy."

"It's you."

She peered up at him. "Do you think so?"

"It's pretty evident I can't take my eyes off of you. You were beautiful before, but the blonde—"

"Okay, Mrs. Applegate, you are good to go." Glenn crossed the floor with a bit of swagger, holding up the Studebaker keys, pointing to the nearest desk. "All you have to do is sign a few papers and you'll be the owner of a new convertible. I hear tomorrow's forecast is sunshine with temperatures in the sixties. Perfect for a Sunday drive."

With a glance at Don, Everleigh took the pen Glenn offered. *Thank you.*

She signed without doubt and bid a tearful farewell to the DeSoto.

After Glenn filled the tank and lowered the top, she stood with Don by her new car.

"What magic did you do to get the car down to thirty-nine dollars a month? And with no down payment?"

He held out his arms, tugging on his sleeves. "No tricks."

"Don."

"I gave you our dealer discount. And you *will* be paying for the next five years."

She tiptoed up and kissed his cheek. "Thank you."

"I should be thanking you. Ever since Valentine's weekend, I've been realizing some things about myself."

"Good ones, I hope." She laughed softly and pointed to her hair. "I've obviously had a few revelations too."

Don hooked his pinky finger with hers and moved toward her. "You dazzle me, Everleigh Applegate."

"Don, please."

"I'm serious. Just when I was beginning to wonder if anything exciting, out of the ordinary, would happen in my life, I ran into you. Don't get me wrong, I'm grateful for everything I have, but every once in a while, a fella needs to have his socks knocked off."

"Do I? Knock your socks off?"

He raised his pant leg to reveal his bare ankles. With a gasp, Everleigh swatted at him. "How'd you do that?"

"I told you, you knock my socks off." His eyes snapped with a teasing glint.

"What about your girl, Carol Ann?" Funny or not, he was declaring something she wasn't ready to receive. She still loved Rhett in a way she couldn't quite explain or understand. Everleigh held up her new car keys. "I should go. Mama has no idea I'm buying a new car."

"Have dinner with me tomorrow night."

"Don, what are you doing?"

"It's only dinner, Everleigh."

"That's what you said last time. Is it? Only dinner? And you never answered my question about Carol Ann."

"I'm ending things with her. We both know we're not right for one another. It's just that neither one of us has said it yet." Don touched her chin, raising her face to his. "Can I kiss you?"

"Perhaps we should just leave things be, okay? You have loose ends to tie up, and I have a new car to take home."

He brushed his thumb along her jaw. "But I'll be back for you, Everleigh."

"Don't arrange your life around mine, Don. You'll be more stuck than you are now."

"But ever since Lauderback's, I can't stop thinking about you." He leaned closer and her heart nearly beat out of her chest.

Heaven help her, but it'd been so long—

"Then kiss me, Don Callahan. Kiss me."

He embraced her, kissing her sweetly, if not awkwardly, as the two took a moment to find their breath, their rhythm.

Tears slicked down her cheeks as she floated on his affections. Don's, not Rhett's.

With a gasp, she broke away, her hand pressing against Don's chest. "I'm sorry, Don, but I can't. I just can't."

———

CHAPTER EIGHTEEN

BECK

"Beetle?"

Beck welcomed the cool, sweet breeze as she raised the bedroom window, glancing around for her puppy, the residue of Bruno's kiss still on her mind, swirling around her heart.

He never called for dinner after their kiss in the backyard and she was glad. She needed time to think. To do some of her own processing.

Then yesterday he flew to South Carolina and Virginia.

Sitting in the rocker by the window, inhaling the morning breeze, Beck gazed across the lawn to Memory Lane as a black Mercedes cruised past the house. Same as the other day.

The driver slowed, almost stopped, but continued to the end of the lane and parked.

Otherwise, the lane was empty, quiet. Peaceful. So very different from the hustle and bustle of New York.

Her thoughts drifted to Bruno. She regretted her memories of him were gone along with Dad's, but the morning light clarified a few things for her. Mostly that a relationship with Bruno was just not possible.

Not now anyway. And in the three weeks she had left in Fernandina Beach, she'd be his friend. No more, no less.

Still, it made her sad. He was a great guy. Another time and she'd easily hand over her heart.

Meanwhile, Baby Girl gave a flutter and Beck needed to eat. But first she'd take Beetle out for his morning constitutional.

"Beetle Boo?" She whistled for him, then searched under the bed. "Bee Boo?"

He was on the bed when she went to the shower. If he jumped off, it was a heck of a leap for him.

"Beetle?" Beck found her slippers, then zipped up a light jacket. The maternity clothes she ordered arrived yesterday, and she was feeling a bit sporty, if not slightly fat.

She called the dog again as she crossed from the bedroom to the upstairs living room, pausing by the tucked-away, narrow stairwell that led to a third floor. She was going to have to inspect that space soon. "Beetle?"

She spotted him on the other side of the BarcaLounger, collapsed on the carpet, blood pooling beneath his mouth.

"No, no, no . . . What's wrong, buddy?" He moaned when she touched his belly. "Okay, okay, let's get you to the vet. Hang in there, hang in there."

She ran to the bedroom, then down the stairs, then back up again, adrenaline flooding her system. Where was her purse? A towel, he needed a towel. Phone, where was her phone? Charging by the bed.

Vets, vets, vets. She searched on her phone, finding Fernandina Beach Animal Clinic with emergency services.

Baby Girl twisted and turned, stretching to see what was going on.

Grabbing a towel from the bathroom, Beck wrapped Beetle as gently as possible. "Mama's here, sweet boy. Don't go anywhere."

The dog responded with a moan, trying to raise his head and attend her voice. His eyes pleaded with her before he gagged and coughed up another spill of blood.

Easing him up off the floor, tears slipping as he writhed and moaned, she exited the back door. Car, she was going to have to take the car.

Settling Beetle in the grass, she knocked over the birdbath for the garage-barn key and soon shoved back the door.

"Stay with me, little guy. Come on, you beat those drug runners.

You can beat this. Don't let what they did to you get you now." But blood stained the towel. His breath was rapid and shallow.

At the car, she settled him on the passenger-side floor and gazed toward the car's ignition. Good, Bruno left the keys in.

"Oh, Jesus, take the wheel. Seriously." Wiping her cheeks, she slid into the driver's seat, mashed in the clutch, and started the engine.

She could do this. Drive. She'd watched Bruno work the gear shift. And Dad had given her a lesson *way* back. At least in the vision she saw.

She closed her eyes with a long intake of the cold January morning and tried to recall the words she'd heard that day.

"Press in the clutch. Up and over for second gear. Straight down for third. There you go."

She gunned the gas and let off the clutch. The car lurched and stalled. Beetle had gone eerily silent.

"Come on, come on." Beck hammered the steering wheel, then started the car again, repeating the process of gas, clutch, stall.

Four more times and the nose of the car just eeked out of the garage.

"Beck Holiday, pull yourself together and drive. He'll die otherwise. Beetle, do *not* die on me."

She started the car *again*, tears dripping from her chin, and got all the way out of the garage before stalling.

"I'm sorry. Bee, I'm so sorry." All this jerking around couldn't be good for him. She ran her sleeve over her eyes, wiping away the dew. "Bee?" She reached down to stroke his head, but he remained still. Lifeless.

She slammed the steering wheel. "Why can't I do this? I knew cars were stupid." She started and stalled the Studebaker for the umpteenth time.

"Hey, hey, what are you doing?" Bruno jogged toward her dressed for a day of sports agenting.

She ignored him, gunning the gas, letting off the clutch, barking to a halt, almost running into him and swearing like a New York cop.

"Beck, stop, where are you going?" He leaned around the windshield, hand on her shoulder. "What's wrong? Are you okay?"

She shook her head with a sob, pointing to the passenger floor.

"Move over." He opened the door, but she refused to move.

"I think it's too late."

"Let's go anyway. Move."

She slid across the bench seat. "I found him collapsed on the floor, blood coming from his mouth. Look at the towel."

"Everything will be all right." He stretched across, squeezing her hand as he turned onto Memory Lane.

She tipped against him, sobbing. "He's just an innocent dog."

"Come on, little guy, stay with us." Bruno shifted gears, blasting the horn when another driver cut him off.

Beck dried her eyes and checked on Beetle. He was breathing, barely, and shivering. So she covered him with her jacket.

Bruno barreled into the parking lot and stopped by the front door, jumping out of the car to run inside while Beck carefully lifted Beetle from the floorboard.

A vet tech met her at the surgery door, his eyes weighted with appropriate sympathy. "We'll let you know what we find as soon as possible."

"Please, take care of him. H-he was a drug mule. His insides were pretty messed up. You can call the vet in New York—"

"Beck." Bruno's strong arm came around her waist. "Let them do their job."

She fell against his chest, holding on to him.

"Tell me what happened." He tucked his arm around her shoulder.

"I went to take him out and found him in the upstairs living room. I can't lose him, Bruno. I can't. He-he's so sweet and trusting.

He's part of this journey. How did I not see this coming? How did I not know? What kind of mother am I going to be?"

"Whoa, wait. You have taken enormous care of that dog." His phone buzzed in his pocket, but he didn't reach for it. "How were you to know if anything was wrong with him? He looked happy and healthy."

"Moms are supposed to know—"

"Moms don't have ESP. But look, you were so desperate you got behind the wheel of the Studebaker."

"I don't want him to suffer, Bruno." As she stood in the middle of the waiting room, the sobs rolled through her. The combination of the pregnancy hormones along with the knowledge of what Beetle had endured in his short life was just too much. "But I can't, I can't put him down."

She took a tissue on the receptionist's counter and made her way to the chairs.

"Let's just see what the vet says," he said, sitting next to her, ignoring his pinging phone.

"Take that call," she said, blowing her nose and tossing the tissue in the trash. "You don't want to miss Calvin Blue telling you he's finally signing with you."

"It's okay. I'm here for you."

"Bruno, I know you have to be somewhere."

"It's just Stuart. If I don't respond, he'll take off without me."

"You're not going to tell him where you are?"

"Maybe I should." He reached back for his phone. "We were going up to Michigan and Indiana."

"Bruno, don't miss your meeting on account of me. Go."

"And leave Beetle Boo to drive home with you?" He tapped out a text. "Can't do that to another guy. You know I can teach you to drive. The kid at Michigan isn't going to sign with me anyway. He only took the meeting because the pro liaison is a friend of mine."

She peered over at him. "You're going to get Sports Equity off the ground, Bruno."

"Still wrestling with the idea of being a nothing. I woke up hearing Dad yelling, 'You're nothing!' When I left Watershed, Kevin yelled it across the office, over fifty heads, as I walked out. I think his 'You're nothing' hooked up with Dad's and they're having a baby."

"Stop." She grabbed his chin and turned his face to hers. "Say it. 'I'm something.' Stop believing in the words of broken, wounded men. If your dad were alive, he'd have a whole different attitude about you."

He brushed his hand over her cheek. "I believe I'm something when I'm with you."

"Bruno—"

"I know." He released her and sat forward, turning his phone between his hands. "You're leaving. Yet I can't get you out of my head. Or those kisses. They were pretty amazing."

"I thought maybe I could have a short, three-week romance with you, Bruno, but I can't. I'm barely surviving my life. I can't worry about your heart while I'm at it." She nodded toward the double doors. "What are they doing in there? Do you think he's okay?"

"It's only been a few minutes." He pressed his hand to hers. "Funny how they get under your skin—animals, babies. New York cops."

"Who can't give you what you need."

"How do you know what I need?"

She tipped her head to one side. "A woman who lives here is a start. A woman not bearing another man's baby. Bruno, seriously, don't get tangled up."

"You know I invented complicated."

"Ha, you wish."

"Beck, I'm not sure I can let you go again. You smooth things out for me, not complicate them."

"Bruno, I never expected to find someone like you here. You're the best surprise, but the previously stated list still applies."

He didn't answer, but she believed, hoped, he heard before he got in too deep. They sat quietly for the better part of an hour until the vet, Dr. Brannon, emerged with a somber expression and pulled a chair around to sit in front of them.

"He has a perforation in his stomach, probably from the drugs. We're prepping him for surgery, but thanks to your good care, he's strong and should pull through."

Bruno asked questions as the doctor explained the surgery, then waited while Beck signed papers and paid the bill. They'd keep him overnight and told Beck to call tomorrow afternoon about picking him up.

Then there was nothing to do but wait. The receptionist promised she'd call with an update the moment he was out of surgery.

Bruno suggested lunch and drove the Studebaker through Fernandina Beach's quaint downtown to the Happy Tomato.

"The Happy Tomato," Beck said as she closed her car door and stepped over the curb. "Are all of the tomatoes happy? 'Cause if mine is sad, I'm leaving."

She walked with Bruno toward the patio, slowing as a black Mercedes turned the corner and eased along the curb. Same one she saw this morning. She angled back to see the plates and froze. New York.

Bruno forged ahead, talking as if she were right next to him, while she made a mental note of the number. It didn't hit on any of the dozens of license plate numbers she'd stored there in the last year.

The driver stepped out of his car, buttoning his jacket. A businessman. Nothing more, nothing less. Beck was just restless. Imagining things.

"Beck, did you hear me? I said your tomatoes will be dancing the Charleston." Bruno grabbed her arm and led her to a table on the patio.

"The Charleston? Perfect." She sat with an exhale, trying to focus on Bruno.

"He's going to be okay. I can just tell."

"Who's going to be okay?"

Bruno made a face. "Beetle. Who else?"

"Of course . . . Yes! He *has* to be." Tears dappled her eyes. *Forget the stupid car. You're not a cop in Fernandina Beach.* "I might have to ugly cry if he's not."

"It's okay to ugly cry. I did with you that day under the bed."

"You were on the phone, not in public with happy tomatoes."

"An ugly cry is an ugly cry."

"One of my first nights on the force, the calls were nonstop. It was like the city went crazy. But I was tough, a new cop, eager to prove myself. Then we went on a call to an apartment where a one-year-old baby girl drowned in the bathtub. The mother was beside herself. I'd never seen anyone so distraught. Made my problems seem minor in comparison. It was an accident, but she blamed herself. It was my job to talk to her while my partner took the report from the father." She blinked back her tears. "I ugly cried that night. My partner pulled over in an alley and just let me go. He is a good guy. Hogan."

"Caring is what makes you a good cop, Beck,"

The waitress, Treena, came by with menus and waters. After they ordered, Bruno made a few calls, rearranged his schedule, his conversation quick and laden with lingo.

"I'll be down tomorrow, Ryan. Ten o'clock. Yeah. What are his times? The forty? What's he bench? Really? And his vertical? I can work with that. Who else is talking to him?"

The air had a winter chill, so a few customers on the patio moved inside. Beck liked the freedom of the open space and the sun on her shoulders.

She breathed out the tension of the morning, grateful to be here with Bruno. When she looked around to capture the charm of the Happy Tomato, the Mercedes driver stepped onto the patio.

His dark, expensive-looking suit spoke of money and influence. With a quick glance around, he sat at the table behind Bruno and ordered black coffee from Treena.

Since Bruno was still on his phone, Beck took a second to observe the man. Clean shaven. Clipped haircut. Manicured hands—unless pregnancy hormones had dulled her powers of observation. Everything about him said money.

He kept his head down, constantly running his hand over the back of his head and down his neck.

But when Treena came to pour his coffee, Beck caught his eye. He quickly glanced away.

Bruno finished his call and tucked his phone into his shirt pocket with the Polo logo instead of Sports Equity.

Beck propped her arms on the table and leaned into the slant of sun falling through the trees. "What do you love about being a sports agent?"

"Everything. The players, the negotiating, I love helping a kid reach his dreams. And, if I do the job right, the money. In LA I had a condo in the hills. Drove a Porsche."

"But here you have your condo on the beach. And your mom." She sat back as Treena brought out their food. "I bet she likes having you around."

"When I came home to take care of her after her accident, I stayed in my old room and did everything but bathe her for six weeks." He inspected his sandwich, removing his tomato.

"What's wrong with your tomato? Is it not happy?"

"It's very happy." He winked at her, and she felt it to her soul. "Not to be eaten."

"I bet. So, you came home to help your mom?" Beck focused on her lunch, trying not to engage the man behind Bruno.

He was probably a just businessman. A shy one. Nevertheless, she felt tense, on the alert.

"I shopped, cleaned, took her to physical therapy. She was so grateful, always telling me to get back to work and not worry about her. But I realized no one had ever looked out for her. Her parents divorced and her mom worked all the time. Her dad traveled so he was never home. Then she married my louse of a father." He reassembled his sandwich.

"I had an offer from another agency last year but I couldn't leave," he said. "For once in her life, Mom deserved to have someone a phone call away. As luck, or God, would have it, I ran into Stuart Strickland right after I decided to stay, and he offered to fly me any-where, anytime."

"You're a good son, Bruno."

"What about you? Once a cop always a cop?"

"'Maybe. It gets in your blood. There's no thrill like being on the job. You live it, breathe it. Even when you're not working, you notice things civilians don't."

He laughed. "Thanks for using your cop vibe to help me."

"Anytime." She glanced past Bruno's shoulder. The man was gone. "But now, I don't know. Everleigh has given me options I didn't have before."

"Bruno Endicott!" A Fernandina Beach police officer with the stars of a chief on his collar popped Bruno on the shoulder.

Ah, so this is why he left. Tailored Suit Guy spotted the cops before Beck.

You're slipping already.

"Chief Bedell." Bruno rose to shake his hand. "Long time no see. Beck, this is Chet Bedell, chief of police. Chet, meet Beck Holiday, an NYPD sergeant. She inherited Miss Everleigh's place."

"Pleasure's all mine," Chet said. "NYPD? What precinct? I have a friend up there. Works in Brooklyn, I believe."

"I'm with the Ninth. Alphabet City."

"So you inherited Miss Everleigh's place. My wife will be jealous."

He flipped Beck his card. "We could use another good cop around here."

"I'm not looking to move, sir." Nevertheless, she tucked the card in her bag. Just in case.

"Well, if you change your mind—" Chet's lunch partner arrived, and they found a table inside.

Beck picked at her sandwich and glanced at her watch. Beetle had been in surgery for at least forty minutes.

"Think he's okay?"

"I do." Bruno finished his sandwich and pushed his plate forward. "I was thinking last night how different everything would be if you hadn't forgotten."

"I used to wonder what life would be like if Dad hadn't been killed. It was his day off. He wasn't supposed to be there."

Beck jumped when her phone rang. "It's the vet. Hello?" He was okay. Her sweet, sweet puppy. "Thank you so much." She smiled at Bruno. "He came through with flying colors. He's going to make it."

Yes, he was going to make it. The little piece of her soul she carried in her arms two weeks ago was going to make it.

CHAPTER NINETEEN

EVERLEIGH

April

"*Walt Disney Presents* looks good tonight," Mama called from the living room. "Of course *Maverick* is on."

"You'll have to watch without me." Everleigh clipped on a pair of pearl earrings. "I'm having dinner with Don."

He'd been in Waco every weekend since he helped her buy the Studebaker. Since he kissed her under the car lot lights.

She'd squirreled away enough money for a little more shopping and spent yesterday at Goldstein-Migel.

Tonight she wore her new blue linen suit with matching slingbacks and a beaded clutch.

"Don again?" Mama rose from her chair, removing her glasses. "Is this getting serious?"

"I don't think so. He's in Dallas, I'm here. I enjoy his company."

"And attention."

"He's a handsome man, Mama. Who wouldn't?"

"You are clearly more than friends, Ev. Is that a new suit? Friends meet for coffee. Maybe a slice of pie at Diamonds, but not fancy dinners every weekend with fancy duds. New shoes too?"

"You knew I went shopping yesterday."

Mama sank down in her chair. "One glance at him in a Lauderback's aisle and you're dying your hair like a Hollywood floozy and trading in Daddy's old DeSoto."

"I said I was sorry about the car." Everleigh sat in her chair next to Mama's. The one that used to be Daddy's. "I shouldn't have traded in the DeSoto without consulting you."

"That was the last car Tom bought. He was so proud."

"It was hard for me to say good-bye, but, Mama, Daddy is not coming back. Neither is Rhett. Seeing Don again made me realize I'm not an eighty-year-old widow."

"What are you saying? I made you live like an eighty-year-old widow?"

"No, Mama, please." She touched her arm. "This is not about you or me—"

"It is every bit about you *and* me. We're partners, Ev. I care for the home and everything that goes with it. You work, pay the bills, and apparently buy the cars. You are a chip off your father, that's for sure. What happens to me if you run off and get married? You cannot leave me here, alone, rattling around this big ol' place. And I hate to bring it up, but there's the little matter of . . ." She looked at the TV, unable to say "the baby." They never talked about it. It was their unspoken pact. "How do you think Don will respond when you tell him?"

"What's to tell? As far as the rest of the world is concerned, I never had a child." Everleigh hated the coarse tone in her voice, but if she was going to walk upright in the world and have some semblance of a life, she couldn't get bogged down with guilt, regret, and sentimentality. It would not serve her well. "Mama, you'll not be alone. I-I won't leave you."

She was forever bound to Mama. As a daughter, as a grieving widow, as a hurting mother. They'd been to hell and back together, which, whether she liked it or not, knotted them in an unbreakable bond.

Still, it didn't mean she had to live in her mother's shadow. Didn't mean she couldn't buy a new dress now and then and go out with a handsome man.

"I'm not opposed to you marrying again," Mama said when

Everleigh returned to the living room. "I'm not as cruel as all that. But Don Callahan? Can't see us tied to that family the rest of our lives. What happened to his fancy girlfriend?"

"Apparently she broke off with him. But he was going to if she didn't. She met someone else, one of the coaches for the new Dallas football team."

"I see." Mama lips were pale and narrow. "Is he coming back to work at Callahan Cars?"

"Callahan merged with Dewey. But Don has other plans for his life, and I don't think they include Waco, or even Texas."

"Then why are you wasting your time with him?" Mama sighed, shaking her head. "Your life is here. Always has been, always will be."

Asked and answered. No use going around that mountain again. "I was going to heat up the coffee. Do you want some?" Everleigh turned for the kitchen.

"With cream but no sugar. I'm cutting back."

Everleigh plugged in the coffee pot and took two cups from the cupboard, dropping a dollop of cream in Mama's cup along with two teaspoons of sugar. *Cutting back, my eye.* She'd complain bitterly if Everleigh handed her a cup of creamed coffee with no sugar.

She gazed into living room where Mama waited for her show, knitting under the light of the floor lamp.

Yes, she'd like to marry one day. When she was ready. But could she love another man the way she loved Rhett?

How would a new husband feel about her loyalty to his predecessor? Everleigh owed it to Rhett, to his parents, to remember them. If she didn't, who would?

What scared her was the unknown of falling in love again. Could she love someone else and Rhett at the same time? To be fair to a new love, she'd have to box away her loyalty to her memories, and she just wasn't ready to do that.

Still, she enjoyed Don's company. He was sweet and charming, loyal and kind, with a wit that made her laugh. She felt at home with him like she'd never felt with anyone. Maybe not even Rhett.

Everleigh mulled over this realization as she carried in Mama's coffee with a plate of cookies.

"Mama." Everleigh handed the items to Mama. "Why'd you fall out with Sher Callahan? After everything she did? How she helped us?"

"We simply have other interests."

"Wasn't she your bridge partner?" Everleigh sat in her chair, cup and saucer in her hand. "But now she's not?"

"She cheats."

"You've known that for years." Everleigh sipped her hot brew. "You used to come home singing her praises."

"The good Lord convicted me."

"Sure took you long enough to listen."

"Hush." Mama pointed to the TV. "Disney is coming on."

Everleigh moved to the window when she heard a car door slam. The McAllisters two doors down had four teenagers. One car or another was always pulling up to their curb.

But it was Don. She carried her coffee to the kitchen and primped in the hall mirror as the doorbell rang.

"Come in, come in," Mama called.

"Mama." Everleigh swatted at her as she hurried to open the door.

Don stepped in and filled the house with his masculine presence, making Everleigh's heart flutter when he kissed her cheek.

"You look beautiful," he said. "Evening, Mrs. Novak."

"Don." Mama hovered over her coffee and cookies like some miser counting her pennies.

Don assisted Everleigh with her new spring coat, then held her hand as he walked her to the Corvette. Closing her door, he walked around to the driver's side and started the engine. But instead of shifting into reverse, he turned to Everleigh.

"I have to say it or I'll burst."

She turned to see his face in the dashboard lights. "You sound serious."

"Ev, I'm falling in love with you."

"Don . . ." Love? Did she really think they were *just* having a few laughs? "Love? What's this? We've only been on a few dates."

"I knew the moment I saw you in the grocery aisle."

She scoffed. "You fell in love with the dowdy widow at a glance?"

"What can I say? I have an eye for true beauty beneath sensible shoes and a granny bun. You have my attention." He ran his hand along her jawline, igniting buried but long-smoldering embers. "I can love you well, Everleigh."

"Mercy." She exhaled, hand to her chest. "You must be reading romance novels."

He touched her chin. "I love you."

"Don, please, I-I don't know what to say." She gripped the door handle and held on for dear life.

What did she expect? He'd come home the last four weekends just to be with her. She'd colored her hair and refreshed her wardrobe for him. What message was she sending?

"Do you think you might return my feelings? Everleigh, I've never felt this way before, and it's a bit unsettling and exciting."

"I'm flattered, Don. Truly. But shouldn't we go? We'll miss our reservation. I don't know about you, but I'm famished."

Don shifted into reverse and eased toward the street. "I know I sprang this whole 'I love you' bit on you tonight, but I mean it. I'm yours."

"Don, I do adore you . . . but love? I-I don't know. I'm still rather attached to Rhett."

"I'm not intimidated by what you had with him. I'm glad he loved you and you loved him. It bodes well for me." He bent to see her face, making a cheeky sound. "Babe?"

"There are things, Don." Mama had to mention the baby, didn't she? Now Everleigh felt the guilt afresh. "Things you don't know. Things that will appall you."

"Like what?" Don slowed for the stop sign. "Robbery? Murder?"

"Not exactly, but shocking nonetheless."

"It's in the past and I don't care."

You would if you knew. "Tell me," she said with forced joviality, "where is this surprise dinner?" She turned up the radio only to hear the Fleetwoods singing "Come Softly to Me."

"I want, want you to know, I love, I love you so . . ."

She coiled her hands in her lap to keep from snapping off the radio. Maybe Don should just take her home. The twist of nerves in her gut made her feel ill. She saw now how she'd been deluding herself.

Don sang with the radio, his smooth voice low and out of tune.

"Mm dooby do, dahm dahm, dahm do dahm ooby do."

Don't laugh, Ev. Don't laugh.

Louder and louder. So off-key Everleigh couldn't match the melody in her head with the one on the radio.

A low snort escaped.

"What?" Don flashed his white, even smile. "You don't like my singing?" He merged onto Hwy. 6 with Corvette speed, heading north. He tipped back his head and howled at the full moon.

Everleigh burst out, her *ha-has* bouncing against the dash and into her thirsty soul.

Don slipped his hand into hers and brought it to his lips. "I love your laugh, Ev."

"Oh, Don . . ." She sank back in her seat, smiling, tightening her fingers around his.

CHAPTER TWENTY

DON

Flashbulbs popped as Dad and Standish Dewey signed the agreement between Dewey Motors and Callahan Cars, making them the largest dealership in central Texas.

The reporter asked questions as Standish and Dad posed for more pictures. Standish's robust laugh was a force all its own.

"We are going to be wealthy men, Harold." He waved Don over. "Get in here. You're still our heir apparent even though my daughter let you go."

Don smiled for the picture, but the basketball-size knot in his chest made it hard to breathe, let alone talk and look happy. He had news of his own to share, and it would not be well received.

He'd met with George Granger last night and he was in, jumping into the insurance business. It was booming in the post-war market with soldiers becoming husbands and fathers, some with kids approaching high school age already.

The world was changing. People needed, wanted insurance. After the Depression and war years, it wasn't enough to live in a decent three-two and pray the factory never closed. People demanded a safety net.

With a bit of hard work, George charted out Don's course. Not only could he help blaze a new trail, but the earning potential was twice that of selling cars. And he'd be helping people prepare for the future.

Everleigh and Mrs. Novak were classic examples. Rhett had no insurance because he was young, sixty years from the threat of death. Mr. Novak, at the age of fifty-seven, had just decided on a policy a week before the tornado but had yet to file the final papers.

Nevertheless, Don was in knots. George was set to move to Florida in two weeks and Don needed to give his final word. George had another prospect if Don couldn't make the leap.

Five hundred dollars was his start-up fee. A small price to pay for such a promising future. For something Don could call his own.

Another flashbulb exploded and spots bounced before his eyes. Carol Ann stood off in the corner with her mother, her arm linked through her new beau's, a statue of a man.

"Champagne all around!" Standish pressed the intercom button. "Denise, bring in the glasses."

As the corks popped and the lawyers shook hands with a wink and a nod, Don made his way over to his parents. Dad was beyond jovial and Mom flittered about, showing off her new green silk suit and regaling anyone who would listen with details of her new home.

"Are you happy, Dad?" Don said. "You won't miss being your own boss, doing things your way?"

"Standish and I have it all worked out. I'll still run things at Callahan. But I won't have to be there twelve hours a day since the sales and accounting will be managed up here. Ol' Brock Lucas was going to retire on me anyway. Look at these." Dad pulled travel brochures from his inside pocket. "I'm surprising your mom with a trip to California next month. Already called the travel agent. We're going to the Brown Derby and Grauman's Chinese Theater." He stuffed the brochures in his pocket. "Why the furrowed brow, son? This is a fine day for the Callahans. Especially you." He rested his hand on Don's shoulder. "That brute Carol Ann threw you over for doesn't have the brain of a bear, let alone a keen businessman."

"He's a football coach, Dad. He doesn't want to sell cars."

"Smile, my boy, and behold your future. Sometimes I think you're afraid of happiness. It's the war, I tell you. It takes something out of a man he can't get back. But these are good, prosperous times."

"The California trip sounds great. Make sure Mom doesn't act like Lucy Ricardo if she sees a real celebrity. And I assure you I'm not afraid of happiness." He was concerned, however, that his pursuit of it would somehow trample on Dad's.

Don set down his champagne with an eye on the door. "I should get to the showroom floor. It's still a work day."

"Did Standish promote you yet? He said he was going to as soon as we merged."

"He's said nothing to me."

"I'll have a chat—"

"Don't. It's okay," Don said. "Let it play out."

No promotion meant one less hurdle. One less way to disappoint. As he hit the showroom floor, the receptionist announced he had visitors in his office.

He'd been working with a local contractor for a deal on a fleet of new trucks, and he hoped they were here to sign.

But it wasn't the boys from RonKen Construction waiting for him. It was George Grange and a man he didn't recognize.

"George, didn't I just see you last night?" Don shook his hand, then reached to close his office door.

"I hate to bother you at work, so we won't take long," George sat across from Don's desk. "This is Joshua Christian. He's partnering with me, with *us*, in Florida, and he was passing through and wondered if he could meet you, see if you had any questions."

Don perched on the edge of his desk, shaking the man's hand. "Have we met?"

"Once, a while ago." Dressed in a brown suit and brown loafers, he seemed rather ordinary. Steady and calm, yet asserting a permeating presence. "In Waco. At the First Baptist Church."

"I'm sorry I don't remember."

"I do." Mr. Christian sat back with a glance at George. "Now, as you know, there are no guarantees in this life." Mr. Christian spoke with a pristine authority. "But isn't it nice to know you can come alongside others with a good insurance policy to ease their minds? Like faith. It's our assurance that God is taking care of us."

"I suppose, yes," Don said. Mr. Christian's insights ignited a strange passion in him. "But, George, Mr. Christian, you don't have to sell me. I'm in. It's just, this is a big day for my family and I need to find the right time. I'm not sure how—"

"Don, when you begin to ask how, you've already killed the dream." Mr. Christian leaned forward. "Leave the *how* to God."

"Excuse me?"

"Leave the *how* to God."

"Yes, of course. Faith, right?" Don sank down to his chair. It'd been so long since he'd considered his faith. Since his return from Korea, he was, as his old granny used to say, a bad-weather Christian.

"Exactly," Mr. Christian said. "So, you're in?"

"Just have to resign my job here and make arrangements to move to Florida."

George leaped to his feet and pumped Don's hand with enthusiasm. "Welcome aboard, welcome aboard. I knew you'd come with us. Mr. Christian said you would. Didn't we dream of something like this back in our Baylor days?" He glanced at Mr. Christian. "Thank you for trusting us with your investment."

"I believe in you both. I do admire your loyalty to your dad, Don, but remember, your father loves you. Trust in that love." Mr. Christian glanced at George. "We should let this man get to work. Don, say hello to Everleigh for me."

"Everleigh? H-how do you know about Everleigh?"

"I was there the night her husband died."

He was there . . . the night . . . "At the Circle A? You were there?"

"Actually, in downtown Waco. George, we best be going. Good day to you, Don."

He exchanged a curiosity glance with George. *Who was this guy?*

Dad appeared in the doorway. "The RonKen boys are here."

"Yeah, okay. I'll be right out."

"They're waiting in Standish's office," Dad said. "See you there."

Alone again with George and Mr. Christian, they set a tentative date for Don to arrive in Florida by the end of the month. George would go on ahead and rent their office and scout out housing.

With a final handshake, the two left. But Don called George back with a husky whisper.

"Who is he again?"

"Joshua Christian."

"How do you know him? Is he really investing in our venture? Can we trust him?"

George looked over his shoulder to where Mr. Christian was greeting the Dewey salesmen and complimenting them on their fine products.

"Dad said he's legit. Comes around when we need him. Even when we don't. Gave Dad great advice about selling our place in Waco and moving to Dallas. He visited my grandmother in the hospital when we thought she was dying. She walked out two days later."

Don shook the chill from his arms. "But *who* is he? Where does he come from?"

George laughed and popped his hand on Don's shoulder. "I don't know. But let's just take him on faith, eh?"

"That's not the answer I wanted, but if you trust him, I trust him." Don shook his friend's hand a final time.

He turned back in his office to get the RonKen file. When he looked around, Dad was in his office, closing the door.

Don's courage abated with a subtle sense of dread. "We'd better get to the RonKen meeting." He held up the folder.

Dad leaned against the door, arms folded, his lips pressed tight. "What was that meeting about?"

"Well, funny you should ask." Don cleared his throat and loosened his tie as a voice shot through him. *Your father loves you.* "Have a seat, Dad, there's something I need to tell you."

———

BRUNO

"I owe you a solid, man." Bruno parked behind Mom's car and ended his call.

He was meeting Stu in an hour to fly down to Ft. Lauderdale, then up to Tallahassee. Bruno would meet with a player at FAU, then with another FSU player *not* named Calvin Blue while Stu dined with the governor. Yeah, *the* governor. Stu rolled big.

He glanced toward Miss Everleigh's, hoping for a glimpse of Beck. She'd picked Beetle Boo up from the vet two days ago and tended him 24–7.

Every text, call, and encounter with her drew him in a little bit more. Maybe she didn't see herself as a mother, but the way she cared for that dog? She was *nurturing* personified.

He hated to think what would happen when she returned to New York.

Could he talk her into something long distance? Despite her objections?

He supposed he could move to New York, take a job with AJ & Co.

He doubted Stuart would remain his personal pilot forever, and he was grateful the man's generosity had helped him expand his recruiting territory.

But there were other things to consider besides Beck's objections and the geographic challenge.

The pregnancy, for one. In his head the baby presented no problem, but he would have to cop to the sobering reality of taking on a kid not his own. He admired men who did it. He just had to be clear *he* was one of them.

So, yes, a relationship with her would be complicated. But worth it, right? One thing was becoming increasingly clear. He loved her. Because he'd always loved her.

With no sign of Beck at the memory house, he let himself into Mom's place, snooping around the kitchen for something to eat. "Mom?" he called up the stairs. "You up?"

No answer. In the living room, he waited, listening, his eye catching the shiny pot on the fireplace mantel. He squinted and stepped forward, reading the bronze name plate.

Stone Aloysius Endicott

No dates. Just his name. What was she doing with Dad's ashes? Bruno flicked the brass urn with the back of his hand. "Hope you're comfy in there."

"Bruno?" Mom bent over the top of the banister. "You startled me."

"Mom, what are you doing with Dad's ashes?"

"I brought them home from Mrs. Ackers."

"Mrs. Ackers?"

"I stored them there." She disappeared. "Couldn't stand the thought of them in my closet or yours so—"

"You stored Dad's ashes at Mrs. Ackers. Did she know?"

"Let's just say she found out."

"Mom, you can't just leave a dead man in another woman's closet."

"It's not like he was murdered."

Bruno carried the urn to his old room and set Dad on the empty bureau. "Shouldn't we scatter him somewhere?" he said, returning to the kitchen.

"I like the idea of him being trapped in that pot." Mom whooshed past dressed in her uniform of sneakers, yoga pants, and a T-shirt, taking her keys from the hook by the door. "Where are you off to today?"

"Lauderdale, then Tallahassee. With Stu."

"Not again. When will you listen to your mother?"

"When she makes sense. Mom, seriously, what are we going to do with Dad's ashes? What about scattering them over the river?" Despite the conflict he carried in his heart over his father's absence, the man deserved a proper send-off. "We could call Aunt Keri and have a little ceremony. Say a prayer."

Though he hadn't seen his dad's sister in years, she sent an annual Christmas card with a photo of her grandchildren.

"She moved to Seattle. There was no love lost between the two of them anyway."

She gestured at her watch. "Got to go. Why'd you stop by? You normally don't make your way over here quite so much." Mom's grin said everything. "Couldn't be the cute girl across the street."

"Can't a guy want to say hello to his mother before taking a trip?"

She patted his cheek. "Don't worry, I think it's sweet. You still have a crush on your first crush."

At his car, he gazed toward the memory house one last time. He'd be late if he didn't get on the road, and Stuart would take off without him. He was serious about his flying time.

Just then Beck stepped out, Beetle in her arms.

She set him in the grass, aiding his weak side as he did what all dogs do. Then she straightened, her long T-shirt stretching over her baby middle, and stared in his direction as she shielded her eyes from the morning sun.

Bruno waved, but instead of responding in kind, Beck ducked down and inched over to one of the ancient, fat-trunk live oaks and disappeared behind its girth.

What the—

She poked her head around the right side, then the left.

Bruno walked to the driveway's edge and scanned the lane. Nothing seemed out of the ordinary. A few cars parked on the street. A blue Ford truck. A black Mercedes. A red Mustang.

"Beck!" He jogged across the street and over the thick green lawn. "What are you doing?"

Wide-eyed, she pressed her finger to her lips and waved him over. When he met up with her, she grabbed his shirt and yanked him behind the tree.

He gazed down at her, his chest against her breast, his heart a locomotive.

"Did you accidentally swallow Beetle's drugs?"

"I'm watching the black Mercedes."

"Where?" He angled to see, but she jerked him back.

"Don't let him see you."

"Who?"

"The man in the Mercedes. Keep up, Endicott."

"Sergeant Holiday, I think you've gone off the deep end. Pregnancy hormones or too many hours of *Gilmore Girls* have fried your brain." Regretfully, Bruno freed himself from her grasp and walked around the tree in search of a black Mercedes. "Are you looking at the car way down at the end? That's Mr. Colter."

"Who?" Beck peeked around the tree.

"Mr. Colter. He lives right there." Bruno indicated the house at the beginning of the lane.

"Then why does he park all the way down there? At the end of the lane? There are no houses there."

"Maybe he wants the exercise. Or the shade."

She pictured the man at the Happy Tomato. "Does he wear an expensive, tailored suit?"

"Only during the week. On weekends he goes naked. Seriously, did you take the dog's meds?" Bruno pressed his hand to her forehead and she smacked it away. "I think *someone* is homesick for her job."

She nudged him with her hip. "Maybe. There's only so much *Gilmore Girls* a cop can take. So, Mr. Colter? And he always parks down here?"

"Not always. But I'm pretty sure that's his car. I'll introduce you sometime. You can ask him. Now, I've got to go. Are you all right? How's Beetle?" At the moment the dog rested in the grass, his pink tongue falling over the side of his mouth.

"He's fine. Healing. Doesn't chew at his stitches, which is good."

"No more blood?"

"No more blood."

"And you? Are you well?" He almost, *almost* touched her belly.

"I'm well." The sweet edge to her reply snapped another rope from his heart and he angled down to kiss her forehead.

"Got to meet Stu. Flying to Ft. Lauderdale, then Tallahassee."

"Have a good trip. Be careful. Those small planes . . ." She laughed as she echoed Mom's speech.

"See you in a few days. Want to do pizza?" He kissed her again. This time a quick peck on the lips. "I'll call you later." He turned to go, slightly stunned by his casual yet intimate gestures, catching the three words dangling from the edge of his lips.

I love you.

CHAPTER TWENTY-ONE

BECK

"I sent you something." Mom, in her pragmatic, simple manner.

"Why? I'll be home in two weeks." Beck prepared Beetle's breakfast, mashing his pills into the soft beef and gravy, and set it on the pantry floor.

She'd made a bed for him in the safe, dark space. He seemed to prefer it. Yet he had full view of the kitchen's light.

When she went upstairs to hang with the Gilmores, she carried him with her. She bought pee pads, spreading them in strategic places just in case he had an emergency. Washed his wounds. Scratched his ears. Even sang songs over him.

She steadied him on his feet so he could eat. But first he licked her hand in thanks before diving into his bowl.

"I thought it might help," Mom said.

"The box? Help with what?"

"You know, your memories."

"You haven't been interested in my memories for years."

"Has anything coming back to you?"

"Not really." She wouldn't talk about the visions until she understood more herself. "Mom, since when do you care about the past? We've all moved on."

"I never said that."

"You didn't have to, you lived it. You packed up all of Dad's stuff. You stopped talking about him. We didn't even go to the 9/11 memorial dedication."

"Well, you didn't remember him, so I thought, why bother? You must have forgotten for a reason. Why try to undo it?"

Mom's comment bounced against Bruno's question. *"Why'd you forget?"*

"You left me behind, Mom. I wanted to talk about stuff but you didn't. Then you got with Flynn and blew me off." Apparently they *were* having the conversation now. Beck blamed the Florida sunshine and the spacious rooms of the memory house.

"Blow you off? When? I never." Her tone broke with a spike of emotion. "That's not fair, Beck."

"I came into your room several nights in a row after Dad died and tried to talk to you about . . . *something,* but you were too tired to talk."

"I was working double shifts, Beck. And I do remember those nights and I told you we'd talk in the morning. When I asked you at breakfast, you said never mind."

"Well, now I have no idea what I wanted to say. I remember I felt bad about something. Guilty. It kept me awake at night." Beck jerked open the fridge for a bottle of water. "I'm sorry for my Flynn comment. But I did feel left out when you two started dating. I spent a lot of time eating popcorn for dinner and watching reruns of *Friends.*"

"I know, and I'm sorry. But I was so alone and he was such a good man . . . You like him now, don't you?"

"Yes, Mom, I like him now."

Beck checked on Beetle. He'd eaten his small morning portion and curled up on his blanket. She raised his leg to check his stitches. If he picked at them, she'd have to make him wear the lampshade of shame, and she refused to do it.

"I'm sorry if you felt—"

"Forget it, Mom. It was a tough season for us both. So, what's in the box of Dad's stuff?"

"Things from his desk at work. They sent it to me about three months after he died. I stuck it in the attic."

What was she going to do with a box of Dad's stuff from the precinct? "Well, okay, thanks. How's everyone?"

"Wyatt scored two goals the other night. A few colleges have contacted him."

"I'll text him later. Hey, Mom, do you remember the Endicotts? Natalie and her son, Bruno."

"Natalie, yes, that's her name. I was telling Flynn about her the other night—I've forgotten so much about those days—and the cute boy who had such a crush on you."

"Bruno."

"Bruno, that's it." Mom laughed. "I kept saying it was a name from *Cinderella*. He said, 'Gus Gus?'"

"He's a sports agent now. Reps football players."

"Tell him about Wyatt. Maybe he can start representing lacrosse players. Didn't Natalie work for some rich lady?"

"Still does. His dad died a year after Dad."

"Did he? I knew he and Natalie had divorced. I guess you two have something in common."

"We do." Beck touched her fingers to her forehead, the imprint of his kiss still there days later.

The way he kissed her and said good-bye, promising to call her later . . . It was a scene from *Married with a Small Dog*.

Baby Girl kicked, bringing Beck back to the moment. "Hey, Mom, I need to tell you something—"

"Can we talk later? I'm not blowing you off. I'm at work. Look for the box, okay?"

Mom's side of the call died, and Beck tucked her phone into her pocket. Opening the kitchen door, she welcomed the sunlight and cold breeze. The high for the day was supposed to be in the fifties. A heat wave in New York. A cold snap in north Florida.

But she loved the chill, the way it cleared away the fog of her amnesia.

When she went to check the mail a few hours later, sure enough, Mom's box sat on the front porch.

Beck carried it upstairs and set it on the bed. She'd grown comfortable in this house, made new memories to cover the old forgotten ones. The flashbacks were a quagmire but nothing to really disturb her equilibrium.

So, the box. Did she look inside? Did she want to disturb the graveyard of her past even more?

Each attempt to call up old images came with an edge of trepidation, caution, as if something horrifying waited for her under the cover of amnesia.

Beck sat in the rocker by the window and studied the box from across the room as if it might explode at any moment.

She patted her belly. "Baby Girl, what do you think?"

A clapping car door got her attention and she glanced out the window toward the street. Beneath the tree limbs, a pair of dark shoes walked beside a black Mercedes.

He was here again. Beck dropped to her knees for a better look, but the second-floor view was too high.

Slipping down the stairs, she felt a little silly. The car was owned by a neighbor. Mr. Colter. Still, she was curious to see the plate. Check out the license number.

Standing behind the narrow porch post, Beck watched Sir Tailored Suit hike down the lane.

She moved barefoot over the grass, tugging her phone from her yoga pants pocket. The New York tag was the same as the one she'd seen at the Happy Tomato.

Ducking behind the car, she tapped a text to Hogan.

Can you run this plate?

Putting her phone away, she skipped back into her yard, picking up broken limbs as a diversion. When he arrived back at the car, she rose up, clutching a handful of twigs to her chest, her loose hair falling over her eye.

"Can I help you?"

"No." He reached for the driver's-side door, turning ever so slightly toward Beck. "My company is looking to develop the lots at the end of the lane."

"I didn't know they were for sale." Because she owned them.

"Yes, well, we just heard from the owner." He slid behind the wheel, the car door slamming behind him.

As he drove off, Beck's cop gut burned. *Text me back, Hogan, and hurry.*

Inside, she dug the local police chief's card from her bag and created a contact in her phone. Then she checked on Beetle, who slept peacefully in his bed under the bedroom window, soaking up the light. He didn't seem to mind not living in darkness.

She was refilling his water bowl when the doorbell rang. She ducked down, then inched up to peer out the window.

Had Sir Tailored Suit returned? Did he catch her reading his plates? Where was her sidearm when she needed it? She prepped a text to Chief Bedell just in case.

Help! Memory house.

But Memory Lane was quiet. No black Mercedes. However, she spied the edge of a blue sedan parked beside the veranda.

The doorbell chimed again. "Beck?"

"Hello?" She went to the stairs and leaned over the banister. "Who is it?"

"Beck, it's me, Hunter."

No! Was he crazy? She gripped the railing. "What are you doing here?"

"Can you open the door?"

Baby Girl fluttered at the sound of his voice, and Beck stared down the stairwell. "What about 'leave me alone' is hard to understand?"

Hunter banged on the door. "Just open up. Please. You'll understand when you do."

Beck eased down the steps, then leaned against the door before turning the knob. "This better be good."

Hunter stood on the veranda with his arm around an aristocratic-looking woman wearing a designer coat and a pained expression. His wife. Beck recognized her from the credenza pictures.

"C-can we come in?"

"I don't know." She exchanged a glance with the woman. "What's going on?"

"Beck, this my wife, Gaynor. I've told her everything."

She fell against the doorframe. "And you brought her here?" She'd considered Hunter one of the smart ones.

"Beck, please, I'm not here to confront you." Gaynor's confession was a cool breeze, blowing away the dirt and debris that covered Beck's shame, and she felt exposed. "Can we come in?"

"I told Hunter he was under no obligation. I was going to handle this on my own. I'm sorry he brought you into it."

"If you let us come in, we can explain." Hunter sounded like her boss. Her friend.

Beck hesitated, then glanced between them. They looked so eager and anxious. She stood aside, her grip on the knob the only thing holding her up.

Gaynor entered like a curious gazelle, taking in the house with compliments and subtle glances at Beck. She created an impressive and imposing presence.

She was the opposite of her tough, thick-bodied cop husband.

They sat on the couch while Beck perched on the edge of a wingback, the three of them arranged in a triangle of tension.

"The place is gorgeous. Hunter said someone left it to you." Gaynor gripped his hand, slightly trembling.

Beck tossed a visual check to Hunter. "How'd you find me?"

"Your mom. I called, said I needed your new address for work business. I figured if you knew we were coming, you'd hide out, avoid us."

"You're right."

The strain of this impromptu tête-à-tête settled in her neck and crept down her back. What was the protocol for sitting across the room from the wife of a girl's married one-night stand?

Gaynor's gaze drifted to Beck's belly before turning to her husband. "Do you want to start?"

She was even more beautiful than her pictures, with kind eyes and an unassuming manner. Beck sank in her chair, strapped down by guilt. This woman was unworthy of what she'd done to her.

Hunter shifted about, nervous. "I told her, Beck."

Beck tried to sit forward but remained pinned, hidden by the wide sides of the Edwardian chair. "I don't—" She shook her head, unable to speak, unable to look at them.

He was a piece of work. Why hadn't he just kept his mouth shut?

"We were lying in bed one night." Hunter paused to clear his throat. "Reading like an old married couple, when she closed her magazine and out of the blue started talking about children. How we never were able to get pregnant and did we have any regrets. When she started wondering what a child of mine would look like, I couldn't stand the secret for another second, Beck. She deserved better. We've been in counseling since I told her about Rosie's. I figured I'd give our counselor an extra challenge at our next session."

"It was my idea to meet you," Gaynor said.

Beck regarded Gaynor. "Did it occur to you I might not want to meet you?" Then to Hunter. "I told you to walk away."

"We've surprised you, and for that I'm sorry, Beck." She was calm. Irritatingly composed.

Beck never imagined meeting Hunter's wife, but if she had, the scene would not look like this.

"I know this is strange, but once we started talking, we saw the silver lining."

"Silver lining?" Her hand rested over Baby Girl.

"A baby, Beck." Hunter freed his hand from his wife's as if he needed every limb and faculty to speak. "We've wanted children our entire marriage. For twenty years. It was one thing when *we* didn't have a kid, but for me to father a child without telling her? I couldn't do it. Then I got to thinking about the baby and what he—"

"She."

"She deserved."

"Is it a girl?" Gaynor's eyes brightened.

"It's a girl."

"Beck," Gaynor said. "We spent thousands of dollars trying to get pregnant. Nothing worked. Four times the adoption process failed. We finally gave up. Children weren't in the cards for us. But now—"

"We want to raise the baby," Hunter said, clear and strong. Like a lieutenant. "Gaynor would adopt her, but we won't cut you out. You can be as involved as you want."

"You want to—" Beck snapped her invisible restraints and sat forward. "What?"

"We want to raise her." If possible, Gaynor brightened even more. "We always said we wanted a girl first, didn't we?"

Hunter nodded with an emotional hue in his eyes.

On her feet, Beck walked behind her chair, digesting their request. "You seriously want to raise your husband's *love* child." She denigrated the word *love* since it was nowhere on site the night Baby Girl was conceived.

"Yes, I do. *We* do." Gaynor wiped a tear from the edge of her eye and her lips quivered. "I know it sounds unusual, if not a bit crazy, but once I worked through the betrayal it was all I could think about."

"So you've forgiven him? It's all good?" Beck scoffed. "Just like that?"

"I know it seems unlikely, improbable really, but I have someone on my side who helps me. Hunter and I are continuing to work on our issues, but we love each other, Beck. We are in this for the long haul. Your child, *Hunter's* child, will be well loved."

"Gaynor has faith . . ." Hunter tripped over his words as if confessing such a thing were akin to confessing a crime.

"Don't choke, babe," Gaynor said with an easy laugh. "He's still adjusting to church. Beck, I met Jesus and my life changed. I'm not ashamed to say it." Beck ran her palm over the top of the chair, the thick upholstery rough under her palm. She'd love to be *not ashamed*. "He rescued me long before Hunter's confession. I was angry and bitter about being barren. Two years ago when my father died I never felt so empty. My hero was gone. I had his money and his possessions, but I didn't have him. I had a void my family, relationships, and career could not fill. So I went seeking, and about halfway down the road, Jesus waited for me. He took all my burdens and I've never looked back. I didn't know such peace existed."

Beck understood bitter and empty. She'd been there. Felt it most in the years after Dad died. Then owned it as a way of life. As the nucleolus of being a tough cop.

The night she'd brushed up against Hunter, drunk and flirting, she'd battled emptiness all week, aching for a purpose, especially after the sting operation went bust.

The job was not enough, yet it was all she knew.

"She changed," Hunter said. "We were already on rocky ground, then the woman I used to party with was going to church and reading her Bible. She played music I'd never heard before. She forgave me instead of fighting with me."

"He gave me an ultimatum. Jesus or him." Gaynor spoke with clarity. "I said Jesus."

He shot Beck a knowing glance. "That explains Rosie's."

So that's why he crossed the line. His *own* pain and loss.

Beetle whimpered from the top of the stairs. Beck ran up to get him, keeping him in her arms when she returned to her chair.

"Is that the drug dog?" Hunter said.

"Yes, and he just had surgery."

"Isn't he sweet?" Gaynor rose up to pet him. "We had a mini schnauzer when I was a girl. Is he going to be okay?"

"Looks like it." Beck waited for Beetle's back-off growl, but instead he lifted his head and attempted to wag his tail, turning his head so Gaynor could scratch his favorite spot behind his ears. "He doesn't let anyone touch him but me."

"Gaynor is the animal whisperer," Hunter said as she returned to the sofa.

"And a baby whisperer?" Beck said.

"We hope so. If you'll let us."

"So you want to raise the baby? Gaynor would adopt her?"

"But you can be involved at every turn," Hunter said.

"You could be Mama Beck," Gaynor said. "We thought we'd tell her the truth from the beginning."

"How will that work? Two mothers? And, Gaynor, how could you not look at her with resentment? That she is his blood but not yours?"

"I don't know, but I have no fears whatsoever. Some things are thicker than blood. If I adopt her, she'll be mine. As for the two mothers, I suppose we should have time with her alone the first few years."

"Then she won't know me."

"Then we'll talk it out." Gaynor's desperation supplied all the answers.

"You really want me involved? Isn't that like having another woman in your marriage?"

Faith or not, Beck couldn't believe Gaynor didn't hate her just a little bit.

"When Hunter first told me, I was hurt and angry. I actually left him for a week. I cried for three days straight, asking God to help me understand, to forgive. I woke up the fourth morning realizing there was another side to this story. A child for us to love." She turned to Hunter. "Can you give us a moment?"

Beetle raised his head, growling as Hunter crossed between Beck and his wife, stepping onto the front porch. The dog squirmed to get down when Gaynor moved to the chair next to Beck.

"I met Hunter when I was sixteen," she said, reaching down to pet Beetle. Little traitor. "He worked at a lake resort restaurant where my family had a summer home. He was tall and gorgeous with those wide shoulders and an incredible smile. He stole my heart with one glance. I've loved him ever since."

"That doesn't answer my question. How will you feel about this, me, another woman in your marriage, in your family?"

When Beetle rested his head on Gaynor's foot, she wanted Hunter and his wife, along with their request, to fly back to New York and never contact her again.

"To be honest, I'm not totally sure how I'll feel, Beck. I've never been in this situation before. But my heart tells me, 'Go for it.' I have a master's degree in international relations, but my number one idea to help the world has always been to raise children with purpose. I've worked at the UN. Traveled the globe. Nothing fulfilled me like the idea of family. Now with the hope of . . . of raising Hunter's child . . . Am I talking too much?" She scratched Beetle's head again, diverting her attention from Beck.

"I suppose I'm trying to communicate forty-two years of desire." She sat back, arms folded. "I was one of those girls who wanted nothing but to be a mom. Hunter and I were going to be the couple who ran the PTA, coached the kids' sports, and traveled the world on summer vacations. You know Hunter as a decorated, tough cop, but he's kind and gentle, more trustworthy than recent behavior would suggest. He'd make an amazing father. Please, if you could—"

Beck shrugged away from her plea and reached down for Beetle. *Whose side are you on?* He strained against her arms for a moment, standing on her legs, wagging his tail for Gaynor. Then settled down, digging his nose under Beck's hand.

"I don't know, Gaynor." Her eyes ran with tears when she finally looked at the other woman. "I should but I don't."

Yet weren't they offering Beck exactly what she wanted for Baby Girl? A mother and a father who loved each other, who cared about their marriage, who would love her and keep her safe.

On top of everything, the woman Beck had wronged was *pleading* with her.

"I-I don't understand why you don't hate me."

"What was it Dr. King said about hate? It's too great a burden to bear? I'd rather love and forgive. Plus, to be honest, I am thinking of the child, what's best for her. She's the innocent one here."

Beck scratched Beetle Boo's ears, Gaynor's words shaking her concept of love and forgiveness, of what the future might hold.

She never imagined a both/and option.

"Have you thought about what *you* want to do?" Gaynor said. "What are your plans?"

"Some. But I ignored the pregnancy until a few weeks ago. Now that you're here, I feel as if time is a locomotive," Beck said. "How would this work between us? Would it be formal? In writing?"

"Formal, yes, but with you as part of the equation. But until you decide, you are in the driver's seat. We are merely asking you to consider us."

"Well, that's a bit scary. I hate driving."

"Really?" Gaynor relaxed and returned to her seat on the sofa. "I do my best thinking behind the wheel." She folded her hands in her lap and studied the paintings on the near wall. "I imagine what we are asking you to do is hard, and a little crazy, but please give it some thought. We can provide a good home. My mother still lives on the horse farm she and Dad bought just outside of Boston. Our daughter will spend her summers there learning to ride. We'll give her music and dance lessons."

"It sounds lovely. My dad died when I was fourteen, and it's impacted me in ways I'm still discovering. In fact, I can't remember him at all." She brushed the dew from her eyes. "I really want Baby Girl to have a father."

"Hunter wants to be a father. He wants to make memories with her, help her with her homework, teach her to ride a bike, then how to drive. I remember when my dad taught me. Oh my word, what a hoot. Lots of screaming and laughter. My family also has a summer home on Nantucket, and I have so many happy memories there."

As she went on Beck saw, knew, Gaynor could give Baby Girl one key thing she could not—a family history. A past. Memories. Stories of summers on the lake, canoeing, hiking, and catching fireflies.

She heard herself ask, "What do you remember about your father and those summers?"

Gaynor's eyes glistened. "Mercy, I don't know. If there's one thing there's a hundred. We hiked every morning. Swam every afternoon. Flew kites. Rode horses. The summer I turned fourteen Dad and I hiked every day. We talked and talked. He tried to imitate bird calls." She pressed her fingers over her laugh. "I swear one morning he had a fifteen-minute conversation with a red bird. When the bird flew away Dad said, 'He's concerned his kids will never leave the nest. He and the missus want to fly to Florida for the winter.' Ah, he had the best laugh."

"Sounds perfect," Beck said, seeing a future for Baby Girl she'd not imagined before today.

Gaynor would be an amazing mom with her poise and charm,

her sophistication, family history and memories, and rich, detailed stories.

"I will love her, Beck. I promise. With my whole heart. I won't keep you from her. I just ask that you let *me* be her mother."

"But we both know I'll end up more on the outside than in. I suppose I would have to be. Otherwise we'll confuse her."

"Maybe. At first. We'll have to establish ourselves, but we want you to be involved."

"I think that's improbable, Gaynor. For both of us. What if I decide to raise her myself? Will *you* want to be involved then?"

Her eyes filled. "Yes, of course. We want Hunter to be her father no matter what. Would you allow him to do that?"

"Now that you know, yes. I'd really like that for her," Beck said. "To be honest, Gaynor, a month ago I might have said yes to your proposition without much debate. But the woman who left me this house also left me some resources for reasons I don't understand, and it's making me consider how Baby Girl is included in this blessing. I'm sorry I can't be more decisive but—"

"I know what we are asking is hard. It's why we asked in person." Gaynor glanced at the front door as Hunter peeked in. "Three people will love her."

"Am I allowed back?"

"Yes, babe, come in. We've just decided the baby's name will be Rutabaga Cauliflower."

His expression made Beck laugh. "Do you think we'd be that cruel?" And just like that, with a plural pronoun, she and Gaynor were on the same side.

"Is that a yes then? We're taking her?"

"Not entirely." Gaynor reached for her bag. "Don't pressure her, Hunter."

"You'll let us know then," he said.

"Yes, one way or the other."

The conversation faded, and Hunter brought Beck up to speed on precinct news and his transfer date. Then there was nothing more to say.

As they walked to the car, Beck leaned against the porch post, her hands locked behind her back. *Say it.* But the confession remained stitched to her tongue. *Say it. Deserve what Gaynor's given you.*

"Gaynor." She blurted out her name because something deeper than Beck's pride wanted free.

"Yes?"

Beck met her halfway, under the lowest branch of the sprawling, ancient oak. "I-I'm sorry. So very sorry."

Gaynor's eyes welled up with watery pain. "You're forgiven, Beck. And I can't help but think something beautiful and wonderful will come from all our mistakes."

Gaynor Ingram was lovely, everything a little girl deserved in a mom.

When they'd driven away and she was alone, Beck collapsed on the couch cradling Beetle against her middle and wept into a throw pillow until all her guilt has washed away.

CHAPTER TWENTY-TWO

EVERLEIGH

The knock came late as the house rattled with the crashes and flashes of a spring thunderstorm.

Mama had retired early to read and Everleigh paced the living room, restless. She'd not be able to sleep until it passed. She had the radio console tuned to the Big Go, listening for alerts. As long as she heard the announcer's voice, she was safe.

But if the sound turned static—

When the wind battered the front porch, she flipped on the porch light, surprised to find Don standing there with his hat in his hand. Rain fell in a thick sheet through the light of the street lamps.

"Can I talk to you?" He motioned to the door, his shiny blue suit rumpled, the lines around his eyes deep and defined.

"Come in, come in. I'll make some coffee."

"I hope I'm not interrupting anything." He dropped his hat on the kitchen table and shook the water from his suit coat.

"Please, interrupt." She took his hat and set it on the table by the door. "The storm had me, well . . . What are you doing here? Wasn't today the big merger? Would you like a piece of cake? Tonight was dessert night."

"With coffee?" He followed her to the kitchen.

"Of course."

When she reached for the plates, his arms came around her waist and he nuzzled her neck. "I've missed you."

She moaned, his touch intoxicating. "Don—"

He turned her about, pressing a kiss to her lips and the plates against her breast. She barely heard the thunder rattling the windows.

"Where's your mother? I don't want her to break in on me making love to her daughter."' His breath brushed past her cheek and down her neck.

"She's . . . she's in bed, reading. Probably asleep by now." Everleigh shivered as dormant, tingling sensations spread through her. "Did you drive down from Dallas just to kiss me?" How lovely if he did.

He tapped his forehead to hers. "Would that be a bad thing?"

She gripped the plates. "I-I don't think so." He made her weak, a puddle of desire, aching for his touch, his devotion and love.

An announcement came over the radio, a voice telling Waco to take cover and precaution.

"This extreme storm comes with dangerous lightning."

Don kissed her again, his broad hand massaging her waist. When he stepped back, he took the plates and set them on the counter.

"You don't like storms, do you?"

"No."

Don leaned against the counter, watching as she sliced the dessert. "The twister still haunts you?"

She reached for the coffee pot. "How do you take your coffee?"

"Cream, no sugar."

She carried the coffee and cake to the living room on a tray and sat with Don on the sofa. His presence steadied her, made her believe everything would be okay.

"Tell me about Rhett." Don reached for his coffee. "What happened the day of the twister, Everleigh?"

She set down her cup and saucer to take up her cake. She felt like she must do something while speaking even though the twister story was rather simple. She'd told it over and over.

"Everyone had gone to town. I was home alone. It started raining and I heard a crash so I ran down to the cellar."

"That's the story everyone knows, Everleigh." He turned her chin to face him. "I want to know your story, sweetheart." He tapped her chest, over her heart, and she shivered at his intimate touch. "What happened here?"

She stared at the cake in her lap. "I try not to talk about it. People mean well when they ask, and certainly enough time has passed, but it robs me, Don, takes away a little bit of my memories and dulls the feelings, the joy *and* the sorrow. So if I answer, pour out my heart, lay myself bare, what can they say or do? Give me a pinched expression with a 'Had to be hell'? Or worse, tell me a comparative story like we're in a contest of tragedies. Meanwhile I know deep down they're praising God that they didn't walk in my shoes."

He set his coffee on the table and pulled her into his arms. She cradled her head on his shoulder, cake still in her lap. "I'm not just anybody, Ev. I'm not *people*. I'm the man who loves you."

"How can you say love, Don? We've only just begun a relationship." She liked the way his hand fit perfectly over her shoulder. The way his thumb stroked her arm.

"Can't explain it myself, but it's true. I see how you take care of your mother, your loyalty, your patience. How you work hard to provide. How you soldier on when this was not the life you wanted. I also see how stunning and sexy—"

"See." She nudged him with her elbow and laughed. "The sensible shoes do it every time."

"I'd never mock your memories, Everleigh. Or try to minimize them. I'm not asking you to forget Rhett." He raised her face to see his. "I'm simply asking you to love me too."

"I'm not sure you want to hear it *all*. I'm not sure I want you to know."

"Then I'm not the man I think I am. The man I want to be." He kissed her cheek. "But I understand. Don't do anything you don't want to do, Ev, but nothing will change how I feel about you."

Between his confessions, the soft lamplight, the low melody on the radio, the scent of the coffee mingling with his end-of-day cologne, Everleigh exhaled her story. The one only Mama had ever heard.

"I saw the rain coming so I went inside. I had chores to do in the kitchen. That night we were celebrating plans to build our new house." She laced her fingers through his, hearing his heartbeat between her words. "And I was three months pregnant."

He rested his head on top of hers.

"I'd brought the last of Lola's puppies inside because the barn was too far. They were terrified. The one Rhett and I were going to keep was the runt of the litter. Rocco. The wind shook the house. I thought it was just another Texas storm until I heard a shatter upstairs. Then the terrifying howl." She pressed her hand to her ear. "I can still hear it sometimes. The rest is a blur, but I ended up in the cellar with the puppies." Sitting up, she set her cake down and stared across the room into a hazy, fading scene. "After the storm, I couldn't move. I was so scared. But I knew Rhett would come. All I had to do was wait."

He said nothing. Just pressed his hand to her back.

"I fell asleep, waking up when someone called my name. Rhett! Finally he was home. The cellar door opened, flooding the dark with light. It was Duke Cartwright from the neighboring ranch."

"How long were you down there?"

"About ten hours. Everything was gone, Don. The house, the barn. Everything that said Circle A Ranch. On the vast prairie there was nothing left but the foundation and the cellar door. Even with all trucks circling and the Cartwright girl giving me a sandwich, I was utterly alone."

He kissed and caught the single tear slipping down her cheek.

"Mr. Cartwright said, 'We need to know what you want to do.' I had no idea what he meant. Two more trucks pulled up with the bodies. Rhett and his parents. I fainted. Next thing I know, it's a gray May day and I'm burying my husband, my hopes and dreams.

"I actually forgot most of that year for a while. But over time, the memories returned." Everleigh glanced up at Don. "That's why I don't share, why I treasure what I have. I don't want to lose them again. Rhett was so young. Only twenty-five. Doesn't he deserve to be remembered?"

"Yes, he does." Don sat forward, gazing at his shoes, then back at Everleigh. "Did you lose the baby too?"

"Please, Don," she whispered, pressing her cheek to his shoulder. "Isn't it your turn to talk for a while? How was your day? The Dewey-Callahan merger?"

———

DON

"I resigned from the dealership today, Everleigh. I told my dad I'm going into the insurance business and moving to Florida with George Granger."

"My word, Don. That had to be difficult. What did he say?" She sniffed and pulled herself together.

"He hit the roof. I think every ear within a mile radius heard him. I realized my desire to please him, honor him, was more out of fear than respect. He's a great guy, my old man, but he's prideful. It's his way or no way. We ended up in Dewey's office with Dad telling Standish to promote me to sales director so I wouldn't leave. However, Standish took the news standing up. Said he was disappointed but a man had to follow his own path. You should've seen Dad's face. Stunned. Then Standish made a big show out of patting him on the back, saying something like, 'It's just us old guys now, Hal. Let's show these young whipper-snappers what's up.'"

"When do you leave for Florida?" She ran her hand over his leg. If she didn't stop he was going to jump from his skin. It was her innocence that baffled and excited him. She'd been a married woman. Didn't she realize certain things, well, lit a man's fuse?

"By the end of the month."

———

"I'm proud of you." Her words, her smile, was worth all the tension and heartache. "Your dad will be, too, when he thinks about it."

"We made a truce, but he's not pleased." Don took her hand. "Are you proud enough to go with me?"

A low, echoing thunder hovered over the house and muffled her soft, "Go with you?"

"It's a small beach town outside of Jacksonville. Fernandina Beach. I've seen pictures. It's beautiful, Ev. It's a chance to start over, leave the pain behind."

She pulled away from him, gathering their coffee cups and cake plates.

Don met her at the kitchen sink. "I'm asking you to marry me."

"But we . . . we barely know each other."

"We know enough and I love you. We can make a go of it."

"You're asking me to leave Waco? It's my home. I've never lived anywhere but here. And what will Mama do? Besides, Don, what's for me in Fernando, Florida?"

"Fernandina Beach. And I'd like to think I'm there for you."

"Don, sweet Don, you are the best thing—" She turned away from him. Well, that was it. He'd leaped too soon. Too far. "But my life is here. Mama needs me."

"What if I need you?" He hurried into the living room for the box he left in his jacket pocket. "Everleigh Novak Applegate . . ." He bent to one knee, raising the box. "Will you—"

"Stop." She cupped her hand over his, covering the ring box, her eyes brimming. "Don't make me answer."

Slowly he stood, tucking the ring in his pocket, feeling the heat of her sweet rejection. "I thought we had something—"

"I'm sorry, I am. I do adore you. But listen to yourself, Don. You want to marry me? You can't mean it. You've not even given the beautiful Florida women a chance. I'm sure there's one waiting for you who is not as burdened and encumbered as I."

He searched her face. "I've never been more sure of anything in my life than this moment. Call me crazy, but I think you love me too. I can't replace what you had with Rhett, but I can give you the things he promised. A home. Children. Security." He bent to kiss her cheek. "All my love."

"I suppose I didn't make it clear when I told you my story, but, Don, I *am* the memory vault for Rhett and the Applegates. *That's* my lot in life. To make sure they are never forgotten."

"I'm not asking you to wipe them from your life. I can't see how staying put here, working at Reed's and living with your mama, is preserving their legacy."

"Don't you see? I'm the living memorial because I allow nothing to override it."

"Well then, I'm sorry for you. And me. Because that sounds like a death sentence for someone so young and beautiful. You're only thirty, Everleigh. Life is long. Don't live with one foot in the grave."

"Perhaps you should go." Her soft command barely penetrated the hot, stale air of the kitchen.

So, that was it then. He grabbed his hat and let himself out, pausing in the doorway, glancing back at Everleigh, who stood at the sink with her back to him.

"Everleigh?"

She raised her head and without a word, turned around, snapped off the radio and the kitchen light before disappearing from view.

———

EVERLEIGH

"Ev?" Mama was at her bedroom door. "Was that Don?"

"You know it was, Mama. Don't pretend you weren't listening."

The house was quiet, too quiet now that the storm had moved on.

———

"Your daddy always said we built the walls of this house too thin. Did he propose?"

"I stopped him before he made a formal request." She changed from her pumps into her sneakers and snatched up her handbag from the dressing table.

"I know it's hard, but it's for the best," Mama said. "Where are you going?"

"I don't know." She moved down the hall, each step churning the disturbance in her belly.

"It's nearly ten o'clock. Everyone is asleep save for the honky-tonks. Everleigh—"

She removed the car keys from the hook by the door. "I'm just going for a drive. To clear my head."

When she slipped behind the Studebaker's wheel, she let her tears go.

She thought she'd changed because she dyed and styled her hair? Because she bought a few new dresses? Because she purchased a red convertible on a whim?

But nothing had changed. Nor would it ever. Not where it mattered, in her heart and mind. She was still the scared twenty-three-year-old pressed against a cold cellar wall waiting to be rescued.

So why had she refused Don? Tonight he opened the cellar door and extended a hand. He offered her love and a chance to come up out of the dark.

But she clung to the headlights of the trucks delivering her husband's dead body, and Don's offer only reminded her of what she'd lost.

While she claimed to be a living memorial to the lives of the Applegates, she was really nothing more than a weak body of flesh who wore her tragedy like a badge of honor.

And she was terrified it would happen to her again.

God, I cannot. I cannot.

Disasters had lasting effects. Ripples that ran through a person's soul and mind, leaving marks no one could see. Fears. Worries. A life locked down.

Lifting her head, she dried her face with the back of her hand and backed out of the garage, letting her heart set her course.

The rain started up again as she crossed Lake Waco and Everleigh snapped on the wipers.

With each mile, the road became her lullaby, and she followed the headlights as they swept over the curves and bends in the road.

Just as the wipers swished away thick raindrops, the lights flashed over a familiar crossbar and swinging sign.

The Circle A. Home.

Yes, here's where her memories remained. On this barren ranch and in her barren heart.

Everleigh swerved right and careened under the wrought-iron-and-beam signpost, the only remains of the ranch. Mr. Cartwright had found the Circle A sign about a mile away a few days after the storm. He rehung it the day of the funeral.

So far, the banks let it be.

The Studebaker dipped and rose in the ruts of the long, over-grown driveway. The car slid over a patch of thick wet grass and fishtailed. Downshifting, Everleigh tried to drive forward, but the tires spun without traction.

"Come on." She shifted into first and tried again, but the spinning tires only dug a new rut in the neglected path.

She squinted through the wet windshield as she leaned for the glove box to retrieve the flashlight. Opening her door, she stepped out just as the clouds twisted, wringing out another sheet of rain.

"What do You want from me, huh?" God and His storms.

Everleigh stepped toward the back of the car to see what was going on with the tires when her foot slipped, tossing her down a small incline and into a wet puddle.

She pushed herself up, wiping her front. But she'd lost her flashlight in the fall, and without the aid of her headlights, the night was completely black.

"Is this funny, God? Watch ol' Everleigh fall in the mud? Did You send Don to propose? What was Your intention? I won't forget Rhett." She balled her hands at her side, her shoes providing no support as the wet earth gave way. "I won't."

A gust of wind drove the rain into her, soaking her hair and her skirt.

"Heaven, please, help me." Without a coat, she began to shiver. The car was still running so as long as she had gas, she could hover in the front seat.

Leaning into the side of the car, she inched along toward the door, but she slipped again and toppled down the incline.

Shoving up, her hands submerged in water and mud, she wept as the rain drove down. "Why didn't You let me die with Rhett?"

Wouldn't it have been easier? But no, she'd had *him* in her belly. Their son. A gift from God. A beacon of hope. But what did she do? Give it away.

Everleigh crumpled forward, touching her face to the mud and rocks, curling her fist around the watery, grainy mixture. "I deserve nothing."

Water ran down her hair and collected around her lips, slinking down her chin. The chill rattled her bones.

Her memories weren't here, on this wasted land. And year by year, her memories of Rhett faded in the light of time.

"God, please, help me."

She startled when a hand touched her shoulder. When a strong arm lifted her up. Don. Dear Don.

"The memories, they aren't here, Don. They aren't here."

"Everleigh, shhh, everything is going to be all right."

CHAPTER TWENTY-THREE

BECK

When she entered Bruno's office, he was on the phone. He waved her over to an old, overstuffed club chair.

Situating Beetle on her lap, she examined the space while he paced. It was small but serviceable, probably once the offices or even living quarters of the store below.

The hardwoods needed redoing and the large pane window a wash, but he had a desk and a credenza bearing a row of books, awards, and an amazing number of old cell phones.

"You've got a player there at Western Michigan I'd love to visit," he said, staring out the window. "All right. Yeah, Florida is my stomping grounds but—That's a good point." He turned, making a face at Beck. She laughed. "Thanks anyway."

When he hung up, he sat at his desk with a groan and ran his hand through his dark, thick hair. "You'd think I'd never done this job before."

"Dead ends?" She casually stroked Beetle's ears, finding the silky touch comforting.

She'd been turning over Hunter and Gaynor's proposition for two days and she really wanted to talk to someone. She was glad when Bruno called asking her to meet him for lunch.

Since his downtown office was close, she walked over.

"Three years ago these college-pro liaisons were calling me."

When his phone rang, he picked up. "Mark, how're you doing? Thanks for calling me back. Your kid Wylie Jones—Did he? Then good luck to him. Can't say enough good about the guys at Sports World."

Beck walked over to the credenza and picked up one of the phones.

When Bruno ended his call she said, "Pretty impressive pile of junk. What is this?"

Bruno swiveled around. "Weird hobby. I used to jail break them for friends. Then people started giving me their old phones so I could fix them up, give them to charities. When some of them became collector's items, I held on to them. Mom found that one for me the other day." He pointed to an ancient car phone.

"Ever find juicy messages on any of them?"

"Mostly business stuff. 'Bill, it's Tom. Did you get the 84XJY forms? We need them for the conference call.'"

Beck laughed. "So glad I'm not in that world."

"I had one really sad one, though. A girl called her boyfriend after he'd broke up with her and man, she was so, so sad, crying, reminding him of everything they'd promised each other. That one stuck with me for a long time."

He reached again for his ringing phone, mumbling something she couldn't make out as he answered.

She examined the awards propped on the credenza's top shelf. Watershed Rookie of the Year. Something called A Sporty Award. And an impressive one. Sports Agent Million Dollar Club.

"I've been working on it, Coach. But these things take time. Sure I called him. Didn't he tell you? Yeah, I'll be in touch."

He dropped his phone to his desk. "That guy is driving me nuts."

"Who?"

"Coach Brown, Tyvis's coach. The JUCO kid I told you about when we met Calvin. They're friends."

Beck listened as he ranted about his reputation, and how, sure, he felt sorry for the kid who'd worked so hard, but how many times did he have to say it? No NFL franchise would touch him. And why was he the only agent Coach Brown kept calling?

"Maybe because he sees you have something the other agents don't. Maybe he knows you're the only one who can make some NFL team consider Tyvis. Isn't that what makes you a good agent? Anyone can sell a Calvin Blue. But only the best of the best can sell a Tyvis Powell."

He got up from his chair and came around the desk.

"That would be akin to selling snow to an Eskimo."

"And the best salesman convinces him it's sunshine."

He laughed, then drew her to him, kissing her without hesitating or checking her eyes for permission. Like his lips belonged on hers. So she tasted of his soul and drank from the well he offered.

Beetle grumbled and snipped until Bruno backed away, hand over his new Sweat Equity shirt pocket.

She stepped back, touching her finger to her lips, feeling woozy. "R-ready for lunch?"

Bruno trapped her between his arms as he rested his hands on the front of the credenza. "I'm falling for you."

"Bruno, can we just . . . not do this now? I really wanted to talk to you about something."

Oh, but she wanted what he was offering. His love. His heart. His affection. Something she craved now that her hunger had been awakened.

But there was the proposition. And Baby Girl.

"Yeah, sure." He sounded disappointed as he grabbed his phone and keys. "Where do you want to eat?"

"First," she said, tapping his arm. "Give that JUCO kid what he wants and needs. Don't make him feel like a nothing. Be generous. If I've learned anything on the job, people can be selfish and stingy for no reason. Or out of fear or greed. What does it hurt to just give freely? When there's nothing in it for you?"

"Free? I'd have to pay for his training and living expenses. About thirty grand."

"So? This kid Tyvis has no one in his corner but his coach. Do you respect this coach? Does he know what he's talking about? Why can't you give him a chance?"

"I'm a one-man shop, Beck. I've got fifty set aside for Calvin, and about twenty for travel for the year, which believe me is nothing."

"Then I'll pay for him."

"What?" he scoffed. "You'll pay for Tyvis?"

"Everleigh left me money. I want to do something good with it." Baby Girl kicked, agreeing with Beck's decision. "Let me help. Please."

"You don't even know this kid."

"But I know you." She did. Not with her mind and memories but with her heart. "You can sell him. I know you can."

"You're too much." He drew her to him with a hungry kiss. She eased down to the chair beside his desk as he made a call. "Scott Fuller, Bruno Endicott. I need a favor for a JUCO kid. Can you work him into your Pro Day tryouts?"

Then he called Tyvis and put him on speaker. She teared up when Bruno gave him the news. Let a trickle run down her cheek when Tyvis broke down, unable to talk.

She loved Bruno's sports-agent swagger as he filled Tyvis in on what to expect in the days ahead.

"You've got a Pro Day at UCF. End of March. You'll only get a quick look from the coaches and scouts who show up, but it's something. I'll start calling some front offices, see if we can get you an on-site visit. Maybe the Buccaneers or the Jaguars. Give me a few days to arrange your training. Do what you have to do on your end to get down here. Welcome to Sweat Equity, Tyvis."

When he hung up, he kissed her again. And she let him, caught up in the celebration and letting herself feel without raising barriers. If only for a moment. "Now that felt good. Really good."

"The kiss or calling Tyvis?"

"Both, but I think the call might be in first place for now." He grabbed her for another kiss. "Nope, now that kiss is in first place."

"You're too easy, Endicott."

He laughed and asked if Jo's 2nd Street Bistro sounded good.

"Can we talk about something first?"

"Sure." He sat on the edge of his desk, giving her his full attention, a dancing light in his eyes. "I feel like a million bucks. I'll pay you back, Beck."

"Let this be my investment in Sports Equity. The money was a gift to me. I'm more than happy to make it a gift to you. Please."

"Thank you." He couldn't stop kissing her. "Now, what's on your mind?"

"Hunter was here. The baby's father." She realized she'd been carrying Beetle this whole time, so she set him on the floor. He hobbled over to the big window and peered out, barking. "With his wife."

"Whoa." He leaned back. "How was that?"

"Weird. She's forgiven me. Us. Then they asked if they could raise her, Bruno. Baby Girl. Gaynor wants to be her mother."

"What do you want?"

"I don't know. At first I thought they were crazy, but the more she talked, the more I thought she would be a great mom. She's beautiful, well-educated."

"So are you."

"She has memories of her childhood."

"So, you'll get yours back one day." Bruno slid off the desk and reached around for his desk chair. "I feel it just like you feel I can do something with Tyvis. But memories don't make a woman a mom. I watch you with that dog and I know you have everything it takes to be a brilliant mother."

"It's not the memories, it's the family history and tradition. Bruno, if they raise her she goes immediately into a two-parent home with a dad and a mom. Gaynor's family has money, so Baby Girl will want for nothing. I know they'll love her. They've never had children of their own and—" Beck glanced toward the window where Beetle looked down on Centre Street. "Wouldn't it be such an amazing gift? I feel half like Gaynor deserves it for what I did."

"First of all, it would be an amazing gift if that's what you want to do. But isn't the core of forgiveness that the debt is paid? You don't owe the offended anymore."

"I guess." Beetle Boo wandered back and curled at her feet. "They said I could be involved. We'd tell her the truth from the beginning, but I see complications ahead. I'd have to fade from the picture."

"Can you raise her and have Hunter be her dad?"

"Yes. They want him to be a part of her life. But, Bruno, Gaynor was special. I can't help but think maybe she would be best for Baby Girl. It's weird, because now I have some money. I could raise her on my own, but when I saw them together . . . Shoot, even Beetle Boo likes her."

"Whoa. What's your cop sense telling you?"

"It's all jammed up on this one." She laughed softly and brushed a slow trickle from the side of her cheek, then sobered, seeing compassion in his eyes. "Tell me what to do, Bruno."

"I can't. But I'll stand by you no matter what you decide. I will."

"Then I think"—she breathed deep and squeezed his hand—"I'm going to let them raise her."

Bruno stood and pulled Beck into his arms, and she dropped her burdens there as tears washed her decision through the cracks and crevices of her heart.

———

DON

June 1960
Fernandina Beach

"Well? What do you think?" George walked the length of the downtown Fernandina Beach space they'd rented over the haberdashery.

With fresh paint, rented office equipment, and a state-of-the-art phone system, the first phase of the Granger & Callahan Insurance Brokers was underway.

Don stood in what would be his office area, separated from George by a partition. The scents of salt and pine blew through the raised window.

"The new secretary starts next week. She's just out of school so I think she'll be perfect for us. We can grow in this together."

Don checked his watch. "I have a Realtor appointment at one. And don't forget, I'm heading to Texas next week to close out my apartment."

"You think your folks will ever get over it?" George seemed fascinated with a new pencil canister and a box of yellow No. 2s.

"Eventually. It's like Mr. Christian said, I have to trust my father's love."

Dad's parting words cut deep.

"Insurance? What kind of man sells insurance for a living? A huckster, that's who. It's a shell game, son."

"Not what I'm doing, Dad. I want to help guarantee an accident or disaster doesn't leave anyone destitute. And sure, make a little money."

"Cars is where it's at, Don. Everyone needs a car."

"Everyone needs insurance. For crying out loud, we have one of the largest insurance companies in the South right in Waco."

Words, words, words. By the time he headed east for Florida, Dad refused to speak to him. Mom wept, wondered what they'd done to deserve such treatment. But she kissed him good-bye and handed over a basket of goodies for the road.

"I'll work on your father."

"What about Everleigh?" George said. Now he was sharpening the pencils with an electric sharpener.

"We're talking every night. I can't mention marriage, but I'm hopeful."

"Women. Took me two years to win over Lila." George clapped

him on the back. "Come on, let's grab some lunch before your appointment."

After a quick sandwich and cold coke at the drugstore, Don walked two doors down to the Realtor, Jason Gill.

"You said you wanted something special." Jason motioned for Don to walk with him. "That your girl lost her first home to a tornado."

"She lost everything to a tornado," Don said.

"I've got the perfect place right here in town. Built in 1895 with expert craftsmanship, it's in good condition. Sure to win your bride's heart."

"I'd like to do a bit of that myself."

Jason laughed. "Send her pictures of this place. She'll change her tune. Got a nice yard. Oversize lot. Lots of trees."

Don slowed his steps as they approached an historic Victorian. Two stories with a large wraparound porch, gables, and turrets. It was lovely. But if he couldn't convince Everleigh to marry him, he'd have to rattle around that big ol' place by himself.

"Number 7 Memory Lane. What do you think?"

"It's beautiful." Don said. But now that he was standing here, on Memory Lane, he wondered if he'd gone too far.

Everleigh and Rhett were going to build their house on a Memory Lane. Would she see this as his attempt to replace Rhett, wipe out her memories?

"The seller is eager so I think we can get a good price. Didn't you say you have a cash down payment?"

"Y-yes."

"Let's take a look at her. There are two floors. Living rooms on both. Downstairs can be more of a parlor. Upstairs more of a family room, what with every Tom, Dick, and Harry having a TV nowadays. Sometimes more than one. There're four bedrooms with a servant's quarters off the kitchen and a butler's pantry. Each bedroom has its own bath, which you didn't see when these beauties were being built. There's a small third-floor turret, which would be perfect for you."

"What's the asking price?" Don swerved around a little boy of about six or seven riding his tricycle at top speed. "Whoa there, tiger."

"My feet start pedaling so fast I can't stop." He offered Don a toothless grin.

"Used to happen to me too." Don crouched down and rang the tricycle bell. "Do you live here? In this big house?"

"I live there." He pointed to a ranch style with a pretty awning across the street. "I'm Lou Jr." He offered Don a firm little-boy handshake.

"Nice to meet you." Don regarded him for a second while Jason showed his impatience with a throaty, "Ahem."

There was something about the boy he recognized. Something familiar.

"Lou Jr., you know you're not supposed to cross the street." A woman stepped from the porch of the ranch house, dishtowel in hand. "I hope he's not bothering you."

Lou Jr. took off pedaling. "Coming, Mama."

"He was no bother—" Don walked toward the edge of the yard. "Aimee?"

"Mr. Callahan?" Jason called, his Realtor smile fading. "Do you want to see the house or not?"

"I so appreciate your patience, but that's my cousin." Don jogged toward the street. "I didn't know she was here."

"Don?" Aimee met him in the quiet, narrow lane with a hug. "What a small world." She wiped her hands on her apron, eyes glancing toward the boy. "Lou Jr., don't ride too far. Yes, the edge of the sidewalk like Daddy told you."

"You live here?"

"We do. Moved here six years ago. Lou got a job with the naval yard. What are you doing here?" She glanced back at her son. "Very good, sweetie. Come back this way now."

The boy whipped the bike around and raced toward home, making motor noises as he sped past them.

"I'm starting an insurance business with George Granger. Do you know his family? He had a relative offer him some space downtown—"

"You're leaving Callahan Cars? Your dad must be beside himself."

"He's not too pleased with me, no. But he merged with Dewey Motors in Dallas and Mom is getting her dream house in Castle Heights."

"Very posh." She watched as Lou Jr. dumped his tricycle and ran into the house. "W-where are my manners? Would you like to come in? I just made cookies."

Lou Jr. walked through the front door, carrying two cookies in each hand. "Here you go, mister." He raised his right hand to Don.

"Why, thank you."

Aimee brushed her hand over his blond hair. "LJ, this is your mama's cousin, Don, all the way from Texas."

"I used to live in Texas."

Aimee peeked at Don with a slow smile. "Daddy and Mama used to live there, that's right. He was born here but he gets confused."

"Mr. Callahan!" Jason said. "Please, you're not my only client."

"Of course, how rude of me. Aimee," he said, handing the cookie back to LJ. "I need to look at the Victorian, but could we meet later? I'd love to catch up and actually eat one of your cookies."

A few years older than Don, Aimee was the daughter of Mom's cousin, Roberta. She married while Don was in high school, and between the war and college, he knew little of her life other than tidbits Mom shared from a Christmas card.

"How about dinner? Lou would love to see you. Is seven too late?"

"Seven it is." He felt kissed by the divine to run into family in this small, faraway community. It felt like home already. "I'd better go see this house."

"It's beautiful. You'll love it. Oh, could we end up neighbors?"

Don crossed his fingers. "I hope so."

The house was spotless, in excellent condition, with upgraded electrical and plumbing. *And* he'd be across the street from his cousin.

"The seller's asking fifteen thousand, but she'll consider your best offer," Jason said as they walked into the spacious, bright master bedroom. "I've got a full set of photos in my office if you want to show them to your intended."

Don gazed out the bedroom window into the green yard, the wind twisting the swinging Spanish moss, then across the road to Aimee's place.

This was home. He knew it. Seeing Aimee was the cherry on top. One day Everleigh would know it too.

"I'll take it, Jason," he said, offering his hand. "Make an offer for fifteen thousand."

CHAPTER TWENTY-FOUR

EVERLEIGH

The shop was quiet, not even the radio playing, as Everleigh and Connie hovered over the workbench, finishing up a large wedding order.

The groom's father was scheduled to pick up the arrangements at nine a.m., but the bride had changed the order one more time late yesterday afternoon.

To Everleigh's relief, Mr. Reed had coaxed the bride back to her original order, because getting the orchids she wanted would've taken all night.

"Speaking of weddings," Connie said. "What's going on with you?"

"What makes you speak of weddings and me in the same breath?" Everleigh reached for a rose and pricked her finger. She snatched her hand back and wiped the blood on her apron. "Did you get Mr. Childers's order done? We may have to send them on the delivery truck. I'm not sure either of us has time to run by there today."

"Waiting in the cooler. And don't avoid my question."

"Nothing is going on." Though she kept Don's almost daily letters tied together with a ribbon.

"I still can't figure why you didn't run off with him."

"I'm still figuring why I told you he tried to propose. You keep bringing it up. Are you done with the bridesmaids' bouquets?"

Ever since Don rescued her from the cold, muddy ground, she woke up thinking of him, eagerly awaiting the day's mail to see if he'd written.

On Saturdays when he usually called she paced anxiously about the kitchen until the phone rang.

She couldn't help it. But she was also desperately trying to cling to Rhett and everything she promised him the day she laid him to rest.

I won't forget. I won't.

Connie set one of the mother's corsages in the cooler, then leaned on Everleigh's work table. "So why aren't you chasing him? You fixed up your hair and makeup, bought a new wardrobe. Purchased that car—"

"So I made a few changes. Doesn't mean I want to run off and get married." Everleigh tied a silk ribbon on the bride's bouquet.

"Surely you're not planning on living with your mother the rest of your life."

"What about the flowers for the altar?"

"You saw me working on them this morning. You can't avoid me." Connie tapped her on the shoulder. "Why do you have one foot in the grave?"

Everleigh slapped her hand on the work table. "Because that's where my husband is! Why can't people understand that? If he's done living, then so am I."

Connie pressed her hand over her open mouth. "Oh, Ev, he wouldn't want you to think that-a way. Not a'tall. You can't *live* half *dead*."

"It's the only way I know how to be. And I'm not half dead because I don't want to marry Don Callahan. Please, just drop it." Everleigh filled a bucket with soap and water and reached for the washcloth. "If you're done with the corsages, let's get this place cleaned up."

"Fine, I'll drop it. But I have one question. Do you think if you died Rhett would be living like you do? No sir, he'd be remarried by now and raising a family."

"You don't know anything about Rhett or what he'd do." The volume of her reply pushed Connie into the workbench. "Just leave me alone, please."

At work, Connie pushed, tried to get Everleigh to step out and change. At home, Mama pulled, pulled, pulled. Wanted her to stay the same, keep the routine. Join the old-girls club.

"The girls were wondering if you wanted to join us for bridge? I was in a club at your age."

"Ev, I signed us up for the Christmas committee. First meeting is Tuesday night."

Mama entangled her tighter and tighter into her world. Then she came home two nights ago to find Mama had set out Everleigh's wedding photo on the breakfront next to hers and Daddy's. She snatched up the picture, staring at two people she didn't know anymore.

"Mama, what's this?"

"I was just missing your daddy and Rhett. That's the only photo we have of your wedding and I thought, why hide it away?"

That was all it took to draw Everleigh back to her old self. Into the familiar ruts.

Connie returned from the utility room with the mop and bucket. "I'm sorry, I can't leave it. I'm your friend. Why do you think you can't move on? Really now. It's not just about Rhett being dead or forgetting him. There's more to the story. Come on, Ev, dig deep and tell ol' Connie."

"Will you shut up?" She tossed a discarded rose at her coworker, beaning her square in the chest. Soft red pedals fluttered to the ground. "I am done talking. This is my life, Connie. My decisions. Do you hear me?"

Everleigh crashed through the shop's back door and into the alley, careening into the chest of the man himself, Don Callahan.

Shaking, she stepped around him to exit the alley for the street. "Oh my word, you scared me. What are you doing here? Why aren't you in Florida?"

"I came home to close out the apartment. I told you in my last letter. Everleigh, what's the matter? Are you all right?"

"I'm fine. Why would anything be the matter?"

He fell in step with her. "Did you see the pictures of my new house?"

"Yes. It's lovely. I hope you have a happy life there." At the corner she wasn't sure where to go. When she started to cross the street, Don gently restrained her.

"What's wrong?"

"What's wrong?" She pulled free from him. "Connie's wrong. Mama's wrong. You're wrong. I don't *have* to move on. Why can't I just stay here in my own world and live the way I want? Why do I have to *let go*? Why do I have to fall in love again? Who says being a wife and mother is the only way to go? You know one day Mr. Reed will make me a manager."

The street lamps had just started to shine through the dusty remainder of the pink summer sunset.

"That's great, Ev." Don leaned against the exterior of the bakery next to the flower shop. "But only if it's what you want and not what you fear."

"This is what I want." She folded her arms, watching the traffic drift through the yellow stoplight.

"Okay, then . . ." He started to move away and she wanted to cry out, but she wrangled her voice into silence. "Just know my feelings haven't changed. I love you. I bought the house for you. It seemed meant to be when I heard the address was Memory Lane."

"Is that supposed to be funny?"

"Not at all. Not at all. And I don't mean to replace Rhett. Just seems maybe the good Lord is giving me a chance to pick up where he left off."

At the curb, he looked both ways and stepped off.

"I can't betray him again, Don. I can't."

He returned to her, the scents of coffee and baking bread wafting on the soft breeze.

"What are you talking about?"

She tightened her jaw, resisting the shivering. "Our child." The confession echoed against the red brick. "I gave him up, Don. This is the kind of woman you say you love. Weak and selfish. He was born early with complications, and someone suggested to Mama a nice two-parent family would be better for him. A couple who was in a good place instead of being raised by two crushed widows."

His eyes narrowed. "You said someone suggested—"

"Your mother, Don. She was the one who said we should let him be adopted."

He slapped his hand to his chest. "My mother?"

"She recommended an agency. No one would ever know. The records are sealed. Don, I don't even know where he is or how he fares. Rhett's boy. I gave his living legacy away. That is why I must maintain his memories.

"You'd think maybe I'd gotten myself sideways with drink or pills in the aftermath of it all. But no, I work and wear sensible shoes. This is my coping mechanism. To just exist. You still want to marry me now?"

"I think I want to marry you all the more." He tried to hold her, but she held herself aloof.

"Out of pity?"

"Pity? You think my love is so conditional that when a financially strapped, lonely, hurting widow allows her child to be adopted by caring parents, I'd walk away? For Pete's sake, Everleigh, I never met a woman who tried so hard not to love or be loved."

"I let him go, Don. I let Rhett's son go." The sorrow of regret burned more than any other kind.

"Everything's going to be all right." When he held her this time, she let go. He rocked her side to side, holding her as she wept.

When her tears finally dried, she patted the wet spot over his heart and took the handkerchief he offered.

———

"I made a mess of your shirt."

"You can ruin a dozen shirts if you'll just say you love me. Will you give me a chance?"

She shook her head. "I feel so conflicted." She pressed his hanky under her eyes. "Don, if I said yes I'm not sure what I'd do if I lost a man I loved. Again."

"They don't have tornados in Florida."

"Then a plane crash or a car accident. Sickness. I couldn't bear it, Don."

"You won't lose me. And, Everleigh, I think you just told me you loved me."

———

BECK

Beck pulled her clothes from the dyer, scooped Beetle into the basket, and carried it upstairs. He wagged his tail as he dug into her warm clothes.

He was on the mend. She had a final vet appointment for him before flying home.

One week from today and she'd be back on the job, in the gray and cold.

Her conversation with Bruno about Hunter and Gaynor lived in her psyche. She'd made her decision and decided to tell them after she arrived home but wanted to tell Mom before.

Today's big to-do was *Call Mom*.

Since deciding Hunter and Gaynor would raise Baby Girl, she felt relieved. A burden lifted. Which made her confident in her decision.

Dumping the basket onto the bed, Beetle frolicked through her clothes until she set him down on the floor.

"I need these folded, not wrinkled."

———

His claws clicked over the hardwood and he moved to his bed in the little hall.

Bruno's Happy Tomato question had surfaced often in the last day. *"Why did you forget?"*

Putting her clothes in the dresser, Beck mused over the only answer that made sense. The amnesia protected her from something ominous.

At the bedroom window, she peered down to the yard, glancing between the garage-barn and Natalie's. Her car was in the carport, a sight that always put Beck at ease.

The rest of Memory Lane appeared normal. No dark Mercedes. Which reminded her. She'd not heard back from Hogan.

She'd made a point of meeting Mr. Colter one afternoon. He was not the man she saw at the Happy Tomato. Or on the lane. And Mr. Colter's Mercedes was blue.

Laundry done, Beck sat in the rocker, propped her elbow on the sill, and dialed Mom.

"Beck? Is everything okay?"

"Yeah, fine, don't sound so worried."

"I'm an ER nurse. I worry. Are you ready to come home? Did you open the box?"

"I meant to but haven't had the chance."

"I imagine you're busy doing *nothing*." Mom sarcasm was shallow. "Are you tan? How often do you go to the beach?"

"Not tan. Beach once. I don't know why I haven't open it yet and by the way, I'm pregnant." Just rip the Band-Aid right off.

"Hunter?"

"W-what? Hello, Mom?"

"I'm here. I asked if Hunter is the father. I knew you were pregnant. I'm a nurse, for crying out loud."

"Why didn't you say anything?"

"I was waiting for you."

"How'd you know it was Hunter?"

"I've been around the NYPD my entire adult life and I've never heard of a lieutenant calling to check on the address of a cop on vacation. Especially when he can text or call her himself."

"He showed up here with his wife the day Dad's box arrived."

Mom's gasp said it all. "That must've been something. Are you all right?"

"Yes, well, all things considered. They want to raise her. I-I think I might take them up on it. They are a good couple and—"

"It's a girl?"

"Yeah, a girl."

Mom was silent for a long moment. "Are you sure you want to give her up?"

"I'd be involved just like Hunter would be if I raised her and married someone else. But, Mom, Gaynor would adopt her."

Beck recounted the Ingrams' desire for children and lack of success and how Gaynor's faith journey led her toward forgiveness.

"I'd be giving her a huge gift."

"I'll say. But, Beck, this is your child."

"And Hunter's. Why can't the father raise her as well as I can? He has a wife. I have a dog."

Mom was silent. Then, "This is breaking my heart, Beck. My first grandchild." She sighed. "But if you choose to let them be her primary parents, then I'll support you. I love you."

"I'll be involved, which means you'll be involved. She'll have more family than she can stand."

"True, and if you include Flynn's side, she'll be sick with aunts and uncles and cousins."

"Thank you."

"Don't thank me yet. Once I've had time to think about this . . . Beck, your father's first grandchild."

Beck sat up. She hadn't considered that angle. "Yeah, I guess so.

You know, Bruno asked me something interesting. He said, 'Why do you think you forgot?" Not why don't I remember, but why did I forget?"

"How's that different?"

"Not remembering feels more accidental. But forgetting is purposeful. Was there anything going on with me after he died?"

"We've been over this, Beck." Dishes clattered in the background, followed by the sound of running water. "Nothing more than usual for a young teen girl who'd just lost her father." She heard Wyatt in the background, looking for something to eat. "Beck, I honestly have no idea, and I've got to get dinner. This is my night to cook. But you call me if you need anything. Seems I taught you to feel like you have to handle everything on your own. I'm sorry."

"You taught me independence. I love you, Mom. Tell Flynn and Wyatt hi for me."

"I love you too. Now open that box. Text me what's inside."

"Will do." She'd retrieved the box from the bedroom floor and paused by the narrow third-floor stairs when she got a text from Hogan.

Got a name on the plate. Call me.

CHAPTER TWENTY-FIVE

EVERLEIGH

It was much too hot for a garden party. Even in September. But Mama insisted she attend.

"It's for Hampton Bing. Your old classmate. Can't you support his town council run?"

"I planned to vote for the other candidate."

"I don't care who you vote for in the booth, you're attending his party. You can't let all that blonde hair go to waste. Wear your pink dress. Leslie Bing will be dressed to the nines."

Of course, the former Waco High head cheerleader and wife of a rising politician would look the part. Leslie was born for it.

Everleigh didn't know whether to envy or pity her.

Envy, because she still had her husband and child. Pity, because she was destined to share Hampton with the public the rest of her life.

She showered because it had been so warm in the shop, then tried to pick something garden party–like from her closet.

The pink dress was ruined. She'd worn it the night Don scooped her up from the mud and rain. If she dwelled on it, she felt his arms under her legs, his shoulder under her head.

The blue dress would have to do. Or she could put on a pair of shorts and go to Cameron Park and read a book.

"Everleigh?" Mama peeked in as she searched for a pair of stockings. "Just wanted to make sure you were getting ready."

"Will you ground me if I don't go?"

Everleigh sat on the edge of her bed, hooked her stocking to her girdle, and stepped into the dress.

At her dressing table, she reached for her brush, knocking over the bottle of perfume that held Don's letters against the mirror. He'd been writing all summer. His latest letter from two days ago sat on top.

. . . I've not given up on you, but George's wife set me up with a friend of hers. Sweet girl, but I couldn't get more than two words out of her. She made an art out of batting her eyes. How are you? What's going on in your world? How's the flower shop? Did I tell you I'd been in touch with Tom Jr.? He's thinking of vacationing here. I miss you and think of you daily, Ev. Write soon.

Forever,

Your Loving Don

Her hand trembled as she slipped the letter into the envelope. When she looked up, her reflection revealed her regret. But she'd made her choice. Now she'd live with it.

She put on her heels and started out of her room, then circled back for Don's letters, clutching them to her chest as she passed through the kitchen.

"I'm off, Mama."

"All right." She got up from her chair. "Don't you look nice. Cinda is picking me up for dinner in an hour, but I'll be home early. Do you want me to press your white linen for church tomorrow?"

The white linen, the one that made her look like a bride?

"I'll just wear my brown suit."

"You wore that last week."

"Good-bye, Mama." Everleigh started out the back door. "Have fun with Cinda."

"What have you got there?" Mama met her by the table and tugged on her arm, angling to see the letters.

"Trash."

"Aren't those Don's letters?"

"You've been snooping in my room again."

"Goodness. I see them against your mirror when I'm dusting. Mind your tone. I don't appreciate being called nosey."

Their eyes met. Mother and daughter. Partners in widowhood. "I'm throwing them away."

Mama released her. "Are you sure?"

"Yes, I'm sure."

At the tin can by the garage, Everleigh dumped the letters without watching them fall. When she slammed down the lid, she sealed her action. Sealed her decision.

Don Callahan was not the way forward. She'd write him, encourage him to move on, find another woman to live in the house on Memory Lane. Take more dates arranged by George's wife.

Leslie Bing was the first to greet her at the senior Bing's lush and sprawling estate. Daisies, fan flower, and bitterweed flourished in the garden while large ornate pots around the pool hosted Mexican sunflowers.

"This is beautiful."

"Please, my mother-in-law is a flower magician. She can make weeds bloom. But look who I'm talking to. Mama Bing won't order from anyone but Reed's and she prefers you do her arranging."

"That's quite a compliment."

"There's Devon Murphy." Leslie waved. "Doesn't she look adorable? Expectant mothers shouldn't be so cute. I was the size of a barn." She touched Everleigh's arm. "I'm glad you came. You are just the bees knees with your Kim Novak hair."

"Les, darling, come meet Agnew Smith." Hampton beckoned his wife with a nod toward Everleigh.

"On my way, sweets. Everleigh?" She motioned to the crowd. "Enjoy." Then she leaned close. "Welcome back. I thought we'd lost you forever after, well, everything."

Leslie buzzed away, chatting to every soul she passed while Everleigh walked free and clear to the punch table.

"Make mine a double," she said to the stiff, formal server behind the crystal bowl.

Then she stood between three conversations. To her right, a group of men comparing golf scores. To her left, three women comparing potty-training techniques. In front of her, two couples discussing the weather. A storm was brewing somewhere.

Storms were Everleigh's cue to move on.

She circled the crowd, recognizing only a few faces. Most of them were business types wanting to get their hooks into Hampton early in the game.

"Everleigh Novak, as I live and breathe." Porter Pyle clapped his arm around her.

"Applegate. It's Everleigh Applegate." She twisted away from his embrace.

"Where in the name of all that's good have you been hiding?" Porter shot her an Elvis-like grin to go with his Elvis-like pompadour.

"Porter, I sold you a bouquet of flowers last Valentine's. For your mother, I believe."

"Naw, naw, that was a dowdy-looking gal with a thing—" He stuck his hand on the back of his head. "Like my granny." He leaned back to glance at Everleigh up and down. "She *sure* wasn't you."

Porter's attention attracted other men at the party. Unattached men. She was about to retreat when a guitar picker and his singer hopped on a makeshift stage and started singing.

Porter grabbed her around the waist and yanked her into a two-step, his clodhoppers just barely missing her toes.

Willie Davenport offered his arm for the next song, then Artemis, whose last name Everleigh couldn't remember.

When she'd danced with every single man at the party, including Hampton's ninety-year-old widower grandpa, who tried to kiss her, she grabbed her handbag from the coat room and ran out the front door.

"You're home early," Mama said. "How was it?"

"I was the token single gal. Danced with every unattached man, including Hampton's granddaddy."

"Well, at least you had fun."

Did she? Have fun? "I'm off to change for bed. Want some popcorn while we watch *Bonanza*? How was dinner with Cinda?"

"Fine, but she's got every ailment under God's golden sun. She went on and on about so many aches and pains I started to feel them myself." Mama followed Everleigh down the hall, chatting, hanging up her blue dress as Everleigh slipped into her pajamas. "Do you think any of them will call for a date?"

"I hope not."

"Why not? It's good to go out once in a while." Mama eased the closet door shut. "I've not said so lately, Everleigh, but I want the world for you. I want you to be happy. We've been a team for a while now and—"

"We make a good team, Mama."

"You are my good girl." The phone rang and Mama darted down the hall. "Mrs. Bentley might need a ride to church."

Everleigh sat at her dressing table to remove her earrings, pausing when she saw a bundle tucked between the mirror and her bottle of perfume, bound by a thread of Mama's pink yarn.

Don's letters.

"Oh, Mama." Everleigh pressed the bundle to her heart, listening as Mama assured Mrs. Bentley they'd be along to collect her in the morning in plenty of time for church.

CHAPTER TWENTY-SIX

BECK

Sitting on the narrow steps up to the third floor, Beck texted Mom the contents of the box.

> One pencil canister with a dozen pencils and pens.
> Six Happy Meal Toys. Mostly Fred Flintstone.
> One picture of Dad, you, and me on Miss Everleigh's porch.
> (I look about twelve.)
> One Nokia cell phone.
> One bottle of aspirin.
> One really old package of Wrigley's Spearmint gum.
> One pair of scissors.
> One ancient Walkman and headphones.

Beck held up the picture of the three of them. Dad's eyes were blue and kind, partnered with an easy smile. Mom, so young and pretty, and completely unaware of what awaited her.

Beck's happy expression would change in a few short years as well.

Setting the picture back in the box, Beck carried the phone to her spot in front of the TV. Bruno was flying home from Mississippi today, and the phone would be a nice icebreaker for the news Hogan delivered yesterday.

BRUNO

She waited for him on the veranda with Beetle Boo curled in her lap. He stepped out of his Honda, a hitch in his step as he made his way toward her.

She was beautiful. Not just the way her hair fell over her shoulder or the curve of her breasts through the blue hoodie. But the softness in her face and the way she mothered that dog.

And how the steel in her eyes the night of Miss Everleigh's memorial had become a feather.

But he had to watch himself. She insisted on going home. Insisted her life was too complicated to consider loving him.

"Kind of cold to be sitting outside, isn't it?" He sat next to her, his lips buzzing to kiss her but mindful of resistance to any further intimacy.

So instead, he attempted to scratch Beetle behind the ears, but the pup would have none of it. He raised his head and snarled.

"You think he'll ever like me?" Bruno said.

"Sure, the day before I leave. Speaking of, will you and Natalie keep an eye on the house for me?"

"Of course. Does that mean you're coming back? I'd like it if you *lived* in the house."

She grinned, tapping him shoulder to shoulder. "How was Mississippi and Tyvis?"

"Good actually." He picked a dry leaf from the porch step and crumbled it between his fingers. "He's very grateful. So am I. He said to tell my partner thanks." He glanced over at her, holding up his phone. "And I just got this—"

"I'm not your partner. I just offered to help a kid out."

"Sure you're my partner. In fact—" He reached into his shoulder bag and took out a newly minted Sweat Equity shirt. "I got you a large for now. After the baby I'll get you a new one."

"Bruno—" Surprise blended with tenderness molded her expression. "Thank you, but I'm not really your partner." Said with more truth layers than Bruno wanted to admit. "Besides, you said you were paying me back."

"I know but, Beck, why not be my partner?" *Why not marry me? Make my fourteen-year-old-boy dream come true?* "Instead of paying you back, I'll give you a percentage of whatever Calvin earns."

She tipped her head in surprise. "Calvin?"

"Read." He tapped the phone's screen.

"'Bruno . . . my man . . . ,'" Beck read aloud. "'I'm in. After what you did for Tyvis—'"

"He signed?" She threw her arms around him. "See? You showed Tyvis kindness—"

"You showed him kindness."

"—and you got the one you really wanted." She held her hand up for a high five. "Way to go."

He held her gaze. "I couldn't have done it without you, Beck." He leaned toward her, but when she didn't respond, he turned the other way. "Stu's flying me to Tallahassee tomorrow."

"Baby Girl and I are excited." She patted her belly. "Did you call teams on his behalf yet? Or whatever it is you do?"

"Not yet. It's early, but I've got some teams in mind. But, Beck—" Bruno brushed her breeze-tossed hair from her face. "Brace yourself. He's not going to make it to the NFL."

"Maybe. But what if he does? What if believing in him changes the tide? You helped him go for his dream, Bruno. Just think how the world would be if everyone gave a hand up to someone else. Look how it changed things for you and Calvin."

"You can't leave, Beck. You're my good-luck charm, the love of my—"

"I have to go, Bruno. You know I do."

"Stay here with me. In the memory house."

"What about her?" She grabbed his hand and placed it on her swelling middle and his chest fluttered.

"I'll love her too." A small kick pumped against his warm palm. His heart thundered.

"Will you?" She raised her hand to his face but pulled away before touching his cheek. "Why would you take on me and Baby Girl, Hunter and Gaynor while building your business? You don't need us slowing you down. Who are you, Bruno Endicott?"

"The man who loves you." Hooking his arm about her, he drew her in for a kiss, the first of many to come. Or perhaps his last.

"Bruno," she said, low. "Do you think you have feelings for me because you remember me from back in the day? Because Miss Everleigh is gone and now I'm here? Because I'm part of your happy childhood memories at the memory house?"

He pressed her hand over his heart. "Beck, it's like we've never been apart."

"Yet we have, Bruno. There have been other men in my life." She set her hand in her lap.

"Obviously."

"And women in yours." She nudged him. "You're too good of a kisser for it to be otherwise."

He made a face, not bothering to hide his wide grin. "I like hearing that from you. To be honest, I haven't had a lot of girlfriends. A few. Mom made sure I had enough Jesus in me as a kid that I'd never be comfortable with the love-'em-and-leave-'em lifestyle. Besides, I think I've always been looking for you." Her hazel gaze fell into his and for a moment, neither of them moved. Even Beetle stopped his soft snoring.

Beck broke away first. "I have something for you."

That's right, she invited him for chili and a movie. "Let's do it. I'm hungry."

"Me too. But first . . ." She pulled an old cell phone from her pocket.

"Wha—A Nokia 8810? Where did you get this?" He held the piece up to light. "This is a collector's item."

"It was in the box of Dad's stuff Mom sent down."

"This was your dad's phone? Did it spark any memories?"

"No more than pictures or Mom's stories. You can have the phone, by the way."

"Are you sure?"

"What am I going to do with it? Not when I'm in the presence of an antique cell phone aficionado." She offered a mock bow. "You can do that jail heist thing with it."

"Jail break."

"Exactly." He turned the phone over for closer inspection. "The condition is pristine."

"Should be. He hardly ever used it."

On his feet, Bruno reached for his bag and offered Beck his arm. "Feed me."

She patted the board next to her. "Sit for one more second."

"What's up?" He loved this moment. That she thought of him. That she trusted him with her dad's phone. He'd extract Dale Holiday's outgoing voice message as a keepsake of her father's voice.

"I have to tell you something," she said, "and I'm not sure how to go about it."

"Just say it." She looked serious.

She breathed in and adjusted Beetle Boo in her lap. If he ever found a way to advance their relationship, this dog would *have* to like him.

"What's going on? Something with the baby?"

"Your dad's not dead, Bruno." The blunt words tumbled from her lips.

"What?"

"Your dad. He's alive."

He shot off the veranda. "That's not funny, Beck."

"I know and I'm not laughing. Remember the black Mercedes? I ran the plates."

"Mr. Colter? He's not my dad. He's a sweet old man. Lives right there." He pointed to the house two doors down from Mom's.

"Mr. Colter drives a blue Mercedes."

"Since when?" He walked across the yard, ducking beneath the tree branches, looking toward the older man's place.

"I had a friend on my squad run the plate. The car is registered to a Stone Endicott. His address is in White Plains, New York. So I did some snooping on the internet. He's hard to find but he's out there. A partner in an investment firm."

"My dad?" He couldn't look back at her. If he did he might just lose it. "Stone 'The Rat Gut' Endicott? Alive? No, he's dead, Beck. For crying out loud, his urn is on Mom's mantel."

"Was he born in October of '53? In Miami?"

He nodded.

"I broke a few rules and regs to get his social and found your parents' marriage certificate. But, Bruno, I couldn't find a death certificate."

"How can he be . . ." *Settle. Breathe. Think.* "Are you telling me my mother has lied to me for seventeen years?" He shook his head, snatching up his bag. "She wouldn't. Not about this. Beck, I don't know *who* you found, but it wasn't Stone Endicott. Was his middle name Aloysius?"

She winced and nodded.

He swore, punching the air, and walked toward his mom's.

———

EVERLEIGH

It was all over the news. Hurricane Donna made landfall in Florida as a category four with winds up to 145 miles per hour.

Connie turned up the radio when the weather report came on. Everleigh hummed to herself, trying not to listen, but the announcer's voice filled every crevice of her being.

Storm, storm, storm.

Her trembling hands dropped Mr. Childers's order of roses, pink alstroemeria, and white waxflower.

"Careful, Ev," Connie said.

"*. . . 150 miles per hour, the storm is expected to weaken slightly as it makes landfall.*"

"My granny was a girl in Galveston the year of the Great Storm." Connie snipped the ends from the orchids she was arranging for Mrs. O'Hare. "For the rest of her life, she never went to the shore, and every time the wind blew she had my granddad board up the windows."

Everleigh snatched up her car keys. "I'm off to lunch and Mr. Childers's."

"Can you bring me a sandwich?" Connie pulled a dollar bill from her pocket. "Roast beef on rye." The bell dinged as a customer entered. "Afternoon. Welcome to Reed's."

In her car, Everleigh settled the flowers on the passenger seat and tied a scarf on her head. It was still convertible weather in Waco and she enjoyed the sun on her shoulders.

The radio popped on as she as she started the car.

"*. . . expecting Donna to head northeast across the state, exiting between Daytona Beach and Jacksonville. If you have family or friends*

---

in the Sunshine State, make sure they are prepared for this deadly storm. Once again, Hurricane Donna—"

She snapped off the radio, her hands shaking as she shifted gears. A hurricane . . . in Florida. Where Don lived. On Franklin Avenue, she nearly ran a red light.

Get ahold of yourself.

She changed the station, searching for music, then cut the radio off all together. But the idea of a major wind blowing over her Don bloomed and consumed. By the time she pulled into Mr. Childers's drive, her bones rattled with fear.

The widower met her at the kitchen door wearing his same dark slacks, stained striped shirt, and tattered blue sweater.

"Come in, come in." He took the box from her and dropped it on the kitchen table next to last week's order. And the week before. "I was just reading my paper."

It'd been a few weeks since Everleigh took this run, but surely Connie hadn't let the flowers go unattended.

"Mr. Childers, don't you want to put the flowers in a vase?" She followed him through the swinging door into the living room.

"Got vases of flowers all over the house." He motioned to the one on the living room table. Another vase of dry, dead flowers sat in the dining room. "Darn things die so quick."

"Not if you water them. Tell your housekeeper to tend them." Everleigh set aside her keys. "Do you have a newspaper I can spread over your table? I'll dispose of the old and set out the new."

"I'm finished with this one." He handed her the morning *Tribune.* Hurricane Donna Ripping Through South Florida

She turned the paper over and spread it out on the table. South Florida. See, there was nothing to worry about. Don was in north Florida. A long way from the storm.

She dropped the dying, rotten blooms on the newsprint. Take

that, Donna, and go away! Then she washed out the vases and filled them with fresh stems.

"If you don't want the flowers, you should cancel, Mr. Childers. Or we can reduce your order to once a month."

He sat in his chair watching her work at the dining room table. "My Mae loved flowers. Couldn't afford them when we got married, but I promised her she'd have a bouquet a week someday."

"She was as lovely as any bouquet." The white-haired, elegant Mae Childers had been Everleigh's Sunday school teacher and spoke of God with such joy.

"That she was. Loved her at first sight. Can't believe she's gone. But you know a thing or two about loss."

"I know you have to *water* dying things from time to time." She paused at her own words, pierced by the subtle truth.

"That you do. Are you watering yourself, Mrs. Applegate?"

"Certainly." She fixed a smile and carried the first fresh vase to the living room.

"I'm old. Lived my life. But you're young." He chuckled. "If I were a few years younger . . ."

"Mr. Childers, you flatter me. Do you have any more vases?" She thought she could salvage a few flowers from the older boxes for an arrangement in the front hall.

She and Connie would just have to come in every week and tend his order.

"In the kitchen. So, what do you make of this hurricane? It's all the weatherman can talk about and we're a thousand miles away. I swear those TV folk love a good disaster."

"Since when has the weatherman ever gotten anything right?" Everleigh collected one more vase from the hall closet.

"They're starting to send up satellites to check on the weather. Come a day when they can see a rainstorm days off."

"Oh please, Mr. Childers, who can predict the rain? Are we God? You've been reading Ray Bradbury books again."

"Nevertheless, the National Weather Bureau has done a fair job predicting Donna. It's a good thing, Mrs. Applegate. People need time to prepare. Can't help but think back to '53 when that tornado ripped through—"

"There." Everleigh held up a fresh arrangement for him. "What do you think of this? Isn't it beautiful? Your wife had exquisite taste in flowers."

She walked the vase to the hall table, happy not to reminisce about the storm of '53, then cleaned up the mess of dead flowers and carried them out to the trash cans, crushing the newspaper declaring Hurricane Donna doom over eggshells and coffee grounds.

"Please, Mr. Childers, remember to add water by Tuesday," she said when she returned to the living room where he'd just lit up his pipe.

"Are you stuck, Mrs. Applegate? I see you dyed your hair, bought a new work dress, but here you are, still a widow, delivering my flowers."

"I'm not stuck. Stuck means I can't get out. I can get out."

"Can you?"

"Anytime I want."

"I heard a rumor you had a fellow wanting to marry you."

"You heard a rumor?" Everleigh propped her hand on the back of a dining room chair and another on her hip. "I'd like to know who's going around gossiping about me."

"Connie said you had a fella."

Of course. Connie. She would wring her neck.

"Well, if that's all, Mr. Childers, I'll be off." Turning on her heel, Everleigh's dramatic exit was ruined when the heel of her shoe fell through the floor grate.

"Have mercy," she said, bending to retrieve her shoe. But the heel was wedged between the narrow louvers.

"Been meaning to replace that." Mr. Childers chuckled, rising from his chair to help. He grasped her shoe and with a backhand, then forward twist, set the red heel free. "Here you go, young lady." He winked. "Don't get stuck now."

"I am not stuck." Everleigh dug her foot into her shoe and headed for her car. "Good afternoon, Mr. Childers."

Stuck. What did he know? She wasn't stuck. She could go anytime she wanted. But as she backed out of the driveway, listening to yet another storm update, she knew more than anyone, she wasn't going anywhere.

She couldn't be any more stuck if she were buried six feet under.

CHAPTER TWENTY-SEVEN

BRUNO

"Mom? You here?" The kitchen smelled of tomato soup and grilled cheese.

"Upstairs," she called. "Finally decided to tackle my closet."

Bruno took the stairs two at a time, ducking under the dormer wall as he entered her room. "Is Dad dead?"

"What?" The garment in her hand slipped to the floor. "Of course he's dead." She stooped to pick it up, wadding it into a ball and stuffing it into a garbage bag.

"Let's not dance around this, Mom. You lied about Dad, didn't you? He's alive."

"Bruno Endicott, I don't have to stand here and—Who do you take me for anyway?" She picked up a pair of shoes, examined them in the light, then set them back in the closet. "I thought you were having dinner with Beck."

"Mom, look at me." His adrenaline had settled enough for a modicum of rationale to return. "Did you lie about Dad?"

She yanked a yellow dress from the hanger and held it against her. "What do you think? Too young for me? Not a good color for my skin? I never felt good in this."

"Mom, stop." Bruno jerked the dress from her hands and tossed it on the bed. "I want the truth. Did you lie about Dad?"

"Could you be more specific? Are you asking if he *was* dead or if he *is* dead?" She twisted her hands together, turning away, gazing out the window.

"Mom!"

"Okay, okay, he's alive. At least last I heard. But it's been a few years. He could be dead now for all I know."

Bruno boomed, swearing against the wall and the ceiling, crushing his angry words under his heel as they fell to the carpet.

"You are unbelievable. You lied to your own kid about his father's death? Who does that?"

Mom spun around, shaking, her face red. "Yes, I lied. But I did it for your own good. Better to have a dead father than a deadbeat one who disappointed you over and over, who never showed up when he said he would, who forgot birthdays and Christmas, who owed me thirty-five thousand dollars in child support. Yeah, you bet your life I *killed* him."

"Just like that?" Bruno snapped his fingers. "You killed him off to make life easy for you. He was out of your hair and you didn't have to look at your sad, rejected kid. Is that it? Did you think of me? How I'd feel? I cried myself to sleep for a month."

"You think I couldn't hear you? It broke my heart. I *cried* over you. But I finally had a hope, Bruno." She tapped her chest. "That sooner or later, you'd heal, find some closure, and stop thinking you were a nothing because Stone Endicott couldn't keep a promise. Because the older you got, the more he treated you like the competition and not his son. I never, ever understood why he had to put you down." Mom growled. "I can still hear his condescension."

The room spun, his reality tilting, as he crashed through his emotions, sorting and tossing everything from anger to compassion, pitting his self-righteousness against hers.

"I have no words. I literally have no words." His phone pinged, reminding him he had a call tonight with the Dallas Cowboys about Calvin.

"I have to go. I have a call . . ."

"Bruno, wait." Mom held his arm. "H-how did you find out? I mean, it's been a secret for seventeen years. Stone has never even approached the barrier—"

"Who's in the urn, Mom? Mrs. Acker's husband?"

Mom turned away, mumbling.

"Speak up, I can't hear you."

"Ashes. Ashes from Mrs. A's fireplace."

"Unbelievable." He turned to go, but about-faced. "I trusted you. If anyone could shoot straight with me, it was you."

"Who told you? My sister? I knew she couldn't keep a secret!"

"Aunt Joy knows?"

"I had to tell someone. I needed help pulling off that small, private memorial."

"Do you hate him that much?"

"For hurting my boy, yes, I hated him. But it took prayer, *lots* of prayer to forgive him, and I have, Bruno. Really, I have."

"How does God feel about your *little* lie?"

"He's not pleased."

"So why didn't you tell me the truth? Fess up?"

"I considered it a few years ago. The first time I saw you on ESPN I was terrified Stone would contact you. When I had the accident and you came home, the boat was sailing peacefully. Why rock it? How did you find out?"

"Beck. She kept watching that black Mercedes slinking around—"

"Mr. Colter?"

"His car is blue. She ran the plates. It was Dad. He lives in New York. Did you know?"

"No." Mom dropped to the side of her bed, her brown curls frizzing around her face.

His phone pinged another reminder. He really needed to go. He started for the door then spun back to Mom. "How did you get him to go along with it?"

"Gave him a get-out-of-jail-free card. I wouldn't hold him to any parental responsibilities, including child support, if he'd go away. Get out of our lives. I was free, you were free. The plan wasn't to kill him off initially. But then I knew you'd start asking questions, wanting to call him, see him—"

"And he agreed to this plan?"

"Not at first. He didn't like the dying part. But he had no roots here, and my family was glad to see the back of him when we divorced. Then his father died and his mother moved to Colorado to be near her sister. That's when I saw my way clear to pull it off. He resisted at first. Then I offered to forgive the thirty-five grand he owed in back support."

"At least we know he has a price."

Mom met him in the doorway. "Bruno, you know I would *never* hurt you. But all I saw was a boy turning into a young man with an angry, broken heart. Why couldn't your dad see it? Especially when he wanted it so much for himself?"

"Want to know a fact you left out of your scheme?" Bruno said, feeling the seconds tick closer to his call. He needed this call. For Calvin. And he wanted to be calm and composed. But his heart was broken and spilling over. "The fallacy in your grand plan? Hope. Sure, I was disappointed every time he missed a visit. Or called to say, 'Something came up. See you next time, sport.' I hated him at times. What'd I ever do to make him treat me like an annoying neighborhood kid? He called me a *nothing*, Mom. He made me feel like a *nothing.*"

"Exactly! Bruno, you are making *my* case."

"But as long as he called, even to say he wasn't coming, at least he called. He hadn't forgotten our number. I had the promise of 'one day' or 'next time.' Next time he'll come. Next time things will go better. Next time we'll find something clever to talk about. One day I'll get my license and drive over to see him. One day we'll drink a beer together as men, as father and son. One day, by some miracle, we'll actually have a relationship. That's what I hoped for, Mom. That's what I promised myself every time a visit didn't go my way or every time he canceled." He charged her with his pointing finger. "But you, in your *stupid* wisdom, decided to take it from me because it was too painful for *you*. I can't even look at you right now."

He banged into the door on his way out, cracking the knob against the wall. Outside, he walked blindly to his car, ignoring his head, his heart, and the trilling of his phone.

———

BECK

She didn't know if he'd ever forgive her. For two days she debated if she'd done the right thing by telling him. But it was done, so no looking back. If she'd honed any skill it was not looking back but pressing forward.

She didn't sleep the last two nights. He told her he loved her and she told him his mother had been lying for seventeen years.

Last evening she finally texted him. Lorelai Gilmore's boldness with Luke inspired her.

Everything okay?
Busy.

Then this morning when she took Beetle out for his morning constitutional, she caught Natalie on her way to work. Beck called to her, but Natalie slammed the car door and backed down the driveway so fast she almost hit poor Mrs. Rover and her slow-moving Camry.

This afternoon she tried to nap, but she was restless. What if Bruno never spoke to her again? The idea wrecked her. Even *Gilmore Girls* season five provided no distraction.

She fixed a light dinner, but the food tasted bland and she swallowed without chewing.

———

Washing up the few dishes at the sink, gazing out the window, her attention landed on the fire pit.

A wave of unusual sentiment—baby hormones?—made her want to knock the leaves and bugs from the dried logs by the garage-barn and build a fire.

She'd sit outside under the clear night sky and find a way to make her world right again.

Oh, Bruno, I miss you.

She worked the fire pit until the flames could live on their own. Back inside, she found an old blanket in the servant's quarters, scooped up Beetle, then dusted off a weather-worn Adirondack, and pulled it over to the fire and sat facing the house, a slice of Memory Lane, and the last of the sunset.

The scene was peaceful, lit with twilight and serenaded by the crackling fire, but Beck felt none of it. It was beyond her grasp.

Bending forward, she let her heart speak. "Lord, please make things right with Bruno and me."

She'd never been a religious person, but one of her counselors used prayer and scripture to help her maneuver through her memory loss and Dad's death.

Beetle settled in her lap and curled around Baby Girl as the night sounds started to rise. She had everything she wanted for the moment, except Bruno.

She wanted him here, sitting next to her, telling her about the good ol' days with Miss Everleigh and the memory house.

In six days she'd be gone, arriving home Saturday, going into work on Sunday, and all of this would be over. With her situation evident now, she'd have questions to answer and quizzical looks to ignore.

Mom called twice to see how she was doing, the idea of her baby having a baby softening her some. She begged to go along on Beck's next doctor's appointment. She wasn't looking forward to *that*, but maybe eventually the walls would come down and they'd start talking about the days before 9/11.

Wyatt wanted her at his lacrosse game Saturday afternoon, so she would make it home in time. Maybe that was a good thing. Mom had invited her friends Sara and Lars for dinner after the game.

And apparently *everyone* wanted to see pictures of the house and hear about *everything*.

Across the way, Natalie's red taillights beamed under the carport. She was home.

Setting Beetle down, Beck made her way to Memory Lane. "Natalie, please, wait."

The woman hesitated, her shoulders heavy, then turned. "He's not speaking to me."

"Me either."

"Why didn't you come to me, Beck? Let me know what you discovered? Let me decide what to do?"

"Would you have told him?"

She brushed her hand under her eyes. "Of course not."

"Natalie, I'm sorry, but if his father is alive, he has a right to know." Beetle finally arrived, panting and leaning against her leg. "Did you know Stone was hanging around town? It was only a matter of time before he approached Bruno."

"How did you know it was him?"

"I didn't." Beck gave Natalie the social media version of Boudreaux, Vinny Campanile, and a black Mercedes with New York plates and her finely tuned NYPD cop sense.

"And that's how you found Stone?" She shook her head and took a sack of groceries from the trunk. "Serves me right. See, our deal was he'd stay away forever. Then about ten years ago he called. Said he regretted his *death* and wanted to meet Bruno. I fought him on it, though if he'd insisted, there was nothing I could do. Bruno had just started law school and I didn't want any emotional upheaval.

An interruption like his father coming back from the grave . . ." She adjusted her bags and closed the trunk lid with her elbow. "Stone agreed to wait until he graduated. But he's never followed through on anything, so after a few sleepless nights, I put it out of my head. Sure enough, he never contacted Bruno."

"Why'd you kill him off?"

"Seemed like a good idea at the time." Natalie detailed her reasons in short, verbal bullet points. Tired of seeing her son hurt. Stone rejected him, made him feel like nothing.

"Beck, you're about to be a mother. How do you think you'd feel if your teenage son cried in his room because his father was a selfish egomaniac?"

"I punched a perp for hurting a dog."

"I rest my case. Know who was great?" Natalie said. "Your dad. Every summer he took Bruno under his wing and treated him like a son. Taught him how to change a tire, change the oil, how to hook and skin a fish. Even how to fix a leaky faucet. He was more a dad to Bruno in the two or three weeks he was here than Stone ever was. And you, he really loved you, Beck. The closer it came to your summer arrival, the more excited he got. He trusted you. He was real with you."

"He's that way now too. But I fear I've pushed him away." She stepped toward Natalie. "I'm sorry I caused problems between you."

"You were doing the right thing, telling him the truth. He can trust you. You two have always had a connection." Tears welled in her eyes. "It's like the last eighteen years rolled up when you came back." She smiled and wiped her eyes. "This is on me. I knew it would bite me in the butt one day. In fact, when I had my accident and he called to say he was coming home, I was scared he'd find out then."

"Why *did* Stone leave?"

"Running from his own fears and wounds. He loved Bruno like crazy when he was born, then the older he got, the more Stone's demons haunted him. I hope he's taken some control of his life now that he's older. Now that he's apparently seeking out his son."

"As do I. For Bruno's sake."

"So, when do you leave?"

"Next Saturday."

"I'd wanted to have you to dinner, but Mrs. Acker decided to do spring cleaning in January—"

"Are you busy now?" Beck motioned to the fire pit. "Come sit by the fire and watch the stars."

"All right, let me put these things inside. Do we need snacks?"

"I'm pregnant. You need to ask?" Now that she'd smoothed things over with Natalie, her appetite was no longer constrained by worry.

"I'll be right over." Natalie regarded her with her head tilted to one side as if trying to assess something unseen in Beck. "Come to church with me on Sunday."

"Church?"

"The place where we had Miss Everleigh's memorial. I think you'd enjoy it."

"Well . . ." She didn't have anything else to do, and Natalie knew it. What was an hour out of her Sunday morning? She'd always wanted to try church and never got around to it.

"I'll need a ride."

"Of course, of course. Dress is casual so don't worry about what to wear. I'll see you in a few minutes. Do you like guacamole? I have fresh avocados."

"Sounds great. Natalie, do you think Bruno will forgive me?"

"I don't think he could ever stay mad at you. The real question is, will he forgive me?"

Beck settled Beetle down by the fire and pulled another Adirondack chair around, then went inside for a second blanket and a bag of cookies she just bought.

Now the sweet night was scented with the heady, rich aroma of wood smoke and forgiveness.

Waiting for Natalie, Beck stretched her feet toward the flames and peered up at the north Florida night sky, the sound of a small plane humming somewhere beyond the horizon.

Bruno. Up, up, and away in his private jet plane. *Be safe and come home.*

CHAPTER TWENTY-EIGHT

DON

The idea started brewing when he came home from church last Sunday. He'd only attended the small chapel on Amelia Island a few times, but since his encounter with Joshua Christian, he had faith on his mind.

There was a feeling, a presence he experienced with the congregation he'd not felt in churches past. It gave him a glimpse of true worship and he hungered for more.

Besides, he was in need of supernatural intervention. One, to build this business. Two, to win over Everleigh.

While their letters passed in the post each week, and their weekly calls were long and engaging, he'd gained no romantic ground. He was about to give up—she was just too stuck in her fear—when the pastor said something from the pulpit that speared him to the pew.

"It is perfect love that drives out all fear."

How did he show Everleigh how much he loved her? It was on the end of that thought, an idea formed.

That afternoon he explored the narrow stairwell just outside the master bedroom that led to the third floor.

Climbing the stairwell filled with the stagnant heat of the Florida summer, he opened a narrow door to find a small, octagonal room at the peak of the turret.

The outside light whitewashed the hardwood through three wide windows. An old settee was pushed against the opposite wall along with a tired-looking wingback.

On his left was a shallow closet but a perfect size for storage.

He could use this room to do something for Everleigh. But what? He'd put the matter to prayer when not an hour later Everleigh's brother, Tom Jr., called.

"I saw your latest adventure in the class newsletter. You moved to Florida?"

Don let it all fly. The new business, the adventure, the beautiful Victorian he bought with cash, and his growing, continuing feelings for Everleigh. Of which Tom had no idea.

"Don't give up on her. She needs you. Mom needs you. I've tried for years to get Mom to move to Austin, be with Alice and me and the kids. But she says she can't leave Ev. They're both trapped in the past."

At that point it was only natural for Don to share his inspiration. Could Tom help? His old friend answered with an enthusiastic yes.

Today, the first box of treasures was on the veranda when he got home from work.

He carried the box inside, then gathered his tools and tuned his new Zenith portable radio to WFBF for weather updates and carried it upstairs to change and get to work.

Hurricane Donna was churning toward Naples on the Gulf Coast, and the weather bureau predicted she'd make a hard right and head toward Daytona, exiting over the Atlantic.

Old-timers around town warned Don and George to be prepared just in case.

Daytona was only 120 miles south, they said. Never know what a wobbly old hurricane will do, so stock up on some water and candles, have a flashlight and radio handy, and lay in some groceries. Bread, canned goods, and a large jar of Jif.

George wanted to make a decision about leaving tomorrow morning. If they didn't leave by Friday evening, they might hit those northeast rain bands on the highway.

Putting the storm out of his mind, Don headed up to the third floor with the box as ol' Cowboy Copas sang about going back to "Alabam'."

He had a memory room to create.

When he opened the windows, the thick, hot breeze swept in and drove out the stale heat and new paint fumes.

He'd just started arranging the photographs on the floor—some would need new frames—when the second-floor phone rang.

A frantic Everleigh was on the other end. "Are you following the storm?"

His heart melted a little. "Hello to you, Ev. How are you?" He sank down to the seat by the phone table.

"Are you following the storm?"

"I am, but you should see it here today. Sunny with blue skies. Beautiful."

"It was a beautiful day when the F5 twister tore up Waco too. The day Moses shut the door on the ark."

"The ark? Whoa, Ev, there's no world flood coming. Not that I know of, anyway. People around here know how to prepare for and survive a hurricane. I'm good. Already got supplies. Besides, Donna is three, four hundred miles south of me."

"Come home until she blows herself out. Hurricanes spawn tornadoes, you know. Do you have a basement?"

"Florida is below sea level. If I had a basement it'd be called a swimming pool."

"Are you mocking me?"

He envisioned her face, drawn and pale, a frown on her pink full lips. Fear robbed her of so much, but his love would restore her joy.

"Everleigh, I *am* home. Fernandina Beach. Only thing missing is you."

A thin squeak came down the line. "Please . . ." she whispered. "Come home. I need to know you're okay. I need to see you, hold you."

If that wasn't a confession of love, he'd be Bob's uncle. He felt it in her plea, and the truth churned in his blood. "I love you too, darling."

"If anything happens to you—"

"Nothing will happen to me."

"You cannot know that, Don. Nothing was going to happen to Rhett either."

"You're right. I can't know. But I refuse to live in fear, Ev. And I wish you wouldn't either. Are we going to live our lives looking over our shoulder for impending disaster? Sweetheart, you could die in the bathtub before another twister rips through Waco. Come here. Marry me. Please. Marry me." He waited. "Ev?" He jiggled the receiver. "Everleigh?"

But she was gone, leaving him with the dull hum of the dial tone.

———

EVERLEIGH

By Friday afternoon Everleigh had made up her mind. If Don wasn't coming home, she would go to him.

Since her encounter with Mr. Childers, she was beginning to believe she was stuck. In the past. In her memories. In fear.

At lunch she asked Mr. Reed if she could have the rest of the afternoon off and he graciously agreed. She filled the Studebaker with gas on her way home to pack.

In order for this to work, in her own mind and soul, she must keep it to herself. One expression of doubt and she'd cave.

Thankfully, Mama was on the phone when she tiptoed her suitcase through the kitchen and out the back door.

Relief. Because if she had to dialog this decision with Mama, Everleigh knew she'd relent and not drive one mile toward Florida.

When she reached the garage, a man in coveralls popped up from the swept floor, startling her, his dark-brown curls peeking from under his crooked cap.

"Hello? Can I help you?"

"She's all good. Ready to go. Tire pressure, oil—"

"I-I'm sorry, who are you? How did you get in here?"

"Josh Christian, at your service." He wiped the grime from his hands before extending one to Everleigh. "I heard you were going to Florida so I thought I'd check your car before making such a long journey." He opened the trunk and set her luggage inside.

"Impossible. I just decided an hour ago." A ghostly chill swirled through her.

"It's my job to know. You best get going while there's a bit of daylight. I'll check in on your mama for you. She'll be just fine." He beamed with confidence.

"I don't . . . Who are you again? Did Don send you? But no, how could he? Daddy . . . Were you a friend of Daddy's?"

"Indeed I was. You go on in and say good-bye to your mama. She's got something to tell you. Go easy on her."

Everleigh turned in stunned obedience and walked back to the house, calling for Mama as she stepped inside.

"There's a man out there. So strange. Do you know a Josh—"

Mama raised a finger, standing in the kitchen, phone pressed to her ear. "I never should've listened to you, Sher Callahan. Well, yes, I know but—" She cast Everleigh a sad, sheepish look.

Well, she didn't have time for this. She needed to get on the road before she lost her nerve. Now that she'd decided to go to Don, she experienced a sense of freedom. Boldness.

In her room Everleigh shoved the doors closed over her nearly empty closet. So this was it. She was dislodging her heel, as it were.

But taking the courage to go to Don left her none to tell Mama. Everleigh picked up the note she'd written Mama.

Dearest Mama,

When you read this, I'll be gone. This may seem the coward's way, but if I told you face-to-face, I'd never leave.

You've been my partner, my friend, my rock for the last seven years, but I have to go to Don. Hurricane Donna has made me realize how much I love him, and if I'm to lose another man in a storm, then let me go with him.

I'm going to marry him, Mama. If he'll still have me.

Please call Mr. Reed for me. Tell him how much I appreciate all the opportunity he's given me. In fact, it would be nice if you'd fill in for me since you're a jewel at floral arrangements.

There is a hundred dollars in the freezer coffee can. The bank books are in the locked secretary drawer. The bills are paid for the month. I'll call you from Florida to go over everything.

I'm taking the car, so ask Tom Jr. to help you purchase one for yourself. There is about seven hundred dollars in savings. You should be able to purchase a right nice car with that.

I know Tom and Alice are always asking you to come to Austin, but you turn them down on account of me. Well, Mama, be free. Move near your son if you want. Play with your grandchildren.

Let's both leave this dull, dark widows' world behind, shall we?

I feel God is with me, so don't worry. But do pray. I'm terrified yet invigorated. It feels good.

I love you so very much. Thank you for everything. For my life.

> Your loving daughter,
> Everleigh

With a piece of masking tape, she anchored the note to her mirror. *For Mama.*

With a final glance at her childhood room, she backed out, closing the door. Her plan was to tell Mama she was going to dinner and a movie with Myrtle.

"I need to talk to you." Mama stood at the end of the hall, foreboding and dark.

"W-what about?"

"Let's sit. Please." Mama moved to the living room, shutting off the TV and turning on the end table lamps.

Everleigh sat in her chair while Mama perched on the edge of hers.

"That was Sher Callahan on the phone."

"So I gathered."

Mama wrung her hands, stood, then sat, her gaze darting about. "There's a bit of a situation." She pressed her fingers to her temples.

"Mama, whatever it is, you can tell me."

"You would think so but—"

"Remember when I was little and too scared to tell you something?"

"I'd go around the wall so you could say it without me glaring down on you."

"What if I do that now?"

"Yes, that might work. Just go around the kitchen door."

When she was on the other side, Everleigh gave Mama the go-ahead. "By the way, I'm going to dinner and a movie with Myrtle tonight."

"That's nice, dear. She's a lovely girl. Listen, Everleigh, Sher called with news about, oh mercy, I can't believe I'm about to say this. She called with news about our baby. I suppose he's a boy now. Nearly seven."

"The baby?" Everleigh stood in the doorway. "My baby? What about him, Mama? How does Sher Callahan know anything?"

"Oh, this is a mess." Mama dropped down to her chair again. "She knows who adopted him."

"How could she?" Had the world gone mad? "The adoption was closed. Through the agency."

"Except Sher went behind our backs and put a couple forward. Her cousin's girl. Aimee."

"And she's just now telling—" Everleigh gasped. "Is this why you two fell out?"

"Yes." Mama lowered her head. "She never said a word about having a connection with the adoption agency when she suggested perhaps you might like to—" In the soft light tears slicked down Mama's face. "I don't think she thought of Aimee and Lou until you agreed, but still, she was a sneaky harpy."

"How long have you known?"

"Almost from the beginning." Mama pulled a picture from her pocket. "This is him about two years ago."

Everleigh stayed by the kitchen, unable to feel her limbs, her heart beating with wild curiosity. After a moment, Mama dropped the black-and-white image on the table.

"I didn't know if you wanted to see him. He's lovely, Everleigh. Built like Rhett."

She eyed the picture, but her legs would not move. "Why are you telling me now? Why did Sher call?"

"She wanted to let me know—"

"I thought I'd never know." Everleigh brushed away a thin tear. But it was an expression of relief instead of sorrow. "My boy is well. He lives with Aimee and Lou? Where? No, don't tell me. I don't want to know."

"Are you angry?"

Everleigh considered her interior state and between Mr. Childers, Don's profession of love, Hurricane Donna, and her secret plan to flee to Florida . . . "No, Mama, I'm not mad."

In fact, she was free.

"But, I need to go." Everleigh glanced at her watch. She'd mapped out her course with one of Daddy's old maps and the thousand-mile trip would take sixteen hours if all went well. But if she drove all night, she counted on beating the storm. "I'll see you later, okay? Don't wait up." She kissed Mama's forehead. "I love you."

"I love you too. Goodness, you sound as if you're dying." Mama held her arm. "Have fun with Myrtle. But, Ev, there is more if you want to know."

"Thank you . . . but I don't believe I do."

The phone rang and Mama went to answer. Everleigh gazed around the kitchen one last time. Then just as she started for the door, she turned back to the living room and snatched up the picture of the boy from the coffee table and exited the back door, racing for her car and a brand-new future with Don Callahan.

CHAPTER TWENTY-NINE

BECK

Saturday afternoon Bruno called. "Mind if I come by?"

"Please do."

Since revealing his father was alive, he'd been on the road. Busy. Since signing Tyvis it seemed all kinds of opportunities had opened up for him.

And she missed him. His absence made her last week in Florida feel hollow.

She brushed her teeth and ran a comb through her hair, then picked up her dishes and trash from a *Gilmore Girls* marathon and carried them down to the kitchen.

Whatever he wanted, she'd listen. A week from today she'd be home, and while her future with Bruno was uncertain at best, she wanted things copasetic.

Back upstairs, she paused by the third-floor stairs.

She'd been meaning to come up the entire time but never made the climb. The stairwell was dark and narrow. Claustrophobic. She didn't seem as fond of those kind of spaces anymore.

Finding the light switch, she flipped on the light and made her way to the top, gently twisting the knob and easing the door open into a small, octagon-shaped room with shades drawn.

She tugged the chain of the floor lamp, and a low, gold glow brought the room to life.

The furniture was sparse—a settee under the windows, a stuffed chair and a tall bureau on the side wall, a colorful area rug.

It was the walls that captured her attention. They were filled with photographs.

Beck turned a slow circle, the images going from black-and-white to full color, a memorial to days and times gone by.

It was more than a few family photos, it was history in pictures. Memories captured and framed so as not to be forgotten.

Drawn into the spell, Beck started with the framed wedding photo, the enormous sun that the other images orbited.

It was of a young woman in a white dress scooped into the arms of a very brawny, handsome cowboy who carried her down the church steps. Head back, laughing, she had one arm around his neck and a bouquet in her other hand. A setting sun spiked through the church steeple and crowned them in light.

Beck raised her hand to trace the woman's smile. Joy. Happiness ruled this day. Everleigh? Was this you? Judging by the styles of the cheering guests, she put this image in the early fifties.

The surrounding photos were more casual. Snapshots in custom frames. They were all of the bride and groom in different settings.

Next to that cluster was another large photo of the same woman, only older, more seasoned and more beautiful, with another man coming out of a small chapel. She wore a tea-length, flared dress and a hat with a short veil.

She carried her modest bouquet at her waist, her left hand in her husband's, a regal-looking man with lean, narrow lines.

The surrounding photos were of the couple moving into the memory house, of a dinner with no fewer than a dozen people at a long table, of two tanned, freckle-faced children.

One with frayed ponytails, the other with a mop of dark curls.

Beck gasped and pulled the stuffed chair over so she could stand on the lumpy seat.

"That's me. And Bruno."

How were they one of the moons orbiting this wedding photo?

Beck glanced between the two large wedding portraits. *Everleigh, what happened?* The woman was the same, but not the men. Who frames two wedding images?

This secret room raised more question than answers.

On the opposite wall was another image of Beck with Bruno. They were older here, maybe thirteen, sitting on the front porch, her arm hooked over his shoulder.

"Two crazy kids." She loved this image of innocence.

There was a picture of Beck with Mom and Dad in the backyard by a bonfire, Dad holding up a fish.

Another of Mom and Dad walking down the beach hand in hand. To her mind's eye, they were familiar strangers.

Raising the frame from its hook, she looked for a notation on the back.

July 2001. Taken by Beck Holiday.
Framed by Everleigh Callahan.

Image after image depicting Beck's childhood. Scenes death had deleted.

One of Bruno holding a surfboard twice his size. Another with the two of them sitting in lawn chairs while Dad grilled. Mom, Natalie, Bruno, and Beck, and who Beck supposed to be Don and Everleigh, sitting around.

Beck teared up at the picture of her as a young teen, shot like a portrait. The sun had spread her freckles across her face and soaked her dark hair with burnished lines.

Her green eyes, rimmed with long lashes, were filled with confidence and love, and Beck envied her.

The next photo made her inhale. With the same tone as the one previous, Beck stared at the camera with Dad at her side. They had the same shape face and aquiline nose, the same snap in their green eyes.

Looking at him was like looking at herself, and the pieces of herself she did not know.

"Why can't I remember?" She slapped the wall. "Why?"

"It's what you said to your father."

She spun around at Bruno's voice. He stood just inside the slender opening.

"I think it's what you said to your father. It's why you forgot."

"What are you talking about? I don't know what I said to my father." She pointed to the wedding side of the display. "Did you know about this room? Is that Everleigh?"

"Yes, a younger version. Probably our age. I don't know this cowboy, but that's Mr. Don." He moved to the other wall, his hand wrapped around his phone. "I'd forgotten about these. Miss Everleigh took up photography as a hobby. In the summer we were her main subjects." He paused at the portrait of Beck, then looked back at her. "This is the image of you in my head. Even now. You're still this girl."

"I'm a long way from *that* girl."

"Not as far as you think." Bruno took another tour of the photographs. "Here's you with your dad." He laughed. "Me with that big surfboard. These pictures tell a story, don't they?" He leaned close to one of Everleigh sitting on the steps of a ranch house. "I wish I knew why these pictures are in this room, arranged this way. Why the two wedding portraits?"

"I wish I understood everything about this house and why Everleigh left it to me." Beck ran her hand down his arm. "Hey, Bruno, a-are we good? About your dad and all?"

"Yeah, we're good. I'd have done the same thing if I were in your shoes. I'm glad you told me." His smile crumbled her concerns. "I just had to process. Still don't know what I'm going to do with the news. Ever since I signed Tyvis I'm getting all kinds of opportunities." He pushed his chair around the desk and faced her. "I spent most of the day with him. His training is going really well and he said to tell you thanks. Told me not to let you go." He took up her hand and laced his fingers through hers.

"I never thought I'd have thirty grand to just give away. Whether he makes it or not, it was worth every penny to give him a chance."

"Can we sit here?" He motioned to the settee. "I need to tell you something. Actually, you need to listen to something."

"Uh-oh. This feels like the night I had something to tell *you*."

He leaned her way and she waited for his kiss. But he stopped, drawing back with a big breath.

"Beck, I broke into your dad's phone." He held up the old Nokia. "There're voice mails on here."

"Did you listen to them?"

"I did." He set the Nokia aside and opened an app on his phone. "Do you want to hear them?"

"Is what I said to my father on these messages?"

"Maybe. But if you want to figure out why you forgot, I'd start with these."

Beck gripped his arm. "I'm ready." She stared at the floor, waiting, her heart skipping.

"Here's the first one."

"Dale, can you bring home a loaf of bread? I'm making hamburger gravy and just saw we were out of the key ingredient."

Mom's voice resonated. It was her former voice. Her younger, lilting, joyful voice. Her before-9/11 voice.

The next one was a message from Dad to himself.

"Dale, this is you. Don't forget Beck's assembly tomorrow."

"Dad," she whispered.

Bruno hit pause. "Do you want to hear it again?"

"No, yes, maybe once. Can you send these to me?"

She brushed the tears from under her eyes. From the bottom of the stairs, Beetle Boo whined, but he'd just have to wait.

Leaning close, Beck listened to Dad's reminder again, his voice like a favorite song she hadn't heard in years.

"I miss him," she said.

"What assembly is he talking about? Do you remember school at all?"

"I do. We used to have school assemblies where a professional talked about his or her career. Entertainers. Politicians. Wall Streeters. Lawyers."

"Cops?"

"Cops." Her eyes rounded with revelation. "Of course, cops. He must have been the speaker that day."

"Want to listen to it again?" Bruno said.

"Please." Beck listened as Dad reminded himself about her assembly. "Is there a date? When was that?"

"September 10th."

"September 10th?" For a split second, the haze around her memories parted and she saw something. Felt a reminiscence.

"Anything?" Bruno said. "Let's play the next one."

"*Dad, where are you? The assembly starts in fifteen minutes. You were supposed to be here already.*"

Beck jerked to attention. "That's me."

"This is September 11th, Beck."

"Play it again."

"*Dad, where are you? The assembly starts in fifteen minutes. You were supposed to be here already.*"

Her voice flared, anxious and angry. If the word *already* was a fist, it'd have punched Dad in the face.

"There're two more."

Beck shifted in her seat, unsettled by a low rumble quaking through her.

"*Dad, call me back! You said you'd be here. You promised.*"

An image flashed, tattered and unframed, faded and washed out. She was in the school office with the phone in her hand.

"I called him to see if he was coming." She was on her feet. "He *was* our speaker, and he was late."

"Beck, think back. Was the secretary upset in any way? Anxious? Were people talking with their heads bent together in a hush?"

She set her hands over her closed eyes, trying to see. "Assemblies were right before lunch, around ten thirty. So the planes would've hit by then, but I can't remember, Bruno. I can't."

"Here's the next message."

A slow burn crept through her as she listened, hovered close to Bruno.

"Where are you? I cannot count on you for anything. Are you working? Of course work is more important than your own daughter. I hate you, Dad. I really do. You're a selfish jerk, and I don't care if you ground me for saying so. Everyone is waiting. I'm humiliated. You're the worst dad ever. I mean it."

Lightning and thunder collided in that small octagon room.

"I hate you—"

Then the revelation from heaven boomed and its meaning became clear. *It's what you said to your father.*

She dropped to the floor with a sorrowful moan. "It's what I said to my father, Bruno. I said I hated him. Then he died."

CHAPTER THIRTY

EVERLEIGH

She'd crossed into Florida on the newly constructed I-10, the eastern sun filling her windshield.

The radio crackled with the news. "... *still a major hurricane ... moving north-northeast ... winds 135 ...*"

The news almost seemed like a fairy tale balanced against the brilliant blue of the western Florida morning. She was hopeful that by the time she arrived at Don's the storm would be well into the Atlantic.

Please! And thank You.

Crossing a low bridge, she reached for the crumpled map and glared bleary-eyed at the red-and-black lines.

She'd just passed the Pensacola signs and Texas seemed a lifetime behind her.

The gas needle bobbed on E, so she exited the next off ramp and pulled into the first gas station.

The attendant sauntered out with a crooked ball cap on his head and a half a sandwich in his hand.

Everleigh's belly rumbled. She might just ask him for a bite.

She'd stopped for a burger in Mississippi last night when she reached the halfway point. But she didn't stay long. Somewhere between sipping a Coke and downing a greasy beef patty, fear slithered up next to her and whispered, "Go home, you crazy dame."

She dropped a five on the counter and beat a path to her car before the darkness clouded her mind. If Don wasn't coming to her, she was going to him.

But after driving all night, fueling her veins with coffee, she was weary. And weakening with each stop.

"Fill her up?" the attendant said. The name patch above his pocket said Earl.

"Please." Everleigh glanced around. "Any place to buy a cup of coffee?"

"Diner right off the exit. But we got some inside. Free." The attendant walked around the car. "Shew-wee, ain't she pretty?"

"Yes, and thank you." Everleigh made her way inside, using the facilities before filling a plastic cup with hot coffee. Her stomach clenched at the strong, bitter scent.

"Where you headed?" The attendant asked when she returned, leaning over the hood, washing her windshield.

"Fernandina Beach. Do you have a pay phone?"

Earl squinted at her through the early-morning sunlight and pointed to the booth at the end of the asphalt. "You know there's a hurricane in those parts? She's done a U-ey and crossing the state."

"You'd have to be dead not to know. It's all over the news."

At the phone booth, she closed herself in and raised the operator, asking for a collect call to Don's office.

After ten rings, the operator informed her there was no answer. *Yes, I know, I know.*

"I'd like to try his home, please." Her voice quivered as she recited Don's number from memory.

Answer, please.

Pressing her head against the hard metal of the phone box, Everleigh counted the rings. She whimpered when the operator returned once again to inform her no one was home.

When she stepped out of the booth, Earl was tightening her gas cap.

"Well?" he said as she paid him for the gas. "What'd he say?"

"How do you I was calling a he?"

"Only reason a woman would be driving toward a storm is love." He tucked her money in his pocket. "You want me to check the oil?"

"No, someone already checked it." Everleigh pictured the man in the coveralls as she took her seat and cranked the engine. "Do you think it's safe? To drive to the East Coast? It's at the northern tip of the state. Do you think the storm will go that far?" Her trembling hand kept slipping from the wheel.

"Well, you got about six, seven hours to Jacksonville, then whatever distance to Fernandina Beach. I'm no weather man, but it seems the storm'll be striking the East Coast sometime tonight."

"So, is it safe?"

"I can't tell you, lady. Got to go with your heart on this one."

"Yes, I suppose I do."

As the engine idled she stepped out, facing west, facing home. In Waco was everything she knew and loved. Her routine, her job, her circle of friends, her seat in the choir, and the graves of those she loved.

But over her shoulder, to the east was something new, terrifying and quite possibly the best man she'd ever met since Rhett.

And there was a vicious and wild storm.

For a split second she was buried under the ground, huddled in that cold, dark cellar waiting for Rhett. Mr. Cartwright might have pulled her above ground that night, but in more ways than one, she'd remained in that cold cellar.

"Give me strength." Everleigh got behind the wheel and shifted into gear, then pointed the Studebaker east toward Tallahassee, and toward Fernandina Beach.

She was coming above ground, and she prayed with all of her heart that Don Callahan would be there waiting.

―――――――

DON

If this was hurricane weather, bring it on. From his second-floor office view, the day promised to be warm and sunny. The river's surface sparkled with light, and he had an itch to go fishing.

George called him not long after Everleigh had hung up on him.

"Let's secure the office in case the storm hits with any velocity."

Don left the solace of the memory room where he'd been arranging and hanging pictures, wondering if he was the world's biggest fool.

Love sometimes walked a close line to crazy.

Meanwhile, Hurricane Donna terrorized the state, making her way through the center toward Daytona. The bass-voiced weatherman predicted the storm's northeast bands would sweep over Jacksonville and the beaches, stirring up the tide and tearing down powerlines.

Their secretary, Alberta, a smart, savvy woman from Bethune-Cookman, came in to help as well.

George handed him a stack of files and Don wrapped them in plastic. "Feels like the days of Noah, doesn't it? Preparing for a storm we can't see."

"I don't know about Noah, but we've worked really hard the last three months to build a client list, and I don't want to lose any of it."

"What time are we leaving for Georgia?" Don stored the files on the shelf in the closet, restless. He walked over to the window and glanced down on Centre Street, where the shops were boarded up and vacant. "It's eerie. Like being in a ghost town."

"Only with a possible tidal surge instead of tumbleweeds." George handed him another box for the top of the closet. "Lila and I will pick you up in, oh, say an hour. That's the last of it. Alberta, thanks for coming in. Are you bugging out for the storm?"

―――――――

"Heading over to my cousin's in Tallahassee."

"Be safe," George said. "Don, Lila is making sandwiches so we don't have to stop for dinner. I've filled an extra gas can in case nothing is open on the road. Or the pumps are empty."

"Do you ever think all this work is for nothing? That we won't even get hit by Donna?"

"I *pray* we're doing all this for nothing." George popped him on the arm with a grin. "Alberta, see you in a few days."

Alberta finished up, wrapping her new typewriter in a plastic sheet as Don took a final glance around the office. The low summer sun tempted him to stay put and ride it out. How bad could the storm be when today was so beautiful?

But Everleigh's plea haunted him. "*Come home.*"

His foot itched with the idea. But this was home now. Besides, he'd gone to Waco twice and she refused him. Now with a hurricane bearing down on him, she plied him with fear.

"Don?" Alberta handed him a canister and an envelope. "These came for you last night after you left. Might as well see what it is in case it's important."

"Thanks, Alberta. You off?"

"Yes, don't want to get caught in the traffic."

Don examined the long tube, then the envelope. The postmark read *Dallas, Texas.*

Inside he found a letter from Dewey senior accountant Len Fenske.

Call me when you get this. Before you open the canister. Len

His work and home numbers were written across the bottom.

Don dialed Len's number, then sat in his desk chair. "Len? Don Callahan." He cradled the receiver against his shoulder and reached for the canister. "What's with the clandestine message? And the tube?"

"You're not going to believe it."

"Can I open it?"

"Go ahead, but make sure you're sitting down."

Don mashed the speakerphone button and opened the canister. The contents slipped onto his desk. He rolled out the pages and examined the title.

RENOVATION OF DEWEY MOTORS. 1961.

"Dewey's making changes?" Don said. "I'm not surprised, but shouldn't it be Dewey-Callahan Motors?"

"Keep reading."

"Can you give me the CliffsNotes version? We're prepping for a hurricane here." Don scanned the pages, noting the lack of references to Callahan or Waco.

"He's closing down Callahan Cars, Don. Laying off the staff. Cutting out your father. In two years he'll build a new, bigger, betch-your-life million-dollar dealership just east of I-35."

Don sank back into his chair. "He can't, Len. He and Dad signed an agreement."

"Look on page fifteen. I highlighted the pivotal paragraph. Dewey-Callahan only had to be in place thirty days before Standish could make unilateral decisions with a quorum of the board."

"But Dad's on the board—"

"He's not, Don. Standish never offered it to him."

Don whistled a word, a dark, dark word. "I knew he'd try something. I warned Dad. 'Read the small print,' I said. But oh, Dad trusted him. Twenty-five years of friendship. Standish never asked Dad to sit on the board?"

"We tried to talk him out of this, Don. Me, Fred, Michael. But he wouldn't hear us. We'll probably lose our jobs."

"This will destroy Dad, Len. If the man values anything it's loyalty. His own father betrayed him by selling the original Callahan

Cars out from under him. Then his son walked out, and now his friend stabs him in the back."

"Standish was never going to give you the dealership, Don. You know that, right?"

"When does he make his move?"

"Monday."

"Len, I owe you. Thanks for warning—"

"Wait, Don, it gets worse. The employees will have no severance pay, including your dad. Whatever he got in the merger is all he's going to get. Dewey classified all employees as working for Dewey Motors after the merger, and there's no payout unless a man has worked here for a year."

He had no words.

"I'm so sorry, Don, but I thought you should know," Len said. "Standish is a greedy guy and an even worse friend."

"Len, I owe you." He sat back with a sigh, running his hand over his head. "Dad is a great friend, a great salesman, but too naive a businessman. This should've been a partnership made in heaven."

Don paced, walking off some of his steam. This was his fault. If he'd stayed he could've looked out for Callahan interests. Then Len's truth echoed.

"Standish was never going to give you the dealership."

"Tell me, Len, did my leaving play a role in this?"

"You got out just in time. Otherwise you'd be caught in the middle. My guess is Standish had plans to get rid of you too."

When he hung up with Len, Don dialed George. "New plans, my friend. I'm heading to Texas where a different kind of storm is brewing."

After he explained, George said, "Don, I'm so sorry."

"Me too. Sadly, I'm not surprised."

"See you in a few days."

"I'll keep you posted."

"And, Don?"

"Yeah?"

"Say hello to Everleigh for me."

He grinned. "I will."

He'd run by the house, close her up, and let Aimee know where he stashed the spare key—under the old birdbath—then hit the road.

He'd come up with a game plan as he drove. Either way, Standish stabbing Dad in the back was just another opportunity for Don to see Everleigh and plead with her once more to come home with him.

CHAPTER THIRTY-ONE

BECK

God was waiting for her on Sunday. From the moment she entered the white clapboard church to the first strum of the guitar, she sensed a touch. A swirl of holy activity.

She stood during worship with Natalie, trying to sing, but emotion choked every word.

Soon the tremor became a ground swell, then the earthquake of emotions brought down the barricades around her memories and they rushed in with the current of her sobs.

Image after image of her dad, of holidays, of birthdays, of riding a bike and building sandcastles. Of crying over math homework and staying up late on Christmas Eve to see him walk through the snow to the house, packages in his arms.

He did not deserve her abuse. Her hate. But it was too late.

She'd wrestled with her behavior, tossing and turning all night, trying to forgive herself, trying to imagine how Dad must have felt hearing her spiteful words.

She'd dreamed of him buried under a pile of rubble, calling her name, and she awoke soaked in anxiety.

She looked up when someone bumped her shoulder. Bruno. "Move over."

"What are you doing here?" she whispered. He looked handsome in a white mock turtleneck and jeans, his dark hair combed into place for once.

"Flew home last night. Got a text from Mom. 'Church.' So I came." He slipped his hand into hers and she leaned against his arm.

She had called Mom last night. *"I remember, Mom, I remember."* And wept recounting the story of her vicious message to Dad.

"He thought I hated him!"

Mom listened without interrupting for once, and when Beck spun the last word of her story, Mom assured her in soft, matronly tones that Dad knew she loved him.

"I'm sorry I wasn't there for you, Beck. I never realized . . . that's what you were trying to tell me."

From the stage, an older woman began to sing about a God who was a good, good Father. Each lyric, each chord vibrated through Beck, pulling her back together.

The congregation sang around her, over her. *"You're a good, good father and I'm loved by you."*

I'm sorry for what I said, for the pain I caused, Dad.

Bruno sang softly, swaying them both from side to side.

God, show me the way.

The music about the good Father faded and the worship leader stepped forward.

"I feel like there's someone here who needs to forgive herself. You did something in your past that wounded you. For years you didn't even remember until suddenly—"

Beck dropped to the cushioned chair, her hand still gripping Bruno's.

"God's forgiven you. Your father has forgiven you. Forgive your-self."

The congregation sang the chorus again as Beck slipped down to the floor, whispering, "I'm forgiven. I have to be forgiven."

Voices murmured over her. Chairs shifted and moved. Hand after hand landed on her back, shoulders, and arms and while the music played, she was covered with love.

And while the people prayed and the lyrics filled in the room, Beck heard the *clank* of chains hitting a concrete floor.

BRUNO

When Beck came up off the floor, she glowed and he loved her. Flat-out loved her.

But he had some other kind of loving to do first. Forgive Mom. She cut him a glance during worship with a pleading in her eyes.

He slipped his arm around her shoulder and whispered, "All's forgiven."

He had some questions, but the atmosphere of God's presence beckoned him to release his grudge. In fact, he had some squaring away to do with God. It started with three simple words.

I surrender all.

After church, he invited Beck to lunch at his place on A1A, stopping by Doo Wops Best 50s Diner for takeout: burger, fries, and shakes.

He grabbed a couple of beach chairs from his deck and a blanket. Beck carried the food, and together they walked toward the shore.

The February sun was out this afternoon, but the warmth was far away.

When they'd settled in and taken a bite or two, he asked, "What happened to you today?" He washed down his bite of burger with his soda.

Beck focused on the high surf, the wind tangling her hair, her legs wrapped with the blanket.

"I'm not sure." Her reply wavered. "I'm afraid if I say what I feel, it will sound stupid."

"What do you feel?"

She grinned. "Reborn. Oh my gosh, I sound like a holy roller."

"What happened when you were on the floor?"

"I asked God to forgive me. Next thing I knew this weight I

didn't even know I'd been carrying broke off. I experienced an instant of knowing God was a good Father. Really knowing."

"I had that sense today too."

She stretched her arms wide. "Hello, world, you're beautiful."

Anchoring his cup in the sand, Bruno held up his hands to the tousled ends of her hair. "You make the world beautiful."

"Bruno—"

"Sorry, Beck. I love you. I've always loved you."

She sat back, chewing on her milkshake straw and shivering. "We should've ordered hot chocolate instead of these cold chocolate shakes."

"It's okay if you don't feel the same way. I can take it."

"What if I did, Bruno? What do we do with it? I'm trying to imagine me in New York, you here, there and everywhere—"

"Who said love had to be easy?" He scooted his chair closer to hers. "For the past ten years I've done nothing but law school and work. I was the guy who wanted to be a big success. Wanted my name known in the sports-agenting world. And I achieved it. I gave up a meaningful social, spiritual, and family life. When I came home to help Mom, I realized how empty I'd been living. But I still had an agency to build, bills to pay. Then you showed up and . . ." He tossed a cold fry at the feet of a scrawny seagull. "I'd forgotten what it feels like to be in love."

If she wanted him to just walk away because something was complicated . . .

"I can move to New York, Beck. There's an agency there who will take me on."

"What about Tyvis and Calvin? All the good stuff happening for Sports Equity? What if you move and we don't work out?"

"Beck, all I need to know right now is if you love me. Do you?"

The seagulls leaned into the wind and clustered at their feet, their dark eyes pleading for a bite.

Her eyes glistened. "Yes, Bruno, I think I do."

CHAPTER THIRTY-TWO

EVERLEIGH

Saturday, September 10

The road to Fernandina Beach was all but deserted. The road out was bumper to bumper.

She'd tried Don's office and home number just outside Jacksonville, but there was no answer and the gravity of her decision began to weigh on her.

What if he'd yielded to her plea and drove to Waco? Surely he would've called.

A little after four p.m., she turned down Memory Lane, the wind gusts pounding the car and scattering horizontal raindrops over the windshield.

The radio announcer called them rain bands, and Jacksonville and the beaches were expected to get hit with the outer edges of the weakening Hurricane Donna.

Everleigh recognized the Victorian home from the picture Don had shown her—7 Memory Lane. She parked along the curb and stepped out of the car.

The house across the street was buttoned up, the awnings lowered over the windows. A car sat under the carport with the trunk raised and the car doors open.

Don's place was dark, but the windows weren't boarded. And there was no sign of his car.

Another gust of wind drove thick raindrops into her blouse and slacks. Everleigh ran toward the porch, stepping in a puddle of muddy water that covered her white sneakers.

"Don?" She rang the bell. "Don! It's me, Everleigh."

Cupping her hand around her eyes, she peered through the sidelight. The dark foyer and living room showed no signs of life.

Running around back, she slipped in the wet grass, crashing to the soft ground. With a moan, she pushed up.

"Don?" She jiggled the kitchen door handle, then seeing the barnlike garage, she tried to slide it open. But it was padlocked.

"Don!"

Back at her car, reality began to sink in. She leaned against the driver's-side door, trembling, exhausted, hungry and weak, her stomach bloated from too much coffee.

She'd driven a thousand miles to see Don, to tell him she loved him, and he was not here.

When a door slammed behind her, she turned to the house with the awnings. Maybe the neighbors knew where he'd gone.

"Hello? Is anyone home?" Everleigh knocked on the carport side door. "Hello?" She exhaled relief when the door opened.

"Can I help you?" The woman on the other side was pretty, her house dress covered in a large apron and her hair wrapped in a kerchief.

"I'm so sorry to bother you but—" Everleigh squinted at the familiar face. "Aimee? Aimee Holiday?"

Her eyes flickered with recognition. "Everleigh Applegate?"

"Yes, it's me. Aimee, what are you doing here?" The wind whipped under the porch, rattling the window's tin coverings and chilling Everleigh to the bone.

"I-I live here. What are *you* doing here?" She glanced behind her, then pulled the door close, blocking Everleigh's view of the house.

"I'm so relieved to see a friendly face. And all the way from Texas. I came to be with Don. Do you know where he is?" She made a face. "Wait, you live across the street from your cousin? He never mentioned it."

"And you're his girl? At dinner the other night he said there was someone but—"

"I'm sort of his girl. He's asked me to marry him, but I turned him down." Everleigh flipped the collar of her blouse against her neck, the air cool and wet. "The storm made me realize . . . I suppose it's a long story. But I had to tell him I love him. Do you know where he is?"

"Mama, who's here?" A boy with eyes the color of a summer Texas sky peeked around Aimee's legs. "Hello."

"Just a friend from Texas." Aimee patted him on the head. "Now, do as I asked and pack your suitcase. Your clothes are on the bed."

Everleigh glanced from the boy to Aimee, then at the boy again. His face. She'd know it even if she hadn't stared at the picture during a gas stop ten hours ago.

He smiled and said, "I was borned in Texas," before dashing away.

"Let me in, Aimee."

"No." Aimee blocked her entrance, her stone posture refusing to yield. "You just go on back where you came from. You shouldn't be here. I can't believe this. Go. Just go."

"Aimee, let me in. Please. I have to see him."

"No, you don't. It's been seven years, and I won't allow it." She pressed the door against Everleigh. "You made this decision. Now keep your word."

"Please, Aimee. I won't say anything to him. Can I just see him?"

"He's settled. He's peaceful. We are all he knows."

"I'm not going to tell him." Everleigh stepped back. "Mama just told me yesterday that she knew who had adopted him. But she didn't give me a name. Only a picture of him from a few years ago. I never wanted to know about him. He wasn't mine any longer." She gave Aimee a weak smile. "Is he a good boy?"

"Very good." Aimee slowly stepped aside. "His room is down the hall."

Everleigh hesitated, then crossed the threshold and found the boy in his room, packing. She sat on the edge of his bed, studying his face, every detail.

"What's your name?"

"Louis Carter Holiday Jr." The little guy closed his child-size suitcase. Aimee stood at the door, hands clasped together, her eyes rimmed with red and steel. "This is my teddy bear. Where I go, he goes."

Everleigh reached for the brown bear, the once-soft fur matted from seven years of use. She'd given this to the adoption worker after she signed the papers.

"So I'll always be with him."

"It-it's a beautiful teddy bear."

"Beautiful?" His high-pitched child's laugh drowned out the storm's bucking winds. "Bears aren't beautiful, are they, Mama? They're ferocious."

Aimee stood in the doorway. "That's right, son."

Her arms moved of their own volition, and Everleigh swept the boy off his feet, bringing him to her. He was warm and sweet, everything she imagined he'd be. And squirmy.

"Hey, you're squeezing me too tight." He pushed against her shoulders and arched back. "I can't breathe. Are you crying?"

Everleigh loosened her hold but studied every inch of his face. He was the miniature version of Rhett, with the same mischievous glint in his eye and the same saucy smile. And the same thick frame.

She brushed her hand over his hair and down his soft cheek. "I never thought I'd see you—"

"Hey, little bug, run get the sandwiches for Mama from the refrigerator. Be sure the door is closed tight, okay? I need to talk to Mrs. Applegate."

With a curious glance at Everleigh, he dashed out of the room. "Women."

Everleigh laughed, the weariness from her seventeen-hour journey fading for a moment. "Where did he hear—"

"Lou. He's always teasing me with it." Aimee sat on the bed with the yellow bedspread that matched the walls. "Don's mother came to us when she heard you gave birth prematurely. You were still in a bad way after losing your family. She thought we could adopt him. We'd been trying for a child for five years with no success. Lou had just signed on here at the naval yard, and we were set to move within a month of your delivery. I said yes without hesitation. Everleigh, he has Novak and Applegate blood. How could we go wrong?"

"You must imagine I'm some horrible mother to give up her child. To be so weak."

"No, I imagine you gave us an incredible gift." Aimee hesitated, then squeezed Everleigh's hand. "I never thought I'd be able to thank you in person. But thank you."

"He seems well. Tell me, does he like school? Does he play outside? Is he healthy?"

"He's the tallest boy in his class. The smartest too."

Lou Jr. bounded into the room. "Are we ready? The wind is really loud."

"Yes, we are." Aimee smiled and tousled his hair. "Get your suitcase. Mr. and Mrs. Carroll and little Tommy will be so happy to see us, won't they?"

Everleigh snatched Aimee by the arm. "Where are you going?"

"We're going to stay with friends in Jacksonville. Lou was supposed to be here with us but got called into work. Now he wants us to leave so we're not home alone."

"Tell me, where's Don?"

"I've not seen him, Everleigh. But there's a spare key to the house under the birdbath. You can let yourself in." Aimee started down the hall. "LJ, let's go. The winds are making Mommy nervous."

"What if he's doesn't come home?" Everleigh gripped Aimee's arm. "Should I go with you?"

"Everleigh, you know you can't." Aimee peeled away her tight grip. "I'm sorry. Why did you come during a hurricane?"

"Because—I couldn't lose another man I loved in a storm."

"Then you must really love him." Aimee passed through her kitchen, placing bread, peanut butter, and a jar of water into a cooler. "There will be a lot of wind and rain, and the electric lines will go down, but you should be safe in Don's place. Lou Jr., get in the car, please." She carried the cooler to the car and settled her son into the passenger seat. "It was good to see you, Everleigh. I've always wanted to thank you."

Everleigh caught Aimee at the trunk of her car. "Do you and Lou love him, Aimee? With all your heart? That's what I wanted for him. A mother and father who love him."

"More than the air we breathe."

Aimee and Lou Jr. pulled out of the driveway as another rain band swept over the coast with thick, cold drops.

Everleigh dashed across the street to her car. Her little boy was happy and loved. If that's all she gained from this crazy trip into a storm, then it was well worth it.

———

DON

He made good time until his car broke down outside of Tallahassee in a little town called Chipley.

He spent the night sitting up in a truck-stop diner waiting for the mechanic shop to open.

It was almost noon before the slow-moving grease monkey got to his Corvette, dinking around the engine while Don paced, finally coming out from under the hood to announce, "Your fuel filter is clogged."

———

"Great. That's a five-minute fix."

"Naw, got to drive to Tallahassee to get the part. And that's if I can find it. Sit tight, won't take but a couple of hours. Three, four tops."

"Four? Listen, I need to get on the road to Texas."

"Don't get your knickers in a wad. I'll hurry."

Yeah, Don would really like to know his definition of *hurry*.

It was almost seven before he got on the road again, foot heavy against the gas.

The more time he had to sit and think, the more he wanted to see Everleigh. Dad's deal was just the "good excuse" he needed to head west again.

He decided to stop for the night outside of Biloxi a little after ten. After checking into a cheap motel, he ran across the road to a diner where the *D*s in the neon sign were burned out.

OTTIE'S INER

The place had a jukebox but no radio. Some yahoo at the counter kept loading the thing with nickels and selecting the same song over and over.

He ordered a sandwich with fries and a glass of water while Johnny Cash's "Second Honeymoon" put him in mind of Everleigh all the more. Absence was doing a bang-up job of making his heart grow fonder.

The car radio informed him every hour that Hurricane Donna was blowing toward the northeast corner of his new home state, wobbling between Jacksonville and Daytona, winds still at category two strength.

The outer rain bands would be hitting Fernandina Beach about now. He was relieved not to be there, trying to sleep in a hot, airless, closed-up house while every knock and rattle kept him awake.

"Refresh your coffee?" The waitress, Liza, hovered over his table with a full pot of black joe. Don slid his cup over. "Where you heading tonight?"

"Texas." He sweetened his coffee with a large drop of cream.

"Better than Florida." She reached for his empty sandwich plate. "That Donna is an angry thing."

"She's taking a toll, no doubt." Don gave her a dismissive smile. His neck was sore from sitting up all night and frankly, he was too weary for chitchat.

"My Dwayne has his ear to the radio constantly. Says it's one of the worst hurricanes since the '28 Miami storm, and he's scared half to death she'll do a one-eighty and come blowing over us."

"Not likely. She's heading into the Atlantic."

"Times like these make you want to hug the ones you love, you know?" Liza moved on with a, "Have fun in Texas," but the truth of her comment rustled up Don's courage.

Call Everleigh. Tell her you're on your way.

He didn't know why he hadn't called sooner. Maybe he wanted to surprise her. Or maybe he needed the long drive to decide if she would ever succumb to his overtures.

Plus, how was he going to break the news of Standish to Dad?

Dumping the change from his pocket onto the counter, he hoped he had enough to make a quick one-minute call. He did. Barely.

At the pay phone, he slipped the coins in the slot and dialed her number. On the first ring he realized the late hour. Ten fifteen. He was about to hang up when someone answered.

"Hello? Everleigh?" Mrs. Novak sounded startled. Fretful.

"Mrs. Novak, it's me." Don cleared his voice. "Don Callahan. Sorry to call so late."

"Don!" She sounded fully alert. "Where is she? Is everything okay? Tell me she's with you. Dear Jesus, she didn't even tell me she was going, just left a note."

"Who's with me? Everleigh? I'm on my way to Waco."

"You mean she's not with you?"

"Why would she be with me?"

"That blame storm. She was terrified it'd take you from her so she left here Friday night on the hunt for you. Did I tell you she didn't even say good-bye but left a note?"

He shot to his feet, banging his head against the top of the low phone booth. "But I'm on my way to Waco."

"Oh my word, you mean my girl drove straight into a hurricane for nothing?"

"I'll find her." Don was about to hang up when he pressed the phone to his ear again. "Mrs. Novak, why did Everleigh go to Florida?"

"Because she loves you, you dolt. Now turn your car around and find my girl. Find her!"

He slapped the phone on the cradle and tripped out of the booth. Tucking a five under his plate, he nodded to Liza and made long, eager strides toward his car.

As he fired out of the diner's narrow parking lot heading east, Don Callahan swore he'd spend the rest of his life making Everleigh Applegate the apple of his eye.

CHAPTER THIRTY-THREE

BECK

March
East Flatbush, New York

Before she started her Sunday-afternoon shift, she'd arranged to meet Hunter and Gaynor at the World Trade Center Memorial.

The day was bright, cold, and filled with emotion as Beck found Dad's name on the north pool kiosk with the rest of the brave souls who died in the North Tower.

Midtown South Dale Holiday

She placed her hand over his name. "Hi, Dad, it's me. Your baby girl."

Beck's own Baby Girl woke up at the sound of her voice, kicking and stretching, wanting to see what was going on in the world.

She pressed her hand on her belly, and Baby Girl pressed back. It'd become their routine the past few weeks. Mini high fives.

Tourists gathered around her, reading the names, wondering what it must have been like to die in such horror, pausing every now and then as if in prayer.

Beck started her soliloquy to Dad until a couple stepped in front of her. She let them pass before starting again.

"Dad, I know it's been eighteen years, but it's never too late to say I'm sorry. Which I am. Terribly sorry. For what I said to you on your phone, the messages I left. I was a stupid, selfish kid who had no idea what you were running into that day. I tried to punish myself by forgetting you, and for a long time, it worked. Then Miss Everleigh died and left me her house, and it set me on a journey. Mom found your old phone and sent it to me. Bruno Endicott, remember him? I'm sure you do. Anyway, he broke into the phone and found my messages. It crushed me hearing how I spoke to you. If I could talk to my fourteen-year-old self now . . . But, Dad, I miss you every day. You were the best." She kissed her fingers, then pressed them over her father's name. "Please forgive me."

"Beck?"

She turned as Hunter and Gaynor approached, hand in hand, an anxious reflection in their eyes.

Gaynor touched Beck's belly. "She's grown. The baby I mean, not you."

"We've both grown. In several ways."

"I can tell. You look even more beautiful."

Hunter motioned to one of the security guards. "Did you see ol' Sergeant Lopez? He works security here now."

"Sergeant Lopez?" Beck glanced back at the memorial building. "I'll have to say hi. I rode with him for six months a few years ago."

Hunter saluted Dad's name, then faced Beck, asking if she wanted to sit on the benches.

It was too cold to have this conversation outside, but she felt the space and the sunlight were on her side.

"I guess I should say what I need to say."

"We've been praying, anxiously awaiting." Gaynor clung to Hunter's arm.

"When you left Florida, I was ninety percent sure I would say yes. Gaynor, your memories of your dad really touched me. The way you talked about your family meant you had something I couldn't give her."

Hunter peered down at his wife. "I feel a *but* in your tone, Beck."

"I wanted to let you raise her. I even told my mom and my friend Bruno. But I can't. I'm already in love with her. Then, through a series of events, including a sports agent who geeks over old phones, I got my memories back. And everything changed. *But* . . . I want you involved. Hunter, *you* are her father."

Gaynor glanced away, wiping her cheeks. "I was so hoping, but I understand, Beck. And yes, we want to be involved."

Her eyes said what her words could not. *She'll be Hunter's child but not mine.*

"We'll help you get into a place," Hunter said. "Anything you need."

"I don't need help with a place. Miss Everleigh left me enough money."

"Who was she again?" Gaynor sniffed, turning to Beck, her face more red from holding back her tears than cold.

"A very old family friend."

"How did everything change?" Hunter said.

Beck explained about Mom's box, the stuff from Dad's desk, and the hateful messages Bruno pulled off Dad's phone.

"I felt guilty so I chose to forget. But now I remember . . . and, well, so much has happened." She patted her heart. God. Bruno. Baby Girl. "I want her to know her grandpa, Dale Holiday, one of twenty-three heroes of the NYPD who died in 9/11."

Was she making sense? It was hard to explain how connecting with who she really was both on earth and in heaven changed *everything*.

Hunter nodded. "I think so. Thank you for considering our request."

"Will you let us know when you go into labor? Can we come to the hospital?"

"Of course."

Gaynor hugged her, no longer restraining her tears. "For what it's worth, Baby Girl is very lucky to have you as her mom."

"And I think she's lucky to have you as her other mom."

With nothing more to say, Hunter and Gaynor bid good-bye. Beck fell against the back of the bench, relieved but sad. Gaynor's graciousness humbled her. If she hoped to be a decent mom to Baby Girl, she needed to take a page from Gaynor's book. From God's good book.

Baby Girl kicked and Beck patted her belly. "You're going to be well loved."

"Beck?" Hunter turned and walked back to her. She braced herself for another plea from a man who dearly loved his wife. "Did you say you heard the messages on your dad's phone? The one in his box of returned things?"

"Yeah, Mom saved it for me. She came across it cleaning the attic and sent it down to Florida."

"Was it a silver phone? A Nokia?"

"Yeah?" Where was he going with this?

"I was the officer assigned to clean out his locker and I found the phone." He smiled. "Your dad was notorious for leaving his phone behind. Hated the idea that the department could get ahold of him anytime, anywhere. Never mind we didn't use them back in '01 like we do today."

"Hunter, what are you saying?"

"He never heard your messages, Beck. If he had, we'd have found his phone on his body not in his locker."

She pressed her fingers over her smile as the beautiful revelation dawned. He never heard her messages. Or her venomous hate.

He didn't have his phone.

All those years of amnesia for nothing. Unchecked grief was an evil friend.

"Oh, thank God. Thank God. Hear that, New York? He didn't hear the messages!"

She ran to the kiosk and pressed her lips without a care over his name.

EVERLEIGH

She awoke drenched in sweat, stiff from a night on the hard floor in the butler's pantry. It was the most interior room in the house. And in her mind, the safest.

She pulled blankets and pillows from the one bed upstairs and made herself a thick pallet. Then waited.

Don had stocked the pantry with water, bread, and peanut butter, candles and a flashlight. So she didn't feel quite so alone when the electricity finally blinked off for the last time.

She had the light to keep her company.

Reaching for her watch, she listened. The silence was a sweet refrain from the hammering winds. Then she blinked at the time. Eleven a.m.

Kicking the blankets aside, she reached for the flashlight and aimed it on the door. She'd not wait to be rescued this time. She'd emerge from the dark and face the aftermath.

She'd driven a thousand miles into a storm for love. She'd embraced her son, then watched him drive away with *his* mother. And she'd spent the night alone while a hurricane passed by.

And when she awoke, she had peace. What could she not accomplish if she let faith overcome her fear? Why had she ever been so locked down? So chained to the past?

A slight twist of the knob and light angled over her foot. A little more and she peeked into the kitchen. Golden rays streamed through the old glass windows and filled the room.

With relief, she clicked off the flashlight and stepped from the hot, stuffy pantry into the wide, sunny kitchen. Opening the back door, she inhaled the stiff, wet breeze blowing through the screen.

Tree branches and leaves littered the lawn. An electrical wire dangled from a distant pole. And the houses stood in defiance of

Donna, and Everleigh stood in defiance of everything that had ever held her back.

Out the front door, a small stream raced along the lane's edge. Frogs belched their continuous song.

"Take that, Donna!" She raised her fist before turning back inside, a laugh bubbling up.

Joy comes in the morning.

Gathering the pallet from the pantry, she folded the bedding and carried it back upstairs, opening windows where she could, replacing the dry, stale heat with a fresh, damp one.

Already her skin glistened with moisture.

After dressing in a pair of shorts and sleeveless blouse, she washed her face and brushed her teeth, then pinned back her hair.

With the storm passing, the day brightened with sunshine, and Everleigh explored the grand house of Don Callahan's.

It was charming with an old-world warmth. The stained glass transoms above the doors were beautiful. When the light hit just right, the stain tinted the living room with a rosy pink and gold.

She toured the empty upstairs bedrooms and peered out the bay window seat to the backyard. In the distance, sunlight flickered off the calm surface of the river. This space would be lovely for afternoon reading. She could watch Don mow the lawn.

Next she passed through an upstairs room large enough to be a family room or library. It appeared Don preferred this space to the one below. He'd set up a lamp and chair, along with a tiny television with tinfoil bunny ears on the antenna.

Exiting that room, she entered a small hall. She'd found the bedding she used in here. To her left was the telephone on a small table. She raised the handset with hope. But the line was dead.

From the bedroom window, she could see nothing but the wind-blown trees, a portion of the front lawn, and a clip of Memory Lane. If she stooped down she could see the house where Lou Jr. lived.

Slowly she sank to the floor. *Don, where are you? Please come home.*

On her feet, she decided to get busy, see what she might do to clean up the yard. Otherwise, panic might ensue, and she was too far from home to feel that alone.

Besides, she and Mama used to be presidents of the Waco Beautification Society. She spent many a Saturday cleaning debris from the city streets and parks.

Passing from the master, she paused by stairs tucked in a small space between Don's living quarters and the bedroom.

Tiptoeing up, she met a narrow door and turned the knob. Light flooded in through the windows and nearly overwhelmed her. The octagonal room with its thick, patterned carpet and leaded windows was magical.

Fresh paint covered the walls above a mahogany wainscoting. A red-and-gold upholstered settee was pushed under the front-facing windows. A cushioned bench fit along another one of the octagon panels.

On the opposite wall was an arrangement of framed photographs. One in particular drew her attention.

"Rhett—" It was their wedding photo. Everleigh stepped for a closer view, her eyes filling. He seemed so alive. So well. "Don, what have you done?"

This picture was her favorite from that day, and one of the few remaining. She'd left it at Mama's to be framed. And now here it was, on the wall of Don's house.

She raised her hand to Rhett's smile.

"My wife, ladies and gentlemen." With almost no effort, he had scooped her up with his strong arms and carried her down the church steps. She cradled against him, laughing. Joy, so much joy. Happiness ruled the day.

As the wedding guests showered them with rice, the last afternoon sun spilling through the church steeple, the photographer caught the scene.

"Rhett, darling, where would we be now?" she whispered.

There were more photos. Two on each side of the wedding shot. More of Everleigh's favorites. Where did Don get these?

One was with Rhett at the country club reception, sitting on the steps outside the ballroom, Everleigh's chin resting on his shoulder as he looked off and away, content, his hand grasping hers.

She always imagined he was gazing toward their future. But now she wondered if he was contemplating his humanity.

The second photo was a casual, everyday shot of life on the Applegate ranch. Everleigh leaned in to see the girl she'd been. Young, exuberant, hopeful.

Naive.

Standing on the bench, she traced her finger over Rhett's handsome face, and her special moments with him paraded across her mind.

Their first kiss. How she giggled, ducking away.

His proposal on one knee at the club. He was so nervous he dropped the ring in the grass, twice.

The candlelight falling over his strong jaw as he gazed down at her on their wedding night.

The sweater she'd attempted to knit him for Christmas. How they laughed when he tried it on. It was so big Daddy Applegate cut it along the seam to use for washing ranch equipment.

The call from the doctor to confirm she was pregnant.

The house plans for Memory Lane.

The first flutter of life in her womb.

The dark clouds. The twister. A night in the cellar.

Everleigh stepped down from the bench. Everything afterward was shapes and shadows, a series of grays that defied light.

The sharp pains that came too early.

Hours of labor.

Weeping into her pillow when she'd given him away.

"I'm not finished."

Everleigh whirled around at the sound of Don's low, sweet voice. She flew into his embrace, drawing her arms tight around his neck. "I was so worried."

"What are you doing here, sweetheart? Why didn't you call? I was frantic on the drive home." His arms gripped her so wonderfully close.

"The hurricane . . ." Tears flushed her voice, her whisper soft against his warm neck. "I was so afraid."

"Of losing me?" Don lifted his head. "Ah, sweetheart, 110-mile-an-hour winds aren't enough to defeat me. I have too much to do. I'd have been here sooner, but the traffic was murder."

"Where were you?"

"Driving to Texas to see you. And Dad. It's a long story." He kissed her, pulling her into him with his presence. With his breath.

She gasped when he released her and faced the photos on the wall. "Don, what is this?"

"You said you didn't want to forget him. That he deserved to be remembered. I decided if that was the only barrier keeping you from loving me, then I'd help you remember."

"Where did you get them? Mama?" She shook her head. "Doesn't seem like something she'd do. Well, and keep quiet about it."

"Tom Jr." Don knelt next to a box on the floor. "He sent these to me."

"Tom? Where did he get them?" Everleigh sat next to him, examining the photos as Don pulled them out one by one.

"Not sure, but I figure this was a pretty good haul. I want to frame a few more, put the rest in an album." He pointed to an empty wall. "Save that for *our* wedding photo and the life we'll build. If you'll have me."

"Have you?" She rose to her knees and pulled him to her, kissing him until every fear vanquished. "I just drove a thousand miles into a hurricane to tell you I love you."

He sighed with a grin. "You keep kissing me like that and we won't make it to the wedding night. Everleigh, if I ask you again, will you say yes?"

She blushed. "Ask me again," she said with a commanding force.

His arms encircled her, pulling her down to the floor with him as he toppled over. She yelped, laughing, as he rolled her over on her back. Gazing down at her, brushing her tangled hair from his face, his eyes searched hers.

"Will you marry me, Everleigh Applegate?"

"Yes, Don Callahan, I will marry you."

He tried to kiss her but was smiling too wide, so he hugged her so hard she complained she lost all her air.

"When shall we get married?" he said, helping her to her feet.

"As soon as you want." Seeing a picture with Rocco, she sat on the floor by the box. "I wanted to keep this little guy, but by the time we finished the funerals all four were happily embedded at Mr. Cartwright's. He raised them all. Probably still has them."

"Define *soon*." He was kissing her cheek, then her neck.

"As legally possible."

In the box there was a picture of her walking down the aisle with Daddy. Another of Tom Jr., Alice, and the kids. The bottom of the box was scattered with childhood snapshots and—horror of all horrors—her toothy elementary school photos.

"Really?" he said.

She peered into his chocolate eyes with the hazel flecks. "Really? I don't need a big wedding or lots of guests. I just need you."

He kissed her again until she saw the stars.

"We'll have to wait for the county offices to open again, but don't you want your mama here? My folks might want to come. If Dad decides to speak to me."

Everleigh held up a handful of photographs. "You did this even though you had no idea I'd ever come."

"That's what love does, Everleigh." Don traced his finger along her jaw. "Makes a man not care so much about himself."

Everleigh shoved the box out of the way and, with a fistful of his shirt, kissed him with her heart and soul, then her lips.

"Can't we get a license today?"

"Everleigh—" His breath brushed her cheek, and his heart pounded beneath her hand. "What about your mama?"

"Let her find her own man." She kissed him again, enveloped in his fragrance and the strength of his arms.

They crumpled to the floor again, kicking the box aside, awakening love. Then somewhere in the distance, a car door slammed.

A child's voice rose from the street, and Everleigh sat up, moving to see out the high window.

She couldn't see him but heard his voice. ". . . ride my bike."

"Not yet. The power lines are still down. Come help Daddy and Mama . . ."

From her third-floor perch, the expanding limbs of a live oak blocked her view, but she could see and hear Lou, Aimee, and Lou Jr. with her heart.

"Ev?" Don's hand brushed her shoulder. "What's wrong?"

She turned to him, touching his strong chin with her finger. "Aimee's boy . . ."

"Why are we being quiet?" He leaned to see out the window, then glanced at Everleigh. "Pretty wild to have her across the street. Lou Jr. is pretty cute. Precocious. Did you meet them already?"

"Yesterday. As they were leaving. But I've known Lou Jr. for a very long time."

His eyes widened with revelation. "Ev . . . their son is—"

She nodded and fell back, resting her head on his shoulder.

"I had no idea."

"Neither did I. Don't know why, but Mama actually tried to tell me before I came here. She showed me a picture, and I recognized him when I knocked on Aimee's door."

"Ah, this is making sense now. I told my mom I bought a house across from the Holidays." He lifted her gaze with a finger under her chin. "She knows I love you so she must have called your mom."

"It was supposed to be a closed adoption. To a family we didn't know."

"But Sher Callahan got involved? Wouldn't be the first time." He lifted her up, his arm firm on her waist. "I-I don't know—Are you all right? Was it weird seeing him?"

"No, it wasn't. He felt like a long-lost relative. He's so cute. I thought he looked like Rhett, but now that I think about it, his smile is so like Aimee's."

"He talked my ear off when I had dinner with them." Don turned to the picture wall. "I'll call the Realtor tomorrow. Put the house up for sale. We can find a new place over on Amelia Island. Get some distance—"

"Why? What will that change? I already know he's here." She gripped his arm. "Besides, you already hung my memories on *these* walls. The boy I gave as a gift to another couple lives across the street. He's loved and healthy. It may sound crazy, but I'd love to see him grow up. Be a friend, maybe even be a voice of wisdom in his life."

Don made a face. "Everleigh, that sounds noble and I love you for it, but could you bear it? When Aimee calls him to dinner, it will be to her house, not ours. You'll have no right to speak into their lives about how they raise him. You can't be on their doorstep every day just for a chance to see him. He'll get suspicious. They have a life to live that's not yours. Or mine."

"I can, Don, I know I can. It's been seven years, and I've finally made peace with the past, including the decision to put him up for adoption. Then I find you, or you find me, and I get a second chance at love. You bought this gorgeous home on Memory Lane, a street by the same name where I once planned to build my dream house and raise a family. Well, this is my dream house now. Look at Lou Jr. Don, what are the odds of you buying a house across the street from him?"

"Astronomical."

"And that house being on Memory Lane. He was the baby in my womb when I dreamed of raising him in a beautiful house on Memory Lane. And look, he's being raised in a beautiful little house on Memory Lane. It's as if God is telling me, 'All is well, Everleigh.'"

"Are you sure? We'll have to talk to Lou and Aimee."

"I'm sure, Don. I am *not* his mother. Aimee is. I feel it. I know it." She tapped her heart. "It's my mind that condemns me, not my heart. And I will no longer yield." She held his face with her hands to kiss him. "Does this change anything between us?"

His kiss covered all of her fears. "It changes nothing. I promise to love you the rest of my days, to kiss you when I come home at night, to not sit on the toilet reading the paper until my legs grow numb."

"Now I know we are meant to be. When I first married Rhett, Betty Jo from Kestner's would tell me, 'One day he'll barely kiss you when he comes home, ask what's for dinner, then sit on the toilet reading the paper until his legs are numb.'"

Don's laugh rang out. "Not me, Ev. I promise. Now, you stay here. I'll be right back."

"Where are you going?"

His quick footsteps resounded in the narrow stairwell. Everleigh giggled to hear doors slam and drawers bang. Then the sound of his urgent return.

He bounded into the room, dropping to one knee, and reached for her hand, slipping a diamond ring on her finger.

"I know you've been here before but—"

"This feels like the very first time."

Because love not only drove out her fears but brought dead things to life. Just when she thought all her rainbows had faded, God sent her Don.

"Now, tell me more about this room," she said, curling into his arms.

"I think over here I'll hang pictures of us and our children . . ."

CHAPTER THIRTY-FOUR

BRUNO

He woke to spring sunlight slicing through the edge of the drawn curtains. Crawling from bed, he stared out over downtown Waco from his fifth-floor room, the Magnolia Silos and the ALICO building in the distance.

Reaching for his phone, he checked the time. He was meeting Stuart at the regional airport in three hours.

He'd flown into Dallas with Stuart four days ago. First stop, a meeting with the Cowboys' front office to talk about Calvin Blue. They were extremely interested but seemed hesitant to talk details. He left a message with Launders Allen, the CFO, hoping to get insight on the team's hesitation. Was there something he needed to know about Calvin?

Allen had yet to return his call.

He also tried to bring up Tyvis Pryor but got cut short. The coach knew of him, of his outstanding record at FSU, and of his criminal trouble and that he ended his career at a JUCO.

Wasn't interested.

Bruno texted the meeting details to Calvin, who responded with about a hundred smile emoticons. To Tyvis, he texted to keep grinding.

While Stuart played golf at Dallas National, Bruno drove down to Waco, met with the pro liaison at Baylor, and evaluated players during their Pro Day, taking advantage of being on the sidelines with his peers and the representatives from a number of NFL head offices.

He squeezed in next to the scout from the Tampa Bay Buccaneers, brought up Tyvis, and to his surprise didn't get a hand to the face.

The scout was interested—no, curious—and promised to check him out during University of Central Florida's Pro Day.

Finally, good news to text the boy from a Scooba, Mississippi, JUCO.

Last night he treated two Baylor players, Jeff Jewel and Damen Worely, to a five-star dinner. He was right in the middle of his pitch when Jeff stopped him.

"Look, man, thanks for dinner, but you're just too small for us. We need a big agency to get us a big deal."

Damen added, "We know you were with Watershed, but they were your clout."

Bruno composed himself. He'd been here before. No big deal. "I appreciate that, boys. Who are you talking to then?"

"Kevin Vrable over at Watershed."

"Is he the one who said I've lost my clout?"

The players exchanged a look. Yeah, it was Kevin. This was his MO. Go after players he didn't really want just to create competition among the agents. Then he'd only sign the cream of the crop and leave the rest stranded at a critical time in their career.

"Look," he said, tucking his napkin under his plate. "I worked with Kevin for seven years. He's got a large client list, to be sure. Names of players you admire. But here's what I can do for you . . ."

They were bored before he even started reciting his résumé. Telling them he'd signed first-round probable Calvin Blue to Sweat Equity also failed to impress.

Kevin Vrable's brainwashing rhetoric was stuck in their heads.

Bruno continued to talk as they texted and scrolled Instagram instead of listening, as they took selfies with the server instead of realizing they were not the caliber of recruit Watershed ever signed.

The night ended with Bruno excusing himself for the men's room and walking right out the door. Yep, he stuck the kids with the bill.

Which now, in the light of day, he regretted. Impulses like that made Kevin Vrable's claims about him look true.

Snatching up his phone, he texted Jeff Jewel.

Send me the tab. I'll reimburse you or make good with the restaurant. Good luck in the draft. Let me know if you need anything.

Tossing his phone to the bed, he started the shower water, then studied his reflection in the harsh mirror lights, rubbing his hand over his night beard. He looked rough. He felt rough.

And he felt like quitting. Maybe he'd run away to Montana or Idaho and be a mountain man. A Jeremiah Johnson. Live away from the grind and completely off the grid.

In a world where he repeated and kept the fruit of his labor. Where arrogant players like Jeff Jewel and Damen Worely wouldn't tell him he wasn't good enough because the fact he survived the winter proved he was.

Where there'd be no lying moms telling stories about dying dads.

But in that world, there'd be no gorgeous NYPD sergeant who captured and owned his heart.

He could do without his private jet rides and the fast pace of the billion-dollar NFL industry.

What he couldn't live without for the next fifty years was Beck Holiday. It was enough they'd been apart for almost two months.

They texted constantly and FaceTimed when they could, but it wasn't enough. Bruno wanted to kiss her good morning, kiss her good night. He wanted to see Baby Girl's face and tell her he loved her. Which was, you know, crazy. She wasn't his kid. But he felt it to his backbone.

"Say, God, help a guy out here. What do I do about Beck? Do I close Sports Equity, move to New York?" He'd move Sports Equity to the Big Apple if he had the money.

Then there was the silent but looming issue of Dad being alive. Bruno had not seen the black Mercedes nor received any anonymous calls since Beck told him the truth.

But he was confronted by his own words, by the wild speech he gave to Mom about "one day" and "next time." Well, here was his chance to live up to "one day" and "next time."

Stone Endicott was alive. Did Bruno want a relationship with him or not?

He stepped into the shower's warm rush, his head pounding. This was too much debate for so early in the day.

The water ran down his shoulders as he bowed his head and baptized himself with prayer. If he was going to figure out his life, he had a feeling he needed more time on his knees, lifting up holy hands without doubt.

He turned on ESPN, muting the sound, as he dressed and packed, figuring he'd grab breakfast and coffee from the hotel breakfast bar before heading north to meet Stuart for wheels-up at ten.

A final sweep of the room and he was ready to go. He was just about to power off the TV when his phone pinged with a text from Coach Brown.

Are you watching ESPN?

Bruno glanced at the screen. Calvin was talking. The overlay underneath read: Top Ten Draft Potential Calvin Blue.

Bruno snatched up the remote and upped the volume.

"Here we go," he said. "Tell them who you are, Blue." He wondered why Calvin didn't tell him ESPN had come calling.

"I'm looking forward to the draft. Yeah . . . I think I've got what it takes. I've been grinding hard. I've got a great team around me. My coaches, my family, my man at Watershed Sports and . . ."

What did he say? Bruno pressed rewind.

". . . my man at Watershed Sports."

Was he joking? Or confused? Bruno used to be at Watershed, but he'd never represented anything but Sports Equity to Calvin. Bruno reached for his phone.

"Calvin, rise and shine. I just saw your clip on ESPN."

"Yeah, who's this?" He sounded sleepy.

"Bruno Endicott, your agent, at *Sports Equity*." He repeated the name, loud and slow.

"Bruno, yeah, man, hi."

"Just saw your interview on ESPN. Why didn't you tell me? And by the way, you're with Sports Equity, not Watershed." Bruno laughed. Too loud. *Settle down.* "Repeat after me. Sports . . . Equity."

"Yeah, bro, sorry. Didn't Kevin call you? He said he would take care of things."

"Kevin? Why do I need to talk to him? Calvin, what's going on?"

"We met with Kevin after I signed with you. My dad wanted to make sure we were with an agent who knew how to negotiate the league. There's a lot on the line."

"Who do you think negotiated Ham Donavan's contract? And Wilson Michael's? Kevin Vrable? No, I negotiated those deals."

"I signed with him two weeks ago. Bruno, he said he'd call you."

"Calvin, I've got money going out of my account to pay for your apartment and training. I've been talking to front offices for you." Now he understood the weird looks from the Dallas guys. "You just sent me a million smileys when I said how interested Dallas was in you."

"I know, and I called Kevin. He promised to take care of it, and look, I'll make sure Watershed pays you back."

Bruno stared at the sunny day beyond his window and every beam of light felt a million miles away. He might as well be in the deep, deep dark. "Unbelievable. After I signed Tyvis too."

"He's real grateful, man. Look, Bruno, I appreciate you, but I had to do what's best for me and my family."

Me and my family. He was sick of that timeworn, meaningless line.

"What about me and *my* family? By the way, I'm the one who would've brokered the best deal for you, Calvin. Trust me, Kevin will do no better. Word to the wise, he never reads the small print and never negotiates bonuses. But I do."

"He bought my mom a Range Rover. She's always wanted a Range Rover."

A Range Rover. Son of a—

Bruno seethed, exhaling hot coals. *Be nice, be nice, this kid may need you in the future.* "Well, I wish you the best. Call me if you ever need anything. I'm here for you. We're friends no matter what."

"I appreciate that, Bruno. Thanks for everything."

"Good luck, Calvin."

Bruno hurled his phone against the wall with such a force it shattered and landed on the tile by the door with a clatter.

He had to get out of here. Had to *goooo.* He stomped his phone with his heels as he walked out and punched the elevator button. But instead of waiting, he slammed through the exit door, ran down the stairs, and burst with a force into the bright Waco day.

Leaning into the March breeze tinted with spring, he started walking.

His steps mounted to a jog, then a run. When he got to Austin Avenue, he was in an all-out run, his jeans tight against his legs. But with each stride, he hammered every emotion into the hard concrete.

The list of people requiring his forgiveness mounted. Mom, Dad, Kevin, Calvin. All of which made him miss Beck even more. He needed to talk to her, hear her calm, sound wisdom.

He stopped when his lungs were burning and dropped to one knee. Running away never fixed anything. So he'd lost this one. But he still had Tyvis to fight for, and if any kid deserved Bruno's absolute best, it was Tyvis Pryor. And by gum, Bruno was going to treat him like he was a potential number one pick.

———

Now to get back to the hotel, pick up his things, and meet Stuart in Dallas.

————

BECK

When she got off shift, she booked an Uber ride home and slept in the back seat. The Cemetery Club was killing her.

It'd been seven weeks since Florida, but her body wanted to keep the lazy-day tempo, sleeping long hours and bingeing on *Gilmore Girls*. She still hadn't seen the last of season seven.

However, the chief promised her the day shift after her maternity leave. If she could endure that long. As it was, her seven-month belly had her driving a desk. Which made the nights even longer.

Yet there was never a dull moment at the Ninth. Last night the boys rounded up a prostitute ring and the holding cells reeked with cheap perfume and cigarette smoke.

When the driver dropped her off in East Flatbush, Beck climbed the brick steps to the house, feeling as if she carried more than herself and a growing baby.

Bruno had been on her mind all night. She texted him a couple of times, but he never responded. Now that she was off tour, he weighed on her even more.

The house was quiet when she entered. Mom's shift had changed to days last week. Flynn was at work and Wyatt at school.

Following the aroma of bacon, she found a plate of eggs and bacon in the oven. With a note.

> Found more of your dad's memorabilia in the attic. His h.s. yearbook. Check him out. XO, Mom.

————

In the past month, Mom had started to open up about Dad, retelling Beck details of how they met and the humorous mishaps on their wedding day.

"Not one groomsman had the right tux. And the ring bearer had his finger up his nose the entire ceremony."

She laughed more, and when she walked past Beck, she'd gently pat her belly.

For Beck, the rebuilding came gently. Not a flood of recall but a flash of something quick that she stored away.

Or if Mom asked *again* what she wanted to do with the house on Memory Lane, Beck would remember driving to pick Dad up from the airport. Or helping him paint the upstairs bedrooms while Miss Everleigh fueled them with milk and cookies.

She thought Miss Everleigh was her grandmother for years. But no, she was just a family friend introduced to Dad by his cousin, Lou Holiday Jr.

Sitting at the table, Beck opened Dad's yearbook to the page Mom marked. There was Dad with his long seventies hair and psychedelic, wide-collar shirt.

Even Flynn told a bunch of rookie cop stories on Dad at dinner last night. Which earned the highest praise possible from Wyatt.

"He sounds like a cool guy."

Beck finished her breakfast, then dropped a couple of pieces of bread in the toaster and turned on the TV anchored in the ceiling corner. News broadcasted from the small flat-screen.

Mom, get help. She was a news channel addict.

Beck poured a glass of orange juice and buttered her toast while the weather girl predicted more cold and possible snow.

She missed Florida. Missed the peace. Missed Miss Everleigh's unseen presence.

While munching on toast, she perused Dad's yearbook and was

about to cut off the TV and head to bed when a crashed airplane came on the screen.

The image raised the hair on the back of her neck as the stiff-haired anchor intoned the plane's tragic demise. She fumbled for the remote.

". . . pilot was found dead after the plane crashed near Jackson, Mississippi. The crash happened after the pilot, whose name is being withheld, flew into bad weather. Investigations are ongoing."

Beck's chair toppled as she stood. Was it Stuart, Bruno's pilot? He'd flown with him to Dallas this week. *No, no, no.*

She patted her pockets for her phone, then ran to her jacket. She had five missed calls from Natalie and about a dozen texts.

Call me please.

Beck?

I can't get ahold of Bruno.

There was a plane crash, but I can't find out the pilot's
name. It's Stuart. I just know it. I'm coming undone down
here. Beck?

Shaking, breakfast churning and burning in her belly, Beck returned Natalie's call, waiting as it rang, anxiety spiking and rising. Baby Girl woke and kicked her in the ribs as if to say, *"What's going on? Your heart rate is killing me."*

Beck swore when Natalie's phone went to voice mail.

"Natalie, it's Beck. I just saw the news. Have you learned anything? Call me."

Then she tried Bruno. Her call went straight to voice mail. *"You've reached Bruno Endicott of Sports Equity—"*

"Bruno, hey, call me." Still in cop mode, she held her voice low. Calm. She hesitated, hand pressed over her terrified heartbeat. "I love you."

She paced the living room, trying to think. She sat on the edge of the sofa, then bounded up again. She needed to sleep, but her adrenaline was on overdrive.

Call me, Bruno, Call me.

"I cannot lose two men I love in disaster, Lord. Dad and Bruno. I can't." Wait. She drew a deep breath. There was absolutely no indication that Stuart was the pilot of that plan. And no reason to believe Bruno was in any danger whatsoever.

She'd let Natalie get under her skin.

He must be busy or in a meeting. She shook off the anxiety and aimed her thoughts in a more positive direction. Bruno was fine. Natalie was panicked for no reason.

Her pulse slowed, and she headed upstairs to shower off the stench of the night. When she reached the second-floor landing, Natalie called.

"You heard from him?" she said, smiling.

"Not a word. I don't even know where he went on this trip. I've tried to call Stuart, but Strickland Industries is like a freaking vault. Beck, do you know where he was headed?"

"Dallas."

"Why isn't he answering his phone? That thing was his third hand."

"Maybe he's in a meeting?"

"For two days?"

Beck's shallow pool of hope drained. "Maybe he lost his phone."

"Never. Even so, he could still call. Beck, hold on." Natalie clicked off and Beck looked over at Beetle Boo, who slept peacefully in his bed. "Trade you places, buddy."

"Beck." Natalie's voice was hollow and empty. "That was Strickland Industries. Stuart was piloting that plane."

CHAPTER THIRTY-FIVE

EVERLEIGH

May 1961

She awoke late, the midmorning sun streaming through the bedroom windows, and rolled over to find Don's side of the bed empty, the sheets cool under her palm.

He rose before dawn to start work. The life of an insurance man was not one of ease. He had mounds of paperwork with each client he signed, but he loved what he was doing and the fruit of his labor was starting to bloom.

Pushing back the mass of curls falling over her eyes, she walked to the window. She'd let go of the platinum blonde and high bouffant style for more natural sandy-brown curls.

She'd started helping out at a local flower shop but was more interested in getting pregnant, a *chore* she and Don both enjoyed rather amorously.

Rhett was the man of her past. Don was the man who brought her reluctantly into the present with his patience and love.

They were regulars now at Fernandina Beach Church, Don serving as a deacon and Everleigh heading up the Women's Prayer League.

Back in Waco, Mama had become Reed's Flowers most popular florist, her arrangements getting regular mentions in the newspaper.

Mr. Childers still took his weekly order, and Connie reported he'd finally instructed his housekeeper to refill the vases once a week.

Taking a page from Everleigh's book, Mama died her hair a soft blonde and was a regular at church socials and the Friday-night dance club downtown.

Tom Jr. helped her buy a new car—not from Dewey, mind you—and she drove to Austin once a month to spend a week with her granddaughters.

Everleigh picked up Mama's latest letter from her bedside table.

> Visited the graves this past weekend. The Applegates have flowers and the headstones are clean. Daddy's was splattered with mud so cleaned it off with a rag and some water.
>
> I'm thinking of selling the house. It's too much for just me. Sharon Hayes bought one of those new little places over by the I-35 corridor and is loving it. Three bedrooms and two baths with a nice yard, but not the large dining room and kitchen. If Tom Jr. and Alice come with the girls and you with your brood once you get going, I think we can still cram together. What's Christmas if we're not living on top of each other? What do you think? I feel like this is your home as much as mine.
>
> Oh, did you hear? The Marshall family bought the Applegate ranch. It'll be a working spread by the end of the year. I think Spike would like Jacob taking over the place. The bank kept it dormant way too long.

Everleigh tucked the letter back in the envelope, absorbing the changes that were happening to her hometown, to her mama, to her.

But she couldn't imagine being any other place or taking a different journey. Every event formed her life and marked her for the woman God created her to be.

Even living across the street from the boy was part of her now. She watched him from afar, and in the nine months she'd lived on Memory Lane, in this memory house, he'd grown and raced down the lane with long, strong legs, catching whatever ball his father tossed to him.

She stayed out of their way, only conversing with Aimee about news from Waco or about Fernandina Beach. Once in a while Aimee bragged on Lou Jr.'s report card, stumbling over phrases such as, "He's smart like his daddy."

But instead of envy or jealousy, Everleigh felt her pride in her bright-eyed, towheaded little boy.

"You're awake." Don walked in with a breakfast tray.

"What's this?" Everleigh kissed him as she walked over to her chair by the window. Don set the tray on the table.

"Well, yesterday was busy . . . I had to leave early for church, then we had the social afterward." He knelt in front of her, offering her the rose from the tray. "You smiled like a champ, never said a word as the pastor honored the mothers. I know it must have been hard. So between you and me, happy Mother's Day, Everleigh." He held her face in his hands as he kissed her, then brushed her shoulders. "For the babies we will have one day. And even if we don't, darling, you are enough for me."

"You are enough for me." She brushed aside his hair. "I mean that, Don. I do."

"Nevertheless, I'd be happy to get to work on our own baby before work if—"

She laughed, tugging on his tie. "We'd be here all day and I know you have calls to make."

"You're right." He kissed her. "Oh, I forgot to tell you, Joshua Christian forgave the loan he gave us. George and I are debt-free."

Everleigh regarded him over the edge of her coffee cup. "Did he now? How generous. We must have him to dinner. Do you have his number?" The bagel was burned on the edges but spread with cream cheese and love. Everleigh bit in with delight.

"You know, I don't. I'll get it from George. He's a bit of an enigma. You never know when he's going to show up and change our lives." Don glanced at his watch. "I do need to go. But we have a date tonight, my love."

"Have a good day. Call me later."

She smiled at his footsteps thundering down the stairs—Don thundered everywhere he went—and when she finished her breakfast, she carried the tray downstairs and filled the sink with dishwater.

She'd just finished cleaning up when the doorbell chimed. Everleigh wiped her hands, and when she opened the door, Lou Jr. stood on the steps, dressed for school, his hair parted, a bouquet of roses gripped in his hand.

"Happy Mother's Day, Miss Everleigh." He jutted the flowers toward her, a sheepish grin on his lips.

She dropped to her knees, taking the bouquet while drawing him into a tight hug. "What's all this?"

"You're squishing me and the flowers." He shoved back and patted the blooms as if to revive them from her crushing embrace.

"Oh my, how right you are. So sorry." Everleigh took a long sniff of the roses. "They are beautiful. Thank you, Lou Jr., very much."

"I bought them with my allowance, and Mama said I could give them to you." He pointed to the tallest and yellowest rose. "You're from Texas, and they like yellow roses out there."

"Indeed they do." She gripped his chin softly, then brushed her hand over his little-boy shoulders. "Thank you for these flowers. I'll enjoy them very much."

He kissed her cheek. "Happy Mother's Day."

Dashing off the porch, he ran toward Aimee, who waited on her side of the lane, one arm crossed over her waist, her hand over her lips.

Everleigh stepped off the porch, her long gaze meshing with Aimee's. She raised the flowers in thanks. Aimee nodded before turning and hurrying her son to the waiting school bus.

She was inside before the real tears fell, clutching the thorny stems to her chest. Eight years after she learned he was coming into the world, her boy, Aimee's boy, wished her a happy Mother's Day.

BRUNO

Walking into his office, he wanted to face-plant and kiss the floor. What an ordeal. After getting stranded in Waco, it took two days, a gazillion-dollar flight, and a hundred bucks in Uber rides to get home.

Without his phone, he couldn't do anything. Couldn't even call his mother. All of his credit cards were on the device, and other than the cash he had in his wallet, he was busted.

But this mess was all his own, *stupid*, immature doing. By the time he got back to Dallas to meet Stuart, the guy had taken off.

He'd warned Bruno they had to have wheels-up no later than ten thirty Friday because he had a benefit for the company that night.

At the hotel computer, he managed to book a flight by reciting from memory one of his credit card numbers. He'd memorized it back in the day before he handed over his brain, his life, to his phone and computer.

Then, just as Bruno was about to leave Dallas, every flight was delayed due to a computer foul-up, and he spent the night sleeping in the airport chairs, the man next to him snoring and exhaling the worst breath. Like, who *died* in his mouth?

Bruno dropped his bags by the office door, then collapsed in his chair. He needed a shower, a decent meal, and to catch up with work. Beginning with a phone call to Kevin Vrable. He wasn't waiting for him to do the right thing.

The debacle had a silver lining, though. He'd run into a former Watershed client just outside the Delta lounge, a lineman for the Cowboys looking for new representation after a bungled contract dispute.

Bruno handed him his card, and they scheduled a call for next week. He opened his calendar and entered *Call with Bryant*. How stupid to kill his phone over Calvin Blue.

Next he launched Messenger to check his text messages. The app pinged nonstop. Forty-eight hours without his phone, and his small world had tilted.

The latest text was from Scott Fuller about Pro Day and Tyvis.

Confirming he's coming next week.

Then one from the trainer.

He's a beast. You'd never know he didn't play D1 ball last year. I hope you're talking him up with front offices.

Next came a waterfall of texts from Mom and Beck.

Where are you? Call me.
Bruno, why aren't you answering your phone?
Okay, this is not funny. CALL YOUR MOTHER!

Well, he would if he had a phone. And the office didn't have a landline. He hit reply on her last message.

What's up? I'm home. Broke phone in Waco. Calvin dumped me for Vrable.

His stomach rumbled, and suddenly he wanted dinner and to hug his mother. To use her phone to call Beck.

But first he ordered the latest and greatest phone online and had it delivered express.

Being disconnected from his world was exhausting. It stripped him of his identity. Who was Bruno Endicott without a phone in his hand, hustling for the next client?

Which concerned him. He'd vowed on that Sunday in church

with Beck to disconnect from work more, from busyness, to just be. Before God. The One who calmed his anxious thoughts.

One thing became clear on this journey. He didn't crash his phone or run down Waco Avenue because he lost Calvin Blue. Or because Mom lied about Dad's death.

He ran like a wild man because he'd lost Beck. He could take any failure as long as she was by his side.

All he'd wanted while trying to sleep next to Snores With Bad Breath was to get home to her.

Except she wouldn't be there.

Bruno faced his computer ready to work, then changed his mind. Not tonight. He'd make the time he promised God starting tonight.

Then he'd get through Pro Day with Tyvis and call Alec Jones at AJ & Co and see if his offer still stood. He'd move to New York and win Beck over.

And when everything had settled down and his life was on track, he'd look up Dad. See what he wanted and why he lurked around Fernandina Beach in January.

He was just about to turn out the lights when someone knocked on his door.

"It's open."

"Hello, Bruno."

"Dad." He looked the same except for the signs of time. Gray at his temples, deep lines on his cheeks that came from aging fast. But it was his dad. "I heard you're back from the grave."

He nodded, somber. "Got a minute?"

Bruno's Messenger app pinged once more, but he reached over and slapped it closed.

"I was just about to go to dinner."

"Can I join you?"

Bruno hesitated, then nodded. "What are you doing here?"

"I heard Miss Everleigh died. She was always kind to me even though I didn't deserve it. And frankly, Bruno, it got me to thinking. It was time to come back from the dead."

"I can't promise you anything."

"And I'm not asking."

They walked down the narrow stairs, then hit the sidewalk, father and son, walking in quiet tandem, their gait making the same scraping sound over the concrete.

———

BECK

Where was he? Natalie had texted he was home, but she'd been waiting for him on his back porch for almost two hours. She shoved up from the Adirondack and waddled over to the edge of Bruno's sandy backyard every time a car pulled in.

But so far he'd not showed.

She returned to her chair and texted Natalie, the pleasant, semi-warm night full of saltwater dew and bright stars lost on her.

Not here yet. You?
No.

She'd just dozed off when headlights flashed over her, starting her awake. Pushing up to her feet, she stared toward the red taillights.

When the driver rose from the car, she caught his profile in the ghostly hue of the parking lot lights.

"Bruno!" She held her belly as she tried to run, her legs like lead. "Bruno!"

He dropped his bag and ran to her, lifting her up as she flew into his arms, her belly bulging between them.

She buried her face in his chest. "You're here, you're here!"

———

"Of course I'm here. What's wrong?" He set her on her feet and kissed away her salty tears. "What are you doing here?"

"You scared the life out of me." She stepped back, wiping her tears. "Where have you been?"

"Texas. Beck, what's going on? You're trembling." He set his hand on her belly. "You're scaring me and the baby." He ran back for his bag. "Let's go inside."

She hiccupped a sob, fingers pressed to her lips. "We thought you were killed. They gave your mom nothing about the wreckage. No hint, no clue."

Beck crashed her head against his chest and clung to his sleeve.

"Beck, wait, killed? What are you talking about?"

"You don't know?"

"Know what?"

"Stuart's plane went down outside Jackson. He was killed. We thought you were with him." She fell against him. "I thought I'd lost you before I ever really found you."

"What? Stuart went down? How?" He paced away from her, facing the night pulling over the Atlantic. "My friend—"

"He flew into a storm. When we couldn't get ahold of you—"

"You thought I was with him. Of course you would. But I'm here, babe. I'm here."

She led him to the sofa and embraced him as he mourned the death of his friend. He'd call Strickland Industries tomorrow. Offer his condolences. Stuart's loss would be felt for years to come.

Sitting forward he brushed his face with the back of his hand, then looped his arm around her.

"I love you, Beck Holiday. Always have. Always will."

She buried her head against him. "Always have, Bruno Endicott. Always will."

CHAPTER THIRTY-SIX

BRUNO

April

For a kid who grew up on the wrong side of happiness, Bruno was certain he'd done well for himself. And it had nothing to do with his sports agent résumé.

At the moment he was broke, a bit desperate, but indisputably happy. The green-eyed beauty with a freckled nose and NYPD demeanor was going to be his bride.

He missed her like crazy, but she had to return to New York and wait for Baby Girl. He had to walk Tyvis through this mid-March Pro Day at the University of Central Florida.

His calls to NFL front offices dashed the sliver of hope he had for Tyvis. If the guy on the other end of the line didn't laugh outright when he said, "He's a JUCO kid," he'd offer Bruno some brutal truth: "There's too many great D1 players ahead of him, Endicott. Is he your only prospect?"

But he'd cheated death in more ways than one this winter so he held on to hope. This morning he woke up with a revelation. A God-inspired, divine revelation.

When he met Tyvis at the University of Central Florida field house, Bruno pulled him aside as the rest of the team ran onto the field.

"Listen to me, you were a top college recruit four years ago, right?"

"Yes, sir."

"And you were All-American your red-shirt sophomore year.

Broke all kinds of school records"—Bruno gently tapped his chest with his fist—"you were a stud."

A slow smile split his lips. "Well, them was the days."

"Those are *your* days," Bruno said. "You're the same Tyvis Pryor. You are not a has-been. You are a not-yet. Or a you've-not-seen-me-yet. But do *not* let your mistakes, which you've paid for dearly, define you. Let them refine you."

A shade of regret fell over the kid's expression. "It kind of did, Bruno. I never got back to D1. No one would touch me."

"Forget those losers. You are an outstanding QB. There are scouts out there who've never seen you. Amaze them. Today they only care about what you can do with your arm. Show them who you are. Prove to them you deserve to be in the league. Let me deal with your past. That's my job."

Before his eyes, the six-five, 230-pound player, sculpted into a living, breathing muscle machine, dropped his head on Bruno's shoulders and wept.

Bruno pressed his hand on the back of his neck and let him go. This was probably a long time coming.

Tyvis lifted his head. "Sorry, man." He wiped his eyes with the edge of his jersey.

"You just grew two feet in my eyes."

"Got to be honest, I wasn't sure you really believed in me until now."

"We're all each other has in this game, so let's go for it. I'll call in every favor I have to get you a fair look. I'll spend myself on you, Tyvis."

Running out of the field house with Tyvis, Bruno couldn't have been prouder if Calvin Blue or Todd Gamble were at his side.

As they emerged onto the field, Scott Fuller caught Bruno by the arm.

"Change of plans, man."

"What do you mean, change of plans? Fuller, come on, we made a deal." Tyvis stood about five feet away, watching, waiting.

"You have your Pro Day, but my quarterback sprained his wrist in practice yesterday. The good news is he had a great combine. Bad news, he can't throw today. I need a quarterback." Scott nodded to Tyvis. "You up for it?"

"Yes, sir."

"Then let's go. I have a wide out who needs a really good day. Tyvis, you're a godsend."

A godsend? *You bet your bottom dollar, Fuller.*

While Tyvis worked out on the field, Bruno chatted up the scouts. "He benches 230. Got a vertical leap of thirty-two and runs the forty in four point five. Take a look, boys. The name's Tyvis Pryor."

The Jaguars' scout pulled Bruno aside. "I remember this kid from FSU. Where's he been?"

Bruno inhaled. "JUCO. He's a superior athlete with a heart to go along."

Once the passing drills started, Tyvis's arm did all the talking. Bruno became a honeycomb and the NFL scouts his bees.

Every pass was textbook perfect. And he did it over and over.

When he finished, the entire field exhaled a collective breath. The UCF coaches, the agents, the scouts patted Bruno on the back.

"Welcome back, bro."

"The Endicott magic lives."

He heard two scouts on the phone with their front office.

". . . a client of Bruno Endicott's. Unbelievable."

"You have to see him. Arm like Dan Marino."

Bruno caught Tyvis's eye and nodded. The kid was beaming.

CHAPTER THIRTY-SEVEN

BECK

April
Fernandina Beach

The memory house was brimming with life. Tyvis with his mom, sister, brother, and cousin. Mom, Flynn, and Wyatt. Hunter and Gaynor. Natalie.

And of course Beetle Boo, who decided Bruno was his best buddy when he saw Beck's lap held a new baby.

Baby Girl arrived three weeks early but in beautiful health. She had Beck's dark hair and Hunter's perfect Greek nose.

Bruno flew up the next day and along with Hunter and Gaynor met Everleigh Holiday Ingram.

When baby Everleigh was released from the hospital, Beck and her family returned to Florida with Bruno.

They were married the next day on the beach by Pastor Oliver in an intimate ceremony with immediate family, and Hunter and Gaynor, as guests.

Hunter held baby Everleigh the entire time.

They hosted the reception at the memory house with Mrs. Acker supplying the caterer, and Beck danced with Bruno in the backyard under twinkle lights.

They planned a Paris honeymoon for the summer.

For now, they were adjusting to being parents as well as lovers. Beck was home. Truly home.

Tonight, however, was the first round of the draft. It was not

Tyvis's night. Nor the next round. Maybe not the round after that. The excitement after his Pro Day had quickly faded.

So Bruno prepared him to be an undrafted free agent and lined up on-site visits with teams in the South. Nevertheless, he was at the memory house to watch the draft.

Upstairs in the master bedroom, in the peaceful quiet, Beck fed and rocked Everleigh, listening to the hum of the house below.

Outside, Wyatt and Tyvis played football with his brother and cousin, plus half the kids in the neighborhood.

In the kitchen Tyvis's mom, Arnell Pryor, along with Mom and Natalie, fussed over NFL draft food.

Bruno came upstairs with Beetle Boo and set the dog down as he bent to kiss her forehead, then the baby's.

"Doing okay?"

"More than okay." She kissed him with a lover's kiss.

When she sent Hogan a picture of the wedding, he texted, The Ice Queen has finally melted.

Then he informed her Parker Boudreaux had completed rehab and his parents shipped him to Montana to work on a dude ranch.

"Hunter just told me the news about Gaynor," Bruno said.

That was a miracle that had taken Beck by surprise. Gaynor was twelve weeks pregnant.

"Everleigh's going to have a baby brother or sister by the end of the year."

"Need a break?" Gaynor peered in from the door.

"Please, come in." Beck handed over the sleeping Everleigh as Gaynor took her place in the rocker.

Bruno shook his head, wrapping his arms around Beck. "This kid's feet are never going to touch the ground."

Hunter called up that the first team in the draft was on the clock, so Bruno headed downstairs.

Beck freshened up in the bathroom, then told Gaynor she was going down to make sure the kitchen was still standing.

"They're having a blast in there."

But she paused on her way, caught by the dark wood of the narrow, twisting stairwell leading to the third floor.

At the top, she opened the door to the room with the pictures, telling the tale of lives once lived with the hope of those to come.

The room was peaceful. A retreat to get away and commune with God. She picked up the picture of the little boy on the tricycle.

She asked Mom and Natalie if they knew who he was, but neither did. Then Mom snapped a photo and made a rare Instagram post.

Turns out it was cousin Lou Jr. from when he lived across the street. Who knew? Small, small world.

A cheer buoyed up from the yard. Beck leaned to see out the glass. Tyvis was running with the ball as four little neighbor boys clung to his legs. He was light with laughter.

Beck turned to Miss Everleigh's wedding picture. "See what you started?"

On the once-bare wall to the left, Bruno had hung their wedding picture. Next to it was Everleigh's baby picture with all four parents.

Yeah, they were going to have some explaining to do.

Inspired by the room, Natalie dusted off her old camera and had become a photography ninja these days. By the time she was done, every wall in the house would be plastered with family photos.

Beck loved this room. It's what made the house on Memory Lane the memory house.

She heard another shout from below and Mom's voice announcing, "Food." The front yard was vacant at once.

With a final look around the room, Beck paused, noticing something on top of the bureau.

Reaching up, she pulled a small leather book down and thumbed through the pages. There was only one entry, and it was addressed to her.

Sitting on the settee, she read the elegant script.

October 20, 2015

Dear Beck,

I suppose you will wonder why I left you the Memory House. We've not seen one another in nearly twenty years. Yet I have fond, dear memories of you and often told Don, "If we had a girl, she'd be just like Beck."

We adored your family, and your father was good to me after Don died. I was devastated at his death, but then I had the comfort of your family.

Your mother, in a rare Christmas card, detailed how the tragedy of 9/11 had robbed you of your precious memories, and I knew one day I'd leave this home with its memory room to you.

We are connected through love, my girl, but also through grief. I understand how you'd want to forget everything when you've lost someone you love so desperately.

You lost your father, and I lost my first husband in a terrible tornado.

For a while, I lost my memories of Rhett and my will to live. It was horrible not knowing who or what I grieved. I was pregnant with our first child when he died, and out of grief I gave him up for adoption.

Eventually I emerged from the darkness and my memories returned. I was determined never to lose them again. So I rarely spoke of my short marriage and enduring love for Rhett.

I lived with and took care of my mother for seven years. I cared not how I looked or felt. I thought love would never be mine again. After all, I'd lost my husband and given up my son.

Then Don came into my life, and his love reminded me I had everything to live for.

Much like what happens when Jesus enters our hearts with love. We want to live again. Or perhaps live for the first time free of guilt and shame.

Still, I clung to my memories of Rhett. He deserved to be remembered. I was afraid of forgetting him if I loved Don. Then Don said so wisely, "I'm not asking you to forget Rhett. I'm asking you to love me too."

If that doesn't win a girl's heart, what will?

Don created this room for me. Instead of being jealous of my first husband, he helped me remember. He said Rhett was part of forming the woman he loved.

In another divine coincidence (wink), we moved across the street from Don's cousin, who just happened to be the family who adopted my son. I watched him grow up from age seven to fourteen.

You might wonder how I could do such a thing, but I was comforted to see how much he was loved. He was healthy and smart, full of joy. I can't imagine who and what he'd have been were he raised by two very sad, very emotionally broken widows. I did the right thing for him.

I hope I am helping you remember. Helping you move on. Joshua is a fine lawyer, and I'm sure he will explain everything to you. If not all at once, as you need to know.

That's how it is with God sometimes.

Don and I never had children. It wasn't meant to be. I have no regrets. My life is very full. We were very happy together. We gave of ourselves and our time to our community. We traveled and saw parts of the world that enchanted our hearts.

I pray by the time you read this, your memories will be restored. Your dad was a man worth remembering.

Enjoy the house. Spend the money! Don worked hard for it.

I hope you have many, many happy memories here in my memory house. And tell Bruno I love him too.

Beck sank to the floor, reading through her tears.

Many, many happy memories here in my memory house.

"Beck?" Bruno's voice climbed the stairs. "Are you hiding out?"

"No, just reading Everleigh's note to me."

His face appeared around the door. "She's writing already? Let me see? Is it print or cursive?"

Beck laughed, swatting at him. "*Miss* Everleigh."

He climbed the stairs and sat next to her, taking the notebook. "She was something else."

"Do you think she knew?" Beck took his hand. "That we belonged together?"

"I have no idea, but I wouldn't be surprised."

"Are you happy?" she said.

He brushed her cheek with the back of his hand. "You have to ask?"

"Look what you married into! Craziness. We haven't even had a real wedding night yet, let alone a honeymoon."

"We have our whole lives for wedding nights and honeymoons." He wiggled his brow and winked. "I'm in this for the long haul, Beck Endicott. Not just one night or two. Either way, we wouldn't have had a honeymoon until after the draft. I couldn't leave Tyvis." He kissed her.

She leaned against him and gazed up at Miss Everleigh's wedding photos. "She was gorgeous, wasn't she?"

"This house was made for gorgeous women," Bruno said. "What are some other pictures we should hang? Your mom and dad? Flynn and your mom? Of course Wyatt." Beck's baby brother was thrilled to have another sports junkie in the family.

"What about you and your dad?"

"Maybe."

Since they'd been married, Stone visited once, though he called Bruno weekly. Bruno still struggled, often walking down Memory Lane after a call with his dad. His healing was a work in progress.

They'd drifted into a peaceful silence when a house-shaking shout rose up through the floors. Beck launched to her feet.

"I think we had an earthquake."

"Bruno! Bruno!" The chorus was almost deafening.

Beck glanced at Bruno. "We'd better get down there."

She saw Tyvis huddled in the corner with a phone to one ear, his hand over the other.

"Yes, sir. Yes, sir."

"What's going on?" Bruno glanced from Arnell to Natalie to Hunter.

"Watch," Hunter said, upping the volume.

Beck took a spot on the couch, sensing a miracle was about to happen. Tyvis roped his arm around her husband, unashamed of his fat tears.

"Do you have something to tell me?" Bruno said, peeking down at his phone, then tucking it into his pocket. He glanced at Beck with a slow nod.

"Here's the NFL commissioner," Hunter said, always the commanding lieutenant.

"For the twentieth pick in this year's draft, the Jacksonville Jaguars pick quarterback Tyvis Pryor."

Well, the room went berserk. Sheer and utter pandemonium. Tyvis had his long, dark arms around Bruno, bouncing him up and down, while Arnell Pryor shrieked, "Thank You, Jesus. Thank You, Jesus. Oh, Lord Jesus."

Then everyone was dancing and cheering, hugging and laughing, even the seven-year-old neighbor girl who, later they found out, thought all the shouting was about ice cream.

That's when Beck knew. Family is whoever fits into your heart. And these people were her family.

Tyvis's phone was blowing up as well as Bruno's. Mom and Natalie wanted to know who was ready to eat and everyone trailed into the kitchen.

Mom squeezed Beck's hand as she picked up a heavy paper plate.

"I have no idea what's going on, but my heart is pounding and I feel like a million bucks."

Bruno ran down some preliminary draft numbers with Arnell and Tyvis.

"They want to pay that much for my boy to throw a ball?"

"Yes."

"Thank You, Jesus. Thank You, Lord."

The evening celebration faded around midnight. The food was eaten and put away. Hunter and Gaynor checked on Everleigh, then left for their B&B.

Natalie walked home arm in arm with Arnell, who stayed in her guest room. Their sons were the surprise hit of the NFL draft.

Tyvis was still grinning when he went up to bed, his brother and cousin not far behind. His sister slipped away sometime in the night to read.

Mom and Flynn had the downstairs bedroom while Wyatt happily took the servant's quarters off the kitchen.

And finally the house was quiet.

Tired, Beck knew she should get some sleep. Everleigh would wake soon for another feeding. But she wandered into the kitchen to help Mom with the cleanup.

"Go on, get some rest. I have this."

Beck reached for a stack of pots and stored them in the cupboard by the stove. "It's nice to be here with you. Where we used to be with Dad."

"Yes, yes, it is." The soft sheen in Mom's eyes made her more real to Beck than she'd been in a long time.

"You know, Mom, Miss Everleigh lost her first husband. To a tornado."

Mom drew a long sheet of tin foil from the roll, listening.

"And she didn't want to move on because she thought she'd forget him."

"And how do you know this? Did she tell you?" Mom tucked the stiff silver foil around the deviled eggs.

"As a matter of fact she did. But when she met Mr. Don, he made her realize she could love him and still remember, even love, her first husband."

"And what does this have to do with me?" Mom slid the plate into the fridge and faced Beck with her arms folded.

"You can love Flynn and still love Dad. Or what you had with him. I think that's why you shut me out all those years ago, and put away all of his things and never talked about him. You were trying not to love him."

Mom's jaw tensed as she stared toward the dark kitchen window. "How'd you get so smart?"

"I had a good mom."

She smiled. "It is so strange being here without him. We used to sit out back late into the night, dreaming of living here instead of Flatbush."

"Well, now you can visit as much as you want."

Mom wrapped Beck in her embrace. "I needed to come back here. It's given me closure I didn't know I needed. Thank you."

"Can I interrupt?" Bruno dropped his phone on the table. It'd been plastered to his ear for the past two hours. "Miranda, can you listen for the baby and take care of Beetle?"

"I'm on it." She shooed them out the door, wiping her eyes. "Go, celebrate."

"Where are we going?" Beck leaned into him as he walked her toward the garage-barn.

"For a ride." He pushed aside the door and helped Beck into the old Studebaker. "With the love of my life."

She curled under his arm as they drove toward the beach and south on A1A. Music played low on the radio and the early-morning hour was still thick with night.

One a.m. was familiar to Beck. She knew the night. But now she saw the beauty of the light that showed through the darkness.

The glow from the dash, the scattered yellow hue from beach house windows. The whiteness of the moon and the distant blue of the stars.

She'd surrendered to the light of love in all of its forms. But she especially loved the light she saw in her husband's eyes when he was looking at her.

The End

ACKNOWLEDGMENTS

Every book is a journey. This one began in my imagination with a house on Memory Lane. Yet it had no inhabitants.

Then while visiting Waco, Texas, with writer friends and learning of the 1953 tornado, the story of Everleigh Callahan came to life. I knew I had to use the devastation of the 1953 tornado as a backdrop.

The name Everleigh was "lent" to me by a reader, Andrea Fuller. When she told me her daughter's name during a casual FB chat, I knew immediately, "I have to use it for a character." So, thank you, Fuller family!

However, Beck Holiday moved into this story from another book idea that was caput and brought her NYPD persona with her.

From the beginning the story was to be about memories. I just wasn't sure how. As I worked on the characters and plotted out ideas with the Story Equation, the loss of memories became the cornerstone.

I've never had memory loss, but I imagine it can be frightening and life altering. I treasure my memories of growing up, especially of my late father. I can't imagine how I'd feel if I couldn't remember him.

Memories, or the loss of them, is what connects Beck and Everleigh and preserves a treasured part of each woman's past.

Special thanks, as always, to my husband for listening, brainstorming, praying, and encouraging me on this writing journey. I am blessed.

To Jesus who inspires me and leads me, dropping story ideas and